Battle Royal

Also by Lucy Parker

Battle Royal

A Novel

LUCY PARKER

AVON

An Imprint of HarperCollins*Publishers*

BATTLE ROYAL. Copyright © 2021 by Laura Elliott. All rights reserved. Printed in the United States of America. No part of this book may be used or reproduced in any manner whatsoever without written permission except in the case of brief quotations embodied in critical articles and reviews. For information, address HarperCollins Publishers, 195 Broadway, New York, NY 10007.

HarperCollins books may be purchased for educational, business, or sales promotional use. For information, please email the Special Markets Department at SPsales@harpercollins.com.

FIRST EDITION

Designed by Diahann Sturge

Cake illustration © ALEXEY GRIGOREV / Shutterstock, Inc.
Ice cream with cone © bioraven / Adobe Stock

Library of Congress Cataloging-in-Publication Data has been applied for.

ISBN 978-0-06-304006-9

21 22 23 24 25 LSC 10 9 8 7 6 5 4 3 2 1

For Emma and Tamara

Battle Royal

Chapter One

Four Years Ago

TOP TV THIS WEEK

Sunday: For the many of us who grab something deliciously
calorific and head to the couch for our weekly fix of
Operation Cake, this Sunday night will see our favorite
British bakers return to their stations for the semifinal. Will
cakes rise? Will soufflés sink? Will judge Dominic De Vere
really end up with a face full of frosting? Don't miss it.

It was the exploding unicorn that finally broke him.

Until she accidentally brained the most eminent pastry chef
in London with a projectile hoof, Sylvie Fairchild had been casually speculating whether—like her ill-fated unicorn cake—
Dominic De Vere *also* contained a hidden robotic mechanism. If
so, his internal programming didn't seem to have grasped that
the catalogue of human expressions offered more options than
Arrogant Disdain and Asleep.

He had remained stony-faced through her polka-dot tart
that turned his tongue every color of the rainbow. While Sylvie

chewed on her lower lip and waited for the verdict from the judging panel, he chewed on three hours of her hard work as if it were a piece of cardboard.

"The bottom," his dark, silky voice intoned at last, "is soggy."

Behind the cameras, the *Operation Cake* production team beamed. They loved a soggy bottom in this competition. Or a cracked surface. Or preferably when a contestant just dropped the whole thing on the floor. Perked them right up.

The voices in the three judges' earpieces obviously told them to stick their tongues out and display the technicolored stains, because Mariana Ortiz and Jim Durham obliged with enthusiasm. Dominic turned his head and skewered the executive producer with a look so wintry that her berry coulis almost became a sorbet.

"I think it's delicious." Mariana's smile was blinding and her charisma tongue-tying. Unlike Dominic, the renowned food writer was a natural on-screen. Sylvie could only assume that Dominic's gold-plated status in the industry was a big enough draw to the network that they were prepared to overlook his stiff body language.

And the unsolved crime attached to his name. The puzzle beyond the abilities of Nancy Drew that would stump even the little gray cells of Hercule Poirot.

The Mysterious Case of the Missing Personality.

Or, alternatively, he'd been chosen as the requisite sex symbol. Sylvie studied him critically as he moved to the neighboring station and forked a mouthful of tepid-looking lemon pie into his mouth. With those wickedly intelligent eyes and strong forearms, he was a visual treat, if you fancied your men large and stroppy.

Personally, she'd forgo muscles for an occasional smile.

Seven episodes in, and if he acknowledged her existence at all, he was dividing his cold stare between her pastel-painted fingernails and the streaks of pink in her brown hair. He'd started visibly bracing every time he had to visit her station.

She'd upped the amount of sparkle in her bakes this week, for the sheer amusement of watching him shudder. Bonus points when he actually closed his eyes against the exquisite horror of edible glitter.

Sylvie had seen dozens of his own, incredibly expensive cakes in his London bakery. His preferred color palette covered a diverse range from white to ivory. Sometimes he really pushed the boat out and ventured into the realms of cream. Once at a black-tie event, she'd spotted a De Vere cake on the banquet table that actually had gold accents, and assumed he was either extremely unwell or suffering an early-onset midlife crisis.

He went in for elegant minimalism. She rarely saw an object that couldn't be improved with sequins.

She was, aesthetically, his worst nightmare.

His control started to waver in round two with her witch's cauldron, a Black Forest gâteau that spilled out sinuous curls of smoke, teasing the taste buds with an elusive hint of . . . toffee? No, bourbon. Honey?

"Caramel brandy." Dominic severed the speculation of the other judges. He was correct. She had infused the dry ice mechanism with caramel brandy. Bending in a very limber motion for a man with those shoulders, he examined the exterior of the cauldron, breaking off a tiny piece with a satisfying *snap*. She'd meticulously assembled the structure from white chocolate that she'd hand-painted to mimic rusted iron, using a customized pigment of a powdered food coloring mixed with—

"The chocolate has a bitter aftertaste." Again, he cut short her explanation, rising to his feet. "Did you taste-test the pigment first?" His face was still carved marble, but as usual when he looked in her direction, his eyes were shooting out darts of irritation.

There was a weak sort of compliment in that. If a contestant had a baseline skill level and made a mistake with an otherwise promising dish, he cared enough for impatience. If you were just irredeemably shit, he plastered on the haughty android stare and mentally went to sleep.

Sylvie had experimented with his signature expression herself this morning, on the neighbor who kept snipping herbs out of her window boxes when he thought she was still in bed. He'd flushed all the way up to his hairline, stammered an apology, and offered her cash.

Handy.

And a very poor lesson in life that strutting about, nastily eyeballing people, netted results.

Dominic's brows rose slightly when she didn't immediately respond, and Sylvie suddenly remembered listening to a radio interview with one of his professional rivals, who'd sarcastically referred to him as the puppet-master.

My right hand and foot are attached to that brow bone by invisible strings. One twitch upward and my fist and boot want to follow suit.

Fatally, with the echo of that acerbic remark in her head, she smiled right in the middle of his continued critique.

And it happened. His controlled demeanor chipped. She was looking straight at him, and she saw it, felt it down to her bones. The driving instinct in his body. His gaze went to her hair and locked there. He wanted to touch it. In that instant of time, he obviously desired nothing more than to slide his long fingers into the fine strands, cup her head with that huge palm, tug her forward, take a slow breath . . . and sling her out the window by her ponytail like the Trunchbull.

She couldn't help it. She outright laughed, and he continued to visibly loathe her.

Most of the *Operation Cake* contestants were petrified of him. They all but dropped their piping bags and scuttled under their benches when he stalked past.

Unless someone she loved was being targeted, in which case she would fight like a lioness, Sylvie was not a very confrontational person. If her meal was too cold in a restaurant, she ate it anyway. Unfair parking ticket? She'd probably just pay it. She'd peeked through the curtain and watched the herb heist for days before she'd tried out the De Vere Glare.

Yet there was not one single second on this set that she'd been intimidated by the man himself. She flatly refused to shy away from a person she found about as likable as a stubbed toe. He was totally devoid of empathy and warmth, she bet he was a bloody nightmare to work for, and she'd wear her apparently "garish, style-over-substance" cauldron cake as a hat before she'd let her knees so much as quiver in his presence.

She was a favorite with the other two judges, so she thought she might scrape through another week despite Dominic pacing around the studio like a sweet-toothed Grim Reaper.

Unfortunately, the final round put the casting vote in his hands.

And Sylvie put a shit-ton of glitter in his hair.

In her defense, when she'd practiced the robotic component of her unicorn cake in the garden shed at home, the results had been significantly less impressive. The treasure chest was to burst open in stages, spilling out hundreds of colored sweets before it set off a chain reaction to move the unicorn's hoof and horn. She'd made dead certain that everything would taste as good as it looked. Dominic had commented before that her foundations were sometimes sacrificed for the exterior glitz. He wasn't wrong, and she did listen to legitimate criticism.

Levers in right place? *Aww. Look, he's waving at you.* Wrong place? *I appear to have constructed this small missile.*

"Fantastic," Jim Durham said, bending to examine the chest as it sprang apart on cue and the sweets cascaded forth. One of his knees gave an alarming little creak, thus providing an unintentional soundtrack for her hinges. Sylvie remembered watching Jim's old cooking show on TV as a child. She and her aunt had taken turns each week making the Friday recipe for dinner. He was in his seventies now and on the list for a double knee replacement, he'd told her. Popping a sweet in his mouth, he winked at her. "I'd expect nothing less from our resident witch. What other magic do you have in store for us?"

He was such a nice man. Always kind and supportive. Smelled a bit like port.

She smiled back at him. "Only the good kind. Promise."

"You couldn't have worked any harder today," Mariana praised her, also circling the display and reaching to toss a sweet onto her tongue.

Dominic surveyed the spectacle from a short distance. His wide chest moved with a silent heave of breath. "Unicorns now."

He sounded like a fed-up character in *Jumanji*, forced to endure one of her ghastly trials after another.

The arrogant dude whinging in the back never fared well in a film.

Sylvie opened her mouth to respond—and became aware of a low clicking sound that she'd initially thought was Jim's knees again. Even as it registered properly, the rhythm of the mechanism stuttered. That wasn't right. The second apparatus should have flicked over by now, setting the unicorn in motion.

She leaned forward to check the control box, and—*shit*. "Duck!"

"Oh, a *duck*." Jim took a few steps back. "*Is* it. I must admit, I did think it was a unicorn, too." He looked slightly doubtfully at the long horn. "His bill—?"

"*Duck!*"

"Yes, *indeed*. Duck. Clear as a bell," Jim said soothingly. "If the creator says it is so, then so it shall be." He reached to pat her shoulder.

Dominic's eyes suddenly narrowed on the control box.

Sylvie grabbed Mariana and hauled her back.

The mechanism came crashing down, catapulting the unicorn off the table and throwing up a cloud of glitter.

Contestants screamed. Mariana swore like a sailor. Jim's knees sounded like chattering teeth. The cameras tracked every movement.

And a large edible hoof nailed Dominic right between the eyes.

The rest of the unicorn continued to smile jauntily as its head sailed past, one eye lowered in the wink of a creature that hadn't quite grasped the gravity of its situation, until it splattered against the fridge.

The cakes were still delicious, Sylvie's fellow contestants assured her as they rescued chunks of chocolate sponge from the scene of the massacre, and the producers were beside themselves with glee, imagining this week's teaser shots.

Glitter twinkled in the stubble that edged Dominic's chiseled jawline.

Hoof remnants smudged his forehead.

He was ominously still as they stood, staring at one another. Only his chest moved with his even breaths.

Without breaking eye contact, he swept one hand through that lush head of thick silvery black hair, and a massive cloud of sparkling particles swirled through the air, as if he'd thrown a handful of stars.

She was eliminated from the show twenty minutes later.

For weeks afterward, she continued to find random pieces of glitter on her clothing, in her pockets, behind her ears—and every time it glimmered in the light, she heard a deep, scathing voice.

Cheap tricks and glitter might get you a gig pulling rabbits out of hats at kiddie parties, but they won't make you a baker.

And every time, the response that came from deep inside her was the same.

Plus or minus a few expletives, depending on her mood.

Watch me.

Chapter Two

Present Day

Sugar Fair, Notting Hill
Proprietor and Head Chef: Sylvie Fairchild

> "You're an entertainer at best. Not a baker."
> —Dominic De Vere, maker of cakes, eater of crow

Royal Wedding Belle? Sylvie's gaze traveled from the *Metropolitan News*'s front-page headline to the inset photograph of Princess Rose. Currently fourth in line to the throne, but likely to be bumped down the queue if her bachelor uncle, the Prince of Wales, or her older brother ever reproduced. The princess was smiling up at a tall blond man. With narrowed eyes, Sylvie scanned the text below, but it was the usual recycled speculation, nothing new since the same engagement rumors last month.

And then, driven by some latent masochistic impulse, she couldn't help flipping through to the arts and lifestyle section to see the article currently being discussed by her staff. Dominic's name immediately jumped out at her—and how lovely, they'd printed a photo of him as well, as if his face plastered all over the ads for the upcoming season of *Operation Cake* weren't enough.

The personality was nothing to brag about, so she supposed they had to milk the bone structure.

It was a lengthy piece about icons of the London food industry. Most of the featured businesses were Michelin-starred restaurants well out of her dinner budget, but they had interviewed a couple of confectioners and pâtissiers, including Dominic— who'd had a *number* of things to say when the journalist had asked about the balance between modern marketing and maintaining artistic integrity.

Cue a bunch of pithy quotes about the reliance of certain bakers on gimmicks and social media algorithms over skill and substance.

It would be pretty unsanitary if her eyeballs actually rolled right out of her head in a commercial kitchen, so it was fortunate that her newest intern called out for help with decorating a tray of truffles. She had learned from experience that it was best to heed those requests quickly. Penny tended to panic at every mishap and turn tiny mistakes into messes that had to be scrapped entirely.

Sylvie was pressing sugar stars into white chocolate truffles when she caught sight of movement through the window onto the main shop floor. With a tickle of welcome amusement, she watched as a dapper little chap in Thomas the Tank Engine overalls sidled another few steps away from his mother. The young woman was engrossed in a display of wrapped fruitcakes, weighing each one in her hands and trying to sniff them through the packaging. Her daughters were transfixed by the chocolate waterfall, staring with wide eyes as it flowed between twinkling tree branches in the center of the room, but her son had his sights fixed firmly on the enchanted castle. He darted a glance between his mum and his target, visibly weighing up his chances. Give him twenty-odd years, and he was a shoo-in for covert ops at MI5.

The Castle—because anything that had taken that long to make deserved to be capitalized—had begun life as a small sugar tower, part of Sylvie's ongoing attempts to exactly replicate the appearance of glass art—*pâte de verre*—in edible form. From the bricks to the turret, the tower appeared to be constructed out of highly textural, glistening ice crystals, as if a fairy-tale witch had cast a spell of perpetual winter. She'd then got a little carried away. For weeks, she'd spent every free evening hunched over in the back room, after full twelve-hour days in the kitchens and storefront. She'd ended up with a record number of blowtorch burns on her hands and wrists, a withered sex life, and a bloody epic five-foot-tall castle. Totally edible from moat to uppermost flying flag.

At least one person appreciated her efforts. The Thomas fan shot a last quick look upward, then set off on his mission, oh-so-casually. Sylvie half expected him to tuck his hands in his little pockets and whistle. With a wiggle of tiny fingers, he took a headlong dive toward her current pride and joy.

"Oy. Kid."

He froze comically, inches from the Castle, as Mabel Yukawa appeared from behind the waterfall. Sylvie's senior assistant was holding an *amezaiku* bird in one hand, the small candy sculpture half-finished, its translucent wings painted in a cascading effect of pink and blue feathers.

Mabel pointed a blue-tipped brush at the guilty-looking child. "Were you going to touch that castle?"

She and the boy gave each other a shrewd once-over, their faces equally skeptical.

"Yes."

As Sylvie handed a completed tray of truffles to a snickering kitchen hand, Mabel nodded and sat back down at the small table where she was painting an entire jungle of sugar animals. "I respect your honesty. Don't."

The little boy drew nearer the table, now fixated on Mabel's deft fingers as she finished coloring the bird. "Could I do that?"

Mabel picked up a candy leopard and held it up to the light. "Not *well*." She reached for a fresh brush and dipped it in a dish of black food dye. "You have extremely small hands," she added disapprovingly.

They narrowed their eyes at each other again.

"So do you," he pointed out, accurately and with obvious indignation, and Mabel tilted her head.

"True." With the tip of her pointed boot, she pushed a second chair in his direction. "Well, what are you waiting for? Sit."

He almost fell over his short legs hastening to join her, and Sylvie shook her head, grinning, as Mabel put a sugar snake on his outstretched palm and handed him a brush. Her instructions were abrupt and drenched with exasperation, but her hand was gentle as she guided his decorating attempt.

When the family had left, Mabel's new number-one fan clutching a rainbow-streaked snake, and his mother loaded down with cakes and sweets, Sylvie spoke without looking up from her notebook. "Some of the staff actually smile at customers. I casually mention."

"Some of the staff are simpering twits." Mabel fluttered her brush over the side of a large fish, iridescent pearly scales appearing beneath her fingertips. A piece of nougat came flying out of the kitchens and smacked her directly on the forehead. Sylvie heard the slap of a congratulatory high five. Mabel didn't so much as pause. "Most human beings are insincere cretins who cover egocentric impulses with meaningless social gestures. At least they buy things. Helps pay for my new couch." She finished the fish, examined the piece of fallen nougat, put it in her mouth. "Kids are usually more tolerable. Stickier fingers, but less bullshit."

The floor-to-ceiling bookcase behind Mabel was full of chocolate boxes, packaged to look like vintage books. As she spoke, the hidden door in the central panel opened and Jay Fforde, Sylvie's best friend and business partner, came in from the staff offices. He was holding a thin sheaf of papers. "Would these be the 'tolerable' kiddies you threatened to drop-kick into the chocolate waterfall last week?"

Mabel was well over a foot shorter than Jay. At the bakery Christmas party, she'd glanced with loathing at the limbo pole, walked straight underneath it, and headed for the bar. She still managed to look down her nose at him now. "Valuable life lesson. If you feel comfortable shoveling handfuls of stolen sweets into your pockets, I might feel comfortable shoving you headfirst into a pipe."

Jay raised his brows at Sylvie. "Have we considered moving Mabel's workstation so she's slightly farther away from the paying customers? Perhaps about"—he made a pinching motion with his finger and thumb—"two postcodes to the left?"

"Have we considered getting a haircut, so we look slightly less like an aging rocker?" Mabel asked conversationally. "It's swell of you to take over potions class while Sylvie's back on telly, Axl Rose, but you don't have to go full wizard cosplay."

Jay opted to ignore that, although his fingers went briefly to his shoulder-length hair. It was quite a bit longer than usual, possibly because of his current girlfriend. Lovely woman. Kept telling him things about his artistic soul. He'd started writing poems and reading them aloud to Sylvie in their shared office.

It had been a trying few months all round.

She closed her notebook. "Are you sure about taking over downstairs?"

At the street level, Sugar Fair welcomed customers into a bright, child-friendly fantasy. The architecturally designed enchanted forest was awash in jewel tones, and gorgeous smells, and the waterfall of free-flowing chocolate.

But it was the Dark Forest downstairs that had proved an unexpected money-spinner, an income stream that had helped keep them afloat through the precarious first year.

Four nights a week, through a haze of purple smoke and bubbling cauldrons, Sylvie taught pre-booked groups how to make concoctions that would tease the senses, delight the mind . . . and knock people flat on their arse if they weren't careful. *High* percentage of alcohol. It was a mixology class with a lot of tricks and pyrotechnics. It had been Jay's idea to get a liquor license.

"Pleasures of the mouth," he'd said at the time. "The holy trinity—chocolate, coffee, and booze."

With even her weekends completely blocked out, Sylvie had almost made a crack about forfeiting certain *other* pleasures of the mouth, but Jay had inherited a puritanical streak from his mother. Both their mouths looked like dried cranberries if someone made a sex joke.

The sensuous, moody haven in the basement was a counterbalance to the carefully manufactured atmosphere upstairs. There were, after all, reasons to shy away from relentless cheer. Perhaps someone had just been through a breakup, or a family reunion. A really distressing haircut. Maybe they'd logged on to Twitter and realized half the population were a bunch of pricks. Or maybe they'd picked up the *Metropolitan News* and found Dominic De Vere indirectly trashing their entire business aesthetic in a major London daily.

Whatever the reason—feeling a little stressed? A bit peeved? Annoyed as fuck? Welcome to the Dark Forest. Through the bakery, turn left, down the stairs.

"There's absolutely no way you can keep your current workload and take up this judging gig on *Operation Cake*," Jay said emphatically. "You'll conk out from sheer exhaustion by month's end. And while I know you'd prefer to blowtorch your own eyeballs than work hand-in-glove with Dominic De Vere—"

"Especially when it was *directly* his vote that booted you off before the final in your series," Mabel cut in, avidly eavesdropping. The comment was heavy with ire. Despite describing most reality TV as "like looking up the devil's colon," the Queen of Doom and Gloom held a grudging fondness for *Operation Cake*. Sylvie had once had to drop a package off at her flat on a Sunday night, and had found her watching last year's series in a onesie.

It's just so damn cozy.

To watch, undeniably. Behind the cameras, it was a business like any other, with the accompanying pros and cons. Sylvie had some fond memories of her time as a contestant, and she was flattered to be asked back as a judge. She also had reservations.

Including one towering, sarcastic reservation who'd just swiped yet *another* major cake contract out from under them.

Trying to hide her dismay in front of the watching staff, she looked at the document Jay handed her. "Hallum & Fox went with De Vere's? That brief was made for us. It's a fantasy novel, for God's sake. They're holding a *carnival* at the launch and they opted for the Dominic Special? Five tiers, blanket white, maybe some fondant work if he's made someone cry and is feeling festive?"

To give the master and commander of De Vere's his due, silently and reluctantly, the cakes inside those tiers would be fantastic. Might-as-well-keel-over-right-now-because-you'll-never-taste-anything-this-good-again quality. *But, Christ, Dominic. Colors. They exist.*

"They went for the old-school prestige."

"Damn," Sylvie said softly, staring down at the Hallum & Fox logo.

She'd badly wanted that commission, and not just because it came with an expansive fee. The launch was for the new installment in one of her favorite book series. She still backed the design she'd submitted. It would have been a beautiful, exciting cake.

"De Vere's has the name recognition and the status." The other bakery had held top-tier status since Sebastian De Vere, Dominic's grandfather, had opened the original pâtisserie decades ago. "They can get away with making snotty comments about tacky fads," Jay said darkly. "We need to utilize every marketing plan we've got."

He glanced around the shop floor, currently devoid of people not on their payroll. He'd always had Resting Brooding Face—way back in their teen years, he'd got the part of Dante Gabriel Rossetti in the school play just by walking into the casting room—but his expression and clothing really had gone full Victorian undertaker lately.

He started to speak, then inclined his chin meaningfully toward the door to the offices. Sylvie stuck her head into the kitchens to make sure everybody knew what they were doing. Nobody was panicking or on fire, so she followed him back through the bookcase.

"Temporary lull," she assured him in their messy little office, easily reading his expression. "It's been busy all morning. We're still riding the wave of Strawberry Bomb sales."

They had pulled a queue right down the street for the Bombs, truffles with a hidden center that burst spectacularly in the mouth, thanks to a visit from a tousled-headed pop star and his model girlfriend, and the accompanying Instagram selfie.

He didn't so much as blink. "But?"

She started plaiting her long ponytail. She was a stress plaiter. There were some very intricate bread loaves and *rocking* hairstyles in this place. "But you're right. Overall momentum is slowing. I'd be more comfortable if we can knock things up to a higher level."

He tucked his hands in his pockets and perched on the edge of the desk. "It is a good thing you're doing *Operation Cake*. I'm sorry, I know you've never exactly been jumping to get on TV."

Understatement of the century. She'd had to be talked into going on the show the first time round, on the grounds it could kick-start their business dreams.

"Ten minutes after I signed the contract, I found a snow-white hair in my eyebrow." She ran a finger over the offending brow. "I expect the rest to shortly follow suit."

Oh, well. Another step toward unlocking her coveted life goal of Cranky Crone.

"It'll be a serious boost for us. People still remember you." A whisper of a grin. "Hard to forget. The slow-motion clip of the hoof whacking De Vere in the face has racked up half a million views on YouTube. I bookmarked it for whenever I need a laugh." Behind the amusement, however, Jay seemed genuinely concerned about any suffering Sylvie was about to endure on their behalf. What a darling. "On the bright side, the studio doesn't waste money. That filming schedule is *fast*. We'll only have to juggle your commitments for a few weeks. And the name recognition for the judges is huge."

Sylvie nodded. They'd already seen a bump in mentions online and in the press. One media outlet, speculating on the show's new judging lineup, had run a puff piece about the perceived competition between Sugar Fair and De Vere's, which she highly doubted Dominic had even seen, let alone read, and would pay no credence if he had.

He viewed her as a temporary, upstart blip on his radar.

So sad for him that she intended to be a permanent, well-established nuisance.

"We need to pull bigger event contracts," she said without preamble, and something flickered in Jay's expression.

She knew that look. Even as kids, it had heralded useful information. He preferred the term "social research" over "gossip."

"You know something."

"Shall we say whisperings have become a loud hum?"

Anticipation sat heavy in her chest. This could be the one they'd been waiting for, for months. The literal contract of the decade. If it was true. "The press has nothing new. Same litany of guesses in the papers today. Princess Rose engaged in heated snog. The princess's new diamond ring. Wrong hand, but still! Ring! Diamond! Et cetera."

He rolled his eyes, all nonverbal scathing of *the press*, and a smile grew from the hopeful flutters in Sylvie's stomach. "Engagement imminent, or has he really popped the question?"

"My royal source"—and only Jay could say that without sounding like a total git—"says it's a done deal. Official announcement from St. Giles Palace any time now. Wedding expected to be in the spring."

"We're ready to go as soon as it drops." She put one hand

down on the desk, resting her fingers on the file that sat on top in priority position.

"And you're quite sure about this video game thing?" Jay looked and sounded skeptical. "She is a princess."

Sylvie snorted. "So her personal hobbies ought to be—what? Practicing ribbon-cutting? Swanning around St. Giles unveiling makeshift plaques? The girl walks her pit bull in a Metallica T-shirt, and showed up to the Easter service at the Abbey wearing a skull necklace. Gamer princess seems entirely on brand. We could do whatever the hell they like for the actual wedding cake, but we need a foot in the door first. The pitch cake has to be memorable and personal." She grinned at him suddenly and buffed her nails against her collar. "You're just pissed because Watson got the jump on Holmes this time. Need to up your game, Sherlock."

Jay's lips were tugging irrepressibly upward. With a surge of affection, she flung her arm around his neck, and he dropped his head to rest against hers.

"If Sugar Fair ever closes," she said, with a note of fierceness, "it'll be at *our* instigation. We will not go under. It works, and it's going to keep working. And if that means going back on TV, fine." She straightened. "If it meant job security for every person under this roof, I'd sign on to a bloody burlesque act with Dominic."

"Wow," Jay said after an extended pause. "That image is going to be the gift that keeps on giving, isn't it?"

The Operation Cake team was sending a car at one o'clock. At five to one, Sylvie stood outside under the shelter of the eaves, checking her watch and pulling her coat tighter across her chest.

Her breath misted in the sharp bite of the air, frosty and ephemeral. Like the steam that flowed silently from Dominic's ears when a schedule ran more than fifteen seconds late.

Shivering as a raindrop hit her eyelashes, she studied the Tudor architecture of the storefront across the street. It was one of her favorite buildings in Notting Hill. Like a teeny version of Liberty. It ought to be flanked by horse-drawn carriages and men in doublets and pantyhose, instead of rain-spattered tourists clutching crisp white bags and boxes.

Her gaze lingered on the discreet, elegant signage above the door. The door she couldn't help noticing was admitting a lot more foot traffic than the one behind her. It swung open again, and a man strode out, with all the appropriate bearing and command of a Tudor king. And increasingly similar amounts of facial hair.

Fortunately, much less formfitting trousers.

The maestro himself.

A ripple of awareness went through the cluster of customers outside De Vere's, and Sylvie started to grin.

Phones appeared, brandished for selfies, and with absolutely no survival instincts, the crowd pounced on Dominic like a swarm of rabid bees.

Even across the street and traffic, with her vision impaired by the rain, she could see the internal battle in his expression. A polite request to piss off and leave him alone wouldn't bode well for repeat customers. He shook a few hands, and she started counting down in her head. When she hit "three," his taut lips moved and the man chattering eagerly at his rigid face took a step back, looking affronted.

Seven seconds from excited greeting to mortal offense. Nowhere near his record. Jay wasn't the only one off his game.

A young woman sidled in close to Dominic and tried to take a photo, and Sylvie could pinpoint the exact moment he lost all will to live.

As a sleek black car with the network logo slid to a stop, easing smoothly into De Vere's private parking spot, he looked up and their eyes met.

His expression changed.

She'd been mistaken.

There was the moment.

Thirty Minutes Earlier, Across the Road in That Gorgeous Tudor Building
Where, unfortunately, running a successful bakery requires occasional interaction with other human beings.

Three layers. Chocolate. Lemon. Pink champagne. The bride wanted lemons grown only in Sorrento. The groom claimed that chocolate made anywhere but Bruges was a waste of cacao. They both refused to consider any champagne but that of a bespoke label that produced only two hundred bottles of that variety a year, most of which were presold to a man in Chicago who, like most multimillionaires, didn't share his toys.

What a boon for the rest of the dating market that two such fucking pains in the arse had found each other.

Dominic's team had the ingredients, budget, and time for one test run. The sample cakes now cooling on the racks were shaped correctly, a good color, barely a crumb out of place. When he took a fork and tasted the spare cuts of the chocolate mud cake, he realized why several members of his staff were staring fixedly at various locations on the floor, ceiling, and nearest exit.

They were already behind schedule this week, and he was out for the afternoon shooting ridiculous promos for *Operation Cake*. Every person in this room was paid a top-tier salary and in almost all cases did correspondingly excellent work. They did *not* usually stand around darting wary looks like he was the bloody Grinch about to invade Whoville, or turn over-priced ingredients into a cake with the textural consistency of cheddar cheese.

He set down the fork. "Who mixed this?"

Glances were exchanged.

Lizzie, one of his chocolatiers, cleared her throat. "Aaron."

He should have known. Aaron's continued employment was starting to hang by a string. There had been multiple incidents when he'd been late and careless. He'd broken so many plates, Lizzie was using the shards to make photo frames for her craft group.

As a side note, he also kept buying hot chocolate from Sylvie Fairchild's bakery across the street. Bakery. Funfair. It seemed to be a matter of semantics. Apparently, Aaron liked the marshmallow unicorns that floated in the drinks like small bloated corpses, and thought Sylvie was "a darling." So not only unreliable and wasting his potential, but questionable sanity.

Dominic counted back from five in his head. "And where is Aaron?" he asked, with whipcord-taut patience.

"Not sure." Lizzie turned to continue placing small pieces of gold leaf on dark chocolate truffles. "But he's definitely not hiding in the bathroom."

"For fuck's sake."

His own workplace was meant to be exempt from the endless stream of sobbing and theatrics that encompassed the short painful weeks on the *Operation Cake* set. It was a grim countdown to that fiasco every year; he didn't need a copycat version in De Vere's.

Aaron finally emerged, full of apologies, and with time Dominic didn't have, he started walking the other man back through the steps he should have taken. And tried to work out what the hell he *had* done, because even the worst cakes produced in the TV studio didn't usually have a mouthfeel more suited to grating on a pizza.

It was Aaron's saving grace that he did have natural talent when he chose to apply it, because that last-chance string seriously frayed after Dominic also tasted the pink champagne cake. Fun new game for the whole staff, working out exactly what bottle of liquid Aaron had mistakenly used for the flavor profile, because it definitely wasn't champagne.

With ten minutes until the network car was due and an aftertaste in his mouth that was going nowhere fast, Dominic was updating spreadsheets in his office when the door came flying open. His sister sailed in, then screeched to a halt on her extremely high heels. He wasn't sure why she bothered wearing them. The stilettos were long and lethal enough to kill a rhino, and Pet would still have trouble getting on half the rides at Disneyland Paris.

Her expression instantly morphed on seeing him. She usually wore a look of perpetual joy in the world around her and sincere interest in the people inhabiting it. Dominic might not be a fully grown adult working in a pseudo-magical tree house like others on this street, but if anything would make him believe in the existence of fairies and changelings, it was Pet's presence in his family.

She hesitated, a frown flickering between her brows. A buzz of tension roped the air between them. "Hello, big brother." Her soft voice was usually cheerful, but artificially so at the moment. She held up a sheaf of papers. "I've sorted the Hallum & Fox correspondence. I was just going to leave it on your desk. I thought you were at the TV studio today."

Dominic finished inputting a column of sums and shot another glance upward. Her gaze was restless and jumpy, darting around like a dazed firefly, briefly fixing on minutiae and finally colliding with his. Big brown eyes that should be liberally laced with laughter and mischief, currently veiled and cautious. His fingers closed hard around a pen. "Hello, extremely small sister." He jotted down a note. "Thanks for dealing with the letters. And I'm leaving soon. If the appropriately hearse-like network car is on time for once."

The wry greeting dispelled some of the strain. Pet noticeably perked up and came to perch on the edge of his desk. "God, I love your show."

"It's not 'my' show. It's a painful source of extra income."

Increasingly necessary income, in the current market. He wouldn't be taking time away from the business for any other reason. De Vere's straddled the boundary between retail and hospitality, and neither industry was exactly a flourishing money tree right now. Event contracts were down on the same quarter last year, and they were seeing fewer sales on the shop floor. The livelihood of every person in this building depended on the decisions he made on a daily basis. As much as he despised almost every element of his unsought side gig, it was paying some of those salaries.

"But it's so warm and cuddly. Like a televised hug." Pet ripped off a piece of notepaper, picked up a pair of scissors, and started making tiny snips. Most chronic fidgeters doodled with a pen. His sister cut intricate silhouette portraits. In less than three minutes, she could reproduce someone's profile with meticulous accuracy. "Not the bits where you make someone cry, obviously." *Snip. Snip.* "I'm still waiting to be invited for a studio visit."

Tucking her tongue between her teeth as she deftly maneuvered the scissors, she sent him a teasing but hesitant look.

That cloak of reserve was seeping in again.

He didn't know how to broach it.

And if he were ruthlessly honest, these interactions with Pet were so far out of his experience that a small part of him would find it easier if she was like his other sister, Lorraine.

A clinical narcissist and living on a different continent.

"Come on," she said lightly, "you're ancient and I'm short. If you can't get a studio pass for a sibling, we could totally pull off a ruse for take-your-daughter-to-work day."

"If you'd like to retain the illusion of the show being 'warm and cuddly,' I'd stick to couch-viewing like the rest of the country." Shaking his head, he took the silhouette Pet handed him, an outline of Mariana Ortiz's head. The food writer had a distinctive nose: narrow, turned up at the tip, and now perfectly captured on the crisp paper.

He turned it over on his palm.

"Should I give this to her?" he asked abruptly. He was not on gift-giving terms with Mariana. Even after six seasons of the show, they hardly knew each other outside of work. But Pet's self-described silly whittling was art. It should be seen.

A faint flush crept into Pet's pointed face. "If you like." She was quiet for a moment before she seemed to shake herself. Tearing off another sheet of paper, she started snipping again. "I see the competition over yonder is doing a steady stream of business despite the foul weather. Please note my staunch loyalty in never having stepped through that adorable door, despite the fact that it looks like my natural habitat and I would really enjoy a cocktail served in a gold cauldron."

Dominic closed the spreadsheet. "If you want to blow out your liver and brain cells at Sugar Fair, have at it." Now that she mentioned it, Pet probably would love the place. If she'd been the one to take over De Vere's, it would be twinning Sylvie's dubious brainchild by now. He rested one hand on the desk, a silent assurance it wouldn't be carved back into a tree trunk and smothered in fake leaves and spangles any time soon. "But I'd make a booking ASAP. It's a miracle it's stayed in business this long."

Pet rotated her paper and made a careful cut. "Is your brother really such a surly bastard, they ask. Of course not; inside, he's a teddy bear, say I." *Snip.* "And then he opens his mouth."

At his raised eyebrow, the left corner of her mouth indented slightly. A ghost of amusement was in her voice as she murmured, "You know, you can stream reruns of Sylvie Fairchild's season. I binged seven episodes last night. Excellent executive decision to bring her onto the judging panel. The woman is a bloomin' treasure."

The woman was a bloody menace.

"Occasional spurts of technical genius wasted on garish, childish, obnoxious concoctions that ought to come with a health and safety warning." A dull stiffness had invaded several muscles around his spine. Cupping a hand around his shoulder, Dominic rolled his neck. "As if it hasn't devolved into enough of a farce. Every half-baked drama-monger in the competition will be rolling out the glitter cannons to win her vote."

He felt more than usually irritated just contemplating it.

The deepening laughter in Pet's eyes momentarily banished more of that god-awful tension in the room. "Think you sank your own ship there, Captain." She grinned as his brooding preoccupation sharpened to acute attention, his gaze narrowing. "You should have kept to the usual Popsicle stare and impersonal critique four years ago. Sylvie was clearly the public darling back then, and Sugar Fair is a production draw now, but if you hadn't needled back and forth like that, I highly doubt they'd have offered her the contract. Sugar-laced strychnine on one side, icy darts on the other. Jab, jab. And she was totally unfazed."

There was a speck of awe in that last remark, and just a hint of bite underscored his response. "She was hardly the only contestant with enough brain cells to differentiate between honest feedback and a personal insult. I don't dick around the truth with pointless bullshit, but if they're giving it their all, there's nothing to be *fazed* about."

It was a small percentage that actually listened and took the advice on board, instead of staring like a headlight-struck rabbit and playing up to the cameras as if they'd just survived an encounter with the Sith, but the number wasn't limited to one.

"No," Pet agreed matter-of-factly, "but she also brings some serious cute factor to the table. She's nice to look at, and the entertainment industry is a shallow beast. And she KO'd you with a sponge cake." Her mouth twitched again. "*Mortal Kombat* with the Sugar Plum Fairy." In a pitch-perfect imitation of Jim Durham's West Country brogue, she drawled, "It's all about those ratings."

He always enjoyed rounding out a grim morning with a few unpalatable truths.

After a moment, he grimaced.

The show was a victim of its own financial success; from a modicum of legitimacy and a few scraps of genuine heart in the first few seasons, it was rapidly unraveling into sensationalized rubbish. Jim's unexpected departure was a boon to a production team that delighted in constantly switching things up.

With a short sound in the back of his throat, he rose and took the files back to the locked cabinet. "If you're not planning to do any more actual work today," he said, "may I offer a suggestion?"

"For the afternoon?"

"For the future in general."

The metaphorical drop in temperature was swift.

"For the last time"—Pet's voice lost all traces of humor—"I am not changing career paths. I'm twenty-six years old, I'm good at my job, and most importantly, I *enjoy* being a personal assistant. We all have a calling, and this is mine." She rubbed her thumb back and forth over the paper a few times. "Why else would I want to help out here so you can fulfill your contractual obligation to scare the living shit out of the nation?"

A question he'd also posed after a motorcycle crash had put his usual executive assistant on leave for weeks and his sister had jumped in to fill the vacancy. Prior to this month, he could count on one hand the number of times they'd been in the same room since she was a baby. So, a bit of a surprise when Pet had promptly showed up in his office with a temp contract she'd drafted, typed, and already signed.

He still wasn't sure how he'd also ended up signing it, and he'd had to controvert her attempt to give herself a pathetically low salary. He wouldn't let anyone work for that, and they sure as hell weren't in such a precarious financial position that he was going to rip off his own sister, whether she needed the money or not.

He leaned back against the filing cabinet and surveyed her stubborn expression. "I know how well you did in school. You were nudging the genius scale in almost every subject, and for a while you wanted to be an astrophysicist."

Once more, Pet's fingers stilled on the scissors. "How do you know that?"

"Sebastian managed to get the occasional update," he said after an infinitesimal pause. After he'd gone to live with their grandfather as a child, his own access to family news had been limited. "We . . . always tried to keep tabs on how you were doing."

Even when she hadn't wanted him to.

He saw Pet swallow.

A bit roughly, he continued, "You could have breezed into Oxford or Cambridge. Instead, you've devoted yourself to pacifying the spoiled whims of people who probably treat you like shit."

"Oh, you're not that bad. At least you come with free chocolate." She wrinkled her nose at him. "I *don't* work for people who treat me like shit, as it happens. I bring a lot to the table, and I expect a lot in return. And if I had the least desire to go back to uni, I'd already have applied. I certainly have the money to pay for it. Shame a whole chunk of it doesn't really belong to me."

He straightened. "We're not going into that again."

"Annoying when people refuse to hear a word you're saying, isn't it?" Pet asked sweetly. Before he could respond, she went on, "Look, I'm happy, and you're . . . well, at least you have your health." She stood up and put back the scissors. "And if the papers are right and there's a royal wedding on the horizon, there's going to be a De Vere's cake on that reception table, photographed for millions of people to see and bringing in a huge paycheck, and I am *pumped* and here to help."

"Enthusiasm on the unconfirmed opportunity noted, Pet, but there's a pink champagne cake out there that tastes like something recently extracted from a drain, and your baking ability makes the man responsible look like Alain Ducasse. I'm not sure this is your forte."

"And is your forte romance, happy-ever-afters, and royal trivia? Doubtful." She handed him the finished silhouette. "See you later. Enjoy intimidating a bunch of nice people who just want to bake cake and massively improve my Sunday nights."

She exited with a lot less noise than her entrance. His mouth taut, Dominic looked at the closed door, and then down at the artwork he held in his hand.

It was a silhouette portrait of Sylvie Fairchild.

For the first time, not a totally accurate portrait. Sylvie's lips had a much more pronounced curve.

The nose and brow bone were dead-on, though.

And in the tilt of Paper Sylvie's chin seemed to lie an implicit challenge.

Chapter Three

Hartwell Studios
Time-honored, beloved home of *Operation Cake*.
Where somebody has made the executive decision to hold a
meeting about baked goods and not serve snacks.

As the assistant producer of *Operation Cake* tapped her iPad,
Sylvie tried to find a more comfortable spot on the conference
room chair, and wished she'd eaten a chocolate bar in the car.
Although even if she'd had one, Dominic's silent, brooding presence beside her would likely have put her off. Nothing like com-
muting with Heathcliff to suppress the appetite.

"Libby Hannigan." Sharon floated another headshot into the
cluster on the PowerPoint. The redhead in the photo had a face
full of adorable freckles and a sweet smile—and a surprisingly
hard expression in her eyes.

"And what deeply traumatic event led to Ms. Hannigan taking
solace in the kitchen?" Dominic turned his ballpoint pen over in
his fingers, regularly tapping out a beat on the tabletop. It had
taken five of these character summaries before Sylvie had identi-
fied the tune. Bonnie Tyler. Unexpected on multiple levels.

She mentally caught herself again. *Contestant* summaries, not characters. Contrary to all appearances—and particularly the appearance of Charlene, the sugar-cookie specialist from North London with four ex-husbands and extremely vague answers as to their current whereabouts—they weren't vetting suspects in a murder mystery game. These were real people. Sylvie had once *been* one of these people.

She'd just had a considerably less dramatic backstory.

At this point, she was amazed she'd ever made it onto the show in the first place. Unlike Sid Khan, the delightfully eccentric bread enthusiast from Middlesex, it hadn't even occurred to her to hint at past alien abduction in her audition tape. She certainly hadn't hand-knit a human-sized cupcake costume, using wool spun by a nun she'd saved from drowning in the Baltic Sea, like retired naval sublieutenant Terence Blaine. If she recalled correctly, she'd introduced herself, Jay had filmed her piping cream into doughnuts, and she'd made a joke about jam that had seemed hilarious until about two seconds after she pressed submit on the application.

"Hard to beat a natural flair for biscuit-decorating and the high probability you've buried four unfaithful men in your basement." Dominic's voice was ominously calm, but his stubbled jaw was set in a long, tense line. One tiny flick of Sylvie's fingernail and his whole head would probably crack like an egg.

So tempting.

"Or maybe she's another Nadine from Bucks," he went on. "Baking through a bereavement and quite sure her late parrot *was* the reincarnated spirit of Julius Caesar."

Aadhya, the nicest of the producers, opened her mouth, but Dominic reached the end of his limited tolerance before she could speak.

"I realize that casting decisions are not my area of expertise."

Every syllable in that sentence had a cutting edge, as if he were snapping off the words one by one, like squares on the chocolate bar she still didn't have. "And that I just need to 'show up, taste the fucking cake, crush a few dreams, and cash my check.'" *Drenched* in cynicism, and clearly a direct quote. Apparently, they'd trod this path before; however, Aadhya's expression barely changed.

Inspiring level of *I do not give one flying shit* from the producer on the left.

"But judging by the relentlessly healthy ratings, your past model worked, and with at least an entry level of sanity." Dominic shot another exasperated glance at the montage of smiling faces. "Did supply just run out on the usual lineup? Pseudobakers with too much imagination, sporadic technical skill . . ." For the first time since he'd ignored her for the entire drive here, his eyes flicked squarely in Sylvie's direction. He'd probably intended to look away just as quickly, but their gazes caught and held. "And the general creative aesthetic of *My Little Pony*."

Languidly, Sylvie ran her fingers through her ponytail, fluffing out her latest pink and lavender highlights. She smothered the most delicate of yawns.

Aadhya studied them both, and then reached for her coffee mug and took a deliberately long, unnecessarily loud sip. "Every contestant has been thoroughly vetted by a counselor. They're interesting people with unique personal experiences, and fully equipped for the pressures of filming, public scrutiny, and minor celebrity." Her fingertips played against the ceramic in a jaunty little tune. "And the potential trauma of a one-on-one conversation with you. It's a new screening process. Sit 'em down and play an hourlong loop of your tactful critiques. Anyone who makes it through with dry eyes and dry pants can grab an apron.

You wouldn't believe how quickly it weeds down the applicant numbers."

Hastily, Sylvie lifted her own cup, and once more Dominic's gaze narrowed on her. His eyes reminded her of his least popular chocolates, the ninety-percent-cacao truffles. Deep, dark, and velvety, with an incredibly sour aftertaste.

"If you've all read your briefings, you'll know we've made format changes this series," Aadhya continued. "A shorter filming schedule to get things moving." And significantly cut their costs on everything from staff catering to contestant hotel rooms. "Stepped-up contestant support services. I'm sure Sylvie can attest that it's disconcerting to go from normal anonymity to suddenly being accosted by strangers at the supermarket." She shot Sylvie a smile.

For all the things Sylvie hadn't enjoyed about her first stint on the *Operation Cake* set, most of the crew had been genuinely kind. There had always been a tacit understanding that shedding a few stress tears or having a spat with another contestant would be well received, but behind the stirred-up drama, there were warm and helpful personalities.

Like Mariana Ortiz. The food writer was flipping through the paperwork in front of her, the gorgeous diamond Art Deco ring on her finger sparkling under the lights. "Good call dropping the mystery-ingredient round." She caught Sylvie's questioning glance. "Finalist last year with an unknown allergy to turmeric. Violent gastro effects. Ever seen the pie scene in *Stand By Me*?"

Sylvie winced.

"We had to reshoot the whole day. I was scrubbing neon yellow out of my ears for a week." Mariana smoothed back a strand of salt-and-pepper hair. "We looked like we'd banded together to massacre Big Bird."

Only this woman could make that anecdote sound almost classy.

"Mystery ingredient is out, new bonus round and theme week are in." Aadhya shoved her papers together and stood. "I think that's all for now. I want you all in makeup, then the studio for a few more promo shots. You're free to head out after that."

Dominic pulled out his phone and shook his head at the frozen PowerPoint display. He shot another unreadable glance at Sylvie before he left the room. He was already dialing, and as he disappeared, she heard crisp orders being issued to some long-suffering underling at De Vere's.

"Sylvie, just a sec." As Mariana squeezed past them with another charming smile, Aadhya stopped her at the door. The producer was a lovely woman in her fifties, who shared Sylvie's delight in all things shiny and pretty. Originally from Jaipur, she'd been working for the network for over twenty years and had steered the *Operation Cake* ship since its very successful maiden voyage. "We're so glad to have you on board. You still head up every poll of most popular former contestants."

That was lovely and flattering. It would, admittedly, be *more* flattering if it were because of her sparkling personality and ingenious bakes, and not because she'd catapulted baked goods into Dominic's skull.

"I've been delighted to see your success with Sugar Fair. There's a framed copy of your *Society* write-up in the greenroom. Bit of alumna inspiration for the newbies." Aadhya was studying her with approval and a tinge of surprise. She looked like a proud mother whose unprepossessing toddler had suddenly come home from nursery with a gold star. "Only three years in business, and you've not only kept a start-up bakery in Notting Hill solvent, you're already gracing the hallowed pages of Matthew Trenery's column. And how did he phrase it?" The words lifted with a provocative lilt. "'Curling your fingertips under the crown of your nemesis'? 'The scorned student preparing to knock her mentor off the throne'?"

Her *mentor*. Dominic. Hell—and she could not stress this enough—no.

"For now," Sylvie said, "I'll be happy with the continued solvency." Her tone was unintentionally grim. Any prolonged conversation with Jay lately and his pessimism started to rub off. She dragged back a lighter note. "Dominic's had a head start. Nudging him off the top spot is more of the *five*-year plan."

Aadhya's nod was knowing. "It's a tough, stressful business. Smart move accepting this contract. I'd expect a sharp lift in profits as soon as the series goes to air."

That was the idea.

And the effect would be quadrupled if they landed the job of all jobs.

There wasn't much better ongoing promotion than baking the cake for the first British royal wedding in almost twenty years.

"You're looking very determined," the producer said, her lips twitching. "And having seen the way your work has continued to develop, I'm not sure Dominic should rest *too* comfortably on his laurels."

Neither he nor anyone else was resting comfortably in the makeup room when Sylvie slipped in a few minutes later.

"Ah, the Chairs of Doom," she murmured, gingerly lowering her butt onto a piece of furniture straight out of Jane Eyre's boarding school. "How much I have not missed thee. This show brings in a fortune in advertising revenue. You'd think they could shell out for a few cushions and a muffin basket."

She bobbed her foot as she looked around. Everything still looked exactly the same. It didn't feel exactly the same, however. As she sat still for what felt the first time in weeks, not merely hours, and stared at a poster on the wall with her name emblazoned next to Dominic's and Mariana's, the sudden unfurling of nerves in her stomach caught her entirely unaware. She'd done this show before, however reluctantly; not for four years and not from this side of the workstation, but still, it shouldn't be so daunting. She taught dozens of classes every month in the Dark Forest, without blinking an eye.

In her lap, her fingers looked strangely pale and bony as she clasped them together.

Very slightly, very subtly, her hands were trembling.

Hell.

There were a lot of people—and a lot of zeroes coming into her bank account—expecting her not to fuck this up.

A chocolate bar appeared in front of her face. Startled, she unraveled her death grip on herself and took it automatically. The calluses on Dominic's fingers rubbed past the calluses on hers, and the wrapper crackled as her fist closed around it.

His attention had briefly left his iPad. His eyes narrowed on her face. "You're shaking. Are you cold, hungry, or scared?"

"Two and three," she muttered, unwrapping the bar. To her relief, the quivering in her limbs eased a bit when the comforting taste hit her tongue. "Thank you."

"Change of pace for you. Some decent chocolate for once." The corner of his mouth indented in an extremely aggravating way.

Midchew, Sylvie turned over the wrapper. She hadn't even noticed she was eating a De Vere's truffle bar. A new flavor. It was delicious. Damn it.

"Why scared?"

She was astonished he even asked. As was he, by the look on his face.

"I don't especially enjoy being on TV." She kept her voice low. It was nothing but the truth, but she had just enough media savvy not to bellow it in the ears of the people signing her paycheck. "And I don't like *personally* being the subject of online discussion. Work, business, is different."

She ate three more pieces of chocolate. Debated keeping the remaining half for later.

Just as she stuffed the entire thing in her mouth, her phone buzzed, and she pulled it out to read the message. An update from Jay. All good on the home front, although he'd argued with Mabel and she'd started making disturbing *amezaiku* lollipops of his face.

Bakery owner. Nursery teacher. In this case, very similar skill sets required.

Dominic flicked to another screen on his iPad. "I'm surprised you could actually commit to this contract. Fledgling businesses usually require twenty-four-seven attention if they're going to have any chance of surviving."

Sylvie finished replying to Jay and set her phone down. Picking up a cleansing wipe, she began swiping off her foundation to leave a blank palette for Zack, the show's makeup artist. "Sugar Fair is almost three years old."

"As I said. Or is it a moot point and things are already going in the same direction as your predecessors?"

She and Jay had looked at twenty-one possible premises for

Sugar Fair. Despite the enormous drawback of it being literally *across the fucking street* from De Vere's, they'd finally selected the space on Magnolia Lane because the former tenant had installed an absolute budget-blowing dream of a kitchen they'd never have been able to afford from scratch. Unfortunately, the erstwhile occupant's culinary dreams—and those of at least six food businesses before him—had hit the rocks. A depressing history for the building that she was choosing to see as a warning and not a precedent.

"If it helps," Dominic murmured, his voice a honeyed drawl as he accepted a sheaf of papers from a passing assistant and scanned the first sheet, "you've outlasted four of the previous failing ventures in that building by at least six months. Not unimpressive for premises that even Willy Wonka would find over the top, and a customer base that appears to be an even split of screeching toddlers and drunken wizards."

The crumb of goodwill over the chocolate bar had lasted a good twenty seconds. Relations were improving.

"Question." With a shiny, scrubbed face, Sylvie reached for the fresh cup of tea waiting on the makeup table and ripped open a sugar packet. "What exactly possessed *you* to commit to *any* of these contracts? This doesn't seem like your natural habitat. Cameras in your face. People trying to take your photo in the street. A name over the front door and it's not yours."

She stirred the tea. As usual, any aversion to confrontation went into hibernation the moment those cool, emotionless eyes glanced over her. A provocative little devil always sashayed out to sit on her shoulder, prodding her more vociferously with every sardonic remark thrown her way. If Dominic could teleport in and fire her up with one of his pillock comments every time she had to negotiate with a supplier, she'd be the freaking queen of haggling.

"And technically," she went on, "unlike your usual workplace, you're not allowed to *completely* decimate someone when they fall short of your ridiculously high standards and dull decorative tastes." Sip. "But let's face it. Anyone who pulls out the glitter is going home with the remains of their ego in a bag."

She truly was curious. He couldn't be here for the same reason she was. De Vere's had always had a foot—and a cake—in every major event and powerhouse in the city. He could hardly be hard up for cash, and she didn't see the Serious Artiste as a closet reality TV fan. He'd lent his brutal honesty and ropy forearms to *Operation Cake*, but the miserable git would probably rather jab himself in the eye with a fondant cutter than curl up on the couch on a Sunday night with a hot chocolate and a slab of Victoria sponge.

Far from unwinding in front of the TV, she'd be surprised if he ever went home at all. He started work as early as she did, and he was frequently still across the road when she tottered tiredly out the door after a Dark Forest session. In fact, he often stood outside the door of De Vere's, practically ticking with annoyance and impatience, and waited until she'd safely made it to her car. In that one singular area, it was surprisingly decent of him.

Jaw-droppingly decent of him.

Because she had manners, she'd popped across once to thank him. He'd looked up from the piping bag he wielded with such ease. His gaze had traveled quickly over her face before returning to meet hers, his lips parting.

As he'd bluntly informed her that she was blocking the way to the stove.

She assumed that once she'd driven off in the early hours of the morning, he went back inside, plugged himself into a power outlet, and recharged his cyborg battery.

He was scrawling his name on the bottom of a paper. She'd noticed before that his handwriting was very messy for a man with the working temperament of Rabbit from *Winnie-the-Pooh*.

"I'd think my motivation for this would be clear," he said after a long enough silence he'd probably been hoping she'd give up and leave.

Sylvie rested her cup on her lap and surveyed him thoughtfully. "Blackmail?"

"The responsibility to share professional expertise with multitudes of otherwise poorly informed bakers." The words were silky smooth. He turned and signed another page. "And a natural inclination for teaching and mentorship."

"I see." She tapped her nails against the hot ceramic. "So, blackmail."

A head popped around the door, then, to summon him back to the studio for his solo promo shots. Apparently, he'd already had his makeup done. Of course there'd be no visible difference.

Dominic lifted his brows at her as he rose and departed, and she realized that her bubbling nerves had simmered down to the point of vanishing completely. His sleeve caught on her hair, stirring the back of her neck as he passed.

She didn't have a chance to speculate further, as Mariana took his place, slipping into the vacated chair and turning with a smile. "So glad to have you here. I've been the only woman on the panel since I came to the network. Jim Durham's a pet, but still, I was *screamingly* sick of the boys' club."

"Lucky for me that Jim wanted to move on." Sylvie remained surprised about that. He'd been on the show since the first season and had seemed like a stalwart.

"Oh, he didn't," Mariana said breezily, leaning forward to

poke through the lipstick selection. "He got arse-over-tit drunk at a network party and told everyone that the head of programming has been shagging his secretary. They retired him faster than a limited-edition Lego set." She picked up a tube. "Word to the wise. If you're going to drink on the clock, stick to a subtle tipple between takes."

Sylvie's smile faltered when Mariana just looked at her placidly.

"Um—any other tips?" she asked lamely, rubbing where the skin itched on the back of her neck, and the other woman shook her head.

"Normally, I'd give a heads-up about the other third of the team, but you already know Frosty, and haven't yet smothered him or yourself. You'll be fine." She hummed. "And Dominic was *not* impressed about your casting, so that's always fun."

"Was he not," Sylvie said, with zero surprise.

"I know you two butted heads from the beginning. He used to say you needed hazard lights attached to your station. And that was before the Hoof Incident." She pulled the cap off the lipstick. "If it sugars the pill, he also found you attractive."

Fun new fact: when a person snorted and swallowed at the same time, hot tea ended up on their chin *and* in their sinuses.

"He once called you the pretty, annoying one," Mariana added, clearing up that little mind-boggler of a moment.

With intense dryness, Sylvie said, "I don't think he intended you to insert a comma into that sentence."

"It's an inevitable personality clash, I suppose. You have a sense of humor. You appear to be open to life's possibilities. And he's . . ." Mariana swatched a line of fuchsia pink on the back of her hand. "Dominic. But perhaps I'm not being totally fair.

He does have his good points beyond those arms and the magic things he does with chocolate."

"He gave her a present today," a passing crew member translated.

Zack bounced through the door like Tigger arriving at Pooh Corner and leaned across Mariana to pluck a different lipstick from the display. "Try the Color Me Coral." Turning, he cast an expert eye over Sylvie. "For you, definitely a rose. Two swipes of Bloomin' Marvelous, and boom. Greta Garbo."

"And I thought *my* work involved magical illusions."

"Is my favorite former contestant excited about the new series?" Zack asked, ignoring that interjection. He held two bottles of foundation against her neck and put one down.

No, but she owed enough to the show and cared enough about these people to at least lie with *perkiness*. "Nervous, but yes."

"It's nice to see some enthusiasm." He pulled a face. His own makeup was gorgeous. Precision of a neurosurgeon when it came to eyeliner. "Especially after the mug on Dominic. Someone needs to tell him that the perpetual glare can drop a bloke who's a solid nine down to a borderline three. And believe me, over the breadth of those six points is a *whole* lot less sex." He started dabbing primer onto Sylvie's cheekbones. "You'd think he was here for a ritual disemboweling, not to be paid my annual salary for a few weeks of part-time work. All he has to do is stand there and tell people they're failing to live up to their potential. My mum's been doing it my whole life for free."

Biting back a grin, Sylvie reached down to her bag when her phone buzzed with another text, trying to keep her head steady for his busy blending. She held it up to read the message and excitement surged in her stomach.

"*Yes.*"

"Good news?" Mariana lowered the iPad she'd extracted from her own bag. There was a paper silhouette of her distinctive head tucked into the lilac case.

"Official press release from the palace." Sylvie followed the link in Jay's text to the actual announcement. "'The Duke and Duchess of Albany are pleased to announce the engagement of Her Royal Highness Princess Rose to Mr. John Marchmont. The wedding will take place in the spring, in London. Further details to follow.'"

As usual, Jay was right on the money.

"Oh." Mariana frowned without much interest. Famously not a royalist. "Remind me. Princess Rose is—"

"Daughter of the king's middle son," Zack said admonishingly. "Especially popular with the under-thirty demographic. Fab fashion sense—like a young Morticia Addams—but she'd retain a spot in my top three favorite royals just for that interview as a teen where she compared her ghastly uncle to a codpiece." He bounced on the balls of his feet. "God, I *love* a royal wedding."

"So do I," Sylvie murmured meaningfully, flipping through to the news sites and clicking on the first link. The press release had been out for almost twenty minutes, so naturally the media had already thrown around names for everything from the dress designer to the supplier of napkin holders.

She scissored her fingers, enlarging the official engagement shot of the couple smiling into one another's eyes. The bride's sleek dark hair was smoothed into an unusually restrained knot, but she'd stuck to her guns with the heavy black eyeliner. Her lacy black dress was a little funereal, but clearly a compromise between her own preference for Victoriana and the palace's idea of appropriate styling for a photo shoot that would make the history books. The groom was wearing a pink shirt, and his curls were fluffy.

It was like a grown-up Emily the Strange marrying Bertie Wooster.

The smiles were natural, the body language extremely affectionate, but their knuckles were white. Nerves or tension?

Sylvie studied the cover shot for a few more seconds, then scrolled down to the article. The journalist would have had a lot of the copy sitting ready to go. This had been on the rumor mill since their first joint public appearance. The union between the king's eldest granddaughter and the youngest son of a baronet, who, according to this tabloid, had inherited neither land nor brain cells from his parents.

The overgrown Goth princess and a stuttering social climber with all the poise and sophistication of a golden retriever.

Charming.

A page-long summary of Rose's past romances and flings followed, basically an illustrated guide to the art of slut-shaming.

Did the editors of the *Daily Spin* actually advertise for their writers or just draw symbols on the ground and summon them from the underworld?

Sylvie zeroed in on the column she was interested in. At least twelve fashion houses had been mooted for the gown. Only one name in connection with the cake. Even the tabloids considered this a done deal.

If Dominic had also seen the breaking news, he was probably out there right now, putting the finishing touches on a sketch for an exquisitely rendered snooze of a fruitcake.

Zack read her mind. "I suppose De Vere's is doing the cake. First royal wedding in years. Dominic's probably a shoo-in. His grandad had the honor in the past. De Vere Senior was the king's pet baker. His Majesty was very fond of their Battenberg." Mariana looked at him, and he shrugged. "Fact of the day on the *Royal Stans* blog."

Mariana's attention returned to Sylvie. She was observing her cannily. "Is that just the slightest touch of scheming criminal mastermind I see?"

Zack made a noise like an overexcited chicken. "Are you going after the royal wedding contract? Literally *the* cake of the year?" He hauled Sylvie's chair around and leaned close. She widened her eyes at him innocently, and he clapped his hands together, a booming *slap* that made her jump. "Oh, *hells yeah*. Judge versus judge. Neighbor pitted against neighbor. The kitten taking on the lion." Sylvie's eyes narrowed again. Zack gave another wriggly little hop. "I do love me some drama. Bring it on, dollface."

Kitten, her arse. This was for her people's future job security. And it was a bake that would be preserved in perpetuity, a part of history. She'd probably have phrased it differently, but—what the hell.

Bring it on, dollface.

Chapter Four

October

De Vere's
Favored establishment of His Majesty the King and his
fondness for Battenberg.
Status: As expected, invited to submit a tender for the royal
wedding cake.

> "Literally *the* cake of the year."
> —Zack Romero, underpaid *Operation Cake* makeup artist

With a flick of his fingers, Dominic sent the fifth and final tier of
the cake spinning onto the upper dowels. Each layer was a clean,
crisp white. Marzipan over rich Vienna cream icing, edged with
sugar lace, a delicate spidery web of lines, the perfect allusion
of the bobbin lace that Princess Rose liked to weave. Or at least
claimed she wove as a useful anecdote. His notes stated that she
gave biannual speeches as patron of the City of London Arts and
Crafts Guild.

Flowers wound up the side of the cake, the blooming vine of
a fairy tale.

He studied the effect with distaste.

A tap of the leftmost flower, and the petals changed color from an iridescent pink to a deep, brooding blood purple, almost black in tone. He swept his hand in front of the cake. One after another, the edges of the peony poppies bled, the dark color leaching over the celestial pink. Still fairy tale, but with the inevitable malevolent element.

Better.

Also better suited to a dungeon or coffin than a reception table, but from the impression he got of the bride, the Tim Burton vibe was strongly in her wheelhouse.

With a stylus pen, he touched the dark petals with the faintest dusting of gold.

"Roses would have been the obvious choice," Liam Boateng commented. Dominic's friend and sous-chef stood at his side, arms folded, studying the screen.

Frowning, Dominic spun the projected image around on the tablet, tilting the angle to better see the intricate lacework on the upper tier, draped in smooth folds around both the royal and Marchmont family crests. He pulled a cluster of the poppies and moved them to the base layer, so the cake appeared to be rising from a frothing profusion of flowers.

"Most other tenders will work with that cliché." He stepped back to cast another critical eye over the design. "And Daciano will ignore the flower brief completely; he's an anthophobic. Won't have so much as a petal in his salon."

"He's also totally overrated and increasingly unreliable."

Dominic made another crisp adjustment and a short sound of agreement. "The embargo on this contract will be ironclad. One drink at his local and he'd be shooting his mouth off about every last detail. He failed as credible competition before Marchmont even popped the question."

Liam scoffed. "Please. Like there's any *credible* competition."

Dominic shot him a warning glance. "Confidence is warranted. Certainty is not. We've lost contracts before. We've lost contracts across the *road* before."

Which was still irritating.

His eyes went briefly to the silhouette portrait he'd tucked into the edge of a photo frame on the desk, to keep Pet's work intact. The outline of Sylvie's face seemed to change in mood daily. Right now, he could almost hear her laughter.

"Noted." Liam plucked a peony poppy of the *non*-digital variety from a vase. "Are we sure these are the groom's favorite flower?" He was obviously skeptical. "Do men even *have* a favorite flower?"

"Ooh." The exclamation came from the doorway. Pet was leaning against the frame, fanning her face. "What was that I just walked into? A sudden puff of toxic masculinity? How doubly disappointing from the blokes who can turn all that gorgeous lace and pearls into three-dimensional, edible reality." She joined them at the table, eyeing both the smaller image on the tablet and the life-sized version on the adjacent projector screen. "And since you ask so obnoxiously, only person who still owes me a tenner for the staff lunch"—she held out her hand, and Liam immediately reached for his wallet—"yes, we are sure."

She pocketed the ten-pound note he gave her and tapped the side of her nose. "I have my sources," she added in a spot-on James Bond voice, Connery-style. "And amongst my vast wealth of knowledge—believe me, I know what men like."

One wink at Liam and the usually levelheaded sous-chef shuffled his feet and coughed several times.

Dominic sent the final images to the printer. It would be faster and easier to submit digitally, but apparently a royal wedding was smothered in enough secrecy and paranoia to stymie a Bletchley Park operative. The staff at St. Giles Palace had requested everything in hard copy, delivered by a private courier. At this point, he was surprised the instructions hadn't included a self-destructing scroll and an invisibility cloak. "If you wouldn't mind horrifying me on your own time, did you finalize the paperwork for the new apprenticeship?"

"Yes, boss." Pet sketched an absentminded salute. She was reading through the assembled proposal on the table, with blithe disregard for the CONFIDENTIAL markings stamped across the heading. She frowned. "You're going with fruitcake?"

Heavy, unmistakeable undertone of *ew*.

Dominic slotted the latest printouts into the folder. "Thanks for the heads-up on the flower selection, but we're dealing with the royal household. There's still a hefty amount of protocol, and even if the bride and groom look like they've respectively stepped out of *The Nightmare Before Christmas* and an *Archie* comic, the royal tradition is—"

"The brandy-soaked, raisin-spotted, intestine-clogging brick known as fruitcake," Pet interrupted. "Will look and taste the same whether it was made yesterday or two decades ago. And at no time during its lengthy existence will anyone want to eat it. I've told you, the bride likes chocolate cake. Specifically and vitally, she apparently likes *your* Death by Chocolate fudge cake. Very little about this couple conforms to royal standards, which is half the reason the bookies are already taking revolting odds on how long the marriage will last, or if they'll actually make it to the altar. Rose is infamously a strong personality and a massive pain in her family's arse. I guarantee that however far she has to bend to tradition, she'll wrangle final say over details like the inside of her cake. You should be pitching chocolate."

Dominic waited for the rolling stream of words to come to an end. "Again, I appreciate your contribution to the proposal, Pet, but—"

"But your judgment is infallible, right?" The words were low. "No regrets, no mistakes for you." Her lips momentarily pinched together, then she turned away.

Liam shot an uncomfortable glance from her departing back to Dominic's taut expression. He drummed his fingers against the folder. "So . . . should we send samples of Death by Chocolate, as well, or . . . ?"

There was something cold and dark between Dominic's ribs. With each passing day of his sister's presence here, it sliced deeper. "Get the proposal sealed and delivered, please. And take the samples of the fruitcake."

"And—"

"You've had the instructions. Do your job."

In deliberate mimicry of Pet, Liam snapped him a salute. His manner was ironic, and his eyes were a little too knowing.

Sugar Fair
Favored establishment of Instagram.
As expected, not invited to submit a tender for the royal wedding cake.

Doing it anyway.

Beneath an encompassing, unflattering net, Sylvie's hair was plastered stickily to her head. To her left, Mabel stood at an oiled marble slab, constantly pulling and stretching a molten sugar mass with her bare hands. The bulging muscles in her otherwise thin arms shifted with the rhythm of her movements, but she never paused. Most of the staff disliked blowing and sculpting sugar, for reasons of both tedium and pain. Mabel was in her element. Humming the Beach Boys of all things, she tested a satiny, pliable piece of the mass between her fingers. It was a finicky, often frustrating process for the uncertain or unskilled—one pull too many, an alteration too far in temperature, and a perfectly workable sculpting medium became a rock-hard, crystallized mess in the bin.

With a satisfied grunt, Mabel grabbed a machete. She gave it a slightly disturbing, almost maternal stroke before she whacked off a long length of deep sapphire-blue sugar and passed it to Sylvie.

"Thanks," Sylvie half sang as she dropped the sugar onto her own workstation under the heating lamps and finished stirring a pot with her other hand. The busier they were, and the more intense the pressure, a vocal tic kicked in and she sounded like an escapee from *Cabaret*, incapable of just speaking at a normal pitch like a normal person. Mabel's continuous loop of "Barbara Ann" wasn't helping. "Time?"

Mabel whipped another pot of boiling syrup solution off the stove and plunged it into a sink full of ice to flash cool. "Exactly three hours until six polite little drawings of fruitcakes and rosebuds toddle along to St. Giles Palace." She waited a few seconds before pouring the syrup into a waiting mold. "And our fuckin' masterpiece storms the gates."

Or, more accurately, tiptoed in the back, via Jay's contact in the inner sanctum of St. Giles. This would either go to plan, or they'd be blacklisted from any future event even remotely associated with the royals. Probably down to and including lunches around the corner at the Prince of Wales pub.

The butterflies in her stomach were muttering derisively.

With a deep breath to steady herself, Sylvie finished rolling the blue sugar mass into a ball. A quick blast with a blowtorch before she inserted a heated metal pump, closed the edges of the sugar around it, and released the air valve. As the sugar inflated, blowing out like a balloon, the sides becoming glossy and ever so slightly transparent, she studied the reference photo pinned on the board. In an unconscious gesture carried over from years in art studios, her eyes briefly closed and her free palm hovered and shaped in the air above and around the sugar as if it were clay. She could see the photographic form in her mind, and with no further hesitation, she set her fingers to the expanding sugar work, pulling, twisting, and coaxing that image into physical being.

Mabel was cutting the remaining blue sugar solution into dozens of small squares. She pinched and rippled each one into the shape of a scale with such skill that even the apprentices edged closer to watch, and most of them had genuinely been known to hide behind the fridges when they heard Mabel's footsteps.

Sylvie bent, ignoring an ache in her lower back as she continued to blow air into the growing sculpture. On the work surface, two wings sat waiting, each a vivid iridescent purple. She nodded to a hovering assistant, who licked her lips nervously before picking up the blowtorch and holding it to the edge of the first wing.

"Christ, she's going to incinerate it," Mabel remarked with great interest and no apparent concern. She kept adding to the stack of scales, tossing them toward Sylvie with the ease of a child plucking a pile of daisies.

"Pull back a little." Sylvie stopped the pump and carefully adjusted the younger girl's uncertain fingers around the blowtorch. "Yes. Good."

Together, they sealed the first wing to the side of the foot-long sugar dragon. He was currently bald and lopsided, but about to be magnificent.

And hopefully win over a princess.

Efficiently, Sylvie attached the second wing, this one unfurling in preparation for flight, and with the aplomb of John Wayne twirling a pistol, Mabel whipped out her own blowtorch to start layering on the scales. She'd customized the handle with purple stripes and diamantés, and really shouldn't be carrying it around in a holster like that. It unsettled the customers.

By the time Jay pushed open the kitchen door and walked in with an air of tangible anxiety and even longer hair, the whole team had temporarily left their own jobs to watch the finishing touches. Sylvie flickered her brush over the dragon, leaving a line of glittering pigment on the spiked tail. The edible paint had an oil-slick effect, shimmering from blue to pink to purple to black under the light.

"What time do I have to—" Jay began.

"Shhh," hissed about fifteen voices at once, as Sylvie picked up the dragon and set it on the lowest tier of the cake.

Three layers of rich chocolate cake, covered in mirror glaze icing, marbled blue, purple, and black, with gold paint etched and feathered to replicate the appearance of the sugar dragon's scales. She wound the tail upward, adjusting the long curve to swoop neatly around the top tier, the very tip coming to rest protectively on the sculpted couple who sat on the edge, their legs dangling, tiny sugar ankles entwined.

One totally edible princess with long black hair and thick

eyeliner. Her endearingly fluffy blond love. And Caractacus, the dragon sentinel from the video game *I, Slayer*, over which the royal couple had apparently bonded, turning an excruciating first private date into an all-nighter. From curt questions and stammering answers to a beer-drinking, ogre-bashing bonk-fest.

Just like all good fairy tales. The Brothers Grimm would be proud.

There was a moment of silence as they all stood and surveyed it from top to bottom.

And then Jay, after weeks of verbal hand-wringing and increasingly unnerving doubt, stood between Sylvie and Mabel and extended both his fists.

Without a word spoken, they touched their knuckles to his.

**INTERNAL MEMO FROM THE DESK OF THE
HONORABLE EDWARD LANCIER**

*Private Secretary to Her Royal Highness,
Princess Rose of Albany*

**HIGHLY CONFIDENTIAL
Re: Project C**

By request of HRH Princess Rose and Mr. John Marchmont,
an initial consultation with each of the prospective parties is
to be arranged on the afternoon of the eleventh of October, in
the Captain's Suite, St. Giles Palace, London SW1A 2BQ.

Each party will be allocated a period of thirty
minutes, commencing 4:25 p.m.

Attendees will arrive at separate locations and be transported by private cars to the north entrance.

Communicate <u>directly</u> with the following persons of interest:

Mr. Dominic De Vere of De Vere's, 8 Magnolia
Lane, Notting Hill, London W11 2DZ
&
Ms. Sylvie Fairchild of Sugar Fair, 11 Magnolia
Lane, Notting Hill, London W11 2DZ

Chapter Five

October the Eleventh

Hartwell Studios
10:35 a.m.

Fortunately for those hoping to "crush a few dreams and cash their check" as soon as possible, the studio still hasn't burnt down, despite the best efforts of certain *Operation Cake* contestants.

Two hours into filming, and Sylvie could already guess who would be going home tomorrow. It was a shame, because Byron, their youngest contestant, had charming manners and a nice smile. The Birmingham student obviously meant well. And he'd already had a challenging year, having recently spent three days trapped in a haunted house at a defunct carnival. He'd been flattened by a rusty statue of a demonic clown, and his mates had been too drunk to remember they'd left him there. As he'd told the cameras and a flatly staring Dominic, it had been in the papers and everything.

Unfortunately, well-intentioned, cautionary-tale Byron could probably screw up a Betty Crocker box mix.

For the sake of both his feelings and the lens zooming in on her expression, Sylvie gamely took another bite of his scone. As expected, that mouthful was also going to sit in her intestines like a rock. It was hard to believe he'd created this . . . object out of unassuming flour and butter.

"It's a lovely color," she offered after a pause, and he cheered up fractionally.

He already looked a teeny bit like a basset hound, and as his eyes tugged irresistibly to her left, the lugubrious lines of his youthful face drooped further.

Doom was approaching, in a very snazzy shirt and tie.

Dominic joined her at the tabletop, keeping a regimental distance between their bodies. She could just faintly smell the oud in his aftershave over the prevailing scent of burnt butter. Poor Byron took a visible breath and swallowed, his floury fingers clenching on the edge of the workstation.

Sylvie had started to relax into the rhythm of the filming the moment she'd seen Mariana's twinkling eyes and heard Aadhya's voice weaving through the mess of tech and wires, but it was the contestants who'd really banished her own qualms. She knew how overwhelming the experience was in the beginning, how intensely emotions amped up. The producers didn't always need to prompt the drama. With camera operators in your face, the judges watching every move, and the awareness of the viewers at home hovering over the scene like a critical ghost, even minor mishaps could come with an appallingly easy threat of tears.

With a sympathetic smile, she gave Byron's arm a little squeeze, and he managed a weak grin in return.

After one long, considering stare, Dominic leaned forward and cut a slice from the scone with crisp movements. A muscle flexed in his lean jaw as he bit down. Sylvie flinched as hard as Byron at the resulting *crack*.

God, she hoped that hadn't been Dominic's tooth.

A handful of seconds passed in which Dominic's expression had all the animation of a frozen video screen, and then he reached up and withdrew a small object from his mouth, turning it in the light to observe the metallic sheen.

"What's that?" Byron blanched, leaning forward to see. "A . . . button?"

Dominic's dark eyes lifted from the button. Wordlessly, he mimicked Sylvie's earlier movement, reaching toward the young man's arm; without making contact, he flicked the air over Byron's sleeve.

They all stared down at his cuff, where a thread hung loose. Tucking his mouth to the side and sinking his teeth into his lip, Byron fidgeted with the other cuff, where a matching silver button was still intact.

"Um. Oops?" he offered lamely, and Sylvie watched as Dominic's wide chest lifted in a silent inhalation.

"And ironically," he drawled, "the button is the most edible part of the bake."

"I think that's a bit of an exaggeration," Byron unexpectedly mustered the moxie to toss back, to Sylvie's pure delight. It was no wonder Dominic was so insufferable in the judging when everyone just toppled over like bowling pins at one severe word.

Admittedly, Byron's tone was so uncertain the retort emerged more like a question, and Dominic's blunt comment wasn't *much* of an exaggeration; the scones were fucking bleak. But as the baby of the group had just demonstrated, it was possible to take on constructive criticism without completely prostrating yourself at the feet of the source.

The room was very quiet, the other contestants all standing sentry at their own efforts, displaying varying degrees of sympathy and apprehension. Sylvie's gaze caught on the workstation of Byron's nearest neighbor, Libby, the redhead with the face so ingenuous she could have been pulled straight from a concept board at Disney. And the blue eyes Sylvie remembered from her photograph at the preproduction meeting—shrewd and determined, at odds with her otherwise guileless appearance. The tiniest smile played around Libby's mouth as she looked at the button in Dominic's hand.

Dominic broke the remaining scone apart, with a concerted effort. "It's like tearing chunks off a baguette. You've kneaded a gluten network that could patch a hole in a 747. It's a scone dough, not a bad back; save the deep-tissue massage for the locker room. This was a flagrant waste of time and ingredients. You fought hard to be here. Prove me wrong and stop fucking up."

Off set, Aadhya tossed her hands up. Between the judging panel and the contestants, a lot of expletives were heading for the cutting-room floor and the blooper reel.

They left the set while the contestants were completing the blind bake round, Mariana disappearing outside to take a call.

"As usual, your critiques have all the subtlety of a Lancaster bomber," Sylvie said as she accompanied Dominic into the greenroom. Dropping into a wheeled chair, she spun back and forth a little. "I've been on the other side of the counter. The pressure is intense. They're trying their best, and most of them are probably nervous as hell."

Dominic unscrewed the cap of a water bottle. "If that was Byron's best, he'd have no business even applying," he said flatly. "There's some marginal skill there, and currently a lot of lazy vanity. He produced a semi-edible pastry in the prelim round, however revolting the filling, but those scones could have been dropped from that bomber during the Blitz. He didn't follow the recipe and he ran short on time because he was too busy checking his reflection in the oven door. We won't even go into the hygiene failure." One hand went gingerly to his jaw, and he grimaced. "Just about lost a molar."

A muffled crash echoed through the wall. She heard the distinct sound of bakeware rolling along tiles.

"*Is* your tooth all right?" she asked, slipping her hands into her back pockets as she studied him. "That was a nasty crack."

His attention briefly fixed on her face, his unreadable gaze colliding with hers before dusting over her cheeks and temples like a physical touch. Like Mariana, the man had undeniable presence; she felt like she was seriously letting the team down in the X-factor stakes. "It's fine." A frown ghosted over his brow. "Thanks."

The light overhead was creating interesting shadows and angles along his profile. Visually, he would have done quite well as a debonair hero in a '40s film. Until the pouty bombshell tried to engage him in flirtatious banter and he cocked a suave eyebrow, swept a slow, sensual look over her body—and told her she was blocking the optimal path of movement in his kitchen.

He swallowed a mouthful of water and rolled one shoulder as if his neck were stiff. He needed to enlist Byron's overly zealous kneading on his trapezius. "I've said nothing that wasn't straight fact."

"I'm taking issue with the delivery, not the content." Sylvie kicked a foot back, holding it in a stretch of her own; she was restless. Obviously, the producers had always got a lot of mileage out of contrasting Dominic and Mariana. Every marketable tale needed an antagonist. But still—"It's easier to absorb and act on constructive criticism if it's softened by the acknowledgment of successes. You could aim for one proper compliment every hour. Maybe an occasional smile."

A fraction of a scowl appeared instead. "Our job is to perform an honest critique."

"I'm not suggesting you go overboard. We don't want to stun the nation senseless. Two or three teeth at most."

"According to the billboards, it's a legitimate competition, not tiny tots' baking hour at the local nursery. They've already got you cradling one hand and Mariana holding the other." Dominic leaned forward to set the bottle on the table. He'd pushed up his shirtsleeves. There was still a small streak of raspberry jam on his forearm. Charlene, the possessor of the multiple mysterious exes, had dropped a jar. The glass had exploded, and her workstation currently looked like a bloody crime scene.

"Probably feels right at home," Sylvie had heard a grip mutter.

"A handshake," she suggested. "When a dish is really spectacular."

"In the unlikely event that situation arises for the first time in seven seasons, I'll consider it." She barely had time to wrinkle her nose before he added unexpectedly, "If *you* were nervous during your time on the show, you didn't show it. You still prioritize flashy decoration over the essential foundations now, but you were never openly rocked by criticism. You took it on the chin and until that last fucking disaster"—a tinge of heat lit up his tone; clearly the unicorn hoof did still rankle—"you listened to all of us and your bakes improved accordingly."

Good grief.

Apparently, bread-baking Sid was right on the money about the alien abductions. She didn't know what they'd suddenly done with the original Dominic, but cheers for the substitute.

Sylvie could feel a reluctantly pleased flush creeping into her cheeks.

"To the extent of your ability," Pod Dominic finished.

Before she could stand up and accidentally insert her metal straw into his nearest artery, a production assistant tapped on the door and approached with iPad in hand to take them through the upcoming schedule changes.

They had finally wrapped things up when Mariana glided in from the hallway and swayed into a chair, with suspiciously perfect timing to skip the tedious briefing. "Judge B. Judge C. How are we doing?"

Sylvie smiled, and Dominic did a sort of man-greeting chin jerk.

"Pretty appalling showing this morning, wasn't it?" Mariana went on cheerfully. "I'm going to be tasting Adam's custard for a week. Did this bunch have to so much as beat an egg during the audition process, or was it *all* about the weird sob stories this year?" She swiveled toward the silent presence Sylvie was going to consider Judge C. "So, how is that talented sister of yours?"

Sylvie had fully intended to spend the rest of their break elsewhere, but for some reason she was still sitting here and now listening to their conversation. Or, more accurately, to Mariana's monologue and Dominic's quiet breathing and obvious desire to not exist in this building.

"I framed the silhouette she made." Mariana crossed her legs and admired her own shoes. "She doesn't work on commission, by any chance? Because friends of mine recently got engaged and they'd love a dual portrait for their wedding invitation."

"Pet works in a matter of minutes, usually while chattering a dozen words a second. I'll give you her number. She'll want to help, and she'll try to do it for free. I'd appreciate if you didn't let her. She has an incurable case of people-pleasing, frequently to her detriment."

"Which one of you is adopted?" Mariana possibly didn't mean to ask aloud, and a sound like a squeaky bicycle wheel escaped Sylvie's throat before she could think better of it.

In an ideal world, the buzzer to summon them back to the studio would have sounded at that moment. However, it was an awkward three minutes of heavy silence before Aadhya's assistant came to usher them back on set for the next round of stomachaches.

"Probably one of those think-before-I-speak moments my wife likes to mention," Mariana murmured to Sylvie as they returned to the studio floor and gazed with equal dismay at the results of the blind bake. The early episode nerves really were hitting this bunch like a sledgehammer. Only one person had produced a dish that was recognizable as crème regis. Ten quid said the entry on the end, the dead ringer for cat sick, had come from Byron's stove. "Speaking of which, she's a big fan of Sugar Fair. She went to a party in your booze dungeon and still rhapsodizes about what she can remember of it. She'd like to meet you properly—I wondered if you'd like to join us for drinks later?"

"Any other day, I'd love to," Sylvie said with genuine regret, "but I have a meeting at five today, and no idea how long it'll run."

A meeting she'd been doing her best to keep simmering in the back of her mind until the first significant event on today's calendar was complete.

A meeting that had been arranged in person, via an inconspicuously dressed, smooth-speaking, plummy-toned stranger like something out of a '70s spy flick.

A meeting at motherfucking St. Giles Palace, because Sugar Fair had been short-listed to bake the royal wedding cake.

She'd hoped like hell, she'd had faith in her team, her own skills, and Princess Rose's badass love of Caractacus, but it still wasn't quite sinking in that they'd crossed the first—*huge*—hurdle. Every time she thought about it, the prospect hopped and skipped around her mind like droplets of oil dancing in a hot pan.

It didn't help that the only person she was allowed to tell at this stage was Jay, who wasn't exactly cool under pressure. He'd rung her at three this morning to propose the hypothetical scenario in which they won the contract, spent months on the cake, and then unintentionally killed off the entire royal family with a lethal dose of listeria from bad eggs. Thoughts?

Her fricking *thoughts* were that it had taken half a bottle of concealer today to control her eye bags.

Speaking of bad eggs—

"The only dish that *looks* remotely correct tastes, for some ungodly reason, like onion soup," Dominic was saying, with obvious exasperation, as they conferred privately over the anonymous dishes. He set down his spoon. "For my part, first place has to go to either the scrambled eggs or the congealed mucus."

"The scrambled eggs are far too sweet." Mariana made a gesture like an old-school game-show hostess presenting a prize. "Blue ribbon to the congealed mucus, it is."

The congealed mucus belonged to Libby, who accepted her status at the top of the leaderboard with a self-deprecating blush. As Sylvie had guessed, Byron fell squarely to the bottom again, with his chunky, burnt mess. According to Aadhya's murmured aside, even Hades would have wiped sweat from his brow at the temperature in that stove.

As Mariana delivered the results, Byron managed a wavering smile for the cameras regardless, but he seemed slightly puzzled. With an air of uncertainty, he looked from the row of unappetizing dishes to his fellow contestants, seated on their stools for the verdict.

Libby smiled sympathetically back at him.

It was probably an unwritten rule of her employment here that judges didn't play favorites, but Sylvie had already ranked the bakers in her head—not from best crème regis to worst, but from morally-deserves-to-win-the-whole-shebang to probably-trolls-people-online. Her personal top spot was veering between Emma Abara, a knitter and pattern designer from Manchester, who'd sacrificed her own bake time to comfort a younger contestant who'd left the set in tears; and Adam Foley from Glasgow, an absentminded former professor straight out of a novel.

"Adam spotted Byron's mistake with the oven temperature," one of the production assistants whispered at her shoulder. "No comment, no fuss, just quietly corrected it. Unfortunately, it was too late to save it. Typical twenty-year-old wannabe 'influencer,'" she added with a scathing glance at the depressed-looking Byron, "too busy admiring himself to get the job done."

"Hmm." Sylvie contemplated the assembled contestants again. "I'm surprised he was that careless again."

After Dominic's unique variety of pep talk, she'd actually thought Byron had looked quite determined going into that round.

The assistant shrugged without much interest. From the crew's perspective, the more disasters, the better.

Sylvie was navigating the winding warren of back hallways to her dressing room when she passed close to the contestants' lounge and heard muffled voices.

"But you did say the oven was meant to be set at—" Byron was cut off by Libby's distinctive Welsh tones.

"That's *not* what I said, but—I mean, it *was* an initiative task,

Byron. Sorry, but you really should have been making your own decisions anyway. We all found that round difficult and it sucks that yours turned out *so* grim, but it's not my fault if you weren't listening proper—"

The remainder of Libby's offhand response faded out as they must have moved into the next room.

Incontrovertible fact of life: even when the exterior was Ewok-level disarming, you could always spot the mean girl at the party.

"Little shit-stirrer," Sylvie muttered, trying to push open the door to the staff corridor. It stuck every damn time.

A large hand reached over her shoulder. "How ungenerous." A silky murmur near her ear. "Don't forget, she's nervous as hell."

Regrettably, it appeared that hours of sugar consumption resulted in Dominic not only remembering but continuing a conversation.

"She's cool as ice, and just as sharp."

"And she's correct. Whatever shit others pulled, he should have been owning his space and decisions."

He managed to jolt the handle upward, but they both stepped back at the same time to let the other pass and ended up nose to nose.

Half her mind was entwined around the approaching meeting at St. Giles; the other was wrapped in annoyance over Libby's saccharine ruthlessness—but as if every bit of noise in her busy brain just whited out for a few frozen seconds, she looked up at him and went completely still.

And just for that instant, beneath the unflappable chill, she saw a flash of startlement and something . . . else.

For the first time, she realized his eyes were very slightly different colors. The left eye was a fractionally lighter shade of brown than the right.

His veiled gaze flickered downward. Returned to hers. A spasm of movement passed through his expression, a sort of abbreviated, curt denial, almost a flinch. He turned away.

With a tiny little breath through parted lips, she ducked her head and slipped through the door.

What the fuck was that?

He walked at her side in silence until they reached their dressing rooms. They were small, poky cupboards located either side of Mariana's, but Sylvie's teeny space contained a mini-fridge she'd stocked with truffles and a pink kettle she'd really fancy adopting on a permanent basis.

Dominic stood with his hand resting against his door, head tilted downward; then he looked at her. "You've obviously picked your favorites from the cast." Did his voice, too, sound just a bit—off?

She cleared her throat. "Emma and Adam." His expression was blank now. Possibly had no idea who they were. Possibly just his face. "She's the—"

"Nice woman who completely squandered her time to pacify the attention-seeker. And he's the Scottish academic who tried to rectify somebody else's mistake but lost half his own equipment and at one point returned from the bathroom and forgot which was his station. Even with the small clue of his name emblazoned in massive letters." Dominic unlocked his door. "They'll both do well in the long run." He met her curious gaze with a very direct look. "Regardless of who makes it to the final, the weeping-heart contestants with the public sympathy vote can always leverage their exposure."

His door shut behind him.

One point in Dominic's favor—that last comment distracted

her from a good five minutes of nerves over her pending royal rendezvous. And any other reactions obviously provoked by the mounting pressure.

Sylvie sat down at the little desk in her dressing room and spun the chair in pensive circles. He certainly hadn't given any indication of it today—she'd never seen him display nerves in any situation—but she'd almost guarantee Dominic also had a meeting coming up at the palace. The man who'd hand-delivered her instructions hadn't divulged the names of other contenders for the contract, but Zack was right—De Vere's was a shoo-in.

For the short list.

As a contestant on the show, as Dominic had just helpfully reminded her, she'd only made it to the penultimate episode.

When it came to this contract, she was taking out the title.

Chapter Six

"In a battle all you need to make you
fight is a little hot blood . . ."
—George Bernard Shaw

Let the battle commence . . .

St. Giles Palace
4:25 p.m.
Meeting with Candidate: Mr. Dominic De Vere

Dominic had anticipated the intense secrecy surrounding the Albany contract. He hadn't expected to feel like a character in a straight-to-TV espionage film. He'd been asked to drive to the Givran hotel at quarter to four, after which he'd sat in the bar for fifteen minutes before he'd been approached by an unsmiling couple in head-to-toe black. They had introduced themselves as Jeremiah and Arabella and looked like cutouts from a paper-doll book, the bodyguard edition. By the time he'd followed them out the rear entrance of the hotel and into the back of a black SUV with tinted windows, he had the unwelcome thought that this was where things took an ugly turn in the film.

Clearly, all this time in Sylvie's company was screwing with his brain.

In more ways than one.

Neither security officer said a word throughout the circuitous journey to the north entrance of St. Giles Palace. Usually, Dominic appreciated people who didn't need to fill any silence with unnecessary small talk, but right now—yeah, a bit unnerving.

The car drew into a private alcove, out of range of prying eyes and zooming camera lenses. It probably wasn't a completely over-the-top precaution. The worst of the tabloids would be sticking their noses and cash incentives into any dodgy corner they could find, trying to pluck out the smallest details of the wedding in advance.

He was grateful as hell he hadn't been born into this life—and he didn't envy John Marchmont marrying into it. He'd met the groom once, at an awards banquet. From the little he remembered—guileless eyes, a bit of a stammer, zero idea what anyone was talking about—the man was about to be eaten alive. Between them, the press and the British public would make mincemeat of the poor sap.

And the marital home wasn't exactly a source of privacy and respite. Dominic took in the plush interior of St. Giles as he followed the protection officers through the winding corridors. The carpet was so thick his shoes were sinking in as he walked, and it was spotless despite the risky choice of winter white. At regular intervals, uniformed staff with ID badges around their necks came in and out of doors, keeping their eyes politely averted from the newcomers. He caught the slight whirring traction of a security camera above his head, twisting to follow their progress.

Thanks to the volley of information Pet had flung at his head over the past couple of weeks, he knew that the princess, her parents, and her siblings each had private apartments in the south wing. Hopefully with a little less foot traffic, but he had a feeling that even occupying the "family" wing would be akin to taking up residence in a fishbowl.

According to Pet, it was "true love."

For their sakes, he hoped it was worth it.

Without any expectation of a useful answer, he addressed Jeremiah, who looked the most likely to drop illicit info. Something about the constant eye twitch and the emerging peek of *Doctor Who* socks under too-short trousers. "How many tenders are on the short list today?"

"I'm not at liberty to divulge that information, sir."

He seemed scandalized that Dominic had even asked.

Weddings topped the priority list of their contracted cakes. They held hugely personal, intrinsic meaning. For two—or in some cases, three, four, or more—people, it was a symbol of an occasion they would remember and shelter for the rest of their lives.

Or at least until divorce proceedings and a subsequent second cake.

But there were limits to how much pretension Dominic could swallow, and this experience was starting to push at those boundaries.

They rounded another corner, and Arabella spoke into her phone. As they approached an imposing set of double wooden doors—the Captain's Suite, according to a gold plaque—the left door opened, and a middle-aged man stepped out.

He inclined his head at the protection officers, and their spines snapped rod straight. Dominic half expected a military salute. Evidently, he was a staffer high up the authority ladder. Dominic surveyed him with one glance.

Small round glasses. Vividly red nose. Bushy white beard.

Probably a heavy drinker. Definitely a smoker; under a whiff of cologne, he still smelled like the rear courtyard of a pub. Visually, he was a dead ringer for Father Christmas. If Father Christmas were the moody old bastard he ought to be, with a job description that revolved around the entitled demands of millions of sugar-hyped children.

"Mr. De Vere," the Santa doppelgänger said crisply, after an equally comprehensive summing-up in return. "Please, come in."

The interior of the room was bog-standard conference suite: an oval table surrounded by backbreaking chairs, a trolley with rudimentary tea and coffee facilities, and a projector screen. A few people in nondescript suits sat in silence, each wearing the ubiquitous staff lanyard. With one exception, it might have been any office building in the city.

That exception, the three people at the front of the room, stood up in a collective movement, accompanied by the rustling of expensive fabric.

The statuesque woman standing front and center studied him from head to foot. Every person in this building was constantly eyeing someone else with suspicion or condescension. Her eyes were infamous, a shade of blue so pale that her irises were almost white, glittering with both intelligence and calculation, like ice crystals reflecting an overcast sky. In an old novel, her features would be described as "handsome." Presently, they were set into a very polite, totally meaningless smile.

At her side was a younger woman in her twenties, whose eyes were at the opposite end of the blue spectrum, almost navy, and heavily accented by thick streaks of black under her lashes. Unlike the pearls the other women were wearing, she had small silver spikes in her earlobes. Her shoulder pressed against the arm of a blond man with a scab on his chin where he'd cut himself shaving. The man was nervous and doing a terrible job of hiding it—swallowing a lot and repeatedly licking his lips.

Princess Rose of Albany and her fiancé, John Marchmont, who ought to be the stars of this particular show, were eclipsed in both authority and X-factor by the bride's mother, Georgina, the Duchess of Albany.

In a literal nod to convention, Dominic dipped his head in a brief bow.

His career had brought him into the path of other royals, but this was his first encounter with the duchess. Supposedly, she ruled her branch of the family with an iron fist. Within two sentences, Dominic believed it.

"This is Edward Lancier, my daughter's private secretary." The duchess nodded in Father Christmas's direction. "He's overseeing the coordination of events in the planning of this wedding."

Lancier looked coldly back at Dominic. His whole demeanor spoke of intense displeasure. Archaic snobbery at having to deal with the local shopkeepers? Or disapproval this wedding was taking place at all?

"You've signed a nondisclosure agreement." The duchess spoke with the certainty of a person whose every wish was carried out promptly. "It goes without saying that we expect every syllable relating to this event to remain strictly confidential."

"Naturally." Dominic's voice was equally cool, and she lifted her finely tweezed eyebrows.

"First of all, we'd like to thank you for accepting the invitation to submit a tender. His Majesty is particularly pleased by the inclusion of your establishment. De Vere's has done excellent work for our family in the past, and I understand His Majesty enjoyed a cordial personal acquaintance with your late grandfather, Mr. Sebastian De Vere."

As a senior and experienced royal, the duchess was prepped and prepared. He imagined a briefing today had also provided the names of his parents and siblings. If he were here to provide a favor and not a highly paid service, she'd probably ask after even his bloody cat by name.

And the seething pile of fur and narcissism he'd inherited in an unbreakable clause of Sebastian's will would expect no less. Humphrey spent his days either sleeping or destroying pillows, confident that the rest of the world existed solely to serve his comforts.

A feline soul mate for the duchess.

"He did. An honor my grandfather appreciated until his death."

The stab in his chest was sudden and unexpected. And at this moment unwelcome.

Dominic thought of Sebastian every time he opened the kitchen door in De Vere's. Part of him expected to see his grandfather standing at the stove, still incredibly adept with his hands, his shoulders broad enough to bear the weight of the business through every financial struggle, every economic downturn.

Broad enough to support the silent cry for help of a very angry teenage boy, a quarter of a century ago.

Sebastian lived in everything that occurred in De Vere's. His legacy and presence were embedded in the very walls. Usually, his memory was faint, lingering solace.

Today, there was pain.

Grief. The ever-changing sea. Brutal and turbulent. Stretches of peace. And out of nowhere, a knockout wave that rolled through dark shadows, stretching so far back in time now their power had thinned to threads.

Or should have.

"De Vere's is always pleased to cater to the needs of the royal household." Rigidly, Dominic closed a mental door on the past and fixed his speculation on the present. Through the industry grapevine, he'd counted at least six salons with the official nod to bid for this contract. A short list should knock that down to no more than three.

Better, it turned out. He doubted if the Duchess of Albany was the royal they rolled out to children's hospitals and aged-care facilities, unless they wanted to scare the shit out of already vulnerable people, but he appreciated her aversion to beating about the bush.

"At present, we've narrowed our choice to two establishments, including your own. We closely considered all submitted proposals." A note of dryness underscored her tone. "And any unexpected ones that arose."

"Or snuck in the back door," Edward Lancier muttered peevishly. "Dragons. Good God."

Dominic heard that bizarre grumble without immediate interest, but within seconds, it settled and sat sparking quietly at the back of his mind.

And provoked a whisper of suspicion . . .

The Captain's Suite
5:03 p.m.
Meeting with Candidate: Ms. Sylvie Fairchild

"The princess was delighted by the attention to detail in your proposal," only the bloody Duchess of Albany was saying.

One thinly plucked brow lifted as she continued to drill a

disconcerting hole through Sylvie's face. She had the extremely pale eyes Sylvie unfairly associated with fictional serial killers. Hopefully not the case here, although the woman definitely looked capable of yanking one of those ceremonial swords off the wall and skewering the maid for putting too much sugar in the tea.

There was still a feeling of profound unreality about this entire experience, heightened from the moment she'd been plucked from a hotel bar by a pair of black-clad protection officers. She was slightly disappointed that she hadn't been taken to an underground facility and asked to join an eccentric gang of codebreakers or jewel thieves. And relieved that thus far she hadn't ended up in witness protection or a woodland grave.

"Your rather *unexpected* proposal," the duchess added, that piercing gaze narrowing to lethal proportions.

Sword-skewering and shallow grave imminent . . .

For all his pessimism, Jay would have passed off this inevitable confrontation with smooth charm. But at this stage of the proceedings, the royals had requested the presence of only one representative of the bakery. Therefore, Sylvie was handling this part alone and could only do a *Sorry, but*—

"I apologize for any—"

The duchess cut her short. "We'll consider that as read. I do not condone the willful breaking of protocol. However, I respect a quantity of initiative."

Over her shoulder, Princess Rose shot Sylvie a very rapid, literally blink-and-miss-it wink. Sylvie had seen the princess in person once before. She was far more put-together today. She also looked less comfortable, in both her attire and wider company.

At her side, her poor fiancé was twitching so much that his left cheekbone kept bouncing up and down. Every few minutes, Rose squeezed his fingers in a subtle show of reassurance, and he looked down at her with all his feelings blazing in his eyes.

Sylvie had been forced to remind herself three times now that it was incredibly patronizing to mentally clasp her hands and *aww* at an adult couple as if they were a basket of baby otters.

"This is a cake that will be photographed for every major publication in the world," the duchess went on. "It will join the annals of history. It's also a very lucrative contract. Our expectations are high. The margin for error is zero. If you have the least doubt in your ability to deliver—"

"Then I wouldn't have broken protocol, and I wouldn't be here today." Her response was firm and adamant. She'd been nervous walking into this meeting. Naturally. But now that she was here, and for all the extraordinary circumstances surrounding this cake, it was a bake like any other. This was her thing. She would always deliver on such an important day for people celebrating their love. And in that respect, *who* those people were made absolutely no difference.

That ice-storm gaze again performed a visual dissection of her every feature; then the duchess nodded. "We'd like you to prepare a second proposal for the finalized cake. There are certain parameters to which you'll need to work. Traditions that cannot be discarded even if your personal tastes are more . . . artistic."

Sylvie bet Dominic wouldn't receive that addendum at his briefing.

Clearly, the duchess was more of a white-fondant than sugar-dragon girl.

The Captain's Suite
4:32 p.m.
Meeting with Candidate: Mr. Dominic De Vere

"You did an admirable job of incorporating necessary details and adhering to tradition in such an *elegant* way," the duchess told Dominic. The heavy note of approval caused a flicker of reaction on Princess Rose's previously expressionless face.

Dominic's eyes narrowed slightly.

The duchess turned her head a fraction, and for the first time since she'd begun her monologue, she actually acknowledged her daughter and future son-in-law. "Within those guidelines, Her Royal Highness and Mr. Marchmont have expressed a desire that the cake still feel intimate—"

"So perhaps we could request those *intimate* details ourselves now, Mother?" Rose was probably the only person in Britain who'd ever interrupted the Duchess of Albany and withstood annihilation from the glare that followed. He'd underestimated the princess. She was outwardly dignified, but something hot and belligerent lurked behind that blandness, and in a very different way, she was suddenly as implacable as her mother.

The duchess stared with more coldness than most people would expect from a parent observing their offspring. To Dominic, it was a sight entirely familiar.

Her lips drew into a thin smile. "Of course." She took a graceful step back, managing to lose no ground in the metaphorical sense. "My daughter and her fiancé will complete the briefing." As she crossed behind John Marchmont, she murmured something. Dominic doubted if the staff around the table could hear, but he did. *"Don't stammer."*

The young man turned a painful shade of red, his freckles standing out in large dots. From his hairline to the hollow of his neck: human strawberry. Marchmont swallowed again, hard.

This job, a lifetime's tenure in the public eye whether his romance lasted or not, really was going to decimate him.

Just for a moment, Princess Rose's public mask shattered, and she shot a look of pure fury at her mother. The anger was covered as quickly as it had broken free, but before she addressed Dominic, she very lightly ran the backs of her curled fingers down Marchmont's arm.

The tiny gesture was so weighted with feeling that even Dominic felt the poignancy.

Perhaps, under the rumpled curls and visible sweat, Marchmont was also burying unexpected depths.

If Sylvie were here, she'd be swooning all over them. Unsurprisingly, the woman who hurled handfuls of glitter at perfectly good cakes was starry-eyed for a love story, real or imagined. He'd seen her light up like a firecracker on set when she realized her pet contestants, Emma and Adam, were both single.

"First of all, I'd also like to thank you for the effort you put into making the pitch personal to us." Rose had produced a smile that looked genuine. Given the turmoil roiling behind that façade, she was a bitter loss to the film industry. "The lace was a lovely touch, and the thoughtfulness in using peony poppies."

A reminder that he owed his sister a bottle of wine.

Twice, Pet had tentatively tried to suggest a dinner to go with that wine. Both times, she'd wandered around the point like a lost rabbit in the woods and bolted back to her comfort zone before he could reply. Which was either organizing his business like a soft-voiced sergeant major, or determinedly flirting with every unattached member of his staff.

"I don't want to keep you from your evening plans." Rose pulled out a handwritten piece of paper. "So I'll keep this concise. Regarding the flavors, for most of the layers we'd like—"

She began laying out the practical details, and Dominic opened his tablet to jot down notes. He inserted the occasional query and suggestion, but largely listened and let idea fragments coalesce in his mind.

"For structural reasons, I'd suggest the chocolate fudge rather than the chocolate mousse," he said when Rose expressed a desire for two layers of chocolate—score two and another bottle of Riesling to Pet.

After a few minutes, the princess cleared her throat and looked at her mother. "That's almost everything. If Johnny and I could have a moment, please, we'll finalize the last details and leave Mr. De Vere be."

Despite her tone, so polite and deferent that the ultimate effect was anything but, it was a dismissal with no room for refusal. And judging by the undulating muscle in the duchess's jaw, Rose would hear about it later.

In front of her staff, there was nothing she could do but gather her regal dignity and leave.

Father Christmas, however, looked more like an angry little prune with every passing second and apparently couldn't resist piping up. "With all due respect, Your Highness, it's my responsibility to oversee—"

"And it's our wedding, Edward." Rose was sugar-sweet now. She checked her black leather watch. "Please do return here at five, but in the meantime, we would like ten minutes alone. Of course, you'll be informed if anything of importance arises in that time."

No doubt Lancier managed to keep himself informed on all manner of things that arose in this building.

When multiple bristling bodies had left the room, and the door had shut with a pointed *click*, Marchmont seemed to grow a good inch in stature. Dominic looked at him thoughtfully before he turned back to the bride. "Your Highness—"

"Rosie." She cut him off, and again her demeanor brooked no opposition, although she softened the terse word with a follow-up, "Please."

"Rosie." Dominic flicked to a new screen on the tablet. "Go ahead."

"With?" She was watching him closely, carefully, her fingers still stroking Marchmont's wrist.

"The details that *will* make this cake personal and intimate for you despite its size and symbolism, and help to shrink a stateroom full of people you probably can't stand down to a bubble of two."

A moment of silence, in which a twinkle appeared in Rosie's eyes.

"I told you he couldn't be as much of a bastard as he seems," Marchmont said with sudden, extravagant relief.

Apparently, when the incoming member of the royal family wasn't too petrified to speak, he operated with complete open honesty.

A rare quality in any human being, and one unlikely to be prized by Lancier and his cohorts.

Rosie cleared her throat and took the wise course of ignoring the last ten seconds of her life. "We each have one additional request for the cake."

"Although I'd like to speak to you about mine privately," Marchmont added quickly.

"It's to be a surprise to me on the wedding day, that Johnny would like to be kept separate on the proposal." Rosie's eyes cast a fond look at her fiancé, before shooting back to Dominic with an explicit silent addendum. *Include only if appropriate.* Noted. "For my part, I'd really love it if the top layer of the cake—our layer—is the flavor of Johnny's favorite drink."

As special requests went, that ranked high on the easy scale. "Which is?"

He was expecting an alcoholic flavoring, Baileys, Kahlúa, Bénédictine—

"Midnight Elixir."

Spoke too soon.

The Captain's Suite
5:20 p.m.
Meeting with Candidate: Ms. Sylvie Fairchild

"Midnight Elixir?" Sylvie repeated, lowering her tablet. Johnny Marchmont couldn't just be a lemon drizzle bloke, could he? "I'm sorry, I'm not familiar . . ."

She had a sudden, horrifying hope that Midnight Elixir wasn't on her own menu. It was a kitschy name for a beverage, flashy, over the top. Right up her street. And Jay had been adding new drinks right and left since he'd taken over the Dark Forest with unexpected aplomb. She was already too busy with *Operation Cake* commitments to keep up. Not a good look.

"It's a hot drink they serve at the Starlight Circus in Holland Park."

Oh, good. She hadn't missed a trick.

It was just the plagiarizing competition.

The Starlight Circus, a coffee shop in a city with more pollution than stars, was owned by Darren Clyde, a colossal fuckwit with a habit of sending spies into Sugar Fair to buy their food, reproduce it poorly, and change the names. They'd first met in a class on advanced sugar craft, and he'd clearly been sent by Satan to test her.

"Johnny loves it," Rosie went on. "His assistant buys him one every day."

Sylvie was petty enough to be glad he wasn't going in person. He was already enough of a public figure to give Darren a boost in sales. She was always glad to see good things happen for good people, even if they operated in her professional sphere, but outside of the bedroom, nobody liked a bigheaded dick.

She rested her stylus pen against her tablet, ready to fill in the details. "And what is the flavor profile of Midnight Elixir?"

"No idea," Rosie said with all the cheerfulness of a woman who wasn't now going to have to spend time and money at the fucking Starlight Circus. "Apparently, it's a house secret. If it helps, I can definitely taste some sort of berry."

"I think there's spice in it," Johnny piped up, and after a pause, Sylvie wrote down exactly that on her iPad.

Spice (?). Some sort of berry.

Well, she'd always enjoyed a mystery. All those nights listening to Agatha Christie audiobooks while she worked were about to pay off.

"I'm not sure how you knew about *I, Slayer*," Rosie said suddenly. "But we adored the pitch cake. You're so clever."

"If it w-were up to us"—on the odd word, there was just a hint of a stutter in Johnny's deep voice—"we'd keep the theme on the big day."

"Obviously, that would be a step too far," Rosie added drily. "Although I'd pay a good deal of money to serve a slice of Caractacus to the Archbishop of Canterbury."

The duchess and her coterie had got to their feet a few minutes ago and abruptly departed, after a pointed remark shot in her daughter's direction—"I believe this is the part of the proceedings where we vacate the room." Otherwise, Sylvie wouldn't bring up—

"I hope I didn't invade your privacy in making that cake. You mentioned the video game one night when you were—"

"Falling down drunk in your business premises?" Rosie filled in the blank with a faint grin. "Amazingly, I do remember the night in question, although I have no recollection of boring a complete stranger with personal anecdotes. I belatedly apologize. I also belatedly thank you for never saying a word about it. It was my dearest friend's birthday. And I wanted to . . . get out. Be out. In hindsight, it was appallingly reckless to ditch my PPOs."

Personal protection officers. Thanks to the covert pair who'd driven her here, Sylvie had that acronym down. It was the only question they'd deigned to answer.

"The reality is that whatever I do in life, I'm always going to be a security risk, to myself and to others around me." Fleetingly, Rosie's look at Johnny was taut. Concerned. And clearly, not for herself. "But that night . . ." A small smile hovered. "Worth it."

"You ditched your PPOs?" Before Sylvie's fascinated gaze, Johnny—Bertie Wooster incarnate—seemed to physically expand. He stood taller, his shoulders dropping and squaring. As worry carved stern lines into his face, he looked both older and temporarily effectual. "Rosie . . ."

"Point noted and agreed, my love." She spoke softly, her fingers still linked through his. "It was foolish. I won't do it again."

Johnny's reply was so low-toned that Sylvie barely heard it and wished she hadn't. She felt as if she'd pried open a doorway into someone's most private refuge. "I wish you felt free. But I need you to be safe."

Again, they looked at each other, briefly, as if there were no one else in the room.

Sylvie liked this pair very much. As young working royals, criticism and rumor were going to dog their every step. She truly hoped that the bond between them proved stronger than all who would test it.

Rosie cleared her throat. "And now I'd better take a cue from my mother and vacate the premises so Johnny can deliver his own request."

When the door closed behind her, Sylvie looked at Johnny with raised eyebrows.

She lifted her stylus, ready, waiting.

And, after the Midnight Elixir request, slightly apprehensive.

The Captain's Suite
4:50 p.m.
Meeting with Candidate: Mr. Dominic De Vere

"Rosie was very close to her great-uncle before Prince Patrick's death." Marchmont's eyes met Dominic's and held gamely. The groom-to-be still looked ill at ease, even with the room depleted of every other occupant. "She saw him as something of a kindred spirit."

Dominic did a rapid mental collation of everything he knew about Prince Patrick, one of the king's younger brothers. Not a lot. Conventionally handsome, but not particularly charismatic. A poor public speaker. Lifelong bachelor. Talented musician. Unlike his siblings, who'd marched dutifully along to military college or straight into royal duties, Patrick had attended a music school. He'd studied classical piano but had pursued a weekend sideline in rock. Pierced his nose, picked up a few tattoos, made a short-lived attempt at putting together a band. The prince had penned several songs about the plays of ancient Greece and one or two about his favorite foods. Apparently, his work had enjoyed fleeting popularity in the more artsy nightclubs in Chelsea, and appalled palace courtiers and the more tedious members of the public, who'd clearly had too much time on their hands. On the scale of royal rebellions, it barely registered. There had been a member of European royalty dabbling in satanic cults back then.

"Patrick and Rosie shared a common viewpoint on many aspects of this life. And that way of thinking can result in friction with other members of the family. But Patrick was important to Rosie. She would have loved her great-uncle to be at our wedding." Johnny hesitated before he added candidly, "In the true meaning of family, he was the closest thing she had to a parent. It's common knowledge that the king's relationship with his brother was strained, but I'd like the cake design to include a special and specific nod to Patrick, even if it's recognizable to no one but Rosie." A faint smile. "Perhaps especially if it's recognizable to her alone."

Dominic waited for a moment, but Johnny seemed to have reached his verbal limits. "Nothing more specific?"

Johnny blinked. Then shrugged. "You're the artist," he said. Blankly, not pointedly. "I thought you'd know what to do."

A longer pause.

"He did like bees," Johnny offered thoughtfully.

Mystery spices. Berries. Bees.

And the most important underpinning fact: one hell of a pay-check.

Dominic closed his iPad cover with a snap. "I'll figure it out."

Johnny beamed.

At exactly 4:55 p.m., he left the Captain's Suite. Right on schedule, he surmised by the satisfied expressions on every staffer's face. The door was held open by one of the biggest human beings he'd seen outside of a Marvel film. Dominic was not a small man, but Johnny's PPO was built like a fucking Airbus. Shaved head, smashed nose, a face so extraordinarily ugly it was conversely fascinating. He might have just walked out of *Game of Thrones* after single-handedly decimating an army. He looked Dominic dead in the eyes and didn't say a word.

If it was Rosie who'd chosen her fiancé's source of frontline protection, she wasn't messing around.

Jeremiah and Arabella reappeared in the space of a blink and with no prior noise, thanks to either the thick pile of the carpet or teleportation. They escorted him back through the corridors. Just in case he was tempted to bundle a few antiques under his arm and make a run for it. Everyone kept efficiently checking the time and murmuring into phones. Presumably, the other name on the short list was also being shunted through the Cone of Silence at St. Giles this afternoon. The as-yet-unknown competition being kept carefully out of his path.

He still had a very strong suspicion as to the identity of his mystery rival.

He hadn't heard so much as a whisper she was putting in a tender for this, and her shop floor wasn't exactly a bastion of secrets.

But considering the personality of this particular bride, her presence on the short list wouldn't be entirely beyond belief. Yet another what-the-fuck in a day that had also included scones with the consistency of schist and custard that fizzed on the tongue like popping candy—but just within the realms of possibility.

"Dominic De Vere!"

He looked up as a heavyset man in military uniform broke off a conversation and came toward him, hand extended.

An old acquaintance of his grandfather's, whose name was either Bill, Will, or Gil.

Or Cyril. As opposed to Sebastian De Vere, who had rarely wasted words, Major General Cyril Blake was like a faulty tap once he started talking. Spilling out everywhere and impossible to turn off.

To the foot-tapping agitation of the bodyguard dolls, Dominic was still standing in the corridor at 5:32 p.m., when a second black-clad escort rounded the corner and he found himself face-to-face with Sylvie Fairchild.

They stared at each other against a background of stone-faced protection officers and Cyril moaning about his grandkids and the price of cheese.

Then: "'Dragons. Good God,'" Dominic quoted in a drawl. "I knew it."

Chapter Seven

De Vere's
Twenty-Four Hours after Dominic Finally Escaped the
Clutches of Major General ~~Bill~~ ~~Will~~ ~~Gil~~ Cyril
(His grandkids are still a disappointment to an old man.)
(Cheese remains expensive.)

The salt-and-pepper truffles—dark chocolate with notes of sea salt and chili—were a De Vere's bestseller. They were also intricate to produce, mirror-glazed by hand and finished with a precise swirl of gold-tinted white chocolate. Dominic was halfway through a batch when he smelled a whiff of burning sugar.

Fortunately, he didn't need to lift his head to see who was responsible.

"Where's Aaron?" He completed a wisp-fine curlicue, moved on to the next, and another. "And somebody please take that pan off the heat."

A quick clash of metal before his sous-chef crossed his line of sight with a steaming pan. More ingredients going straight in the bin. "Aaron's . . ." Liam looked around the busy kitchen and grimaced. "Well, he *was* here."

Dominic completed the tray of truffles and slid them onto the racks for packaging. Pulling off his gloves with a *snap*, he gestured Liam toward the remaining sweets on the assembly line. "Finish up, would you?"

He found Aaron in the back hallway, just coming in from the alleyway. He was clutching his phone. "My office. Now."

They were short-staffed in the kitchens today and the busiest they'd been all month out front, thanks to a blasting of promos for *Operation Cake*. No complaints about the increased foot traffic, but he'd already endured five hours of mostly mediocre bakes in the TV studio this morning, culminating in the elimination of Byron. He of the clown phobia, lethal scones, and today, a shortbread sculpture of the Victoria Memorial that looked like a toddler had got into the biscuit tin and emptied the contents onto the floor.

The kid had cried. Tears dripping down the peach fuzz on his cheeks—before he'd double-checked which camera to sniff into and delivered a speech straight off the cutting-room floor of a third-rate battle flick. The wounded hero, reluctant to abandon his comrades to the encroaching evil.

Insert clip of Dominic.

Unless there was a genuine reason for Aaron's increasingly poor efforts, he was not in the mood for this.

He perched on the edge of his desk and eyed his employee, who was currently demonstrating both shifty eyes and shuffling feet. "Aaron," he said, his tone obviously not what the other man was expecting; Aaron stopped fidgeting and looked at him. "I shouldn't need to point out that your work is not up to standard. You're struggling. If it's a health issue, either physical or mental, we can offer multiple avenues of support. Life deals a fucker of a card sometimes, it happens frequently, and with respect to work it's not a big deal. We'll help you through it. If it's the work itself, again there's assistance available, but if things don't improve soon—"

"I'm sorry," Aaron interrupted miserably. "It's my nan. My grandmother. She's not well, and I've had to move in with her. There's no one else. And I've asked her not to call me at work unless it's an emergency, but . . . but she forgets . . . And I'm tired. God, I'm so tired."

"Right." For a moment, Dominic said nothing. Then he nodded at a chair. "Take a seat."

When Aaron left the office ten minutes later, some of the strain had left his features.

Dominic wished he could say the same. And when he opened his emails and read the message from his lawyer, any hope of salvaging this day from the scrap heap went out the window like a rocket.

He jerked open his door, ready to stalk out in search of his sister, but at least the universe was prepared to offer the sop of hand-delivering his target. Pet stood with her hand partly raised. He'd give her the benefit of the doubt that he'd interrupted her midknock, but her style was more shove-open-and-sail-merrily-on-in.

"Hello!" Her smile faltered when she saw his expression.

A few seconds ticked by.

"I genuinely can't tell if you're pissed about something, or if that's just your face now."

"I just received an email from my lawyer. Regarding a substantial financial deposit."

"Yay?" Pet suggested without much hope.

"Chair. Sit. Now." Dominic jerked the door wider, and she sighed.

Looking extremely put-upon, she brushed past him, bypassed

the chair, and hopped up to sit on his desk. "I know you were already practically collecting a pension when I was born, and I might be currently between fathers," Pet muttered, "but I'm a good decade past the parental lecture, bro." She looked at him. "That money is rightfully yours. Mum left it to you. You're never going to see the half you generously and stupidly gave to Lorraine again, but *I'm* not keeping your share."

"I don't have a clue what latent burst of remorse or guilt prompted Lana to leave me a third of her estate, but we hadn't spoken for over twenty years. I severed those ties at thirteen years old, and that cut was permanent. On both sides. I have no interest in her money. It belongs to you and Lorraine. And you'll take it."

"No. I won't. You were still her son. And she owed you." The tiniest quaver rocked Pet's instant rebuttal, but her gaze was solid. Stubborn. "Stop giving it back. *I don't want it.*"

Dominic looked at her. Those big dark eyes, fixed on him. Twenty-five years ago, those same eyes, in a round little baby face. Trusting. Loving.

Abruptly, he turned away. "Then donate it to charity. Feed some cats. Clean some rivers. Set up a scholarship fund for gifted bloody chihuahuas, if you like."

His office had been cleaned only this morning, but the air felt thick, as if it were layered with dust.

Voice clipped, he spoke solely to break the intense silence. "What do you mean, you're 'currently between fathers'?"

Gerald Hunt—Pet's father, Dominic's . . . stepfather, for lack of a more specific term for a man raising the living, breathing proof of his wife's extramarital affair—was dead a good five years now. As their mother had also passed, Pet would find it difficult to acquire a new parent.

The silence took on a new quality. Frowning, he turned.

Pet had pressed her lips together. For an appalling moment, he thought she was going to cry. The last time he'd seen her in tears, she'd been crawling around in footsie pajamas, clutching a piece of bedraggled, drool-encrusted blanket she'd named "Fizzy" for a reason she'd kept to herself. It had been her first word. One of only two words she'd been able to speak when he'd left that house.

Fizzy. And "Mink."

Dominic.

"So, funny story," she said in a sudden rush, as if once she'd decided to speak, she had to get the words out as quickly as possible. "Last year, thanks to a medical test . . ." At his jerky movement, she shook her head. "It's fine. I'm fine. And also, genetically not the daughter of Gerald Hunt."

"What?"

"Not a single strand of common DNA. Add my bio dad to the mystery list with yours."

He shook his head, not a negation, just—*the fuck?* "And was Lorraine . . ." He cut off that pointless question before it could fully form, and Pet's obvious tension briefly relaxed into a snort.

"Lop off Lorraine's hair, paste it to her chin, and behold! Gerald walks again. She's his mirror image."

In both face and personality.

"I . . ." Her voice wobbled again. Again, in his mind, he saw the baby she'd once been. The ghost of chubby arms around his neck. She took a deep breath and lifted her chin. She was a fighter. Disastrously soft heart. Spine of steel.

"There was no sense of loss in that discovery," she said quietly. "I was relieved. He was a hypocritical, judgmental bully. As I got older, I saw him for the man he was. I saw the way he treated others. I—I know now how he treated you." She held out her hand, and Dominic realized she was holding a card. He took it automatically. "The DNA is just a technicality. I haven't felt like a Hunt in a long time." She nodded at the card. "It's finally official, so I'm just . . ." Her chin rose higher. "Informing you."

He looked down at the business card advertising the credentials and contact information of Petunia De Vere. His thumb moved to rest over the surname.

"I didn't know Sebastian the way you did, but he was my grandfather, too." Her bravado seemed to falter. "I hope he wouldn't mind my taking his name."

Across the distance between them, her anxious gaze fixed on his.

"I hope you don't mind, either."

Without waiting for him to respond, she turned and left.

He stared at the business card for a long time, before he tucked it into the photo frame on his desk, next to the silhouette she'd cut, the rendition of Sylvie's profile.

After the day he'd had so far, he'd rather flash-boil his own eyeballs than trek across to the Starlight Circus in Holland Park for a few rounds of Johnny Marchmont's daily vice, but one obstacle stood between De Vere's and the Albany contract, and she wouldn't be wasting time.

For all Sylvie's rainbow-hued, bejeweled frivolity, there wasn't a lazy bone in her body. Nor was she a procrastinator—

—as she proved when Dominic pushed open the ivy-covered door of the coffee shop, set off a night-themed soundtrack of owl hoots and nondescript rustling, and found her perched cross-legged on a floor cushion.

The door swung shut behind him with a *thump*. He tucked his hands in his trouser pockets and swept his gaze over the packed interior, from the glow-in-the-dark stars on the ceiling to the scattering of picnic rugs and cushions.

There were no tables. No chairs besides two beanbags, both already occupied.

"If it isn't Judge C." Sylvie seemed equally unsurprised to see him, and not at all bothered by the strangers sprawled around her.

To be fair, most of them were in a world of their own. Many were wearing headphones. One guy had just starfished out on a rug and was napping in a happy pool of his own drool. Only one was paying Sylvie any attention, a young man with a Manchester United cap sitting staring fixedly at the side of her head, lost in admiration of her pink- and lavender-streaked plait. He had "postgrad student" and "optimist" written all over him.

One look at Dominic's face and the budding lothario just about hid in his backpack.

Sylvie was eating a biscuit. She'd been chewing on the same bite for over thirty seconds. "What do you think?" she asked, finally swallowing. Her head inclined in the general direction of—everything. He'd seen less junk packed onto the odds-and-ends stall at a village fair. He didn't know what to avoid looking at first. "Seventy percent toddler's bedroom, thirty percent crack den, or the other way around?"

"I'd throw in at least ten percent low-budget slasher film." With horrified fascination, Dominic locked stares with an enormous plastic clown and found he couldn't look away.

He couldn't even blink.

This wasn't ideal.

"I was pretty sure you'd turn up tonight, too." A pause, during which he could hear Sylvie chewing again. It sounded like hard work.

The clown's pupils were spinning. Literally spinning.

Unless that was his own eyes.

Or his brain.

Nausea was kicking in a good ten minutes earlier than he'd expected. He hadn't even ordered yet.

"This is like a cross between everlasting bubble gum and sawdust. I . . . Dominic?" Sylvie cleared her throat. "Dominic."

Two fingertips touched his wrist. Dominic drew in a long breath. Briefly, he closed his eyes.

Turning deliberately away from the clown, he looked down into a bright hazel gaze. "I currently despise every atom of my existence."

The faintest of lines feathered out from Sylvie's lashes. They deepened now. "Poor baby. Completely out of your comfort zone." She unwound her long legs to free a foot and nudged a plush purple cushion in his direction. "Pull up a pew and join us commoners. I saved you a cushion, and I hope you're grateful. The bloke in the bobble hat was eyeing this spot, and in my efforts to secure it for you, I collided with the mechanical bear."

She turned her arm and brandished her elbow, where the skin beneath her pushed-up sleeve was pink and scraped.

Dominic was fucking exhausted, and now addled by the Hypno-Clown. He almost reached out and took her arm. The unheard-of instinct that had just propelled into his muscles was to bloody *stroke* her.

Politely, Sylvie caught the attention of the barista. "Could you make it *two* Midnight Elixirs, please? Thank you."

She was playing with the remainder of her biscuit, dropping crumbs. Everywhere she went, strewing small atoms of chaos.

"I would cling to the faint hope this is a dream." He needed to get off his feet. Unwillingly, he hooked his boot around the cushion. When he lowered himself to sit, an arsehole vertebra midspine screamed that he was edging up on forty and spent his days leaning forward with a piping bag. "But even in nightmares, my imagination doesn't pull up indoor tents and popcorn cannons."

"No shit. I've seen your cakes." Sylvie took another unenthused bite. "This place is way busier than I was expecting. I am *seething*." She looked at the remaining piece of biscuit. He could see from here how overbaked it was. It was also glistening under the overhead spotlights and streaked with pink, although that could be traces of Sylvie's lipstick. Her lip curled. "This tastes nothing like my Celestial Cloud Cookies." She set it down on a napkin and shot a glance at the demonic clown. "And the décor is ugly." With obvious satisfaction, she finished, "'Emerging competitor to Sugar Fair,' my arse."

There was a piece of card under Dominic's foot. He flicked it around without interest and realized it was the menu.

Popcorn Cappuccino
Penny Pops
Star Bright Fudge
Darren's Daringly Delicious Dewdrops

"Mmm." He lifted the menu and turned it over to see if it got worse. Darren Didn't Disappoint. He appeared to be surrounded by escapees from an Enid Blyton book. "I can see where the comparison came from."

In life, there were many sudden silences. Awkward silences. Companionable silences. Confused silences.

And those moments when the world abruptly went so quiet that all you could hear were the icy breaths of your approaching demise.

He lowered the menu. Any hint of amusement had disappeared from Sylvie's face. She leaned forward, and her palm landed on the remains of her dry biscuit. She squashed it flat.

Judging by her expression, she'd prefer it was one or both of his testicles.

In lethally sweet tones, she inquired, "Are you seriously putting this nightmarish profusion of thrift-store rejects and *unparalleled* tackiness on remotely the same level as my gorgeous, magical dream come true?"

"Weak tea, dude." For a moment, Dominic thought Sylvie's admirer, the Man U fan, was delivering an unsolicited review of his beverage, but no. Just an indictment on Dominic's recent life choices. The kid shook his head in heavy disapproval. "Insulting your woman's work. Not cool, man."

And the day edged further into surrealism.

"I'm not *his woman*," Sylvie said, with a level of revulsion usually reserved for blocked drains and maggot infestations.

Her ally brightened. He whipped the cap off his head and edged closer with a coaxing smile. "In that case, would you like to—"

"No," she said uncompromisingly. She shifted her weight sideways so she could pull a small pink ticket from her pocket. "But I appreciate a wise man. Have a voucher for free cake."

He looked at her, looked at the voucher in his hand, made an *all right, then* face, and wandered off.

The smiling, ponytailed barista bent and placed a steaming metal flagon at each of their feet. "Two Midnight Elixirs. Sorry about the wait. We're packed tonight."

"I noticed." For the other woman, Sylvie found a smile. "Thanks." Completely ignoring Dominic now, which would usually be a gift beyond compare but, as the cherry on an endless stream of unsettling experiences, perversely annoyed him more, she picked up her flagon and took her first sip. "Hmm," she said, and wrote something into her phone.

Dominic's jaw shifted a few times, then he picked up his own drink and dubiously examined the contents. Johnny Marchmont's favorite drink was a dark indigo color, shades of purple when the light hit it. The consistency was thicker than he'd expected, midway between creamy coffee and a milkshake. He brought the cup to his nose and inhaled. There *was* spice in it. And he was pretty sure . . . He took a mouthful, considered it for a second, and swallowed. Star anise. Followed by a strong hit of berry and intense sweetness.

He'd rather have an espresso, but the drink wasn't actually that bad. When he broke down the rest of the contents, it would make for an unusual but palatable cake flavor.

"So, 'Darren,' whoever he is, isn't amenable to disclosing his recipes," he murmured aloud as he jotted *star anise* onto his tablet. An earlier call to the coffee shop had netted only an irritating giggle from the staffer at the end of the line, and "Ooh, no. All our recipes are a Clyde family secret. Darren would *never* tell. Shhh."

"*His* recipes. Please." Sylvie's dislike of Darren and his saccharine alliteration was apparently strong enough to break the silent treatment. "He regularly steals ideas from Sugar Fair. I'd bet my stake in this contract that he didn't concoct this himself." She took another sip, a frown of concentration in her eyes. Then she wrote down something else. Dominic's eyes traveled to her fingers against his will, and she lifted both her chin and her phone, covering the screen. "Unfortunately, he didn't rip this one off me. And it's way too . . . not beige to come from your kitchens."

"A neutral palette is universally appropriate."

"That's not how you pronounce 'dull.'"

They both drank more.

Dominic wrote down *Boysenberry? Definitely vanilla; no more than two drops.*

Finishing their drinks, they ordered another round from the barista.

"This place would be Byron's worst nightmare," Sylvie commented after a few minutes of silence, staring at the clown again. Dominic wasn't repeating that mistake. "I thought he handled the elimination well today."

He accepted another flagon of Midnight Elixir and swallowed a mouthful. It burnt a warm trail down his throat that he quite liked. "He cried for an hour. I've seen less moisture expelled by hydraulic dams. Ironic, considering his gâteau opéra was dust-dry."

"Don't be horrible."

"Every poignant, quivering teardrop was straight out of school drama. Are you planning to let *every* evictee faux-snivel into your neck?" Dominic's thigh was starting to cramp. He shifted irritably. "It's inappropriate."

"Some of us have compassion for others. It's called empathy."

"Some of us would hug a rabid squirrel if it shed a few tears and burbled an improbable sob story. It's called gullibility."

If she kept hurling her eyeballs around her skull like that, he wasn't going to be the only one with a headache.

He must have grimaced unconsciously, because Sylvie stopped rolling her eyes and narrowed them on his face.

"Are you feeling okay?"

"I'm fine."

"You're all strained here." Without warning, those cool fingertips touched him again, this time glancing over his temple, a light kiss of a movement. He stiffened, his hand curling around the flagon of Elixir.

Sylvie's own hand folded into itself. A tinge of color invaded her cheekbones, until they matched the patchy remnants of her lipstick. "Sorry. Instinct. I didn't mean to . . . infringe on your . . ." She cleared her throat.

"I . . ."

Had apparently experienced a human touch so infrequently lately that one silk-soft tap and the rest of his body almost separated from his skin.

Except he could still feel that prickle through his nerves.

Not exactly a reaction he had to every bit of casual physical contact.

"Headache," he said shortly, sitting back. He touched his temple. "It's been a very long day." Each word came out with grim emphasis.

"Staff problems?" Sylvie guessed warily. She was frowning into her Elixir. After burying her nose in the cup and inhaling deeply several times, she wrote down three more things on her list.

He was falling behind, as his mind wandered down several unsettling avenues. Raising his flagon, he drained half the mixture in one go. The more he drank, the more cloying the sweetness in the aftertaste. It wasn't so much complementing as cloaking the other flavors. Not honey. *Sucralose?*

"Those as well." He felt damned sorry for Aaron, but hopefully the interim measures they'd taken paid off, because he also couldn't afford an endless stream of expensive mistakes.

Especially if they secured the Albany contract. The short-term pressure would shoot into the stratosphere at that point, and he confidently expected a significant increase in knock-on sales once the name of the bakery was released in connection with the cake.

The royal effect on trade was no joke. Princess Rose could single-handedly exceed the impact of thousands of pounds of advertising budget.

He could almost hear Sylvie's voice in his head: *She's a person, not an algorithm.*

What nontheoretical Sylvie said aloud was "Me too."

A combination of fatigue and high sugar content was slowing his reaction time. It took a second before he connected those words to a meaning. He glanced up. "You're having staff problems?"

"Problem, singular." Sylvie wrinkled her nose. "Unless you count Jay and Mabel, our senior assistant, constantly squawking and pecking at one another like territorial budgies. Which is doing my head in, but nothing new."

Jay . . . one of those surnames with an unnecessary repetition of consonants. Fforde. Dominic had met him a couple of times, and they occasionally crossed paths in the street. Sharp head for figures but flapped under pressure. He'd crumble in a crisis.

"Jay's your business partner?"

"Business partner. Lifelong best friend. We've known each other since we were babies. We were born in the same maternity ward, twelve hours apart. Our mothers apparently bonded over how useless our fathers were during the onset of labor. I literally learned to walk holding Jay's hand." The dimple by her mouth deepened again. "My aunt said we were crawling around the floor together, playing as usual, and I spotted a packet of biscuits. Motivated by sugar even then. I was determined to get to it, but I kept falling over when I tried to stand up. So Jay clambered to his feet as well, grabbed my hand, and off we toddled." She lifted one shoulder. "He's my brother, for all intents and purposes." As Sylvie spoke of the other man, her preoccupied expression diffused into affectionate softness. The door opened to admit yet another customer, setting off the soundtrack of birdsong and a few piano notes of Moonlight Sonata to accompany her raptures.

An odd, unfamiliar sensation was prickling at his spine. Not quite impatience, not quite discomfort. Literally shrugging it off, Dominic rather curtly addressed her original observation. "Maybe it's personal."

She cocked her head.

He could be at home right now with a glass of lager, his homicidal cat, and no constantly talking people. "Maybe Jay and Mabel are skating around an always-inadvisable workplace relationship," he clarified. "According to my sister and the book she's currently reading and for some reason thinks I need a daily briefing on, squabbling like enraged parakeets is an early sign of attraction."

"In the nonfictional world, it might be easier to skip the verbal pigtail-pulling and just ask someone out for a drink."

They finished their flagons, and he scribbled down a few more ingredients.

Cranberry juice.
White chocolate.

Raising a hand, he asked the barista for a third round.

A spark of wicked humor suddenly lit up the green in Sylvie's eyes. She grinned. "Jay and Mabs—God help the entire planet. But despite the lessons of literature, courtesy of this book I'm privately convinced you're reading yourself, that's a negative on pissing me off because they secretly want to bang. Mabel's asexual and already in a committed relationship, and Jay has a girlfriend." After a beat, her brows compressed. "I think. I just realized he hasn't mentioned her for a couple of weeks. He's still writing poetry, though, so I assume they're still together."

Intense gloom invaded that sentence.

"Poetry?"

"He writes poems. He reads them aloud for feedback. It's a deeply distressing subject for me. I don't want to talk about it."

A small smile tugged. It felt like the first minuscule release of tension all day. "You said you were having an actual staffing problem."

"Yeah." All traces of smiles on Sylvie's part fell away. "My intern, Penny. She's really struggling with the work. I've had to move her to four different stations so far, and nothing seems to be clicking. It's not an issue of effort—she is trying." On a very dry note, she added, "Every mistake is made with an impressive level of enthusiasm."

"So she's not suited to the job."

"But she *wants* to be." Sylvie caught her lower lip between her teeth. He'd been right about Pet's silhouette drawing falling short on the full curve of her mouth. "And I get the feeling there's something going on outside of work. She's frequently distracted, and a couple of times she's taken a phone call and seemed odd afterward. Jay's over it and wants to let her go, but if the rest of her life is falling apart, I don't want her to be unemployed as well."

His answering grunt was neither agreement nor immediate dismissal. "I've got an employee myself with extenuating circumstances that we'll do our best to accommodate."

"You see." Sylvie leaned forward, brightening. Her right hand tried to twitch in his direction again. She sat on it. "You get it."

That was probably the most genuine smile she'd ever directed at him.

"In my case, the employee in question has a lot of talent when he's in the right mind to access it, and is very definitely in the right field," he said warningly, and Sylvie blew out a breath. "Do you think your employee might be having family issues?"

She shook her head. "She doesn't have any family. It came up at her interview. Her parents have passed, no brothers or sisters, no eccentric aunts, no drunk uncles. Not even a cat."

Despite the light, lilting addition at the end, a strange note underlaid Sylvie's response.

It was in her eyes, too. Pain. A deep well of emotions that coalesced into, simply, pain.

"I see," Dominic said.

She blinked a few times, and a self-conscious stiffness came into her posture.

Two more portions of Midnight Elixir were delivered to their bit of floor. They both knocked them back like huge shots of tequila.

Simultaneously decided to order another.

"If your employee is wise enough to live a cat-less existence," he said at last, while they waited for the next round, "it may be worth keeping her on."

He pulled back his sleeve and revealed a long, angry scratch slicing through the hair on his forearm.

Sylvie's expression cleared of shadows as concern yanked her back to the present. This time, she seized hold of his arm without hesitation, her fingers wrapping gently about his wrist as she pulled it into her lap. His own fingers curled into a light fist. "Oh my God. What kind of pet do you *have*?" she asked, horrified. "A Bengal tiger?"

"Similar bulk, worse temperament. A tabby menace, inherited from a relative whose affection for me has since been called into question."

"I hope you put something on this; it's really nasty. What provoked that?"

"The vet suggested I cut his dry food allotment by a quarter cup. Humphrey suggested I get sepsis."

Her fingertips were absently stroking the back of his hand, another glide along his nerve pathways.

The barista approached with two more flagons of Midnight Elixir, and Sylvie released him to grab the drinks.

Her cheeks were flushed again.

She took a hasty gulp from her cup. "Definitely cranberry," she said aloud.

"Agreed." His own mouthful was a more intense throat-burn than the last glass. The barista returned behind the counter, and he studied the array of treats in the glass cabinet. They ran a gamut from children's party fare to wouldn't-even-feed-it-to-his-hellcat. "Is the owner of this place really ripping off your menu?"

"Yes, and with the exception of this . . ." Sylvie waved her flagon at him. Her voice was slightly slurred. She really was pink in the face. ". . . this fantastic concoction, he doesn't even have the decency to plagiarize *well*. It's like a counterfeit purse, all cheap plastic and bad stitching. And freaky clowns."

"Pretty shit of him." The tension was draining out of his muscles, and his headache had eased somewhat as his body relaxed.

"I know," Sylvie agreed fervently. She leaned forward and pointed at him. Having stuck her finger in his face, she didn't seem to know what to do with it.

Dominic considered the problem. "I should punch him."

She looked absolutely thrilled. "*Could* you?"

"Of course I could," he said, vaguely offended. He held up a hand. Fisted it. "I have hands." He turned his wrist to examine his fist from multiple angles. It was very satisfactory. "Big ones."

"Yes, you do." In the dim light, Sylvie's wide eyes looked more black than hazel. "Huge. I've noticed that before." The last words dropped, low and husky.

Sexy.

"Have you?" Deep. Gravelly.

She nodded solemnly and put her fingers back over his, and they studied the result.

"Your hand is quite small," he had to point out.

Her sigh was all sad resignation. "It is." Her lower lip was pink and damp. She sank her teeth into it again. "I'm sorry about that."

His view of anything farther than her head was beginning to haze. Dominic's brain was currently fixed on one subject, but a spike of suspicion penetrated.

Over their entwined fingers, they stared at each other. He could see the movement of her chest with her quiet, quick breaths. A loose clot of mascara clung to the end of one lash, and her eyes really were quite . . .

Dilated.

Sitting there with Sylvie's hand in his, her herb-scented breath a warm tickle against his chin, he saw a reflection of his own rapidly dawning realization.

Releasing her, Dominic reached for his tablet. With a decisive motion, he deleted the top line.

Across from him, Sylvie retrieved her stylus pen and her phone. As it clicked on, she picked up the flagon by her foot and set it aside with an emphatic *thud*. The nearly empty flagon. Their fourth helping. She drew a crisp line and made the necessary amendment.

Midnight Elixir's mystery ingredient number one: *not* star anise.

A grim murmur, in unison: "Absinthe."

Chapter Eight

Hartwell Studios
Contestants Eliminated: 3
Contestants Quitting: 1
Contestants Crying: 1, but give Judge C a chance. He's not even properly awake yet.
Judges Hungover: 2

Nadine from Bucks needed to leave the *Operation Cake* studio and hook an immediate turn into the casting office for *Days Gone By*. With that wavy hair and uptilted eyebrows, she even looked like the fictional family in the long-running soap opera. And she'd nailed their signature acting technique. Gaze into the distance. Deep, shuddering breath. Close eyes. Square shoulders. Exude aura of self-sacrificial courage. And—scene.

"I'll always be grateful for this experience," Nadine said tearfully into Camera B. Her breath quivered inward again. She pressed her palm to her chest. Her apron, pretty floral top, and neck were all splattered in lumpy cake batter. "But it's made me realize where I truly need to be right now. With my family. I miss my husband. I miss Roget."

"Roget?" Mariana asked over Sylvie's shoulder. Her mouth was full of Victoria sponge. They'd both been going back for thirds and fourths of Emma Abara's exquisite morning bake. The cake was light, fluffy, and one of the best Victoria sponges Sylvie had ever eaten. It more than compensated for Emma's disastrous first round.

And it was creating a nice spongy layer in Sylvie's stomach to soak up the remnants of alcohol.

"Her parrot."

"The beaky resurrection of Caesar? I thought it had taken that last great plummet from its perch."

"That was Roget's predecessor."

"Are you okay?" Mariana licked the cream from her fingers and peered at her. "You look a bit peaky."

"Unintentional absinthe binge." Sylvie could still taste anise in the back of her throat when she swallowed.

Thanks to Darren Clyde using the world's smallest font to warn of extreme alcoholic content, she'd held hands with Dominic, gushed over his . . . hugeness, and woken up with the mother of all headaches.

"Wow. You other judges really know how to party. Dominic's also exuding alcohol fumes." Mariana inclined her head toward Dominic, who was currently staring at the lighting fixture over Nadine's head. Probably hoping it would collapse and bring this endless monologue to a conclusion, so they could break for lunch. Sylvie needed coffee, stat. There had been a bowl of cold espresso on a benchtop for a contestant's trifle, and she'd come dangerously close to just dropping her whole head in and absorbing the caffeine like a sponge.

"Even he doesn't have the bone structure to pull off the vampiric red eyes." Mariana reached into the pocket of her tunic and pulled out a folded napkin. She unwrapped it, revealing several more pieces of cake she'd been hoarding. "And his normal mood is sufficiently unattractive without a hangover dragging us all into the deeper pits of hell."

Sylvie had been trying not to look at or speak to Dominic all day. She was . . . Honestly, she was a bit horrified. There was a unique mortification in revealing private pieces of yourself to someone who truly didn't give a shit.

Even if he could be surprisingly nice when he was sozzled.

When she peeked at him again now, she saw that he *was* very red around the eyelids. She was fairly sure her entire insides were a similarly angry shade. It felt like she'd scoured her gut with steel wool.

If she'd ever been youthful enough to tolerate absinthe, those days had passed. Cranky Crone could not handle her booze.

Nadine finally wrapped up her lengthy resignation speech. The moment the cameras clicked off, she turned and stalked toward Libby's station.

The other woman was watching the departing contestant with that same teensy smile she'd directed at Byron before his elimination. She was still currently in the lead, just to add to the hellfire of this day. That little twitch to her lips was infuriating— and apparently not just to Sylvie.

"I hope you're happy." Nadine's jaw set tight as she stopped in front of the countertop. "You nasty little cow."

With no warning, she picked up the remains of Libby's unfortunately perfect toffee cream tart and shoved it straight in its creator's face.

Sylvie had never seen anything like it—the gelatin in the tart held so well that almost the entire contents of the tin transferred smoothly to Libby. Two beady eyes were glaring out of an otherwise largely intact circle of toffee.

When the eyes blinked and Libby's new face slid off like the Wicked Witch melting into the pavers of Oz, Mariana succumbed to a coughing fit, spraying crumbs over Sylvie's shoulder. Hazard of screeching with surprised laughter while stuffing one's face.

Even Dominic's eyebrows had shot up.

"Did we get that on camera?" a voice asked urgently behind her, and a lighting pole poked her in the back of the head as the crew scrambled into action.

"No."

"*Fuck.*"

Within earshot of the contestants, it was all consoling, tactful comments as the production staff began soothing Libby's wounded feelings and getting her a towel. More helpful people rushed after Nadine, who was stalking off set, tossing back her hair.

On a scale of one to ten, how unprofessional would it be to applaud?

"What was that about?" Mariana asked in a low voice.

"Somehow I don't think Libby's character matches her face."

"Well, nobody could be *that* ingenuous, could they?" the other judge intoned cynically. She looked down at her hands. "I need more cake."

"I know. Most of your previous slice is sliding into my best bra."

"Wowzer," a new voice said as Mariana made a beeline for the food tables. Speaking of ingenuous, those tones were so soft and melodious, a Disney princess might have hopped the Channel from Disneyland Paris and gone for a wander. "Talk about upping the drama ante," the newcomer continued. "Last season, it was thrilling if someone dropped an egg."

Not so much Rapunzel, Sylvie discovered when she turned around, as a young Phryne Fisher. The woman grinning at her was midtwenties-ish, with fine-boned, fairylike features, a short, glossy bob of black hair, and crisply outlined red lipstick. Even her clothing was vintage.

"Hello, Sylvie," the very pretty girl said, shoving a hand toward her. "I am *stupendously* pleased to meet you, o genius behind that fabulous creation across the road. Which sadly I can never step foot in, because my flag is planted squarely in enemy territory. I'm Pet De Vere. Dominic's beloved sister."

Her cheery tone took a decided dip into sarcasm on those last two words. And ironically made the sibling relationship more believable.

"She of the incredible talent with a piece of paper and a pair of scissors," Sylvie said, shaking Pet's hand. A few painful dregs of hangover were brushed aside by curiosity. Dominic was more than a few years older than his sister—and light-years apart in personality from this perky, wee sprite. "Wee" being the operative word. She was at least six inches shorter than Sylvie.

Some of that buoyancy in Pet's face had faded as Sylvie spoke, morphing into something more complex. "Oh," she said, a bit uncertainly. "Has he actually . . . Has he mentioned me?"

She glanced across to the studio to where Dominic was deep in conversation with the executive producer. As he was probably purposely not looking in Sylvie's direction, he also hadn't seen Pet yet.

"He gave Mariana a silhouette portrait you cut of her." Sylvie must be almost a decade older than Pet, but she didn't want to be condescending. Nevertheless, she found her voice gentling. "She showed it to me. You're extremely talented. Are you a full-time artist?"

"Thank you." Pet cleared her throat. "No, I'm not. I'm a full-time PA, and right now I'm temping for Dominic while his executive assistant is out on sick leave." She held up an envelope. "Hence the personal delivery service with urgent documents he needs to sign."

"Well, if you ever wanted to practice art as a profession, you could. We're all jealous of Mariana's portrait. Count me in if you ever need a model."

"Sure. Anytime" was the response after a noticeable pause and a slightly odd glance.

"Pet!" Mariana returned with more cake and offered them both a piece. "How nice to see you again. Have you come to watch the filming?"

"Officially, and if my brother asks, no." Pet tasted the cake and immediately brightened. "This is really good cake."

"Courtesy of Emma." Mariana inclined her head to where most of the contestants were whispering amongst themselves. "In the red apron. Next to her in the blue apron is Adam. And the matchmaker here would like to see them team up over more than a group challenge."

They all watched as Emma leaned forward to wipe up a puddle of spilled lemon juice. She stumbled, and Adam just about threw himself across his neighboring station to grab hold of the bow in her apron strings. He pulled her back before she could fall and ended the performance with a reassuring pat on her upper arm. Emma said something, and he blushed on every visible patch of skin on his body.

As he turned away, fiddling with his badly knotted tie, Emma self-consciously adjusted her glasses and patted the multitude of tiny braids twisted under her headscarf.

"Oh, wow." Pet had pressed her hands together before her

face, Dominic's urgent envelope currently forgotten, squeezed between her palms. "I so ship it."

"I will concede they're sweet," Mariana said. "And that I shouldn't be surprised the resident unicorn enthusiast is a hopeless romantic."

Sylvie had returned to rubbing her temples. "Pardon me if it's obvious when two people are into each other."

"Is it?" Mariana murmured. And smiled at her blandly.

"Speaking of sweet," Pet said, "those little unicorn marshmallows you put in your hot drinks at Sugar Fair are the best. I'd like to steal your idea and add them to the menu at De Vere's, but unicorns are not on Dominic's radar."

"Unless they're catapulting straight into his skull." Mariana examined another piece of cake and prodded it between her lips.

"Have you been giving me illicit patronage after all?" Sylvie teased Pet.

"It's evidence of my ironclad willpower and loyalty that I'm not facedown in a booze cauldron every Saturday night, but no. Sorry. Dominic's apprentice is the one putting coins in your coffers. He loves them. And it sounds like he could do with the treats right now, poor guy."

"Going through a rough time?" Mariana asked incuriously through her mouthful of cake, and Pet nodded.

"Yeah. He's sole caregiver for a family member with high needs, and his work's really been slipping. Dominic's shortened and changed his hours so he can spend more time at home, on full pay, and given him a bonus so he can pay for some home help."

Sylvie looked up. "Dominic did that?"

"Surprising." Mariana's response was blunt. Apparently, the warm fuzzies over her gifted silhouette had reached their expiry date.

"I don't think it's surprising at all." Pet folded her arms, but the belligerent gesture turned into something more like a self-hug. Sylvie was pretty sure that only she heard the soft follow-up: "But I suppose I don't really know him well enough to say."

Sugar Fair
Where everything has been running like clockwork in the boss's
absence and it is, as ever, one big happy family.
It's nice to have something to rely upon in a world of constant
change and unwanted skin tingles.

"For the third time," Jay was saying when Sylvie finished decorating a golden anniversary cake that afternoon and walked through to the central shop floor, "could you mix up the lollipop selection? We're almost out of birds and jungle animals, and we have way too many of these weird walrus things."

Mabel didn't look up from the ball of sugar she was molding. "That's you, dipshit. Just balder this time. I took the liberty of giving Lollipop Jay a haircut since the breathing version seems to have lost the address of his barber." Helpfully, she added, "Imagine the walrus with a Steven Tyler wig, and look again."

Jay stared at her before his gaze dropped to the lollipop in his hand. Sylvie was eight feet away and she could already see the perfect likeness of his face sunk eerily into the sweet, like a tiny trapped spirit.

An alarming crimson flush rose up Non-Lollipop Jay's neck. She prayed for strength.

"I have to go out for an hour or two," she said loudly, "to do some research for . . ." She glanced at Mabel's lowered head. "For a commission. Is everything going to be all right here?"

"Sticky hands keep touching my art, and if this scraggly-haired idiot doesn't stop interfering with my vision, I'm going to sculpt a six-foot-tall *amezaiku* voodoo doll and shove an ice pick in his dick," Mabel returned pleasantly. "Business as usual."

Sylvie made the executive decision to just let that go. As she turned away to collect her coat, Mabel added, "Have fun poking about dusty old papers at the Royal Archives."

She stopped. Mabel was engrossed in her work. Fortunately, all their current customers were in the right atrium, beyond the waterfall, which muffled sound.

"I won't ask how you know that."

Mabel's snort was scornful.

Jay caught her up in the back cloakroom. "Do you want me to come? Lend an extra pair of eyes? I'll let you borrow my magnifying glass."

Sylvie frowned, buttoning up her coat. "Don't you have an early group in the Dark Forest soon?"

"Oh . . . right." He ran his hand over his jaw. "And another group later, yeah. We're doing well for bookings. All this promo for *Operation Cake* and the social media campaign is really boosting sales." He reached out and pulled her plait free of the coat collar. While his hand was in the vicinity, he gave her cheek a fond stroke with his thumb. "Sorry it's at the expense of daily run-ins with De Vere."

"Yeah," Sylvie said after a moment. She stretched her lips into a smile. "The sacrifices we make for the bottom line, right?" Reaching up on her tiptoes, she took his shoulders in a little hug, and pressed an affectionate kiss to his cheek. "Call me if there are any major disasters. Please try not to murder Mabs, and vice versa." She turned back at the door. "Oh, I meant to ask . . ."

Jay's hand fell from his cheek and he looked at her inquiringly.

"How are things with Fiona? It's been so busy lately we never had that dinner together, and you haven't mentioned her for a while."

Something in his handsome face closed off. His smile became as forced as hers. "We're not seeing each other anymore."

"Oh no." Sylvie's hand fell away from the doorknob as she stared back at him in dismay. "Oh, Jay, I'm so sorry. I know you really liked her." She returned to wrap her arms around him again. After a beat or two, his hand fisted in her coat, at the base of her spine. "Can I ask what happened?"

He continued to hold her a second longer. One broad shoulder lifted. "We just weren't right. One of those things."

"But—" Sylvie's phone buzzed. "That's my taxi." She didn't move, undecided. "Look, should I stay? Do you want to talk?"

"No." He softened the abrupt rejection with another smile, more genuine now. "Honestly, it's fine, but I appreciate the offer." He jerked his head. "Go forth and discover what made Prince Patrick tick."

She could hear the distant tooting of a car horn now.

"Okay, but if you *do* want to talk—"

"I'll track you down somewhere between a bowl of cake icing and a stack of dusty papers."

When she was halfway through the door, Jay said, suddenly, "Syl."

She looked back.

"I love you."

"Back at you, slick." She blew him a kiss and ran to catch the taxi, which was already starting to pull away from the curb without her.

The Royal Archives were spread amongst multiple institutions, but as the main repository for information relating to the king's siblings, the natural starting spot was Abbey Hall. Located perpendicular to St. Giles Palace, the archival stores had apparently received most of the effects they'd bequeathed for preservation.

Sylvie had already made use of the modern treasure hunter's first aide, Google. But Johnny wanted the top tier of this cake to be incredibly personal and special for Rosie, and so far, no bald, dry detail of Prince Patrick's life pulled from a webpage was jumping out to be included in the design. The king's younger brother had been popular with lower-level palace aides, but reputedly despised the topmost advisors. Never married. A passion for people, philanthropy, and the arts. A close bond with his young great-niece.

And that was about it.

After some well-publicized exploits in his youth, Patrick had kept a low profile outside of his official appearances. He'd carried out his public engagements with bland correctness and generally sailed under the radar. During his teen years and twenties, he'd been photographed with a number of women, each resulting in a press frenzy. The tabloids had shredded every girlfriend like sharks circling bloodied meat, analyzing their past relationships, their appearance, their clothing, their smallest gesture. Anyone who appeared with the prince more than once was mooted as a potential wife.

That appeared to have stopped abruptly in his late thirties. From the age of about thirty-eight until two years ago, when he'd died from cancer at sixty-three, the prince had really never been the subject of even the most tepid romance rumors. No more women with an arm hooked through the crook of his elbow as they left a restaurant, not a hint of an engagement on the horizon.

Considering that he'd been a handsome, kind-looking man in the prime of life even without his royal status, she found that interesting from a purely nosy point of view, but it was hardly helpful for the cake design.

She had found a few covers on YouTube of some pretty terrible rock songs he'd written as a student, the existence of which he'd understandably chosen to ignore in later life. One was titled "The Staring Eye of Death," which she'd assumed was going to be a metaphorical reflection on mortality, but had turned out to be an ode to the prince's favorite childhood meal: poached haddock in milk.

She might have more "artistic" tastes in cake design than the Duchess of Albany would like, but even she drew the line at dead fish.

Sylvie seriously hoped that Abbey Hall could provide a metaphorical key, turn an elusive shade into a personality and a soul with hopes and dreams and loves. She needed there to be *something* that would give her the edge here.

De Vere's was formidable competition in this race. She didn't underestimate Dominic. He had the existing prestige and probably the backing of the more traditionally minded royals. He also had an advantage in the other half of the quest, the transformation of Midnight Elixir from beverage to bake. His handling of flavors was literally second to none.

Where he slipped back a step was sentiment and connection to the material. He was all technique and cold perfection, all the time. Rosie and Johnny wanted heart. And therein lay her opportunity, the small gap through which Sugar Fair could slip.

If she could somehow reach back across the years and catch hold of Patrick.

The person, not the prince on paper. The man Rosie had loved.

When the taxi let her out at King Charles Square, she shivered and tugged her hat down her forehead as she walked around the cobblestoned boundary of St. Giles Palace. Her boots slipped on the icy ground, and she wiggled empty gloved fingers at a pigeon that hopped closer, ever hopeful.

"Sorry, little chap." She suddenly remembered something. Reaching into her bag, she pulled out the napkin containing one last square of Emma's Victoria sponge, shoved at her by Mariana when the other woman had been called back to set. She crouched and tossed the cake to the hungry pigeon. "Enjoy. And make sure you appreciate it," she said severely. "It's the best cake you'll ever taste."

"Unless he manages to snatch a crumb of the royal wedding cake. As baked by De Vere's." Unlike Emma's sponge, the words behind her were dry. Sylvie swung around, and Dominic raised his brows. The wind was blowing his thick hair around. He looked, as she'd already vocally noted once before, *huge* in his wool coat, the fabric stretched taut over his broad shoulders. "Talking to pigeons now?"

"Better company than a lot of human beings. Just ask Nikola Tesla." She straightened. "I would say fancy meeting you here, but it appears that right now our wavelengths are crossing so often we're weaving a veritable fucking lattice."

"Abbey Hall?" Dominic cast his eyes up when she nodded. In the silence that followed, she could hear the pigeon making little bobbling sounds.

Dominic stepped back and made a short gesture. "After you."

He walked more or less at her side, however, and Sylvie felt . . . ruffled. Self-conscious in a way she usually was not.

The *tip-tip* of her boot heels was loud on the stones. It was a quiet time of day for the square, with minimal foot traffic.

"So, your sister's lovely," she said mostly to suppress the urge to flat-out sprint the remaining distance to Abbey Hall.

"Yes, she is."

She peeked a glance sideways. He was scanning the square with narrowed eyes, his hands tucked into his pockets. No bowed head and shoulders for Dominic; always alert and aware of his surroundings.

"Did you get your urgent correspondence sorted out?"

"I did," the Master of Loquacity confirmed.

With all these words constantly spilling out of him, it was amazing she could get a phrase in edgewise.

He'd obviously prefer to walk in silence. She considered gifting that wish.

Decided no.

"Secret business to do with the Albany contract?" she pried, with another sidelong glance through her lashes.

"Odds I'd tell you if it were?" Dominic stopped and crouched to pick something up from the pavers. When he stood, there was a worm between his fingers. He looked around before walking over to deposit the little guy in a plant pot. "But as it happens, no." He dusted his hand off against his trousers. "Upcoming function for Farquhar's. Six cakes. Eight hundred chocolates."

There were horribly starchy insurance firms, and then there was Farquhar's. Their current CEO had once been Sylvie's local councillor during his short-lived political career. The man was so unbending she was surprised he didn't snap in half like a twig every time he sat at his desk. A perfect match for Dominic's repressive aesthetic. They were never likely to be a client for Sugar Fair, and she murmured as much.

"We do have distinct markets." His tone was reciprocally unflattering about the parties who preferred her own work.

"But could both thoroughly benefit from the prestige of this contract."

His gaze collided with hers. "Yes."

"A lot of ups and downs for the whole industry lately," she murmured, an automatic exchange of commiserations with a fellow pâtissier, temporarily forgetting *which* pâtissier.

However, he responded frankly. "The industry has been in turbulent waters for a good five years. Hence the need to boost income."

She blinked. Twice. "Is that why you do *Operation Cake*?"

"Of course that's why I do *Operation Cake*. I have staff who need paying; they have families to support. And that bloody show brings in a hell of a lot of associated business."

Well.

Layers of things in common. Who would have thought?

He was close enough that she could smell his cologne again, overlaid with the familiar scents of sugar and caramel. He smelled both delicious and like hard work. The wind blew loose strands of her hair against his face and he reached up to catch them, holding them away from his skin.

A shiver followed the gust of cold air slipping down Sylvie's spine.

They both tucked their hands into their pockets, and she started walking again, more briskly. She wanted out of the cold. And she was privately quite psyched about the next hour or so. Museums were her jam, the pokier and dustier the better, and she rarely got a chance to indulge.

They mounted the long strip of stone stairs, and Dominic held open the glass-paneled door for her.

The interior of the repository was a bit of a disappointment. Sylvie had hoped for hidden treasures, and lush tapestries, and lots of old volumes with that nice dusty-book smell. Instead, she got very neat filing cabinets and display cases, and the smell of lavender floor cleaner.

"How . . . antiseptic," she said glumly, examining the floor plan of the public areas.

"What were you hoping for?" Dominic's shoulder touched hers. "Abandoned attics, mysterious objects, the odd ghost or two?"

"Yes."

"It's Abbey Hall, not Thornfield Hall." He shook his head. "All right. Consider this my yearly good deed."

Curiously, she followed as he went to the service desk and spoke in low tones to the clerk.

After a minute or two, another door opened and a beaming elderly Black woman bustled out, hands extended to take Dominic's. "Dominic De Vere. How wonderful to see you."

She gave his fingers an affectionate little shake and reached up to kiss him extravagantly on both cheeks.

After years of failing to rise to any bait, rarely cracking a smile, *never* losing his composure—the back of Dominic's neck reddened.

If the most interesting thing Sylvie found in this building was Patrick's laundry receipts, this entire excursion had already justified itself.

Dominic's very gallant lady friend released his hands and patted him on the arm. Her lively eyes moved to Sylvie. "And who is this lovely young woman? Introduce me."

A killing stare dared her to even *look* at his sweet wee lingering flush. The tips of his ears were red, too. "This is Sylvie Fairchild, owner and head chef at Sugar Fair in Notting Hill. Sylvie, meet Dolores Grant, curator of rare books for Abbey Hall, and the woman with the magic keys."

"Ah, you want access to the inner sanctum." After shaking hands with Sylvie, too, Dolores rubbed her palms together. "May I inquire why?"

"The late Prince Patrick." Without turning his head, Dominic touched Sylvie's arm, pulled her closer to his side, then immediately let her go. Simultaneously, a patron reaching around her for a book dislodged a whole shelf of folders, which now fell on the ground instead of her foot. "What do you know about him?"

"King James's younger brother. Never married. No offspring. If you mean beyond the basic biography," Dolores said, "I met him a number of times throughout my career. By far the nicest member of the family with whom I've had professional dealings. Unfailingly polite. Always interested. An unusually moral man." She looked suddenly thoughtful. "Not by the measure of royalty. By the measure of humanity. Prince Patrick was a thoroughly decent human being."

Sylvie was listening intently. "And a talented musician, I believe."

Dolores's ready smile put the most beautiful light in her eyes. "When that man sat down at a piano . . . There are no words," she said simply, before adding with intense wryness, "There are also no words for his short-lived foray into metal, for an entirely different reason."

"I did listen to an impassioned performance of his breakfast anthem."

"Youth is a time for making an arse of oneself, and His Highness excelled at the brief." Dolores bent to her computer and pulled up a catalogue entry. She scrawled a series of numbers on a Post-it note. "But there's a recording in the archives of him playing Rachmaninoff's Piano Concerto No. 2. Listen to it. The man wove magic." Her silky-smooth voice was low and musing. "He treated his instrument with the skill and respect of a devoted lover, and it responded to his touch like a woman in the throes of desire. Every sound, every sigh, coming together in pure harmony."

The skin over Sylvie's cheekbones felt slightly taut. Fleetingly, compulsively, her eyes slipped sideways again to where Dominic stood quietly listening to Dolores.

And silently scrutinizing *her*.

Her heart, increasingly unreliable the past few days, did another skippety-hop, and her stomach muscles clenched.

She swallowed, dragging her gaze away, and saw that the smile in Dolores's dark eyes had deepened into intense speculation.

Perhaps taking pity on Sylvie's obvious discomposure, Dolores tilted her head and switched that perspicacious stare to Dominic. "And why the sudden fascination with Patrick?"

There was a fractional pause before he responded blandly, "Just a small research project. But we were hoping to have a look at the private collections."

"A research project. I think it can be arranged." She exhaled. "Good heavens, I owe you a good deal more than *that*."

"You owe me nothing. But we would appreciate the short-term loan of that key."

"I owe you my whole world." The words were soft, but slipped immediately into normal tones before Dominic could reply. "You're lucky with your timing. I'm on leave after this week. But I can certainly give you a couple of hours now."

Stepping back from the desk, she held up the electronic key card and spoke with the resonant burr of a tour guide. "Follow me, lady and gent, as we enter these hallowed halls and step back in time."

Despite her initial enthusiasm to fossick amongst antiques and lovely old letters, Sylvie was feeling a little uncertain in general now, but she followed them through a locked door behind the desk and into a chilled corridor. Which, in turn, led into an absolute tangle of hallways. If she got lost in here, she'd probably emerge back into the square at about age fifty-three. She was pleased to discover that the farther they receded into the building, the messier and more archaic-looking things got, and by the time Dolores let them into a large chamber, they might be in the country house attic of her dreams.

High wooden beams across the ceiling were spotted with the odd cobweb, and shelf after shelf was stacked with labeled cartons and bubble-wrapped picture frames.

"When members of the royal household pass," Dolores said, "often their personal belongings extend into hundreds of boxes. These came from Patrick's own properties. Some of it has been catalogued. A great deal has not. We've only had this set for eighteen months. You can be assured that if you return in eighteen years, the archivists will have at least half of these boxes fully classified."

"Are we allowed to just . . . touch things?" Sylvie asked.

"As I'm personally vouching for you and not telling anyone about this, yes," Dolores returned cheerfully. "Just put on a pair of those gloves, don't break anything, or take anything, and put things back where you found them. If any long-lost crown jewels fall out of a file, it's not Finders Keepers." She gestured over to a long worktable and handed Sylvie the Post-it. "There's a tape deck on the far table. Here's the shelving reference for the music recording. It *has* been logged and digitized, but I think you're a woman after my own heart. You'll always seek the original source."

She studied them for a further moment. "What are you hoping to find?"

Once more, briefly, Dominic's eyes met Sylvie's. "Inspiration."

"I see." Dolores's response was a little enigmatic. "Well, that's what we're all looking for, isn't it? I'll leave you to it."

She was already heading out in a brisk stride, but popped her head back around the door to fix Dominic with a stern stare. "Postscript. I've chased enough snuggling students out of the public stacks lately. No hanky-panky in front of Will." She patted a bronze bust of Shakespeare on the head. "You're old enough to know better."

The door slammed shut behind her, dislodging a wave of dust particles in the cool air, sending them spinning past Sylvie's hot cheeks.

She was very aware of Dominic standing a few feet away but wouldn't have looked at his face just then if a *million*-pound contract and her life itself were at stake.

"Dolores seems very, um, energetic," she offered into the echoing silence.

"Yes," Dominic said, intensely drily. "Doesn't she?" He was already slipping on a pair of white gloves and reaching for a carton, lifting it down from a shelf and reading the detailed label on top. The sleeves of his shirt and wool pullover were pushed back, his famous forearms on full display.

To be quite honest, the more he kept shoving his shirt up, the more she could see why they had their own fan account on Instagram.

"How do you know her?" Not planning to lose ground on the battlefield, Sylvie pulled on gloves and chose a stack of wrapped photographs.

"She was a customer, a long time ago. One of the first I handled after I finished my qualifications and started working for my grandfather full-time."

Sylvie wanted to ask what Dolores had meant by a favor owed, but there was something about Dominic that made her cautious of prying too far. He was like a human fortress, seemingly impenetrable. But no human being was beyond hurt. She was beginning to have the strangest, prickliest feeling when she was with him, that she could tap, tap, tap against the stone wall— and, just maybe, stab through the tiniest of cracks.

And the feeling it was very important she didn't.

"You know," she said suddenly, lifting out a photo of three ascetic, anaemic-looking people with guns and spaniels, "your grandfather is one of my earliest memories."

Dominic was leafing impatiently through a thick file. His fingers paused on the paper. "Sebastian is?"

"And his chocolate." Sylvie grinned. "Figures. Most of my strongest memories are food-related. And of those, most of them chocolate. It was my fifth birthday. My aunt Mallory took me to De Vere's. Your grandfather was out in the storefront. He shook my hand, wished me happy birthday, showed me the front page of the paper, and asked which of these people should win the general election. I chose the one with the nicest eyes, and he said, 'Excellent. A wise young woman.' He gave me a cupcake on the house, and Mallory let me pick out a whole box of chocolates. A dozen of Sebastian De Vere's signature truffles, all for me. I didn't even have to share." Her smile flickered. "But I did. Mallory and I went to Kensington Gardens, we sat near the Peter Pan statue, and we gorged ourselves on milk caramel creams. It was . . . a really good day. I'll never forget it."

She didn't really expect Dominic to reply, but he looked across at her. "In the bare bones of an anecdote, I can hear his voice."

"You were close."

He said nothing. And then: "We were. Despite a rocky beginning."

Sylvie frowned.

He must really want to change the subject. He actually voluntarily encouraged her to speak. "And you were clearly close to your aunt."

A pang. And a flood of love, always, forever love, from her heart to the tips of her toes.

"She was the great love of my life so far." Sylvie looked down at the second photo she'd unearthed. It was—must be—a mother and daughter, two women a couple of decades apart in age, their features so similar. The daughter was seated, her mother's hand resting on her shoulder. And at their feet, yet another spaniel. Royals and spaniels seemed to go hand in paw. "My parents died when I was a baby. I never knew them. Mallory was my father's younger sister. She was barely twenty-one when she was landed with custody of me. There was no one else. My mother was an only child of only children. My father had no other siblings, no cousins, or aunts or uncles. If Mallory hadn't taken me, I'd have had to go into foster care. I don't think she even hesitated."

She traced her fingers lightly over the photograph. "She used to strap me to her chest and take me to her uni tutorials. She was an artist and became a curator, an expert in nineteenth- and twentieth-century glass art and sculpture. Any time she had a contract or speaking engagement outside of London, she made sure I was okay with it, and off we both went." Finally, simply: "She was always there."

"Until?" Dominic asked quietly, and a film of blurriness distorted the strangers in the photo.

"Until I was nineteen. When the universe put a very bright light into the sky, a lot too soon."

There was a clock somewhere in this room. She could hear it ticking, a repetitive dull sound.

A drop of wet touched the corner of her mouth, and she caught it on her tongue before it could fall farther. Blindly, she set the photos aside, reached for the nearest box, pulling it onto her lap.

Something scraped against the wooden floorboards, and then he was there, crouching before her. Her hands gripped the sides of the carton.

He didn't touch her, but she could feel the warmth and solidity of his presence.

Strange, that the man she'd always considered one of the coldest people she'd ever met could get down on the floor with her and radiate such utter solace.

Neither of them said a word. She listened to his deep, even breaths, until her own came freely and her shoulders relaxed.

Only then did she look up into his eyes, fixed steadily on her face. His black brows were pulled together.

"It was a long time ago," she said softly.

"Does it feel like a long time ago?"

Her smile was crooked. "It feels like a hundred years ago. It feels like yesterday."

He nodded, and that small movement wasn't acknowledgment; it was understanding. Another fragment of grief, splintering the quiet in the room. Memories of his own.

"Me and Rosie," she whispered. "I think we both know first-hand that love and family is something you're born into if you're lucky, but hopefully you'll also find it along the way. And parenthood, it's not always the person who gave birth to you."

His eyes flickered.

She hesitated. "You too?"

A long silence before one word. "Yes."

As her mind retreated from both the pain and shelter of the past, recentering in the present, Sylvie became hyperaware of her surroundings. The ticking was coming from an old grandfather clock; she could see the antique face now, just beyond Dominic's left ear.

There was a bit of dust caught in his thick hair.

A muscle pulsed beside his lips.

Sylvie swallowed and lowered her gaze to the open box. There were more photographs inside, mostly of strangers, more official settings and public occasions than candid shots of the family's leisure time. She studied a studio portrait of the prince, aged perhaps forty. He sat rather stiffly on a bench, shoulders very straight, lips a little tense and narrow. With the lingering remnants of her own sadness tugging at her, the expression in his eyes spoke of desolation.

With painstaking care, she returned the photograph to the box. Standing up, she glanced at the numbers on the Post-it Dolores had given her and plunged into the rear stacks. That section was meticulously organized, and she located an envelope containing a cassette tape without difficulty.

A welcome smile spread through her body as she plugged in the very retro-looking tape deck and slipped in the tape. She could suddenly see the tiny kitchen of Mallory's first flat, sunlight filtering in through pink curtains, books and plants everywhere, and cassette tapes scattered across the table. Standing on her aunt's feet and holding her hands as they danced around the tiles.

Eight-year-old Jay already sporting a romantic coif of dark hair and a melancholic expression, rolling his eyes at her taste, but using months of hoarded pocket money to buy her a Spice Girls tape for her birthday.

She sat down slowly at the table, aware of the faint rustling sounds behind her as Dominic continued his efficient search, and pressed play.

As the first piano notes wrapped around her, Dominic's movements slowed and stopped.

Pulling off the gloves, Sylvie set them down neatly. Leaning her elbows on the wooden tabletop, she rested her chin in her hands and closed her eyes.

There were rare moments when the passing of time, the significance of the clock, the entire world beyond four walls, drifted into nothingness. She existed in those endless minutes in a bubble, suspended only by the music and the rhythm of her own breaths and Dominic's silent presence. There was no physical connection between them, she couldn't even see him—and it was as if she could feel the skin of his hands, the steady beat of his heart, the comforting rasp of his fingers sliding between hers.

When she eventually reached out and turned off the tape, she felt the echoing quiet down to her bones.

Her cheeks were wet against her hands. She ran her pinkie fingers under her lashes, collecting the lingering traces of tears, before she turned.

Dominic was standing motionless, looking down at the box he held. When he lifted his head, the faintest sheen lent those dark eyes the endless depths of the midnight sky.

"If it were possible to bottle sound and sculpt it into visual form," he said simply, and she nodded wordlessly.

Releasing a long, shaky breath as she put her gloves back on, she stood and removed the tape, returning it to its envelope.

"I'm not sure how to translate that experience into a cake design," she murmured—and honestly, part of her wouldn't want to. It had been something profoundly, transcendently personal, somehow, as if every note had hung in the air like the most delicate of lace, drawing around her and Dominic and the haunting spirit of Patrick. And whatever emotion in the prince's life had slipped from his soul and into those piano keys. "But it's going to be difficult to top that."

She took the envelope back to its drawer, reluctantly closing it away.

Leaning lightly against a pillar near Dominic, she nodded at the box he was sifting through. "Have you found anything interesting yet?" She coughed to dispel the lingering huskiness.

"Trying to form a task force with the enemy?" He seemed to take refuge in the sardonic, as quick as she was to step back from that sudden, almost overwhelming sense of intimacy.

"What's that saying about keeping them close?" Sylvie watched as he turned a small velvet box over in his hands. "Don't worry. That end contract is ours—"

"Ours?" He arched a brow.

"Sugar Fair." She'd woven glittery strands of ribbon through her fishtail plait, leftovers from the golden anniversary cake. One slipped loose now and she wrapped it around her thumb. "Fair warning, in the final leg of this race, I will sail airily past you and scoop the honors with very little remorse. But in the meantime, if you're planning to show up everywhere I go, it's too much effort and a little too Agent Ninety-Nine to sneak around

you in covert circles. I'm prepared to extend a level of coopera-
tion."

Dominic paused. "All right. A *complete* walkover would be a
sour victory. I will also cooperate. To an extent."

"Very magnanimous."

"I thought so." He ran his fingers over the seal of the velvet
box, looking for the opening. "And for the record, if you want me
to be worried about credible competition, you're going to have to
do better than fondant stars, sugar dragons, and pseudo-magic.
It's a wedding." He found and popped the lock. "Not their sixth
birthday."

The usual retort was tickling half-heartedly at Sylvie's tongue,
but if anything had magical properties, it was this room. For at
least the next five minutes or so, she didn't really feel like argu-
ing with him.

In fact—

"You know," she said slowly, winding the fallen gold ribbon
tighter and tighter around her thumb, "you have the tableside
manner of the shark from *Jaws*, but the actual basis of your criticism on the show *is* usually sound. You know what you're talking about, and you bring that experience to the set."

Dominic removed some padding from the box and lifted out a
bundle of more velvet. "My *experience* tells me that's not ending
in a compliment."

"But," Sylvie went on with emphasis, "you have an awful lot
to say about my business, none of it good, for someone who, as
far as I'm aware, has never actually stepped foot in the place."

His veiled gaze raised from the unknown object held so gently
in his hands.

"Tomorrow night, the last booking in the Dark Forest ends
at nine." The ribbon tore in her grip. This was likely the biggest

mistake since she'd screwed up the mechanism in that unicorn cake, but apparently she was dedicated to committing it. "Consider this your official invitation into enemy territory. Meet me downstairs at quarter past nine, and I'll give you your very own potions class. If you're going to denigrate my hard work, you might as well know what you're talking about."

The offer ended in just the shade of a taunt, and his jaw tightened on what had likely been an instinctive "not a chance in a hell."

In the silence, the ticking of the grandfather clock sounded like a warning.

Bad-idea, bad-idea, bad-idea.

Tick-tock, listen to the clock, tick-tock, the man's a cock.

With deft, sensitive hands that had rescued a stranded earthworm and eyes that could betray the most profound understanding . . .

"I have a business meeting tomorrow." She imagined he'd sound similarly enthusiastic if she'd invited him to a joint colonoscopy. "Half nine?"

She slipped her phone out of her bag, tapped it into her calendar, and wiggled the screen at him. "Done. See you there. And unlike the Starlight Circus, I make no secret of high booze content." She refastened her bag. "Speaking of, Rosie should probably have a heads-up that Johnny's daily pick-me-up contains enough alcohol to anesthetize a horse. Even sober, he's pretty disastrously frank for a public figure."

"I wonder if that relationship is going to last the long haul."

"I hope it does. The way they look at each other. Not everyone gets that in their life."

For just a moment, they looked at each other again.

Bad-idea.

With a tiny, abrupt movement of his head, Dominic unwrapped the velvet bundle on his palm and lifted out the object within.

"Oh!" Sylvie's exclamation was involuntary. "How beautiful."

It was a tiny cast-glass sculpture of a globe, a perfect little Earth on a minuscule glass stand. Immediately, before she remembered a few manners, Sylvie reached out for it, her gloves brushing over Dominic's as she touched the exquisite piece of art. It was a working model, turning on a hinge as she stroked the surface.

"Amazing," she said fervently, spellbound by the sparkle of light around every curve. "The skill in this. May I—?"

He passed it carefully into her hands, his attention on her face rather than the miniature masterpiece he'd uncovered. "You said your aunt was a glass expert and an artist. Your sugar work has always been exceptional." One of the few areas of her work he'd commended without reservation four years ago, usually accompanied by mutterings about wasting perfect technique on such frivolous subject matter. "There's the hand of an artist in your sculptural pieces. Are you a glass artist, as well?"

"Mallory started teaching me when I was six, and I went to art school before I switched to the culinary field. Glass art was my specialty. Inevitably, after being carried around museums every weekend as a toddler, I'd grow to love it or hate it. I love it." She'd combined the best of both worlds with her sugar art, but sometimes she still missed creating works that lasted longer than a party. She couldn't stop staring at the globe. "But I'll never in my life be able to make something like this."

Very, very delicately, she turned it over, looking for a clue as to the artist. On the base of the stand, engraved in elegant, neat letters were the words: ALL THE WORLD AND STILL ONLY YOU. And underneath, simply: JESSIE.

"Jessie," Sylvie murmured aloud. This was a piece that ought to be in a museum, not merely a gallery, but she was very familiar with British glass artists both past and present, and that didn't ring any bells. "Was this just shoved in a carton of random files?" She was massively offended on behalf of the globe, the unknown Jessie, and Patrick, because nobody could have owned this and not treasured it.

Frowning, Dominic was looking through the rest of the box. "This hasn't been catalogued yet," he said, "and I'm not sure it was meant to be here. I suspect all of these items came straight from Patrick's bedroom, and probably ought to have been taken by Rosie. She seemed to be the only one who really cared about him." He held up a pretty little antique clock, a well-dog-eared copy of *Murder on the Orient Express*, and poignantly, a hand-drawn old birthday card, inscribed in a childish hand. *Loves and hugs and the moon and back, from Rosie.*

A couple of vinyl records were sticking out the top of the box, and curiously, Sylvie pulled one out. She could almost guess what it would be before she saw the sleeve. "Rachmaninoff. Probably not performed as well as his own interpretation." She turned it over and the record slipped out; as she hastily caught it before it could fall, two items drifted to the ground. "Crap."

She bent to pick them up and stopped, looking down at what she held in her hands. An envelope, yellowed with age. Just an ordinary envelope that had obviously once contained a gas bill. But it was covered with little pencil sketches and notes, still visible despite the passing years, in two different hands. Playful line drawings of a couple lounging by a stream, the figure of a man with his head in a woman's lap. The same man climbing a tree, his face teasing and alight with laughter. The woman standing with hands on hips, her visible disapproval justified as her lover—for lover he obviously was—tumbled to the ground in the next vignette. Despite his own folly, she bent to kiss his head.

In a neat cursive, a hand had written: *I don't know what you'd do without me.*

And a man's scrawl in return: *Never leave me then and we won't find out.*

Sylvie knew the handwriting of the latter. She'd already seen several examples of Patrick's correspondence today.

The envelope was addressed to Jessica Maple-Moore at Primrose Cottage in a village near Oxford.

Pulling her gaze from the drawings, she looked at the other fallen object. A photograph. No posed studio shot this time. A candid photo of two people sitting on stone steps leading up to a wooden door. The railings either side of their bodies barely held back a profusion of blooming primroses.

A thirtysomething Prince Patrick, wearing an exquisitely cut wool suit, couture in every line, sitting with an arm hooked around his bent knee. With a watch chain hanging from his pocket, he looked more *Downton Abbey* than the wannabe rocker of his younger days. His dark hair was combed back, slicked to his head, and a smile played about his mouth as he turned his head toward the woman beside him. Relaxed and obviously happy, he looked like an entirely different man.

Sylvie raised her eyebrows. She'd recognized that Patrick had been conventionally handsome, but she hadn't before considered him *attractive*, which was a very different beast. Here, however . . . In the sexiness stakes, she'd personally rank a three-piece suit with a waistcoat well over visible abs, and she could understand the light in his companion's eyes.

With laughter in every line of her fascinating face, a vivacious brunette looked into the camera, but one hand was caught and held tightly in Patrick's, their fingers linked together. Even in a photograph, the woman emanated an aura of restrained energy that reminded Sylvie a bit of Pet De Vere.

She wished it were a digital photograph so she could zoom in—so used to Instagram that any time she saw a photo, her finger twitched toward an invisible "like" button—but really, no higher resolution was necessary. In the instant when the camera flash had captured this moment for posterity, their body language was baldly explicit.

The woman had quite rounded cheeks and a very pointed chin, and she'd depicted both features with ruthless accuracy in her pencil drawings on the envelope.

Without a word, Sylvie handed the envelope to Dominic, as she continued to stare at the photo of Prince Patrick and presumably Jessica Maple-Moore.

Jessie.

Dominic studied the pencil drawings without comment, before reaching for the photograph.

"Clearly," Sylvie said, "Rosie was *not* the only person who cared about Patrick."

When Dolores came to collect them at the end of her shift, Dominic indicated the box they'd meticulously repacked and set aside, and suggested quietly that she might want to double-check to whom the contents had been bequeathed.

Dolores glanced at it—and them—curiously, and took the box under her arm. "Found what you were looking for?" she asked them when they returned to the busy, blessedly warm public rooms.

A tiny beat, before Dominic said, "Not yet. But I think the first stones have been laid."

"Coming back tomorrow?"

A small glint replaced the thoughtful look on his face. "I have to see a man about a horse tomorrow. Or a woman with enough alcohol to anesthetize one."

When he went to retrieve their coats, Dolores twinkled at her. "Goodness, was that almost a smile I saw? I'd assume that Patrick and Rachmaninoff worked their magic even on Dominic, but I suspect the credit belongs a little closer to home."

Sylvie's mind had been half back in the archives room, and it took a moment to register Dolores's smiling inference. For the fiftieth time that day, a spreading flush was a pulsing beat in her cheeks.

Before she could voice a denial in what would likely be an astounding display of inarticulacy, Dolores said, "I've never seen his body language like that. And I've known him for some time now. My love has known him even longer." She nodded over Sylvie's shoulder, warmth and delight suffusing every line of her face.

Sylvie turned to see another elderly woman sitting patiently on an armchair near the doors. Her dark brown skin creased into countless wrinkles with the most gorgeous smile as she saw them looking. She blew Dolores a kiss.

"Isobel." Acres of emotion in a few syllables. "My fiancée."

"Congratulations." Sylvie returned Isobel's wave when it moved to her. Smiling, she pulled a card out of her bag. "If you need a cake for the wedding, please give me a call."

Dolores laughed and took the card. "I'm afraid Dominic won my loyalty a long time ago, but I've heard some very interesting tales of a magical forest and bubbling cauldrons in Notting Hill. The cake I can't commission, but a cocktail?"

"On the house. Anytime." Sylvie couldn't help it. She had to ask. "What did you mean about his body language?"

"So entirely tuned into someone else." Dolores considered. "Somehow *curved* into someone else, without moving a muscle. Aware of their every movement, without so much as a glance."

Sylvie shook her head slightly, but it wasn't quite "no." She wasn't sure what it was. She hesitated. "You said you owed Dominic a favor—"

"I owe Dominic my life. Quite literally." Dolores gestured *five more minutes* to Isobel, but the other woman was now talking to Dominic, who'd spotted her and walked over to crouch by her chair. "Years ago, he was catering the desserts for a function I'd organized. When he arrived to deliver the cake, I was forty-five minutes late to the venue. I made it clear to him in our initial meetings that I prized punctuality in myself and expected it in others. I'm never late. He barely knew me, and he had another commitment that evening that would have resulted in a lucrative ongoing contract, I was later told by a member of his staff. But he had a feeling something was wrong. He came looking at my former workplace, and he found me. Fallen through the floor of a rotting heritage building, cold, bleeding, and alone." A shadow momentarily darkened her eyes at the memory. "For hours. Dominic called emergency services, he stayed with me, he *talked* to me even though he's clearly about as naturally chatty as *The Thinker*, and when the structure collapsed again before help arrived, he dislocated his shoulder keeping me from falling another level."

Sylvie didn't know what to say.

Before she had to find words, Dolores continued, "It's no exaggeration to say I would have died that night without him. But he gifted me my life twice. It was through him that I met Isobel. She knew his family when he was a young child and met him again as an adult. He introduced us at an awards dinner." Where before she had been open, almost garrulous, here she stopped. She looked into Sylvie's face, and there was something so . . . dissecting in that look, Sylvie felt as if a sci-fi scanner were running over her body, somehow drawing out every last secret of her past, every minute facet of her character.

She felt oddly nervous suddenly, but whatever silent test Dolores was conducting, apparently she passed. The older woman gave small nod. "Isobel has told me," she said very quietly, "a little of what she knows of Dominic's early childhood. She wasn't in a position to intervene, but she wished desperately that she could, on more than one occasion."

Something cold and angry clutched in a ball in Sylvie's stomach. She wanted to ask. And she didn't want to invade Dominic's privacy so acutely behind his back.

Dolores answered the unspoken. "Not abuse in the form that the law would recognize. Grievous neglect couched in luxury. He was entirely given over to the care of a nanny, who didn't believe in coddling children, as she put it. The woman shouldn't have even had the care of a houseplant," she added with a distinct bite. "Let alone a child with nowhere to go and no one for whom he could reach. *I've never felt so helpless,*' Isobel said to me once. *'A touch-starved five-year-old. I'd have liked to load his parents into a cannon.*'"

Dominic had said goodbye to Isobel and returned then with their coats. He cast a glance between them, that laser focus sharpening on Sylvie's face. She was trying very hard to keep her expression clear of emotion. His eyes narrowed. After a moment, he merely queried, "Ready?"

Silently, Sylvie nodded, and Dominic shot her another look before he held out her coat so she could slip her arms into the sleeves.

Dolores patted his own arm fondly. "I'll look into the items you've flagged." Her gaze softened on Sylvie. "Have a good evening. Bring her again."

When they opened the door to walk back outside, the icy wind was a frigid blast, rocketing down Sylvie's spine. She drew her coat tighter across her chest, and couldn't help noticing that he stepped to the left, apparently unconsciously taking the brunt of the wind.

Dominic stood looking down at her. His query was abrupt. "Are you all right?"

"I am," she said slowly. She looked back at the stone walls of Abbey Hall. All things considered, and in a comparatively short amount of time, she felt as if she'd stepped into that building with one path on the horizon, and suddenly someone had opened up a dozen different avenues of possibility.

Her gaze returned to dust over the taut line of his stubbled jaw, the sprinkling of pale freckles above his collar, the unreadable expression in his eyes.

Evenly, he commented, "Not quite what I expected to find in there."

No.

Nor her.

Chapter Nine

De Vere's
Mission: Midnight Elixir, the Cake
Attempt 8
9
~~10~~
11

> "Yes, I did think we were going to be there all night."
> —Liam Boateng, highly paid, highly annoyed sous-chef, De Vere's

The cake was perfectly golden, rich, with a good crumb. And it tasted like nothing on Earth.

Liam lowered his napkin from his mouth. His shoulders were still wracked with small shudders. "Literally the first time I've ever had to spit something out in this kitchen."

Dominic leaned both fists on the countertop. If he could develop telekinesis powers through sheer will, that platter would fly into the bin on its own and save him the trouble.

"Reduce the vanilla," he said over his shoulder to the assistant currently mixing the next batch. "The boysenberry is giving a

note far too sour. Need to counterbalance with the white chocolate. And the absinthe—"

"Has to go." Liam was physically scrubbing his tongue with
the napkin.

"It's an important component of the flavor profile, but it's overwhelming. And cut the theatrics. I've had enough on set." He reached
for a piece of paper and started scrawling with a pen. "Maybe if we
introduce that note in the second icing layer. Could use a spray . . ."

"May I make a suggestion?"

He scribbled a diagram, added a ratio of liquid to dry ingredients. "Yes."

Liam smacked a massive tablet of dark Belgian chocolate on
the counter next to the hell cake. "Stick with chocolate."

Sugar Fair

Sylvie leaned on the counter, darkly eyeing the array of cakes.
Two looked great, one would be acceptable if it'd been pulled off
a supermarket bargain shelf, the other two would net a failing
grade as a school project.

Gingerly, she poked one of the decent-looking examples with
her fork, brought another small mouthful to her lips.

Which puckered as soon as the renewed taste of that cake hit
her senses.

She dropped the fork and looked up at Jay and Mabel, both
lingering for the verdict.

"They're all disgusting. And pace yourself with those," she
added warningly to Mabel, who was slurping at another of the
Midnight Elixir takeaway cups Sylvie had asked Penny to pur-

chase. Partly because they needed the drink for comparative purposes. Partly to keep the intern occupied and not dissolving into tears for the third time that week. "It's all fun and games until it throws a punch like Mike Tyson and you start complimenting people on their fleshly assets."

"Sorry?" Jay finished hiding his cake sample in the bin and shot her an amused glance.

"Mabs, how many of those have you had?" Sylvie asked, and her assistant lowered the cup.

"Four. Neither my brain nor my stomach is weak." Mabel finished the remaining Elixir in the cup, extended an elegant hand and tapped the bottle of absinthe. "And this isn't going to work in the mix. You need a more subtle delivery agent for the flavor note."

She sailed out in a perfectly straight line, steady as a rock.

"I'm aggrieved," Sylvie remarked, and Jay rested his hand on her head.

"Welcome to my world."

De Vere's

"It's not purple." Pet sounded personally offended.

Dominic looked up from the Midnight Elixir cake. Version #WhoTheFuckKnows. "Why would it be purple?"

"Because the drink is purple." She took another sip from the takeaway cup. "It's good, too." He didn't need her pointed look at the cake to fill in the unspoken: *Unlike that.*

"I thought it was black," Liam murmured.

"Isn't it brown?" A cluster of assistants gathered around to peer into the cups.

Dominic pressed his thumb and forefinger against his brow-bone and speculated on the sensation of an imploding brain.

Sugar Fair

"It's better," Jay said, chewing thoughtfully. His jaw shifted as he turned the cake over on his tongue, weighing the flavors. "*Much* better than the last one."

Sylvie took another bite. The cake was packed with flavor, not in the least dry, and it looked pretty, since she'd added a tiny sprinkling of gold glitter dust. "It *is* much better," she agreed slowly, and took another bite. Chewed. Thought. Flung down the fork. "It's still horrible."

"Foul." Jay shoved his own plate away and reached for a bottle of water. He cracked the top and drank a third in one shot. "How goes the second part of the mission?"

Sticking a piece of plain white chocolate in her mouth to melt on her tongue, Sylvie opened her bag and took out her phone. She handed it to Jay, and he flicked through the photos she'd taken of the envelope, the photograph of Patrick and Jessica at Primrose Cottage, and the little glass globe. She'd resisted a latent Bonnie-and-Clyde impulse and not put the latter in her pocket.

Jay zoomed in to read the little handwritten words on the en-velope, before he turned to the snapshot of the couple, studying it closely. "Is this relevant to the cake design?"

She propped her hip against the bench. "I don't know. My instinct says yes."

Also, she had literally no other ideas right now.

He leaned forward to rest his arms on the wooden surface, running the fingers of one hand through the fall of hair over his forehead. "He was a bachelor prince of the British realm. He must have had lovers by the barrel-load."

"That's not a given. But there did appear to be a number of short-term flings, analyzed by the tabloids in tedious, painstaking detail." She nodded at her phone. "Until he was about thirty-eight. Approximately the age he must have been in that photograph. I can't find a single press mention of Jessica Maple-Moore. From a research point of view, she's invisible. A handsome prince, constantly in the public eye, hounded by the press—and not a peep of that affair leaked to the public."

Reaching out, she flipped back to the drawings. "Teasing. Intimate. Clearly the best of friends." She returned to the photograph, that moment frozen in time on the steps of Primrose Cottage. "His eyes," she said. "Look at his eyes. He loved her." And obviously, Jessie had loved him. A flick of the screen, and she traced the tip of her finger over the inscription on the base of the globe. "All the world and still only you."

Jay's own eyes lifted slowly to her face.

"A whole world outside and it could only ever be them." Her mind was preoccupied, the words coming from some hidden part of her brain in almost a whisper, but in the periphery of her vision and attention, just for a moment, she thought that Jay had stilled.

De Vere's

Pet was hovering.

Dominic's eyes were on the bubbling pot of berry syrup under his spoon, but the waves of tension emanating from his sister were stronger than the lingering scent of anise. "Everything all right?"

"Yes."

Her feet shuffled. Side to side. A few steps forward. Stop. Side to side.

The syrup turned, thickening to the correct consistency in the space of a single stir, and he pulled it from the stove. Nearby, Aaron was dipping truffles into melted dark chocolate and decorating them with sugar flowers.

"Aaron?" Lizzie stuck her head apologetically through the door. "Phone. It's your grandmother."

Aaron's glance immediately went guiltily to Dominic.

"Take it," Dominic said, taking the chocolate from him. "I'll finish these."

When Aaron hesitated, he inclined his head pointedly toward the door. "Go. You're more than earning your keep."

Guilt faded into a flush of pleasure, and Aaron stripped off his gloves and went to answer the phone.

"How are you with flowers?" Dominic asked without looking at Pet.

His sister's feet stopped shifting about.

"As a person landed with the name Petunia, I ought to have an affinity." She grabbed a pair of gloves and took the bowl of sugar flowers he proffered. "Just plop one on top?"

"I'd prefer 'neatly place.'" He rapidly dipped one truffle after another. "But essentially, yes."

As Pet placed a Cosmos on each truffle, she did so with painstaking care. There was nothing pointed or sarcastic about her measured movements.

He finished the last tray of truffles and went to transfer a completed batch of croissants from the pastry ovens to the racks. The hot, buttery smell was a reminder he'd had to skip lunch to reshoot a scene for *Operation Cake*, and he apparently had plans to burn out his stomach lining in Sylvie's booze basement this evening.

"Croissant?" he asked over his shoulder, nudging a couple onto a plate.

"Free food? Yes, please." Pet had a little blooming garden of Cosmos around her.

Dominic set the croissants on the bench in the side alcove. Sitting down for the first time all day, he hooked one boot into the leg of the stool and silently watched his sister finish her work.

Everything she did, she did with the delicacy and attention to detail of her silhouette portraits. As a baby, she'd been endearingly wobbly, tripping over her own knees, knocking over toys. As an adult, she was . . .

In many respects, a stranger.

The fault for that, now, rested largely on his shoulders.

"Have you spoken to Lorraine lately?" He wasn't particularly interested in the answer to that question, and her sideways glance spoke volumes.

"I speak to Lorraine as infrequently as I can manage." She pressed the last Cosmos into place. "I can't stand her."

Stated placidly.

"You probably ought to keep up at least a minimal connection with her."

Pet set down the bowl in her hands and turned to face him. "Why?"

Actually, he couldn't think of a single reason why, other than a token nod to the adage that "family is family."

But as he'd never believed in maintaining a toxic relationship simply because of a few common threads of DNA . . .

"Because otherwise I'm currently lacking in the family stakes?" Pet inquired. "Mum's gone. Gerald's gone, and not who I once thought he was. In more ways than one. I might have a bio dad out there somewhere, but that seems irrelevant as I have no idea who he is, and if he knows who *I* am, he's never bothered to drop a text to say hi. My sister's about as pleasant to have around as a dodgy mole." She took a deep breath. It shook. "And my brother wishes I'd just go away."

There was a sharp, sour taste in Dominic's mouth. He pushed away the plate of untouched croissants. "Pet . . ."

She stood still, staring at him, and he wanted to get up.

He wanted to make this right.

He was unable to move.

Pet bit her lip so hard she left an imprint in her lipstick. When she turned, the words caught in his throat tore free.

"I don't want you to go away, Pet," he said roughly, and her head turned a little toward him.

"No?" Her voice was very low.

"No."

Her eyes searched his. Finally, she came toward him. Momentarily, he thought she was going to hug him, and his hand unfurled from a tight fist. She reached out and took a croissant from the plate.

"I'll be in Vivienne's office. I have a line to follow on Prince Patrick." Her fingers plucked at the pastry. With a tiny spark of animation, she shot him a little smile. "I like Sylvie a lot, and when this contract is over, I have grand plans for drinks at hers, but she's still going down."

With a faint curl of his own mouth, he said, "Team De Vere?"

This time, her smile reached her eyes. Tentative and shadowed, but legit. "Team De Vere."

A cold, heavy weight twisted in his chest. He watched as Pet started to walk away, hesitated, came back.

Her hand closed over the other croissant, and she clutched both to her chest like a squirrel jealously hoarding nuts.

His brows rose.

Her chin, likewise. "This half of Team De Vere is an emotional eater, okay?"

The Dark Forest
9:30 p.m.

Sylvie was sitting at the head table in her—to quote Mariana—booze dungeon when Dominic's tall form appeared through the trees.

Through curls and swirls of rising purple smoke, she surreptitiously studied his face. He looked deeply tired, beyond the simple exhaustion of a long day and several reshoots on set that had culminated in the elimination of Charlene.

Their Black Widow had taken the decision very well. She hadn't forgotten to thank the rest of the contestants and the crew for making the experience so memorable.

The whole crew. By name. While smiling gently and looking directly at each face for a full three seconds.

Not unsettling at all.

Dominic reached out to gently touch a tree trunk, his long fingers playing over the embedded lights like piano keys. In the flickering shadows, he turned, boot soles a soft rasp on the stone floor. "Impressive."

Carefully, Sylvie set a gold-toned cauldron over a burner. "That sounded sincere."

"I feel like I'm in Disneyland Paris." His footsteps echoed amidst the quiet bubbling and hissing. His hands came down to rest on the table. "Not a bakery."

Not coming across as a compliment.

Without pausing in her movements, she opened a beaker of elderflower syrup and poured the contents into the cauldron.

"But I agree," he murmured in that dark, satiny voice. "Any comparison between Sugar Fair and the Starlight Circus is an insult." He was examining every smallest detail. "It's not my taste any more than De Vere's is yours."

"No," she agreed.

His head turned back toward hers. "It's brilliant, Sylvie."

She looked straight into his eyes, searching their expression. The side of her lips slowly curved, and she saw him flick a glance in the direction of her dimple. "I know," she said complacently. "But thanks."

A reciprocal flash of amusement in those hard, sculpted features.

She worked amidst the steam and fog down here all the time, but it was making her a bit light-headed tonight. Returning her attention to her work, she made a face. "Apparently, my raspberry toffees have now appeared on Darren Clyde's menu. As 'Darren's Dewberry Dreams.' Gag. We've only been stocking those for three weeks ourselves. He's on the ball." Opening a small metal box, she added a pinch of blue salts to the syrup mixture and blew on the cauldron. A burst of smoke puffed up, sending a dusting of glitter particles spinning in the lights. He turned his head to follow the twinkling trail, and she slanted a sideways smile. "Magic."

"Predictable chemical reaction," he returned, examining the

box of salts. "And once again in your company, I have glitter in my hair."

"And your stubble. Bit of technicolor glam to liven up the grays. You're welcome."

He rolled his eyes, but she thought she saw a slight relaxing of his shoulders. "So Clyde's still nosing about nicking your work."

"Mmm." In a second cauldron, she started mixing cranberry juice and vodka. "Having spent hours today deconstructing his top seller, I should probably feel on shaky ground in my moral indignation. But as I remain convinced that he ripped off that recipe from someone as well—I do not."

"And how's your version of the Midnight Elixir cake?" Dominic hooked a stool closer and sat down, watching the motions of her hands.

"Great, thanks," Sylvie said, plucking a mint leaf and dropping it in the first brew. "As delicious in crumb form as it is in a flagon."

She handed him a vanilla bean, and with expert precision, he sliced it open and scraped out the seeds.

"So, as inedible as mine, then?" he asked, handing her a knife coated with pure vanilla.

"Tongue-curlingly vile." Mixing the vanilla into the sugar syrup, she kicked a lever under the table. "But I'll get there."

Flashes of lightning lit up the forest, revealing the silhouette of an old country estate house through the branches, a hologram against the far wall. Flapping wings crossed over their heads, dipping close to Dominic's stool.

He didn't so much as flinch.

"Throw me a bone and at least squeak," she muttered, stirring the cranberry vodka.

A second kick of the lever, and six large cauldrons along the central bench lit up one after another: blue, purple, red, green, pink, yellow. Smoke spiraled upward to the ceiling, where little flames licked.

Sylvie lowered her eyes from the burning roof and looked at Dominic.

He looked back.

"Eek," he said solemnly.

She grinned. Shaking her head, she moved down the bench to where more cauldrons bubbled, keeping sugar solutions on a low boil. Taking a spoon, she took a decent blob of the thickest solution, transferred it to a heated pad, and started rolling it, kneading and pulling.

"Teflon hands." Dominic turned on the stool. With the bulk of his chest and shoulders, he took up a fair amount of space, was still within touching distance even after she'd shifted position; but his movements were always so light and fluid.

She held up one palm, kept kneading with the other. "Calluses for life."

He turned his own big hand. "Likewise."

On sheer instinct, she almost high-fived him. Her special effects might have zero impact on his nerves whatsoever, but she imagined *that* would have him doing a spooked-cat scarper out the door.

Although . . .

Dolores's words yesterday. *A touch-starved five-year-old.* It made her feel like crying every time she thought about it. It made her furious.

And it made her wonder.

Attaching a tiny piece of sugar mass to the end of her blow

pipe, she started blowing air into it, keeping an eye on the density as it stretched and expanded. With a thin, delicate syringe, she injected a flavor emulsion into the bubble that instantly flooded the interior with sparkling rainbow. She sealed it off, released it carefully, and started on another.

Dominic glanced over at the silhouette of the old house on the wall. "I understand the location shoot has been moved up."

Every season of *Operation Cake* had a special episode shot out of the studio, usually on location in a stately home. This year, they were going to Middlethorpe Grange, an hour outside of London. On the initial schedule, it had been booked for a later date but the owners were planning to fumigate. As nobody wanted insecticide in their cakes—some of the bakes emerging from the contestants' ovens were bad enough this season without the extra help—they were shooting on Monday.

Sylvie laid a third bubble next to the others, progressively smaller in size, all twinkling under the lights. "It'll be nice to get out of the city for the day. And I like stately homes. Lets me indulge my Pemberley fantasies." She realized she was singing softly under her breath and stopped before he pointed it out. "Hopefully it'll be really romantic."

His head lifted, and a traitorous heat spread down her neck.

"For Emma and Adam." Too much emphasis.

There was a heart skip of silence before he reached out and gave her sugar syrup a stir. Just when it needed one. "Thanks for getting Pet hooked on *that* fantasy," Dominic said sardonically—and with a note of something else when he spoke his sister's name. "Evidently, my new daily routine will involve a summary of her reading material, followed by my own contribution, a detailed update on the imaginary romance between two total strangers."

"It's not imaginary." Sylvie had accumulated a little pile of bubbles in various sizes. She took her mint-scented syrup off the boil and poured it into the cranberry and vodka. Turning around, she scanned the towering shelves of little bottles and jars, took down a pink one. "Emma laughed at Adam's joke today."

He waited.

She added a few drops of a shimmering lilac solution to the cauldron.

"And?"

"And he's not funny. Trust me, if she mustered more than a polite titter, she wants to ride him like Space Mountain."

At one point, Dominic had rarely addressed her with more than two words together.

She appeared to have sent him back into the realms of total silence.

Carefully, Sylvie decanted the whole mixture into a long beaker. Collecting a handful of the sugar bubbles, she floated them in the drink. She popped in a sugar straw and set it in front of him. "The bubbles contain our signature Sorceress emulsion, which releases as they dissolve."

He picked up the glass, examined it under the light. Ignoring the straw, he tasted it from the side, curling his lip when he realized she'd rimmed it in popping candy.

"Well?" she said, realizing—to her faint horror—that the sensation twisting in her stomach was actually nerves.

It shouldn't matter whether he liked or approved anything that she did.

It definitely hadn't four years ago on set.

But it was starting to now.

He took another mouthful. Set the glass down. "It's delicious."

Simple, restrained, and obviously truthful.

As she bit down on the inside of her lip, a small crease appeared between his brows.

"In fact . . ." He reached across the table for a spoon and fished out one of the dissolving sugar bubbles, slipping the remnants onto his tongue. "Hmm."

"What?" She peered into his glass. "Is there something wrong with the bubbles?"

"No." Dominic retrieved another and held out the spoon to her. Sylvie shot him a curious look, but obligingly opened her mouth, and he fed her the bubble. "Think about what we've both been doing for hours today. And re-taste your mystery bubbles."

Running her tongue over her lower lip to catch a drop of the liquid, she shook her head with a prickle of tiredness and frustration. After a subpar day on the *Operation Cake* set and a kitchen full of virtually inedible cake, her brain was inching along like a grumpy tortoise right now, and—

And her Sorceress bubbles tasted *exactly* like one of the main flavor notes in Midnight Elixir.

She snatched up the syringe containing the Sorceress emulsion and shot a stream straight into her mouth.

Judging by the way ever-stoic Dominic was startled into a slow blink, the result was slightly pornographic.

But definite confirmation on the flavor. The anise in Midnight Elixir sat strongly on top of any other notes, and the sweetness was so intense it even drowned out the tang of alcohol, but strip that out and underneath was something very close to her Sorceress bubbles.

Suspiciously close.

"Fucking Darren Clyde." Sylvie was pissed. She self-soothed with another long stream of emulsion. "How did I not recognize this before?"

"To begin with, the other night we were both boozed to the eyeballs within half an hour. And there's a fair whack of . . ." Dominic cut himself off, letting the unknown ingredient hide behind silence. No matter. It was only a matter of time before she had that recipe down to the last pinch of sugar. "There's another ingredient in the Elixir that hits as a top note and initially distracts. Your 'Sorceress' concoction is the middle note, before it ends with a lingering renewal of anise."

He picked up another bubble and examined it. "You were quite right," he said grimly. "He *did* rip off the recipe. Or at least part of it."

"Yup."

"Going to tell me what's in this emulsion?"

"Nope."

He settled the bubble on his tongue. "Boysenberry. White chocolate." He made a little considering noise in the back of his throat, a honeyed purr that she somehow felt as a twitch on the back of her neck. "Agave?"

"Sorry," she said, with zero remorse. "House secret." She wiggled a bottle at him. "But I'll throw you a bone. You can take this with you. Study to your heart's content."

"Which you confidently anticipate will come to nothing." By his tone, he expected to have the recipe in its entirety in about three minutes. "Thank you." As he moved to take the bottle, he knocked over her propped-up iPad. "Sorry," he murmured, rescuing it before it shot to the floor.

Sylvie took it and thumbed back to the news item she'd been reading earlier with disgust. "Did you see the latest headlines on Rosie and Johnny? Having failed to dig out any hot titbits about the wedding, the *Daily Spin* has resorted to fabricating stories in which Johnny is both a callous heartbreaker, who left a string of weeping maidens around his parents' estate, and a thwarted lover, still pining for his ex-girlfriend." She turned the screen and he gave it a cursory glance. "Imagine having such a hate-on for Johnny. He wouldn't make the most effective figurehead, but it's not like he's in line for the top job. And he's adorable."

Dominic's brows shot up. "Is he?"

"*Adorable.* Like a puppy that hasn't grown into its feet yet." He looked slightly revolted. Unperturbed, she went on, "There's a lot of critical press about this wedding. I know the royals are perpetual cannon fodder for the tabloids, but I always thought Rosie was popular—"

"With younger people, very, according to Pet, the font of royal gossip. Less so with the older guard. Rosie's not quite the standard pearls-and-pillbox-hat royal, is she, and the press loves to punish individuality."

"Pet sounds usefully connected, like Jay."

"Name anyone in London and my sister could probably tell you where they went to school, what they like to eat, and which train they take in the morning."

Sylvie was smiling. "Has she always been so . . . exuberant?"

Apparently, that was the wrong thing to say. The traces of amusement disappeared from his face as if she'd hit a button.

The silence stretched before he said, "I don't know."

Averting her eyes to give him some semblance of privacy, she bent over the cauldron she hadn't touched yet, in which a thin sugar solution simmered. It was a milky white in color, touched with gleaming pastels when it caught the light. She stirred it as delicately as if she were collecting unbroken cobwebs.

"May I ask you something?" Her voice was low, blending in

with the rhythmic *pat-pat* of raindrops falling on leaves, winding from hidden speakers.

"Can I stop you?"

Her hand paused midstir. Their eyes met. "Yes."

That muscle in his jaw jumped. "Go on."

"It's extremely nosy."

The faintest flicker of another smile in that watchful gaze. "I would expect nothing less."

Outwardly, Sylvie redirected her attention to the contents of the cauldron, watching a little bubble rise and pop in a sparkling second. "When Pet came into the studio, she was obviously so proud of you. But she also made a comment about not knowing you very well. Is that just because of the age difference, or—"

"I . . ." Dominic broke in, and then stopped. She shot a quick glance sideways, and saw his hand on the table, fisted so tightly that his knuckles were showing white.

Sylvie dropped the stirring stick and impulsively moved to place her hand tightly over his. "Don't," she said softly. "I'm sorry I asked."

He stared at their stacked hands. "I haven't talked to anyone about this since my grandfather died."

"And you don't have to." Sylvie started to draw her hand back, but his fingers suddenly turned over and caught hers.

It was a light hold; she could have broken it easily if she wanted to. Her skin was tingling again.

"I was born nine months after my mother had an extramarital affair." The words were expressionless. "From an early age, I suspected it was one of many affairs, but at the time, I was the only living, breathing result. And Gerald, my stepfather, hated me. Not resentment, not antipathy—hatred." He looked at her. "I don't know if you've ever looked at someone and seen pure, undiluted hatred seeping out. Gerald's aggression was of the passive variety—occasional digs if he thought they'd strike home. Which they rarely did. He was a blustering, pathetic, relentlessly dim man. For the most part, he just ignored my existence. But when he did look at me, I could see it."

Her mouth was dry. "What about your mother?"

"Lana generally backed up Gerald in whatever arrogant, shortsighted comments he made on any topic. I don't think she actually liked him very much, but she didn't want to deal with problems in the household."

"Problems." The welfare and well-being of her own child.

"I was left in the care of a nanny most of the time." Dominic's tone was typically matter-of-fact. "She wasn't exactly Mary Poppins. Thank God," he added. "I can't imagine anything worse than spontaneous outbursts of daily musical theater."

He *had* noticed her tendency to bust out random lyrics when she was deep in concentration; his look was both sarcastic and amused, and invited a retort.

For once, Sylvie couldn't oblige.

Her life so far had been punctuated by periods of soul-shattering loss, but that grief had come amidst decades of warmth and love. She'd known herself the light and center of someone's existence. No, she'd never experienced hatred.

But as she wrapped her fingers tighter around Dominic's, she could feel the flickering beginnings of it for two strangers who didn't deserve to be called parents, and a woman who ought to have been a child's only hope of comfort.

She was under shrewd observation. "You know some of this already," he said, and it was a statement, not a question.

"Only that you had a nanny. Dolores didn't say much more than that."

His expression didn't change. "She doesn't *know* much more than that. Isobel worked with my mother and used to come around to the house when I was very small. She would always have something for me in her bag. A chocolate bar. A small toy. I've never forgotten the scent of her perfume." A flicker of a smile. "She still uses it now." There was deepening warmth in his voice. "I'm thirty-eight years old and she still occasionally presents me with a bag of sweets."

Sylvie was very conscious of the feel of his hand in hers, the skin so silky-warm along his fingers, so shivery-rough on the tips. "Is Pet your only sibling?"

"I have another sister, Lorraine, who's four years younger than I am. Gerald doted on her, and she's still his carbon copy in every way. But Pet, she was an unexpected, very welcome surprise, born when I was twelve."

"And you loved her."

Another of those semi-smiles. She'd do quite a lot to see a real one. "From just a few months old, she was such a cheeky, happy little kid. Once she started crawling, she followed me everywhere. She almost made living in that house tolerable." He was looking at their linked hands again, turning them slightly, absently measuring his fingers against hers. "Almost. But when I turned thirteen, I couldn't take it anymore. I'd been saving scraps of money doing odd jobs around the neighborhood. I was tall for my age. People usually thought I was older. On my birthday, I managed to get a train ticket, and I left for London. I came here. To Magnolia Lane, to find my grandfather. Who took me in without the slightest hesitation. Like your aunt, I don't think he ever regretted it."

Opening the door of De Vere's that day must have been like walking through the Narnia wardrobe: a whole new world and way of life.

Ultimately, the way home at last.

"And Pet?"

"Initially," Dominic said, "I left a note and took Pet with me. She was still a baby, not even walking yet."

"You . . ." Sylvie pursed her lips with a silent breath. Barely aware of what she was doing, she stroked his fingers.

"I wanted the only member of my family who *felt* like my family to be with me. I thought my grandfather could adopt us both." His thumb ran along her palm before he suddenly released her, sitting back with a grimace of self-derision. "As we weren't living in a Disney film, however, it didn't quite work out that way. Lana and Gerald had Pet back by dinnertime, and Gerald contacted the police to see if he could have me charged for abduction, as a minor—"

"Oh my God." Sitting on the edge of a stool, she stared at him, appalled.

"After Pet was returned home, Sebastian went to see them and spent over an hour talking to Lana. When he came back to the bakery, they'd agreed to abandon any punitive course and sign over full custody of me. I think the former required considerably more finesse and persuasion than the latter," Dominic added wryly.

There was a slight burn behind Sylvie's eyes. She blinked it away almost viciously. He'd think she was offering pity. And of the multitude of emotions she'd felt listening to the bare bones of his early years, pity didn't enter into it. But she was intensely sorry, and helpless, that it was impossible to somehow reach back, to help. "And your grandfather started training you in the family business."

"A gold-plated legacy to live up to."

She was quiet. Then: "Sebastian was a marvel. An absolute icon. But you've made De Vere's your own, you know. You're forging a new legacy here. And I suspect your grandad would be pleased as punch about it." There was a glimpse of something in his eyes, then, that made her stomach explode into flutters. She looked back at him steadily. "You were happy with Sebastian."

This was her main professional rival. The man who'd repeatedly insulted and undermined her work. Whose own aesthetic she belittled in return. The man she had, at one time, profoundly disliked.

And if he still hurt, it mattered.

"Yes, I was." No hesitation now. "He'd been alone since my grandmother died five years before, and my mother rarely contacted him. She'd both inherited and made enough money that she had no use for him or De Vere's. There was very little emotional attachment on her side. On his, she was a constant absence, a forever loss. He wanted me. He was always interested in what I'd done, what I thought, what I wanted to be. And he made it possible."

The Dark Forest encouraged confidences, and not just because buckets of alcohol were consumed amongst these tree branches. Sylvie knew from experience that it was easier to talk down here, to open up in the dim light and dancing shadows, to be truthful; with others, with yourself.

Carefully, she said, "In the archives, you said that you and Sebastian had a rocky beginning—"

When he finally responded, she was very aware of how far he was stepping out on the precipice with her right now.

"When I moved in with Sebastian, he enlisted an excellent

therapist for guidance in how best to . . . redirect the emotional path I was on. And, hell, did he try. He pushed himself out of his comfort zone in every way to counteract as much of my previous life as he could. He was incredibly generous with his time, no matter how busy he was, and provided everything I needed in a material sense. Including a piano and music lessons, because he believed everyone needs at least two creative outlets for their mental well-being. But . . ." Dominic's jaw shifted. The tinge of dull red under his cheekbones could have been a reflection from the pink cauldron, but she didn't think so. She folded her fingers together to avoid slipping a hand back across the counter. In clipped staccato, he confirmed a little of what she'd begun to suspect. "I was a very guarded teenager. I found it almost impossible to initiate any gesture of physical affection. I would want to, sometimes very badly, and I couldn't. I struggled less on the receiving end, but—that, too. Sometimes."

Because before the advent of Sebastian, the only person in Dominic's life who would have offered the comfort of their arms—or wanted his own—was his baby sister.

Jesus. His fucking parents.

He didn't need to voice the obvious inference, but he added, still curtly, "Thanks to Sebastian, I left the worst of it behind a long time ago. But engrained instinct is hard to shake completely." And buried pain periodically raised its head; Sylvie knew that. "Outside of purely casual or sexual touch, and unless there's significant inherent trust, my brain can still throw up a barricade in that respect."

Exhaling, Sylvie gestured at the table surface where their hands had rested, entwined. "A few times recently, I—we . . ." Heat was pressing back into her own cheeks. "Does it make you uncomfortable when I . . ."

Seemed to be increasingly drawn to reach out to him—and with nothing casual about it.

Abruptly, he rescued her from the pit of awkwardness. "No." Then, more slowly, with a frown in his eyes, as if he were acknowledging something to himself tonight, as well, "It doesn't."

They were both silent again until Dominic said tersely, "Pet was upset today. She thinks I want her to leave." One brow lifted. "What did you once call me? A human ice block?" She grimaced, hard. "I looked at her and just for a moment, I was back in that house and I couldn't move. It's been twenty-five fucking years. Her parents are dead, Sebastian's passed on as well, and if I'm an ice block, Lorraine could have single-handedly sunk the *Titanic*. Pet's a family-oriented person with, to all intents and purposes, no family. I'm not what she's obviously looking for and needs."

That comment caused a tiny, deep-buried personal pang, but every instinct in her mind and body was focused outward right then. She leaned forward. "Dominic. At thirteen years old, you loved that girl enough to take her and run. A child and a baby, all the way to London, with only a few pounds in your pocket. Everybody should have someone in their life who cares that much."

It was some time before he spoke again. "I tried to see her a number of times when I was a teenager, but Gerald blocked contact. I finally managed a meeting when she was eighteen, but she wanted nothing to do with me then. He'd probably been feeding her God knows what poison." He shook his head. "She asked me not to contact her, so I respected her wishes, and mentally closed a final door on that side of my family. In retrospect, though, she was profoundly uncomfortable that day. Shutting *anyone* out, it's not in Pet's nature. Even when it should be."

Tiredly, Dominic rubbed his hand over the dark shadow on his jaw. "She started tentatively reaching out a few years ago, just showing up at the bakery for ten minutes at a time, making phone calls on some weak pretense. And then she installed herself as a full-time fixture. At least temporarily."

"Maybe temporarily in your workplace. In your *life*, the plan is obviously to become a permanent fixture." Sylvie hesitated. "And underneath, it sounds like that's what you want, too."

The only sounds were the continuing *pad-pad* of the raindrops and the occasional birdcall.

"Sylvie."

"Yes?"

"I think I might have hurt you when I said Pet needed a family and doesn't have one. I'm sorry."

He caught her so off guard that an unexpected wash of vulnerability made her vision misty.

Feeling like a Beatrix Potter character scuttling back to hide in her burrow, she returned to the cauldron, stirring with extreme concentration. If she didn't have hips, boobs, and a fairly large head, she might have just climbed on in.

He was still watching her levelly, but with something very unsettling in that usually saturnine face.

It shook something loose. "I'm not alone," she said, with just the tiniest hint of a wobble. She stopped to steady her voice. Continued. "I still have family—I have my friends. Particularly Jay. I couldn't love him more. Even Mabel, as horrified as she would be, I think of as a sister. Or a really irascible grandma. Depends on the day. And I have the business."

Dominic was very quiet, all his attention focused on her. Even his body was angled toward her, his muscles tense and tight.

Keeping one hand on the stirring stick, Sylvie pointed. His gaze traveled to a little ceramic pot, in pride of place on the shelves. It was painted with the simple words: YOU MAKE MY

WORLD A BETTER PLACE. "Mallory was a beautiful glass artist, but she dabbled in pottery. She made me that. Not for any special occasion. Just one afternoon, on a Wednesday. She really loved me. I'll live my entire existence knowing someone loved me that much. The way Sebastian loved you. Death is not the end of love. In any and all of its forms." She stared blindly into the sparkling pot. "I'm not alone," she repeated. The sugar solution moved in waves and curls, an iridescent sunset shimmer. "But every so often, just for a second or two, I'll be in my flat or standing on a busy street surrounded by strangers, and I *feel* so alone my heart hurts."

She reached for the smallest size of blowpipe and dipped it in the mixture. "I still have Mallory's phone. I keep it charged so I can look at her photos. Sometimes, if there's something I really want her to know and I can't get to the cemetery, I send her a text message. And once I texted myself from her phone. Just to see a new message from her on my birthday." Her mouth twisted. "How pathetic is that?"

"It's not pathetic at all." Straightforward, implacable.

She stood still and silent, then placed the blowpipe to her lips and drew up a little of the mixture, carefully exhaled. An iridescent sphere slipped effortlessly from the pipe and floated toward Dominic, caught by the faux breeze that rustled the Dark Forest leaves.

His eyes never left hers as he raised a hand and let the bubble come to rest on his palm. This was a finer solution than the Sorceress bubbles, would never stand up to a filling, but it was much hardier than a soap bubble.

He ran his thumb over it, so carefully. "Pretty."

"Small pockets of beauty, everywhere you look. I hope it's much more beautiful wherever Mallory is now, but this world has a lot to offer." Sylvie wasn't aware of moving, but suddenly she was standing in front of him, touching a fingertip to the bubble.

She had the fleeting thought that they probably looked like a pair of fortune-tellers, hovering over a crystal ball. Looking for portents of the future.

Dominic lightly tossed the bubble back into the air, and they watched it turn and bob in a peaceful current.

Her pulse was a rapid flutter in her throat, a darker thrum low in her abdomen. Nerves, and—not really arousal, her emotions were still too torn on the surface, but that disquieting *wanting* that kept creeping up on her.

The rise and fall of his chest had quickened. On the table, their fingertips brushed, and they both looked down, Sylvie's breath catching as his index finger ran, so lightly, along hers.

Slowly, she lifted her gaze back to his. He was close enough that she could see the finest of the lines around his eyes, whispering away from short, incredibly thick lashes. Those eyes were locked on hers, intent, shadowed, growing darker as she watched.

Without breaking that contact, they both moved, crossing a distance both tiny and significant. Their lips touched. Soft. Gentle. Coming apart just long enough that she drew in a shaky breath and felt his fingers tighten on hers, before their mouths were sliding back together, as surprisingly easily as interlocking a puzzle piece.

It was still featherlight and almost dreamy, as if she'd sent her mind floating in a flagon of Midnight Elixir again. His skin was silky, his lips parting a little, just starting to coax hers open. Shivers slipped down her spine, and she moved a little restlessly on the stool, pushing the pads of her fingers against the wooden tabletop, pressing her thighs together.

A tiny sound rose from her throat as the kiss very briefly deepened, and she lifted her hand. Hesitated.

Dominic raised his head, his breathing as unsteady as hers. They stared at each other. Before Sylvie could pull back, his warm hand closed around hers and he drew her palm to his cheek. Swallowing, she cupped the strong bone there, feeling the rough abrasion of his stubble beneath her skin.

Her gaze dropped to his lips. They were still slightly parted. She ran her thumb across the full lower curve and felt his quick inhalation.

Even when his phone rang, vibrating on the countertop, it barely intruded into her warm haze.

Dominic had gone very still. For just a second, his forehead leaned against hers and their noses nudged, the tiniest nuzzle.

Then he was reaching for his phone and a tinny voice on the other end wound out to her ears. One of his suppliers had canceled a weekend shipment at the last minute.

He hesitated, looking at her. His expression was guarded, but there was still a trace of heat there.

Also, a fair whack of *how the hell did this happen*, which— ditto.

Her fingers were still trembling.

That first soft touch of Dominic's mouth—why did it feel like turning the corner in the labyrinth and finally, finally seeing a glimmer of the right path?

She managed a half smile. "Business happens. Go deal." They couldn't seem to tear their eyes from each other. Quietly, not quite certainly, and not even sure which of them she was talking to, she said, "This is okay."

Another flicker in his expression.

Something twinkled in her peripheral vision, and she realized with some surprise that the bubble was still drifting in the lights.

It felt as if an hour had passed since she'd sent it toward him, not merely minutes.

Dominic's mouth was set tautly.

Small pockets of beauty.

Without a sound, in a tiny sparkle of glitter, the bubble burst.

Sylvie hoped that wasn't an omen.

Chapter Ten

Middlethorpe Grange, Surrey

Haunted by rumors of discontented spirits for over seven hundred years. Throughout the centuries, locals spoke of lights in the wood, voices in the dark, words on the walls. Legend foretold of a dark, chilling force that would someday strike wide the door as the people cowered in fear—

> "I mean, to be fair, Dominic did knock first."
> —Sylvie Fairchild

> "Not amused."
> —Dominic De Vere

During Sylvie's first stint on *Operation Cake*, the stately home episode had been shot at the property that was also used as a stand-in for Rosings Park in the latest adaptation of *Pride & Prejudice*. Extremely grand, well heated, and the dining room had a chocolate buffet. She'd been so busy she hadn't even searched Middlethorpe Grange online, but her expectation had been something similarly Austenian.

In reality, the Grange was a Gothic monstrosity more suited to Bram Stoker. And under a glum gray sky, the surrounding fields scattered with a light dusting of early snow, it was an inconveniently long commute to work on a Monday and a reminder that her own poky little flat was at least *warm*.

She had a private driver, but the car ran into three backups in traffic, and it was already midmorning by the time she sat down in a makeup chair. The hair and makeup team had set up in a hideous stone-walled parlor, in which some Middlethorpe of old had indulged his melancholic streak by hanging massive, scowling gargoyles from the ceiling. She assumed there was a suitably bloodthirsty curse attached to their removal or disturbance; otherwise, there was no excuse for not ripping them down and trying a nice plant.

Zack picked up a concealer bottle and looked between her sleep-deprived face and the leering monstrosity beside her. His fingers fluttered in feigned confusion. "I'm sorry, *which* is the patient?"

"Ha-ha," Sylvie said, but a small grin broke through. He wasn't wrong—at this rate, the bags under her eyes would be drooping to her clavicle by the final.

She'd spent much of the weekend with Sugar Fair's most difficult customer, a wealthy Mayfair businesswoman with five daughters. Each daughter celebrated her birthday with a party so extravagant that there had actually been cause, at the fourteen-year-old's gala festivities on Sunday, for somebody to whisper, "What carat do you think those diamonds are?"

In reference to the birthday girl's *straw*. Her diamond-encrusted straw, which probably cost more than Sylvie's annual rent.

The mother was an absolute nightmare, and every time Sylvie had to deal with her, she seriously debated the benefits of a reclusive lifestyle in which human contact was limited to pizza delivery and fictional characters.

And when she hadn't been changing a million details at the last minute, and usually changing them all back again when Madame reverted her whims, she'd been thinking about Friday night in the Dark Forest.

She could still feel the pressure of Dominic's lips, the strength of his fingers, the hard warmth of his chest beneath her palm.

"The smudge-proof claims of that lipstick have been highly exaggerated. If you don't stop touching your mouth," Zack said, swatting her hand away before he continued circling a blush brush over her cheekbones, "I'm feeding you to Quasimodo's chums here. What's with you today? Visions of wedding cakes dancing in your head?"

His wiggling eyebrows invited expansion on that topic. Sugar Fair had been officially mentioned as a possible contender for the Albany contract in yesterday's tabloids. De Vere's was still leading the odds at the bookies' by a massive margin, but nobody could say the gutter press wasn't thorough when it came to wild speculation. Several reporters had come sniffing around the shop floor over the weekend. They'd all zeroed in on Mabel, sitting quietly at her table carving sweet little candy kittens. Young, female, probably naïve and easily flattered—a prime target to bully into a stammering disclosure.

Sylvie had almost felt sorry for them.

Silencing the first queries with a delicately raised finger, Mabel had paused for three majestic seconds before slamming the blade of her sharpest knife into the cutting board and resting her chin on the handle. Her gentle smile had lowered the temperature of the room about thirty degrees.

She'd torn them to shreds and strewn the remnants of their egos like confetti.

"We spent a fucking fortune decorating this place," Jay had commented with reluctant admiration. "Ruins the vibe when you have grown men almost pissing on the floor."

Restlessly playing with the tube of lipstick on the table, Sylvie glanced up at Zack. For all his garrulous delight in gossip, she would actually trust him to be circumspect. After that burst of glee when they'd first discussed the possibility, he hadn't breathed a word of her intentions on set. However, her lips were now contractually zipped.

The pressure was starting to mount on the contract. The clock was ticking on their deadline. For all intents and purposes, she'd *invented* Midnight Elixir, and she still couldn't produce an edible facsimile in cake form. And despite returning again and again to the photograph of Patrick and Jessica, with an odd, tugging fascination, she was no further forward on the design elements.

There was every reason for Rosie's wedding cake to keep her up at night.

It would be a far more comfortable explanation for her exhausted jumpiness now.

She forced herself still. He had a job to do, and she was being a pest. "Sorry. I didn't sleep well."

For the first time in a very long time, she'd lain in bed last night and experienced the physical ache of missing a particular person's body, their touch, their scent. More personal than simply thwarted arousal, it was a feeling she'd *never* had for somebody she barely knew in a physical sense. It was something she associated more with a separation in a long-term relationship, when her body was used to sleeping entwined with another.

Not with a man she'd previously have fancied chucking under a nonmetaphorical bus.

And that light, whispering kiss was the least of the intimacy that had started to weave between them.

Yesterday at the party, when she'd been unusually tired and frustrated, there'd come one moment when her patience had been stretched to the finest of threads—and her sudden instinct had been to call Dominic.

As if in response to that thought, her phone buzzed on her lap, and she glanced down at the screen. Her heart jumped at his name on the display. He'd hit the traffic jams as well, but his car was well and truly stuck, and he was running late. She sent a quick reply, confirming she'd arrived safely.

They were just simple, no-frills messages—thankfully he hadn't broken out the emojis. If he ever smiley-faced her, she'd have to assume it was some sort of SOS and report his kidnapping.

But still . . . He'd texted to let her know.

If she were not a grown woman with increasingly crackly joints and white hairs in her eyebrows, these rapid developments might have distracted her from the job she was being paid to do today.

Fortunately, she'd racked up a lot of life experience that included multiple short-lived infatuations, two serious relationships, and a failed one-night stand with a man who'd recognized her from TV and thought she'd find it hilarious if he smeared himself with icing and dipped his dick in sprinkles.

She'd survived an encounter with Cupcake Cock. She was not going to be earth-shatteringly flustered by one tiny kiss.

One tiny, really great kiss.

Oh, look. Residual sex tingles. From a memory.

This wasn't potentially life-upturning at all.

Zack was looking for somewhere to put his muslin cloth. He hung it from the clawed hand of the nearest gargoyle, like a Gothic towel rail. *Addams Family* chic. "This is all so weird," he pronounced with great satisfaction.

Yes. Yes, it was.

With her eyebags sufficiently camouflaged, she followed a grip to the ballroom where the team was prepping for the day's competition. Leaning against a pillar out of everyone's way, she watched the contestants setting up their stations. The usual format was temporarily dropped for the location shoot. Instead of multiple rounds, the contestants would have five hours to produce four types of sweets—petit fours, sugar cookies, tartlets, whatever they chose. The selection had to include an occasion cake; it must adhere to the chosen theme, which this year was current West End musicals, and it must involve elements of sugar craft. Four years ago, this was the episode in which she'd topped the leaderboard, and she was hoping she'd see some spectacular art today.

Emma was helping Adam unpack a variety of molds and stencils at his station. Their heads were close together and they were laughing. Transparently, endearingly smitten. Smiling, Sylvie's gaze passed on, coming to a stop on Libby.

At her counter, the redhead was efficiently sorting her ingredients for each component of her menu, checking them off against a handwritten list. She frowned suddenly, her finger pausing on the page. After a moment, she walked over to a neighboring station and spoke briefly to its habitant, Sid Khan, the jovial alien abductee. Libby beamed at the elderly man when he obligingly handed her a small box. Returning to her station with it, she caught wind of Sylvie's scrutiny, and her eyes widened.

Innocence personified.

Aadhya came striding over, Mariana trailing languidly behind with a coffee cup perched on one elegant palm. The producer opened her mouth to speak, then followed the direction of Sylvie's pensive stare. "Don't tell me you've got a down on the poor girl, too."

Sylvie chose to focus on the last part of the accusation. "Too?"

Aadhya's eye roll was masterfully expressive. "Dominic. At our last meeting, he was typically obstructive. Just lounged there like a bloody Roman emperor, ready to turn his thumb down and condemn every idea I put forward," she said with obvious lingering irritation.

Sylvie had to suppress faint amusement. She wasn't surprised Dominic hadn't jumped for joy at whatever brain wave Aadhya had sprung on him. Just last Friday, she'd tried to push through the idea of thematic costumes for today's shoot. Emma had been assigned *Grease* as her musical, so wardrobe could supply her with a Pink Ladies bomber jacket. And Adam Foley had *Beauty and the Beast*; wouldn't he be a *scream* as Cogsworth? The health and safety officer had put her foot down then, painting a dire picture of what was likely to occur if Adam was forced to maneuver pots of boiling sugar around a minuscule work space while kitted out as an anthropomorphic clock.

As much as Sylvie liked and respected Aadhya, it was an illuminating experience being on this side of the kitchen counter.

"Having contributed absolutely nothing of use," Aadhya went on, "he mildly suggested that I ought to keep an eye on Libby, because there ought to be a line between 'manufactured soap opera bullshit' and cheating." She fixed Sylvie with a piercing look. "Do you suspect nefarious activity as well?" Her tone was not encouraging.

"I suspect she's a bully at best," Sylvie returned matter-of-factly. "Nobody's reacted quite as"—*epically*—"forcefully as Nadine, but I've seen some of the contestants giving her a wide berth." Her gaze traveled back toward the contestant pool, but the lighting team had clustered in front of Libby's station, unrolling a long spool of cable and blocking her view. "And admittedly, some people in this room are quite capable of setting their own ovens too high or leaving the freezer door ajar, but there do seem to have been an unusual number of incidents. She clearly misled Byron during the ingenuity challenge, even if he shouldn't have been asking for help." She drew her lower lip between her teeth in a brief tug. "It was the look in her eyes when that button wound up in his scone."

"It's a competition," Aadhya pointed out. "It's natural to be privately relieved if a competitor does poorly."

"It wasn't relief in her face," Mariana said unexpectedly, watching her tea swirl as she moved the cup. "It was satisfaction. Of the *clever wee me* variety."

"I haven't received a single complaint from any contestant about Libby." Aadhya looked faintly harassed. Sylvie wasn't surprised about the radio silence behind the scenes. She recalled very well that with the grand final prize money at stake, nobody had wanted to rock any boats and prejudice their chances of winning. "Do you have any evidence the girl is waging some invisible scheme of sabotage and harassment?"

"Not a scrap," Sylvie said, and the producer's response was crisp.

"Then I hope you'll retain an impartial view of her performance today and going forward. Excuse me; I need to deal with this latest disaster."

As Aadhya departed, Mariana supplied the necessary footnote. "There's a problem with the electricity source in this wing. A real ace card, this place. Freezing cold, poorly lit, *and* ugly as sin." She sipped her tea. "I wouldn't dwell on Libby's behavior. Unfortunately, there's always going to be a rotten apple in the barrel. Have you seen the art gallery yet?"

It took a moment to register the sudden change in topic. "No. What—?"

"The Middlethorpe family have an extensive art collection in the third-floor gallery, and apparently the lady of the house has an especial interest in glass works. I know you also like pretty glass, although unless you can pour a bottle of wine into it, I don't quite understand the appeal," Mariana teased, before her face settled into softer lines. "Your aunt, *nena*—Mallory?" Her voice lifted into a tentative question. "You told me she was an artist, yes?" When Sylvie nodded silently, the older woman patted her arm. "Go have a look."

It was very tempting, but—they *were* supposed to be working here.

Mariana correctly interpreted her second lip bite. "With the lighting gone kaput and Dominic stuck on the M4, we're delayed at least half an hour. You might as well seize the opportunity for a quick peek."

Libby chose that moment to cruise past Adam's station and say something to him that made his sweet, thin face fall, his eyes darting toward Emma, back at her own counter. He looked down at himself and touched his crumpled tie. His shoulders folded inward. Even at that distance, crystal clear stance of someone who had just taken a hit to their self-esteem.

Sylvie decided to take up Mariana's suggestion. Lest she pick up a dessert from the snack table and follow Nadine's example with the tart.

If nothing else, this job and working side by side with Dominic was doing wonders for her usual aversion to confrontation.

Halfway up the grand stone staircase, her phone vibrated in her bag and she pulled it out with embarrassing haste.

Unknown number, which she almost ignored as a possible scammer.

However, as the lord of the manor was coming down the stairs and casting her a lascivious glance, it was advisable to close off every opportunity for conversation. After their brief introduction upon her arrival, even speaking to a faux bank or purveyor of penile enlargements seemed favorable.

"Sylvie Fairchild speaking," she said into the receiver as Lord Middlethorpe continued on his way with a regretful backward glance. The man reeked of the old boys' club. She bet he regularly sat over a whisky with his cronies and reflected on the good old days, when he could behave as atrociously as he liked with impunity. "To save time, I'm not giving you any financial details, I possess no appendages that need enlarging, and if you're claiming to be a member of a royal family, I'm going to need multiple sources of evidence."

There was barely a pause before the very cut-glass voice of Rosie's secretary said, "I make no claim to royal birth, merely employment, madam. This is the Honorable Edward Lancier."

Of course he used his full title even on the phone. She bet he entered it in the address field when he was doing his online shopping, hitting up Marks & Spencer for his Honorable hankies and jammies.

Sylvie exchanged a companionable grimace with one of the

gargoyles on the landing wall. "Sorry," she said, clearing her throat. "Yes, Mr. Lancier."

"With respect to the previously discussed commission, one requests a short meeting at your earliest convenience. Would tomorrow afternoon be suitable?"

She agreed without hesitation to a meeting with *one*, drawing out her notebook to jot down the directive. Not a meeting at St. Giles Palace this time, but an office on a street she'd never heard of. Apparently, every step of this commission was going to be laced with intrigue.

Still a lingering chance of that recruitment into a band of misfit do-gooders.

When she reached the third floor, it was eerily quiet after the pandemonium downstairs. The walls in the Grange must be a good twelve inches thick, and where it fell down in central heating, it provided in spades for soundproofing.

If that particularly malevolent-looking gargoyle *were* actually moving and had grand plans to reach out and strangle her as she went past, her demise would likely pass unnoticed until they needed her for the opening shots.

Dominic was possibly correct that her attraction to all things fantastical had grown to epic proportions since she'd taken this job.

Nevertheless, she was fascinated when she found the gallery and discovered an art collection with all the eclectic disorganization of a junkyard, nestled in a dramatically spooky setting—and contents that wouldn't be out of place in a national museum.

The silence was even more cavernous here, and she jumped at the distant squeak of a footstep.

She had the passing neck prickle that usually heralded watching eyes, but her attention had caught on a large oil canvas. They hadn't *seriously* just tossed a Caroline Beckwith onto the wall, with no obvious security? If she wanted to whip out her keys right this second and scrape that £50,000 painting into shreds, there was literally nothing to stop her. And given the abrasive personality of its owner, she wouldn't be surprised if half the neighborhood would quite happily wreck the family valuables.

Living truism that you couldn't buy common sense.

Several glass works were arranged on podiums. She was immediately drawn to a beautiful little sculpture of clear glass shot through with shimmering silver, as if it had caught a forever sheen of moonlight. Lovers, their heads lowered together in a perfect curve, limbs entwined in a sinuous twist, two bodies forming one continuous shape. One figure was cradling the head of the other, hand cupped in a protective shield. She'd been raised by a curator; she knew better than to touch an exhibit without permission, but her fingers almost went out and traced the gentle lines of that revealing gesture.

She pulled out her phone and bent to snap a few close-up photos.

A strange skittering sound brought her head around sharply. There was nobody behind her, but one of the long wooden panels in the wall appeared to open a few centimeters. It closed again just as quietly. The dizzying effect of the black-and-white floor tiles was messing with her eyes, not helped by the leering gargoyles sprouting from every corner, but she was quite certain that *was* a door.

Cautiously, Sylvie rose and approached the panel. When she tugged on a protruding beam, it slid back easily, revealing a narrow corridor. Her vision slipped into darkness beyond a short distance, and she couldn't see where it ultimately led.

This was now entirely too *Famous Five* for first thing on a

Monday. She ought to have sandwiches and lemonade in a rucksack, an intelligent dog at her leg, and a gang of smugglers to foil.

As it was, she had a roll of breath mints in her handbag, Middlethorpe Grange was miles from the coast, and if any lost smugglers had walked these fields, they would now be very old bones.

From somewhere in the creepy abyss, a board creaked, and a murmuring susurration drifted on a gust of cold air. At least she knew there was a window somewhere.

"Hello?" she called, purposefully raising her voice and injecting a note of cheerful normality.

Another creak, another singsong murmur.

Okay.

Rapidly becoming less *Famous Five*, more *The Haunting of Bly Manor.*

"For God's sake," she muttered, flicking on the flashlight app on her phone. She took several steps forward and flooded the cramped interior with light.

Her eyes adjusting rapidly, she looked around a musty hallway that led to a door, about fifteen feet away, and to her side, a few rickety-looking shelves containing the odd unloved book and a bowl of the most disgusting, desiccated potpourri.

Potpourri that appeared to be . . . undulating.

With the feeling she was seriously going to regret this, Sylvie reached out and poked the bowl. Just as a hairy twig-like leg nudged aside a shriveled petal and delicately waved at her, she caught sight of the pale blur of a face in the darkness.

By time her brain had caught up to the facts of *mirror* and *own reflection*, her poor heart was doing its best to wrench out of her chest.

For all Sylvie's love of everything whimsical and extraordinary, she actually considered herself quite a straightforward person, not prone to panic. She could have handled the horror of whatever was living in the potpourri. The fright over her reflection was a passing blip.

But what was written *on* that mirror, smudged very, very clearly into the dust, wrenched a sound from her that she'd never made in her life.

Her left foot skidded on the floor and she almost fell. Something moved behind her, and on instinct, she fought back with the ultimate weapon: a direct shot of infested potpourri to the face.

The unknown presence in the dark screamed loud enough to wake every gargoyle on-site.

As he or she thrashed about and a piece of potpourri rebounded into Sylvie's chin, she turned back down the passage, almost hurling herself into the comparative brightness of the gallery.

Her breath was coming in small, squeaky hitches, and her legs were shaking.

All she saw then was Dominic, standing alone in front of an ugly metal sculpture of a tractor, a heavy scowl on his face—and she acted on sheer, driving instinct.

"What the fuck is going on up here—?" He didn't have a chance to finish the incredulous snap of words before she was at his side, only just catching herself seconds before she could follow through on the immediate plan announced by her brain.

Basically, to throw herself into his arms, burrow into his body, and stay there for a while. Five minutes. An hour. A decade.

Her chest was rising and falling rapidly. One of her hands still hovered in the air millimeters from his chest.

She had hesitated; he did not.

As he'd done once before, Dominic took her hand in his, this time drawing it around his neck and pulling her into him. Her hot cheek coming to press against the cool silkiness of his shirt, Sylvie exhaled through her mouth and felt the first tension wash out of her muscles, as if her body were melting into his.

His fingers stroked her hair, gentle, unbelievably soothing, and then his hand moved to cup her cheek, holding her head as she nestled into the curve of his neck. She could feel the steady movement of his pulse beneath her fingertips.

"Sylvie," he said in a low voice. His arms tightened on her as she struggled to stop the residual trembling right down through her wrists and ankles. "What the hell happened?"

Her eyes were squeezed closed. All she was aware of in that moment, as she forced her breathing out of that asthmatic wheeze and into long, juddering inhalations, was his scent and his warmth wrapping around her. "*Dom.*"

It was nothing more than a whisper, but he heard her. His hold, already tight, drew her in even closer to the long planes of his body. She felt the abrasion of his jaw against her temple, and the weight as he rested his cheek on her head.

The fingers entwined in her hair played gently with the fine strands.

"I know all this place is missing is a young David Bowie before it goes full *Labyrinth*," Dominic said against her temple, the words light, the underlying tone anything but, "but I don't think there's much danger beyond appallingly bad taste."

His thumb ran lightly down her nose, before his fingertips touched under her eyes. Sylvie hadn't realized that she was crying a bit until he made another low sound, and was so horrified that she immediately stopped.

He was just pulling her back to look into her face when the panel door banged back open behind them, and she almost jumped out of her skin yet again.

With complete and total outrage, a high-pitched voice roared, "You *threw a spider in my face*."

She twisted, Dominic's hand falling to hold the curve of her waist, and saw a small, furious-faced boy with violently red curls, extremely round freckled cheeks, and waving fists. He shook one at her, like a crabby policeman in an old-fashioned children's book. She half expected his next words to be *Look 'ere!*

"It ran down my neck," screamed the very loud child. "It had *legs!*"

Dominic was running his fingers up and down Sylvie's back. She thought he probably wasn't even aware he was doing it. Normally, that would provoke a renewed rush of sensation, but the initial shock of that experience with the mirror was creeping back.

"Friend of yours?" he inquired mildly, eyeing the child with a distinct lack of enthusiasm.

Even in the light of day, holding on to Dominic's body, her heart was starting to beat too fast again, throwing another little catch into her breath.

His hand came up to cup her cheek again, but that typically shrewd gaze swung back to the child.

The little boy clearly had some brain cells to go with the lung power, because he'd stopped hollering at her and was giving Dominic a slightly wary look.

One small foot edged back.

"Don't move." It was Dominic's most grim sergeant-major tone, usually reserved for the absolute worst offenders on *Operation Cake*, and the kid's hair almost stood on end.

Amazingly, for a child who looked as if he'd never heard the word "no" in his life, he did *not* move. Even when Dominic squeezed Sylvie's hand and crossed the distance to the panel door in long strides, both she and her erstwhile spook-in-the-dark stood in silence.

Dominic activated his own phone light and disappeared into the corridor. He was back in less than ten seconds, and when he closed the door behind him with a slow, deliberate *click*, Sylvie wasn't surprised the little boy quailed.

In all these years of icy words and withering looks, she'd never seen Dominic so angry. There was nothing cold and restrained about the expression on his face now; it was intense, burning fury.

The kid reanimated with a vengeance. Scooting behind a metal statue of a soldier, much taller than his own four-foot-nothing, he peeked out at the Angel of Death descending upon him. "You can't do nothing to me," he said, chin jutting. "My daddy owns this place and he can have you killed."

"Your *daddy* and I," Dominic said, his eyes lethal, "are shortly going to have a chat. You cruel little brat."

The freckled chin lifted higher. "I'm a *Middlethorpe*," he retorted, as if that should say it all.

Actually, having met his daddy, it probably *did* say it all.

Middlethorpe Junior shot her a quick look. "It was a joke." A sullen note was creeping in.

"It was a disgusting thing to do. And I'm betting it's not the first time you've tried out your 'joke' on unsuspecting visitors." Dominic's hard stare hadn't wavered, but he looked at Sylvie now, and she swallowed hard at the immediate change in the depths of his eyes. Very gently, incredibly gently, he said, "Did you mention your aunt's name at some point this morning?"

A fine tremor had come back into her hands. Tucking her fingers under her armpits, she took a steadying breath, trying to clear the last of the fog that had netted her thoughts since her light had landed on that mirror.

And she'd seen Mallory's name smudged in the dust and grime.

She closed her eyes for a second. "Mariana did," she said, and her voice cracked. "Just for a second."

A muscle ticked in Dominic's jaw as he turned to the belligerent, wary boy. "It's not a joke. It wasn't funny. Don't you *ever* do something like that again."

The child stuck out his lower lip, darted out from behind the statue, and took off. Sylvie heard the echo of his footsteps on the stairs a moment later.

Her arms were still crossed tightly. "A kid's prank. I completely freaked out. That's really embarrassing. I'm sorry."

Dominic stood still; then, as if in the passing of mere seconds, he'd come to a decision, he crossed to where she stood. Their eyes locked as their chests moved with ragged snatches of breath. His hand lifted to touch her cheek, the lightest, softest heart clutch of a caress. Trembling again, she reached to fold her fingers back over his, and he exhaled.

And then his hands were slipping under her hair, lifting her lips to his own, and Sylvie's whole world shrank to that warm bubble where nothing existed but them.

In a sound almost like a tiny sob, her breath hitched again as he kissed her—nothing tentative or exploratory this time; it was hard, hot, deep, his tongue a silken stroke around hers. Her hands fisted against his ribs, her fingers curling into the fabric of his shirt.

It was an intense kiss, but not a long one. Neither his hands nor his lips had traveled lower than her collarbone. Yet, when he lifted his head, her mind was swimming and her stomach was clenched. Her heart had jumped into thumping beats, pounding so hard it was almost painful.

Powerful chemistry was quite a ride.

With his thumbs under her chin, voice husky, he repeated, "It was a repellent thing to do. The kid's a nasty little shit."

She reached up and held on to his wrists. "I just—I was already thrown, and . . . in the dark, when I saw Mallory's name—"

"I know." His gaze very steady, he traced his thumbs in circles over her cheeks.

Sylvie could feel heat creeping into the skin under his touch. Suddenly, ridiculously, shy, she lowered her eyes to the base of his throat, where his pulse beat quickly.

A thread of renewed tension etched into the air between them, and Dominic released her, his hold dropping away.

"You made it out of traffic," she said at last, foolishly, to his top shirt button.

"Eventually. They're almost ready for us downstairs." That same sense of constraint had come into his body.

"Oh, good."

"Your favorite contestants were holding hands when I left the ballroom." A flicker of amusement broke through the complicated, conflicted expression in Dominic's eyes. "I think you just bounced up and down without moving a single muscle."

She couldn't help the return smile. "I have a text bet with Pet. She says they'll be living together by Easter. I'm slightly less optimistic. My money's on June."

Dominic shook his head, but the amusement was still there. "My sister's texting the enemy now, too, is she?"

Her smile faded as she asked, quite seriously, "Do you mind?"

He was, as usual, difficult to fully read. But there was nothing uncertain in his response. "No. I don't mind."

They were still standing very close. Suddenly, impulsively, she reached up and kissed him again. Just a soft, dancing press of her closed mouth against his.

"I suppose we should go down, then," she murmured, and he moved his head, a slight gesture of assent.

As they walked back through the artworks, she stopped, her attention fixed on a wooden cabinet. Behind the display panel was a selection of smaller pieces of blown glass.

One in particular—an exquisitely rendered little sculpture of a deer.

And in the space of a blink, a heartbeat, the indrawing of her breath, it was fifteen years ago. In a room that was a sterile blur in her memory, but for the oddly specific details of a crack on the wall that looked like a butterfly and the blue-and-white star-print curtains. Someone had hand-sewn those. A valiant effort to introduce some cheer into four walls where hearts were inevitably going to break, over and over and over again.

A machine beeping, so familiar that her blood seemed to be pulsing in rhythm with the sound. And on the bedside table, amidst a jug of water and an array of medication bottles, a few scattered items. Beloved objects, a small piece of the home that would never echo with her aunt's laughter again. A doll, the last remnant of Mallory's childhood, a present from a doting older brother. The doll's rosy cheeks had a dull sheen, worn away by years of kisses, but her hair and clothes were still immaculate. Mallory had kept his gift safe.

As she had later kept his child safe, and so very loved, for nineteen years.

There were well-worn copies of her favorite books. The necklace she'd never taken off until drugs had left her skin so sensitized that the friction of the chain was unbearable. And a tiny glass sculpture of a deer. During a trip to Paris for Sylvie's sixteenth birthday, they'd visited the studio of the renowned animal sculptor Arielle Aubert, and Mallory had fallen in love with that one little deer. It was utterly beyond her reach financially, but Arielle herself had seen the look on the face of her visitor. As they'd prepared to leave, the artist had appeared from the private room out back. Vivid features, shining white hair, sparkling light-gray eyes; Sylvie would always remember her as looking like the spirit of a midnight star. She'd silently taken the little deer from his companions and placed him into Mallory's hands.

Arielle Aubert had been killed a month later in a random act of violence on the streets of Montmartre.

Sylvie remembered curving over with her cheek resting against her aunt's bed on that last night, her eyes parched and tight with exhaustion, staring at the little deer. *La Belle Étoile*, Mallory had called it. *The Beautiful Star.* In that dim, airless room, with the weight of the coming hours pressing down upon her and dread a sick clawing at her gut, the deer had seemed to be standing guard over them as they lay in the dying light.

Mallory had been largely drifting by then, heavily medicated, already a step departed from Sylvie's world. With their fingers entwined against Mallory's chest, Sylvie had watched as the taut, grayish skin over her aunt's high cheekbones seemed to pull tauter as the sun slipped away. So quiet and still, as the disease raging through her blood and bones made its last advance, and her tired body rallied for the final, futile stand. She had been unwavering since the diagnosis, relentlessly strong, ever cheerful, keeping her sense of humor until the end.

But in those last hours, her hand had suddenly tightened on Sylvie's, with a strength Sylvie hadn't known she still possessed.

"I don't want to go," her aunt had said fiercely, her feverish eyes fixed over Sylvie's shoulder. "I promised him. I promised him. I promised him." The words low and urgent, a refrain of anguish. "She'll be alone. *I don't want to leave her alone.*"

Sylvie had cried, then, for the first time in Mallory's presence, her face pressed against their joined hands, contorting as she tried to hold back the tears that wet both their skin. She was glad her aunt was too delirious to know.

And as the sky turned black and it got really bad, Mallory's pain increasing, her breath taking on a labored rattle, a nurse standing in constant vigil, Sylvie had pressed that little glass deer into her aunt's hand, wrapping her fingers around it.

She had lain beside her on the narrow, hard bed, cuddling her one last time, her forehead touching Mallory's temple. "It's okay." A whisper in her ear, for her alone, for them alone. The hardest thing she'd ever done, to steady her voice and dry her eyes and put every bit of love in her heart into those last words. "You've given me everything you had and everything I need. It's okay." Her eyes had squeezed closed. "It's okay to go now."

In a place neither of them wanted to be, but under the starry sky they both loved, Mallory had slipped away.

And the deer had fallen from her fingers and shattered against the black linoleum floor, a thousand fragments of crystal sparkling in the light.

Cool, firm lips were pressed against her temple. Closing her eyes for a moment now, as she had then, Sylvie breathed deeply before she turned her head and looked up at Dominic. He was holding her, his arms wrapped around her without hesitation, his body sharing its warmth.

For once, the expression in his dark eyes was transmitting clear as day. Deep concern, but primarily empathy. The bone-deep understanding of someone who had walked a similar path.

"Which piece?" he asked, inclining his head toward the glass cabinet without taking the comfort of that steady connection away from her. "Which one took you back there?"

"The deer." As she slipped her hand into his, she looked at it again. It was unmistakeably an Arielle Aubert, so similar to Mallory's that it might well have been on the same shelf that day in Paris, a sister work. "It's the deer."

She felt a slight tug on her hand, as if he were unconsciously trying to pull her away from the source of obvious pain, and she shook her hand.

"It reminds me of the worst night of my life." Like that long-ago companion in the dark, this deer had incredible eyes, so expressive in such simple lines. She could feel the tight traces of tears on her cheeks, but her body felt calm now. Peaceful. Comforted. "But also—*more* so—some of the best times. And it's beautiful."

When she looked up again, Dominic said nothing, but very lightly, once more, he touched the back of his free hand to her cheek.

And once more, she repeated the words in her mind and in her heart. "It's okay."

They'd progressed from soggy bottoms and burnt crusts in previous seasons to outright assassination attempts.

Death by incineration.

Dominic knocked back another half glass of milk and exhaled through his mouth, trying to suppress the residual flames burning through every taste bud. Mariana was still bent over Sid Khan's countertop, her face cradled in her hands, muttering to herself. Once she'd regained the ability to speak after her mouthful of Sid's *Hello, Dolly!* cake, he'd heard a rasping repetition of "*Mierda.*" Followed by an equally blunt "Fuckin' A." The moment the first burn of chili had hit his tongue, he'd knocked

Sylvie's piece out of her hand before she could bite into it; unfortunately, he'd been a second too late in preventing Mariana from putting her entire slice into her mouth. He was surprised she was still conscious.

The cake—seven layers of chocolate with a "hint" of chili, according to Sid's initial intro—lay abandoned on the countertop. The elderly widower's structural design—Horace Vandergelder's top hat—wouldn't have scored highly for either ingenuity or difficulty, even if the man hadn't packed in enough heat to sear the hide off a rhino. However, any official critique on this one seemed a bit redundant.

The poor bloke was just about in tears, turning his own hat over in his hands as he apologized profusely for the thirtieth time. Sylvie had her arm around him, trying to gently tease him out of his misery, while Aadhya and the medics bent over Mariana.

Draining the last of the milk, Dominic shook his head at the medic who tried to approach him with a blood pressure monitor. "I'm probably about thirty percent grayer than I was five minutes ago," he said wryly, touching his temple. "But it was only one bite. I'm fine."

"Are you?" Sylvie had left Sid to the sympathy and support of his fellow contestants. She searched his face. Her hand moved to touch his chest; he doubted she was even aware.

Certainly, she'd appeared to be entirely driven by instinct when he'd been bent forward, coughing his guts up after his bite of the aptly named Lucifer's Sponge. Sylvie had been at his side, rubbing his back, pushing milk at him. It hadn't passed unnoticed that she'd gone straight to him before she'd tried to help Mariana. Quite a few crew and several contestants were sending speculative glances their way.

And Dominic's own instinct was to shield her from the scrutiny. She was still pale after the events in the third-floor gallery, a star scattering of freckles standing out on her nose. A fresh dusting of powder had removed the traces of tears from her cheeks, but he could still see her in his mind, standing staring at the little glass deer. Completely still, her mind obviously miles away. Or rather, *years* away. Despite the misdeeds of Middlethorpe's mini-me, the true haunting had been in her eyes then. Before she'd returned to the gallery, to him, her arms had come up and folded around her body, as if she was holding herself. Or remembering reaching for someone, holding someone, who was no longer there.

Over the years, he'd had relationships with women, generally playing out at a very surface level on both sides and ending amicably. None of those experiences had left or inflicted scars.

But there were other bonds in his life that had—not broken but splintered his heart, chiseling fragments away.

Today, part of his heart had fractured for someone else's pain.

It would have been quite possible to step away, mentally and physically, from the intimacy that had unexpectedly ramped off the scale last Friday night.

But the way he'd felt today at the Grange, when Sylvie had been genuinely frightened and she'd burrowed straight for his arms, when she'd stood alone with her memories, her chin held high and her eyes wet with tears—

Understatement of the millennium to say this was not what he'd expected from this period of contractual proximity.

He could still feel the press of her lips, the teasing dart of her tongue, a satin stroke against his own, and the sense of utter . . . *rightness* sinking into his bones as she wriggled close.

It was as if she were settling inside him, a constant warm little light in his chest.

"I'm fine," he repeated in a low voice.

Mariana had recovered her composure and the full use of her lungs. "Mother of God," she said, coming over to join them. Her eyelids and cheeks were red, and even the single strand of silver hair stuck to her forehead was extreme dishevelment by her usual standards. "His recipe called for a quarter teaspoon of cayenne pepper. That was like inhaling a Carolina Reaper. How the hell do you make that mistake?" Barely pausing to draw breath, she added severely to Dominic, "But don't go and ask. The poor man feels bad enough without a De Vere decimation."

"He wouldn't do that when someone's *genuinely* upset." With a small frown, Sylvie had turned to look over at the contestants. She spoke absently.

He looked at her for a long moment.

Mariana was watching him. Her glance also flickered momentarily to Sylvie, with a ghost of a smile. However, when she spoke, it was merely to incline her head toward one workstation in particular, where Sylvie's scrutiny was focused. "Are we directing a few faint and fiery suspicions at Libby?"

"I mean, you said it yourself." Sylvie shifted at Dominic's side, her hand brushing his again. Just for a moment, one finger slipped inside his cuff, teasing the skin of his wrist. The tiny shiver of pleasure that danced down his spine was increasingly reliable. "It's a hell of a mistake to make, isn't it? Sid's a careful, meticulous man." Alien abduction claims aside, which had clearly been a blatant lie to get on the show. And had succeeded; so—well done, Sid. "Libby did borrow something from his station earlier."

"Chili?" Mariana asked doubtfully, and Sylvie shook her head.

"I think it was baking soda. But it was chaotic with the lighting crew throwing cables everywhere, and Sid was away from his station when I left the room. She *could* have messed up his other ingredients. But once again—"

"No proof," Mariana finished.

They all looked over at Libby's station. She was one of the few contestants who weren't standing with Sid. If she *were* responsible, at least she wasn't compounding her sins with hypocrisy. They had already judged her *Chicago*-themed display. Other than a few minor errors, her dishes today were excellent. The home economist on the crew had privately pronounced her caramel brownie tart the best bake of the series so far, and Dominic didn't disagree.

Only one remaining contestant still had to present their work, and unless Adam pulled off something spectacular, Libby was going to top the leaderboard again.

It was a high bar to clear—and Adam clambered over it.

"Oh my goodness," Sylvie said with obvious delight, immediately leaning down for a closer look at the former professor's *Beauty and the Beast* spread.

There were iced biscuits, piped well, each in the shape of an animated character. Happily chomping down on a smiling teapot, Mariana cooed, "Look at the gingerbread houses."

Adam had re-created the central square of a small French-inspired town in gingerbread blocks, chocolate beams, and blown sugar fountains. He'd mechanized the latter to spill out a cascade of syrup, which fizzed like sherbet and tasted far better than Dominic had expected.

Most of the sugar-craft requirements had been checked off on the cake, however, and the sculpted objects that stood atop the icing. Even for a highly skilled, trained sugar artist, it was difficult to pull off a human figure, and Adam had wisely opted for the Beast's enchanted household: the clock, the candelabra, and so on.

With one exception.

Mariana emitted a strangled squeak, and Sylvie went suspiciously still and quiet.

After a long stare at Adam's mild-mannered, reserved face—and the twinkle in his eyes—Dominic crouched to look at the figure of Gaston in pride of place.

The legs were a bit malformed and the ponytail more of a mullet, but it was clearly the show's arrogant, narcissistic villain.

With Dominic's face.

Dead-on likeness.

Unlike the character, Dominic didn't spend hours gazing at his own reflection, but even he had no trouble recognizing Adam's tongue-in-cheek mimicry.

The silence stretched.

From the beginnings of twitching lips, Sylvie was now openly grinning.

Adam was starting to shuffle his feet.

"Some of the sugar work is clumsy," Dominic said very coolly. "The proportions on a few of the figures are off, and you clearly overboiled this batch. These biscuits are overbaked and there are lumps in your custard."

Out of the corner of his eye, he saw Emma Abara's face. She had been entirely unbothered through the critique of her own more mediocre *Grease* bake, but she was glaring at him now.

Sylvie also noticed that. She perked up even more.

Dominic reached out and plucked Gaston from his perch, carefully holding the sculpture on his palm.

"Just a little joke?" Adam suggested with a shade of caution.

"I wouldn't call it a joke." With his other hand, he reached into his pocket and pulled out the little gold disc all the judges were given at the beginning of the season. Engraved with a crown, it could be awarded by each of them only once and earned the recipient an instant cash prize of £1,000. "From the neck up, I'd call it fairly exceptional work. Well done."

A blinking Adam took the disc, looking a bit stunned as the other contestants broke into applause—notably unenthusiastic clapping from Libby—and Dominic extended his hand.

The other man was completely flabbergasted now.

As he shook Adam's hand, he turned his head and raised a brow at Sylvie.

Laughter was a dancing light in her eyes. She inclined her head in a silent *Touché*.

His own amusement was tested when they headed out into the grounds for some fresh air before the journey back to London. He'd been distracted by Aadhya, chattering at him with yet more lunacy—did he think it would be a good idea to stage one of the final rounds on a Thames barge? No, he fucking did *not*. And nor should she, after what had occurred last year, when she'd made them film an episode on a train to Edinburgh. Rocking surfaces, three saucepans of highly flammable liquids, two blowtorches, and one elderly former judge's toupee. Jim Durham's drinking had noticeably worsened after that disaster.

So it wasn't until they were standing on ice-crisp grass in a spectacular winter garden that he noticed what Sylvie was holding.

She blinked placidly as she gave Gaston-Dominic a pat on his mullet.

"Unless you're planning to eat that," he said, "you'd better not be taking it in the car."

Her look was drenched with pity for his poor straggling wits.

"Obviously, I'm taking it in the car." She smiled beatifically at it. "I'm going to put it in the kitchens at Sugar Fair as our new mascot."

Before he could voice one of several comments on that, she reached into her bag and pulled out another item she'd purloined from the tables. It was a pink sugar Cadillac, reasonably identifiable and Emma's one real success today.

Carefully, she propped up G-D in it.

"What—"

"How else is he going to get around with those teeny legs?"

Absolute last straw.

When he started to laugh, the smile in Sylvie's eyes lifted her mouth. But the humor in her face faded, transmuting into something else. An emerging hint of an emotion that made him feel slightly less alone in new territory here.

Spontaneously, she reached up and touched his cheek, dusting her lips across his jaw in a feather-soft kiss. She paused there afterward, fleetingly, obviously checking his reaction. Lightning fast, Dominic cupped the back of her head before she could lower from her tiptoes and kissed her mouth. Her smile grew against his, and she nuzzled her nose against his cheek before she drew back.

He took a slow, deep breath, trying to clear his head.

Sylvie touched the tip of her tongue to her lips before she pressed them together. Her hands gripped the sugar Cadillac, cradling it against her chest.

Suddenly, she sighed. "And I once *swore* that I'd never let my knees quiver in your presence."

Chapter Eleven

Sugar Fair
Currently in Mourning
RIP the victims of the Great Gingerbread Witch Massacre.

Sylvie tried not to flinch as the entire trolley of gingerbread witches crashed to the ground. Broken biscuits skittered across the newly cleaned floors. A decapitated witch head landed on the tip of her shoe. They decorated these as *good* witches, with correspondingly friendly expressions, but the fall had knocked this one's face askew and she peered up with gleaming malevolence.

Considering that the rest of her body was six feet away under the truffle fridge, she was entitled to be a little peeved.

Mabel pushed through the kitchen door, took one look at the mess on the floor, shot Sylvie a very pointed stare, and turned straight back the way she'd come.

Sylvie lifted her head to meet the wide-eyed, naïve gaze of Penny.

Even as she opened her mouth, the intern's gray eyes started to fill.

Oh no.

"It was an accident," she said hastily, but it was too late. The meltdown commenced.

"I'm hopeless!" Penny wailed, flinging herself down onto a stool and scrubbing her hands over her face. She was still wearing her gloves, so green icing smeared all over her cheeks.

With a massive internal sigh, Sylvie stripped off her own gloves and went to pat her on the back.

"It was like sad Elphaba," she said a quarter of an hour later, knocking back coffee in the office. "Tears streaking down her green face. Have you *seen* her when she's crying? She has Disney eyes at the best of times. The slightest upset and she goes full-on Bambi."

Jay was leaning against the filing cabinet, arms folded.

Before he could say the words obviously *scrambling* toward his tongue, she set down her mug. "Don't say it. I can't fire her over a dropped tray of biscuits."

Jay tossed down the papers he was holding. "It was an entire trolley of biscuits, and this is only one more catastrophe in an endless stream of incompetence."

She was tired and on uncertain ground about a lot of things right now, and she was really not in the mood to argue about this again. And it was admittedly becoming frustrating that however hard she tried with Penny, whatever angle she took, it netted no positive results at all. "I know you think I need to be tougher in this part of the business."

Jay seemed about to respond, probably in the emphatic affirmative, but when he took a closer look at her face, he sighed and came to sit on the edge of the desk. "Look, when it comes down to it, you can't be anything other than what you are. And nor should you be. You're almost entirely the reason this business is successful at all."

His eyes were very warm and affectionate on her, and she reached up to squeeze his hand. "The business is both of us. We built it together, and I couldn't do it without you."

Letting her fingers drop, she sat up straighter with a sigh. "I think—I *know*—I've probably been a bit . . . softer on Penny because of her family situation."

"Her family situation?" Jay reached for the bowl of mints on her desk and unwrapped one, slipping it into his mouth.

"Not having living family anymore. Like me." It had been something of a bonding moment during Penny's interview, after the other woman's nervous small talk had veered into the area of Sylvie's private life. There had been several candidates with roughly equal qualifications that day; if she were honest, it was Penny's similar circumstances that had sealed the deal on the job offer. However, as soon as the words were out, Sylvie quickly touched Jay's knee. "*Biological* family. I know I still have a family."

Something in his expression deepened, then. She couldn't quite read it. And when he spoke, after a noticeable pause, his voice was gruff. "You and I will always be family, Syl."

Adamant. Obviously sincere.

Yet something in the air was raising a tickling sensation down the back of her neck. Only a couple of times in her life, the most notable instance in the hours before Mallory's death, Sylvie had experienced that creeping sense of foreboding.

Jay pushed back a falling strand of his dark hair. His muscular chest moved with a long in-drawn breath. "Sylvie," he said, and although their eyes met, she still couldn't get a grip on what he was feeling, at all. "Can we talk? Not now. I know you have this meeting with the Albany team. But later. Soon."

"Yes. Of course we can." She tapped the tip of her shoe against the chair leg. "Is something wrong?"

"I . . . hope not wrong. No." He exhaled, some of the stiffness leaving his frame as he smiled at her. "Don't look so worried. It's very un-Sylvie. I'm meant to be the family pessimist."

She smiled back, but that hard, tight feeling remained.

Jay had been a rock in her life for a long time, so why did she feel like that foundation stone had just wobbled?

He stroked her head as he straightened. "I have to go, too. Meeting with that supplier who's gone rogue." After grabbing another mint, he headed for the door, but suddenly turned back. "By the way, why did you think Penny doesn't have family? I heard her talking to her mother on the phone recently."

She looked up from where she'd been frowning at the desk. "I don't think so. She definitely said at her interview she doesn't have family."

He made a noncommittal gesture. "Maybe I got it wrong." He touched a finger to his temple in a glancing salute. "See you later. Good luck with the princess's pompous PA."

It was a relief to fall back on irony. "Darren Clyde would like to inform you that the title of Asshat Alliterator is already filled."

Which reminded her that she needed one more unenthusiastic trip to the Starlight Circus. She was missing one ingredient in the Midnight Elixir, the linking note that brought everything else together. It was suitably elusive, slipping away into the darkness every time she thought she had it.

Jay's low laugh followed her as she grabbed her coat and went out the back door into the side alleyway. It was freezing outside, and she pulled her woolly gloves from her coat pocket as she walked.

Freezing, but busy. After almost five minutes of waiting for a break in the traffic, and a quick selfie with a passing *Operation*

Cake fan, she managed to cross the road safely, and stood looking at the classy frontage of the love of Dominic's life.

Even with the constant gray drizzle of rain, his windows were perfectly polished under their awnings and the gold fittings gleamed.

With a small smile, she pushed open the door. Immediately, a rush of warm, delicious air hit her in the face—the most welcome knockout blow she could imagine. She breathed deep. Interesting how two businesses with similar wares could smell so distinct. Sugar Fair was caramel, candyfloss, popcorn. De Vere's was dark chocolate and bourbon—deep, indulgent, sensual.

The front rooms of the salon were beautiful and not her personal taste at all. White walls with just the smallest hint of mint, oak accents, and a general vibe of Paris. The expensive end.

A kind-eyed assistant smiled at her from behind a massive glass cabinet of chocolates. "Welcome to De Vere's. May I help you find something?"

"Bring forth the siege engines. The enemy walks amongst us."

At the dramatic pronouncement, Sylvie turned, startled—and grinned. Pet De Vere was sitting on the window seat, perched amongst the cushions with an open laptop on her knee.

Pet winked at her. "Just straight through the front door. No army. No unicorn bombs. Not even a concealing cloak. Bold. Very bold."

Still smiling, Sylvie walked over and leaned against a wooden beam that was crying out for some fairy lights. "You look busy."

Pet picked up the hot chocolate at her side and took a sip, looking as if she were bracing herself to continue an unpleasant task. "Job-hunting. Always a blast."

"He hasn't given you the sack?"

"Amazingly, not yet." Pet waved a hand at her laptop screen. "But it's only a fixed-term contract, until his permanent assistant can come back." She lifted a shoulder in an incredibly Dominic-esque gesture. "And at some point, I need to find my own place, you know? In the world, I mean," she added, in a way that could have come across naïvely, but didn't.

"I do know," Sylvie said quietly. She tilted her head at the laptop. "If I hear of anything—"

"Thanks. I'll know the right thing when it comes along." Pet set the computer aside and stood, smoothing down her top and skirt. Her silk blouse was neatly pressed and tied in a jaunty pussy bow under her chin. "I'm guessing you want Dominic?"

There was a slightly wicked glint in her eyes, but Sylvie worked on a daily basis with Mabel. It was a far higher bar than that to discompose her with subtextual innuendo. "We have a meeting, and I thought we might as well share a ride."

Now that the cat was out of the bag between them regarding the Albany tender—and as they were currently colleagues on set—the palace had directed one big cozy Super-Secret Cake Meeting. Bit of a switch-up from last time, but it saved everyone some time and subterfuge, she supposed.

Pet shot a quick glance around and leaned close. "The atmosphere suddenly went very sly. Is this a meeting regarding a certain commission, or is 'meeting' a complete euphemism, in which case, I'd like to put up a hand and say I both highly endorse this and also don't want to know any details, ever."

It took a second to untangle that stream of words. The genetics gods had clearly forgotten to give any garrulous genes to Dominic and stuffed a few extra into Pet instead.

"The former," Sylvie said emphatically, eyeing her.

A rear door opened, and she sensed Dominic seconds before

he appeared. Like a personal Bat-Signal. He was wearing a navy peacoat, strands of silver at his temples glinted under the lights, and her stomach did a dizzy little flip-flop.

All the surrealness and confliction aside, she'd forgotten how—*fun* it was, to feel that little leap of excitement, just from someone walking into a room.

When he saw her standing with Pet, his dark gaze moved slowly between them before coming to rest on her. "Hello."

Typically guarded, but she could have sworn that a little inner light appeared in his eyes when he looked at her. As it had multiple times overnight, the sight and sound of his laughter yesterday returned to her mind.

Obviously, Dominic was handsome. He'd lucked out genetically where his face was concerned. But when he had laughed, properly laughed, for the first time ever in her presence, he'd made her want to draw in close in every way. Physically, sexually, emotionally.

As she'd said. Knee-weakening.

"Hi." She unnecessarily tucked a strand of hair behind her ear.

"I just need to stick these in the office." Holding up a couple of files. "And we can go." He shot a glance at the Baroque clock near the counter. "That's running fast again, but traffic's horrific today, so we shouldn't cut it too fine—"

"I can do that," Pet said at once, snatching the files from him. "You get going."

"I haven't signed them yet—"

She was already gone.

"Well, she's efficient," Sylvie offered.

"That's one word for it. Come on back. It won't take a minute."

With avid interest, she followed him back into the inner sanctum. She'd never been farther than the kitchens of De Vere's.

Unsurprisingly, even their back rooms were decorated in polar-opposite styles.

Dominic's office was spacious, highly equipped with tech, and surprisingly messy. She was envious of the large plushy couch. She only had space in her own office for her desk chair. On the rare occasions she had time for a breather—or tiny nap—she usually lay on the floor in the Dark Forest and looked up at the fairy lights in the trees.

As she stood near the door, he signed his papers, and Pet hovered by the desk, chewing on her lip. When Sylvie had first spoken to her out front, she'd been sparkly, confident, teasing.

In here, in the quiet, it was much more apparent how Pet and Dominic changed around each other. The vibe became wary. Not at all combative—quite the opposite. Trying, but battle-wounded. She knew he wanted to connect with Pet, but it was crystal clear how badly Pet, too, wanted that bond back.

She spoke instinctively. "We're allowed to involve our most trusted inner circle in the final bids for this contract. Why doesn't Pet come to the meeting today as part of yours?"

Pet's head jerked around, and Dominic looked up from the document he was signing.

Neither said a word. Sylvie realized how presumptuous the suggestion was. She still didn't regret making it. "I'm sure she has good insight for your team."

Pet's eyes darted to her brother.

Dominic raised his brows. "How altruistic of you to give the competition any advantage."

Sylvie smiled at him. "Wasn't it?" Then, ever so slightly, she inclined her head toward Pet, who was still standing silently. The younger woman was starting to twist her fingers around her pen.

Dominic put down his own pen. "You do have good instincts, Pet, and you're an excellent judge of character. If you could spare an hour or two and come to the meeting, I'd appreciate it."

Her lips parted and moved silently, before an actual word emerged. "Okay."

He nodded. "Okay."

She hesitated a few seconds longer, and then seemed to reanimate as if she'd come off a battery charge. "I'll just get my coat!"

The door slammed behind her, and the walls of that large, spacious room seemed to close in. Sylvie was very aware of the rhythm and sound of her own breathing.

"I should have involved her myself." Dominic's voice was low and deep. "Thank you."

"She just wants time with you. To be part of your life." She finally looked up. He was watching her very intently. "I . . ." She sought for something to say. "Um. I checked the public records for a Jessica Maple-Moore in the region of Oxford and I found her death certificate. She died almost twenty-seven years ago, of catastrophic injury. By the measure of Patrick's age, that can't have been all that long after the photograph was taken at Primrose Cottage." She hesitated again. "I thought about it, and I think after the meeting with her team today, we should try to contact Rosie directly and see if the name means anything to her. I can't shake the feeling that this is the key to—well, to understanding Patrick."

Even outside of the cake, setting aside the contract, she was drawn to that photograph in a way she couldn't understand. Maybe it was the look in Patrick's eyes, or the pure joy in Jessica's face, the sense of two souls intimately connected.

Or maybe it was pure nosiness. Either way, she felt compelled to follow the path a little further.

"Okay," Dominic repeated simply, still quietly.

Her absurdly nervous gaze suddenly stopped skating around and returned to an object she'd just skimmed on his desk. It was a framed photograph, an old-fashioned shot of a youngish Sebastian De Vere standing outside De Vere's in an earlier decade. At any other time, she'd be fascinated to see again how handsome he'd been—and how much his grandson resembled him. But it wasn't the photograph that caught her attention. It was what was tucked into the frame.

Dominic's eyes followed hers. And a tinge of color appeared in his cheeks.

Walking over, the butterflies skittering about her stomach, Sylvie reached out and touched the intricate little silhouette portrait of her own face. Her eyes lifted to Dominic's in-the-flesh face, which was currently much stiffer than that paper.

"Pet," he said. "She cut a couple of portraits in here one day when we were talking about *Operation Cake*. Yours and Mariana's."

"Yes. I saw Mariana's after you gave it to her." She ran her finger around the paper contour of her plait, dropped her hand to the desk. "You didn't give me mine, though."

"No. I didn't."

"Because . . . we didn't get along? And you wanted to keep Pet's artwork?"

"I did want to have some of Pet's art." Dominic's jaw ticked. "And somewhere along the line, I wanted that one in particular."

Sylvie swallowed.

When he walked forward and slowly reached for her, sliding his hands around the curve of her waist, she touched his jaw almost wonderingly, feeling that increasingly familiar prickle of stubble. The softness of his lips when she ran her fingers over them, before his head lowered the short distance to hers.

The coming together was quiet and searching, but as soon as their mouths met, the kiss was hard, urgent. He pulled her up into his body, and Sylvie wrapped her arms around his neck, holding him tightly as they pressed closer to each other. His hand stroked up her ribs, his thumb lightly tracing the under-curve of her breast.

Little whispers of kisses on each corner of her mouth and the tip of her nose, before he roughly caught her lips again, pushing deep, a shivering rush of awareness that echoed in her heart.

If she'd rubbed a magic lamp and wished for the most head-spinning, gorgeous kiss, even a genie would struggle to top this.

Dominic's fingers slid into her hair, cupping her neck, and his teeth closed on her lower lip.

"Oops," Pet said from somewhere in the mists beyond Sylvie's immediate consciousness.

Her lashes fluttered open, and she looked into Dominic's darkened eyes. His hand tightened on her and he tore his gaze from hers, turning his head.

"Um. I'll just wait at the car."

Sylvie finally clued properly into Pet's presence. She was standing at the door, clutching its edge, and looking equal parts thrilled and squicked-out.

She flitted away again, and Sylvie's hand curled against the front of Dominic's shirt, feeling the movement of his chest.

"That was—" Her voice was a crackly mess.

"It was." Low and velvety, just one simple statement that made her shiver again. He ran the edge of his thumb down her nose.

Touching her with an ease that would mean so much less from someone else. "Rain check?"

She nodded, and their fingers brushed, briefly interlocked.

As they left the office, Dominic rang ahead to the contact number they'd been given, to warn of an extra visitor.

Sylvie sat in the back of the car during the long, traffic-stalled trip to the mystery office building, partly so Pet could talk to Dominic. Partly because she had a mind all over the place right now—and frankly, enough sexual frustration that she felt awkward even sitting in the same car as his little sister.

Pet seemed to have gone unnaturally silent, however, and after about ten minutes, Dominic turned on the radio, which Sylvie doubted got much airtime in this vehicle.

A song finished, and the DJs filled the car with boring chat about a movie she'd never heard of. She couldn't remember the last time she'd watched a film. Life at the moment revolved mostly around cake, with snatches of sleep when possible.

She looked at the back of Dominic's head, his forearm resting on the steering wheel.

Although one or two other things were starting to take precedence.

The inane chatter suddenly turned to the royal wedding.

"They're putting the whole thing on telly, so I hope the groom can get his vows out by dinnertime," one of the shock jocks cracked.

Sylvie shook her head with a low sound of disgust.

"Sounds like Marchmont is still boffing his ex. The Eton set usually wait until after the wedding before they hook up a bit on the side . . ."

Emphatically, Dominic reached out and switched the radio off.

In the renewed quiet, Pet said, "These stories popping up about John Marchmont. It's bullshit, surely?"

"It's definitely bullshit." Sylvie had no doubts whatsoever on that score. "He loves Rosie. I've met a lot of engaged couples in this business, and I've rarely seen a couple with such a strong, private connection."

She expected a cynical rejoinder from Dominic at that, but he surprised her. "I agree. The connection between them seemed genuine."

He changed lanes, turning into a quieter street. This was a part of London Sylvie rarely visited, mostly expensive commercial zones. Very old and exclusive-looking properties converted into office and loft space.

When Dominic had found a parking space, they stood looking at a heavily fenced Georgian property.

"And the battle resumes," Dominic murmured.

"Hmm." Sylvie started forward. "Countdown until the final proposals is on. I'd start preparing your gracious concession speech now."

"Oh no," she heard Pet say behind her, with a perfect blend of condescension and sympathy. "Does she really think they have a chance?"

Without turning around, Sylvie lifted her hand, made a very unsporting gesture, and heard Pet's laughter ring out.

Dominic snorted softly.

Fortunately, none of the intimidating guards at the entrance had seen that lapse of professionalism. They were all too occupied with the woman having an almighty tantrum on the steps.

"I'm sorry, miss," a grim-looking man in black said, stepping to block another attempt by the curly-haired blonde to get past him. "Entrance is by appointment only. And you're not on our list."

"I know they're in there," she snapped. She was probably quite pretty, but right now her face was red and screwed up with fury. She stamped her foot like a stymied toddler. "And I demand to see Johnny. I'll even talk to *her* if he's supposedly so 'busy.'"

A woman in similarly funereal attire said something into her phone, which provoked a renewed screech of outrage.

"I *need* to see him. And who are you?" In a momentary break from her wild gesticulating, she'd caught sight of Sylvie and Pet, standing awkwardly at the bottom of the steps. "More of his discards?"

She suddenly made a break for the doors and was scooped up by the biggest of the guards. He tucked her under his arm like a football and calmly walked past them and out of sight. Flailing arms and legs and a stream of profanity exited with him.

Pet ran her fingers through her hair, mussing the sleekly straightened bob. "That was a bit . . ."

Disquieting. Sylvie totally agreed. She suspected any premises with a celebrity connection, royal or otherwise, copped their share of unhealthy attention, but there had been something about the look in that woman's eyes.

Dominic's words came back to her—*I don't know if you've ever looked at someone and seen pure, undiluted hatred seeping out.*

His hand touched her back. "Hazard of being in the public eye, especially in this day and age, when tech creates an illusion—or *delusion*—of intimacy. I think the source of the Don Juan rumors might have just revealed herself at some volume."

"You don't think that's really John Marchmont's ex?" Pet shot a disbelieving glance back. "It would be like a rabbit shagging a wolverine."

"Thank you for that image." Dominic pulled out his credentials to give to the waiting guard. "And no, I imagine that was a woman who's never met Marchmont in her life, and probably needs a bit of help and compassion."

Pet bit her lip.

Sylvie also produced her ID and checked in, and a guard escorted them inside. The foyer was expectedly plush, with a marble floor and a crystal chandelier. A gold-printed board stood next to a glass elevator, but there were no names, simply suite numbers.

She checked her notes. "Suite 4B?"

"That's what I have." Dominic reached out and hit the button, and the doors slid open.

When the lift reached the fourth floor, Edward Lancier was waiting for them. "Ms. Fairchild. Mr. De Vere. And I received a very last-minute request to approve a third party." He'd couldn't have sounded more put-upon if they'd asked him to personally escort Pet to the meeting, having first fetched her from the peaks of Everest.

"My sister, Petunia De Vere. She's part of my team," Dominic said briefly, and some of the pensiveness in Pet's face was replaced with shy pleasure.

Edward turned smartly, knocked on a door, and held it open.

Dominic stood back and nodded Sylvie and Pet forward. She stepped into the room.

She'd been expecting a short and impersonal progress meeting with staff.

She had *not* been expecting to find the royal couple themselves, lounging about with takeaway cups from the Starlight Circus and an open bag of crisps.

"Good afternoon," Rosie said, rising to her feet. "Thank you for coming, team. *Teams.*"

Johnny, who was wearing jeans and a Bastille tee, also stood and looked expectantly at Pet.

Rosie politely thanked and unceremoniously booted Edward from the room, and Dominic introduced his sister. Pet had gone uncharacteristically quiet.

"I like Bastille" was all she said before turning bright red.

Johnny immediately beamed at her. Sylvie could almost see the cartoon thought bubble above his head: *A friend!*

Rosie was dressed more formally than her fiancé, in a high-necked black lace dress. A leather blazer was slung over a nearby chair. Her sharp navy eyes performed a rapid assessment of Pet before switching to Sylvie and Dominic. "You were expecting to meet with Edward today."

"Yes, we were." Dominic's response was equally blunt. The princess nodded for them to sit down. "I wouldn't have thought your schedule would allow time for further meetings in person until we're actually contracted and ready to move forward with the final cake."

"Sadly misguided with the 'we're' there, De Vere," Sylvie murmured. "But otherwise—ditto."

"There are some further last-minute elements we'd like included in the cake tenders . . ." Rosie correctly interpreted Sylvie's expression and cracked a small grin. "Nothing complicated, I assure you. But I'd like to be sure that our requests are relayed . . . correctly."

That pronouncement echoed into a short, expressive pause, broken by Johnny's interjection.

"Lancier knows the ropes at the palace," he said flatly. "But his appointment as her right-hand man was not Rosie's choice. He used to work for a different branch of the household, and his loyalties remain firmly in that camp. She can't sneeze in the night without Lancier sending a report up the family tree. Her relatives like to passive-aggressively meddle. They *don't* like the increased spotlight on us since the announcement of the engagement, and that we draw m-more than our allotted share of attention. Somehow any ideas we shoot down the pipeline emerge looking very different to what we intended."

The silence extended.

Rosie's gaze slid sideways, and Johnny looked fondly back at her.

She cleared her throat. Patted his arm. "First order of business. On Sunday, a ball will be held at St. Giles to celebrate my twenty-fifth birthday."

"Happy birthday!" Pet blurted, and Rosie's smile became more genuine.

"Thank you. My actual birthday was last month, but . . ." She shrugged. "Networking."

That visible unbending was enough to unplug Pet's nervous chattiness. "I hope you celebrated privately, too."

Sylvie had been watching Johnny. Whenever his face fell into lines of repose, she thought there was a certain strain there, a tension far weightier than his nerves and awkward shuffling at their first meeting. But at Pet's words, a twinkle appeared. "There may have been an all-night gaming tournament. And a very p-poor showing by the birthday girl."

"It was four to three. In my favor," Rosie retorted, and her fiancé reached out and took her hand, bringing it to his lips in a natural, affectionate gesture.

"I threw the last round as a gift. Gentleman's code."

"Nice try, babe."

Pet looked absolutely fascinated.

Rosie cast a final laughing glance at Johnny—but Sylvie

thought there was still underlying tension in her own demeanor, as well. "The final cake tenders are due on Sunday. I'd like to invite you both . . ." She looked at Pet, and her expression settled into something gentler. Kind. "I'd like to invite you *all* to attend the ball as our guests after you submit, including your business partner, Sylvie. Regardless of the outcome, your hard work is enormously appreciated."

Sylvie was completely taken aback, and surprised that Pet wasn't shooting about the room like an out-of-control firecracker. She was almost vibrating in her seat.

Dominic was clearly not as enamored as his sister by the prospect of a black-tie ball in a royal palace, but when he saw her excitement, the habitually hard edges of his expression softened.

Sylvie could very easily imagine what Pet had been like as a little girl, and suddenly she saw them in her mind's eye—an emotionally battered, stoic small boy, clutching the baby girl who loved him, clambering onto that train.

She blinked away the burning in her eyes when Dominic looked at her with a small frown.

"Attendance obviously isn't mandatory," Rosie added. "A ball is not everyone's idea of a delightful Sunday evening."

Johnny managed not to pop up like a disastrously honest jack-in-the-box again, but the unspoken *It's not ours, either* hung in the air.

Rosie dutifully pushed on. "With regard to the wedding cake, how difficult would it be to add an additional two tiers?"

She'd done a sketch of the changes they wanted, and Sylvie took a photograph of the drawing for later reference.

"This is a beautiful building," Pet said suddenly. "Is it a permanent base for business? Or just a one-off hire for today?"

"For a number of reasons, we prefer to run some of our engagements outside of the palace." Rosie was seemingly unbothered by the rapid-fire questions. "We keep an external suite of offices here, although we don't advertise that fact."

There was a very slight, very polite warning in those words, which Pet immediately discarded. "It can't be that secret," she said, so bluntly that her resemblance to her brother was momentarily marked. "Somebody was trying to get in to see you downstairs, and she obviously wasn't invited."

Rosie frowned. "Probably a member of the press," she said, with an ironic twist on the last word. "If she may be so called. We have a reciprocal agreement with the media, but one of the tabloid papers in particular respects very few boundaries, and their photographers have been increasingly invasive."

"Yes, my staff have had to shoo a few out of Sugar Fair." Sylvie clicked off her pen. "But I don't think your visitor today was a reporter. She was quite insistent about speaking to Johnny, and she was rather . . . cross," she finished inadequately.

Flicking over a new page in her notebook, she looked up and caught the looks on the couple's faces. In Rosie's expression, she saw nothing but faint irritation, no obvious concern or suspicion.

Johnny, however—just for a second, something flickered. Alarm? Guilt?

Interesting. Worrying.

"That's why we have security." Rosie dismissed the subject and clasped her hands together. "We do want a quick word with you separately. We don't expect you to divulge your secrets in front of each other." The princess started scrolling through pages on her tablet. "But with regard to the design honorific to Uncle Patrick . . ." She saw their mutually raised eyebrows. "I'm afraid that surprise lasted about half an hour."

Johnny pinkened. Whatever Sylvie had just seen in his face had gone, vanquished by a rush of self-deprecation. "When I'm excited about anything, my first instinct is to tell Rosie. She's my best friend."

Pet had heart-eyes again.

"It was a really lovely thought," Rosie said, her gaze lingering and gentle on Johnny. "I miss him a lot." Her smile twisted as she turned back to Sylvie. "Patrick—he genuinely cared about other people. He was interested in their lives. Truly happy when things went well for them. Just . . ." She made a little gesture with her hand.

"A good man," Dominic said.

"Yes." Rosie glanced at her lap, then drew in a deep breath. When she straightened her shoulders, getting back to business, the professional demeanor slipped back over her like a veil. It was like a holographic image—turn the picture one way and see the royal trappings, the well-trained princess; tip the image and catch a glimpse of the normal human woman. "As I was saying, with regard to that element of the design, I'm aware it's quite a difficult brief. I was closer to Patrick than probably anyone else in the world . . ."

Another break in the trained exterior; her face was fleetingly stark. Bleak. Then it was gone. "I have no idea what to suggest for the design. Patrick was an intensely private man, and for as long as I knew him, he was primarily focused on his charities. And his music. But unfortunately, you can't put his piano sonatas on a cake. Nor do I want a sugar facsimile of his pet bees." A wry postscript. "Short of straight-out writing his name on a tier, which would go down like a bucket of cold sick with my grandfather," Rosie added with graphic bluntness, "I can't provide much help. But it occurred to Johnny that you might want access to the private records at Abbey Hall . . ." Closely observing their faces, her shrewd eyes narrowed. "You've already been there."

"We both have, yes," Sylvie said, and exchanged rapid glances with Dominic. Ask about Jessica Maple-Moore now, or when they split groups shortly and someone could speak to Rosie privately? She was inclined toward the latter and Dominic clearly agreed. He raised his hand to push back a strand of that lush silvering hair—and made a tiny gesture with his forefinger and middle finger. It was *Operation Cake* language, a smattering of hand signals that the crew used to communicate while the cameras were rolling. In this case: *Wait.* A full dialogue in a matter of seconds, without saying a word. She inclined her head. "It opened possibilities."

Rosie lifted her brows. "Impressive." She picked up her Starlight Circus cup. "And how about progress on the Midnight Elixir layer? Does it also advance?"

It advanced straight into the bin. Layer upon disgusting layer.

"I don't know about De Vere's," Sylvie said primly. "But we're very close." Dominic cleared his throat at that, and she lifted her chin. "*Very* close."

Johnny took a sip from his own cup. "God, it actually is ghastly."

The end of Dominic's tapping pen hit his paper hard, and Sylvie looked up from her own notes. Having put money into Darren Clyde's cash register, and the world's most revolting cake onto her poor, abused taste buds, she couldn't even begin to hide her expression.

Belatedly, Johnny explained, "My assistant picked up the wrong drink today. I don't know what this is exactly, but it's the most horrible thing I've ever tasted."

Yet, he kept drinking it, looking perfectly happy to do so.

"Johnny's assistant is leaving after the wedding," Rosie explained, probably to smooth over their unblinking silence. "He's getting married himself. Naturally, he's become a little distracted. But I'm pleased to hear you're so close to translating the flavor."

They split up, then, Dominic and Pet going into an adjacent room with Johnny. Sylvie answered a few of Rosie's questions about her progress and asked for clarification on several points. She was probing into which flavor notes of the Midnight Elixir the couple most enjoyed when she realized that Rosie was answering on autopilot. Very polite, very practiced, but very definitely worried.

If she saw anyone upset or stressed, Sylvie asked if they needed help. She was quite sure it wasn't in the etiquette books to ask a princess what was up; nor would it be protocol to receive a truthful response. Nevertheless . . . "Your Highness. Are you all right?"

Rosie didn't stiffen or startle. She looked up smoothly, her face serene. Sylvie fully expected an immaculate brush-off.

The other woman's eyeliner was smudged, just a tiny bit, at one corner. Those large eyes searched Sylvie's face. And she spoke. And it was neither a brush-off nor a social lie. "I don't take for granted the privileges of my birth. They are many and legion. In many ways, I'm one of the most fortunate women in this country."

Sylvie said nothing.

"There is a flip side to those advantages." Rosie paused. "I'm sure you can understand that it's rather difficult to know whom one can confide in, at times."

"I can very much imagine that would be the case." Especially if Rosie's senior staff were spying on her every move and reporting any small misstep to her relatives and *their* staff. It would be like living in a game of Minesweeper, constantly trying not to step on the bombs.

"I learned, the hard way, to make swift judgments as to character," Rosie said crisply. "And instinctively, right from the beginning, I've trusted you. You could have sold the story of my behavior in Sugar Fair that night to the gutter press. You didn't."

"I wouldn't."

"Not everyone in my family is happy. With me, with my engagement. Or in general." She briefly pressed her lips together. "I'm not sure what I would do without Johnny at my side. Through all the pressure, all the press, all the . . . dissent, he's been there. He's on my team, all the time. Just this morning, he saw I was about to blow my fuse and he took me out to the mulberry tree in the palace gardens. Patrick's thinking spot. It's the only part of my home where I feel like I can truly breathe."

Her words had dropped to a whisper, as if she'd forgotten Sylvie was there; but her eyes focused again. "When I met him, it was like something out of someone else's life. Some people couldn't understand it. They don't *see* him. I saw him," she said simply. "And he saw me. The way I felt, I've never experienced anything like it. When I was growing up, I didn't have . . . Daddy and my mother . . ." Rosie trailed away circumspectly on that point.

The body language between the Duke and Duchess of Albany did not speak of an immensity of love. In every photo, every video clip, it resonated with total indifference. It was fairly common knowledge that the duke spent more time with his horses than with his wife.

"It was a total game changer for me. But it isn't easy for him."

Her voice went through a lightning hitch. She stopped. Cleared her throat twice. "There have been moments lately when he's been preoccupied. Distant—"

"Your Highness."

"*Rosie.*" The princess set her teeth.

"Rosie," Sylvie said softly. "I've struggled to deal with the tiny notoriety of a television show. I can't even begin to imagine the pressures on your relationship. But if I may say so, it's very, very evident how you feel about each other. It's a privilege to be involved even this far with your wedding, for that reason alone." In this instant, she was talking only to a very stressed, not particularly happy woman. "I truly don't think you need to doubt that Johnny is where he wants to be. I expect it's where he *needs* to be."

Rosie's jaw worked. "But is it fair to him?" In anyone else, that might have been a passionate outburst, yet the very soberness of the princess's response was all the more powerful. "Is it fair to him?" she repeated, and that bleakness was back in her eyes. "I'm sure you've seen the press lately. I've had it since the day I was born, and I'll be dogged by it until I die. But Johnny—he doesn't have to live like this. He doesn't deserve any of it. He's *enduring* it because of me. For me. I love him," she said with sudden fierceness. "I love him more than anything. So much more than myself. And yet I'm pulling him into a way of life that's going to make him miserable."

"Rosie—"

"It happened to Patrick." Suddenly, there were tears in Rosie's eyes. "It happened to Patrick, years ago. He loved someone desperately. But she'd seen how his previous girlfriends had been treated. She knew what her life would become, the moment they went public. And in the end, it wasn't a path she could walk."

Sylvie reached out and took her hand, and Rosie gripped on to her very tightly.

"He loved her all his life," she said, rubbing her back of her free hand under her wet lashes. "There was never anyone else, ever again. He—he *mourned* her, all his life." She turned a stark look on Sylvie. "But he never blamed her for the decision she made. He said . . . He said, so simply, 'She was the light. She was everything that was beautiful and kind, and she would have struggled every day, for the rest of her life. I would have caged a bird that was always meant to soar. I had to let her go.' I've never forgotten the *way* he said it." Another tear slipped down her cheek. "I think his spirit—the Patrick he would have been then—went with her and never returned. He was the light in *my* life, until I met Johnny, but he carried his sadness with him."

She looked down at their joined hands, and Sylvie had a suspicion that very few people had ever reached out and held on to Rosie. "In the last days before he died, he wrote a final piece of music. I have it in my dressing table. I've never told anyone else about it. I'm not musical, so I've never heard it played." A faint smile that spoke more of grief than pleasure; and not an old grief. Sylvie heard in the princess's tone *anticipated* grief, and she tightened her grip. "I suspect it would make me cry, though. And the laundry is probably already wondering why I'm going through so many hankies." She lifted her gaze back to Sylvie's. "He wrote it for her. It's called—"

Even later, Sylvie wasn't sure exactly why she was so certain in that moment, as she saw in her mind that small glass globe and the simple inscription that encompassed—everything. "Jessie."

If nothing else, it shocked Rosie out of the dark spiral that obviously had icy fingers on her, pulling her down. Sylvie knew what it was like, those moments when it felt as if you were drowning in the absence of light.

The princess stared at her, lips parted. There was a dead silence, before she said, "As far as I know, there isn't another person living who knows about Jessie. Either you found something at Abbey Hall, or you're *way* more qualified than I thought to spend your nights hovering over a cauldron."

Sylvie reached into her bag and pulled out her phone. Bringing up the photos she'd taken in the archives, she passed it across to Rosie, who looked down at the inscription on the glass globe.

Immediately, a new sheen appeared in her blue eyes. She flipped to the envelope with its intimate little sketches, zooming in, tracing her fingertip over Patrick's handwriting. "Jessica Maple-Moore. I never knew her full name. Patrick only ever called her Jessie. And he was typically circumspect about any private details."

Sylvie waited, watching Rosie's face as she turned to the last image. The other woman went very still as she looked down at the photograph of her uncle and Jessie on the steps at Primrose Cottage. The pure love and absolute happiness in both of their faces.

After a full minute in which they sat in silence, Sylvie asked quietly, "The originals are at Abbey Hall and I think they'll be returned to you, but in the meantime, do you want me to send you that photo?"

Rosie nodded wordlessly. She finally looked up. Her eyes were drenched, and there was a deeply sad twist to her mouth, but she was smiling.

"Thank you," she said, through her tears. "I've never seen him like that. That light in him—he brought so much happiness to so many lives, I'm so *glad* to know that at least for a short time, he knew that sort of joy."

And then her face crumpled, and Sylvie leaned forward to put her arms around her.

Eventually, Rosie lifted her wet face from Sylvie's shoulder and took a deep breath, swiping at her cheeks. She exhaled heavily. "I have to go out there and be Princess Rose. Quick, tell me something lighter. A joke. Ask the most inane question you can think of. Something."

Because Sylvie's brain was frequently a complete twat, what popped into her head then was a limerick she'd heard at her local pub. It involved both Rosie's grandfather and the Archbishop of Canterbury's penis, and might as well be subtitled "How to Hand Dominic This Entire Contract in One Smutty Poem."

In lieu of that option, she went with Thought B. "Our initial meeting was understandably kept well under wraps. And very separate."

She emphasized the last word.

Rosie had pulled out a hand mirror and was dabbing face powder under her reddened eyes. "As you noted, my schedule is busy. This was more time-efficient." Despite her residual sniffles, her voice was back to very calm Trained Royal. She looked straight at Sylvie—then, fleetingly, her gaze flicked over to the adjoining door, where the others had gone. "And now, somehow I don't think you mind having to share the space."

Pollyanna couldn't have presented a more innocent front.

Even the busy, beleaguered, worried princess appeared to have noticed Sylvie's increasing desire to climb Dominic like a fireman's pole.

Marvelous.

Before she left the little meeting room to rejoin Dominic and Pet, Sylvie hesitated with her hand on the door and looked back at Rosie. "Rosie. It's going to be okay."

Rosie had fully adorned her armor now. She nodded slightly, her chin held high, eyes very straight.

But in their depths, buried beneath protocol and pride, remained something small and scared.

As Sylvie walked with the De Veres back out into the wind-tossed rain, Dominic looked at her with a frown. "Everything all right?"

She turned and looked up at the pretty stone building, the tinted windows, the guards at the door. "I hope so."

Chapter Twelve

The Starlight Circus
Round two.
The clowns are multiplying.

This time, the doorway into hell set off a crescendo of fox screams. Darren Clyde was mixing up his playlist.

He'd also switched around the décor. The glowing stars on the ceiling were now purple, the previously white rug on the floor had turned pink and shaggy, and he'd put red bulbs in the floor lamps. Behind the counter, an oversized Union Jack hung from gold chains.

The whole room was overheated, the temperature immediately bypassing comfortable warmth and raising sweat along Dominic's neck.

"If you ever wondered what Austin Powers's sex dungeon would look like," Sylvie remarked conversationally at his side, "ponder no more."

He snorted, his hand going to her back without prior decision. He played absently with the end of her plait, running it through his fingers.

She moved slightly into his side. "Brace yourself," she informed him solemnly. "Your best buddy has a gal pal."

Dominic had already seen that particular horror. Wherever Clyde had obtained his demonic clown, the evil had spawned a companion. Same leering face and wide hypnotic eyes. Distinguishable by its earrings and painted-on spikes of mascara.

"It sort of looks like a possessed Betty Boop," Sylvie said. Accurately.

"Let's get these bloody drinks and get back to work."

It had been almost four by the time they'd left the meeting with Rosie and Johnny, so he'd told Pet to clock off and dropped her near Oxford Street at her request. He and Sylvie had plans for the remainder of the day that involved a takeaway service at the Starlight Circus and another round of flavor trialing.

When they joined the line to place their orders, Sylvie suddenly swore. Her expression evolved from deeply meditative to wrathful. "Unbelievable. He's mocking up a whole new menu on the . . . the fucking *fruits of thievery.*"

In a new glass cabinet, an array of desserts now included a so-called Midnight Elixir cheesecake.

"And I expect he's used my Sorceress emulsion in that, too."

"I'd imagine so."

She spun on her high-heeled boots. "He's profiting off *my* work. Is that acceptable?"

"It is not."

"It's outrageous. It's probably illegal. He's done this one too many times now." She raised a finger. Not the one she'd undoubtedly like to direct at Clyde. "And do you know what I'm going to do about it?"

Leaning against the mechanical bear, Dominic crossed one ankle over the other and regarded her with great interest. When she poked him lightly in the chest for emphasis, he caught her finger, hooking it with his own. "What *are* you going to do about it?"

Sylvie glared at him, before she yanked her hand back with an exasperated gesture. "Nothing. I am probably going to do *nothing* about it, because at the first sign of confrontation, I generally fold like a bad round of poker."

They'd reached the front of the queue.

Without a pause, she said very politely to the server, "Eight Midnight Elixir drinks and two slices of Midnight Elixir cheesecake to take away, please. And if you could package that order in two halves—four drinks and one cheesecake each—that would be great. Thank you."

Then she again looked at Dominic as if he were responsible for every ill that ailed her and snapped, with extreme crabbiness, "My treat."

It was probably slightly perverse to feel that growing warmth in his chest as she directed her list of grievances at him.

And yet here they were.

The more Sylvie stared daggers at him, the more inclined he was to pull her in.

For a fucking cuddle, no less.

She was increasingly bringing out parts of him he'd thought were long gone.

"We're actually eating the cheesecake?" he asked mildly, tapping his fingers on the mechanical bear's head.

"Clearly, you're still not one hundred percent on the makeup of my Sorceress emulsion, and I'm missing one ingredient that you're smugly keeping to yourself. Maybe it's more obvious in the cheesecake version." Sylvie hunched her shoulders and muttered ominously to herself. Stick her in front of her cauldrons and it would be like a Weird Sister from *Macbeth* had gone walk-about in twenty-first-century London.

Confirmed: increasing instinct to cuddle.

He could be disingenuous and wonder what the hell was going on with them, how things had come to this—but he'd never spouted naïve bullshit, even to himself. He hadn't been living in a bubble. It might not have ever happened before, but it was pretty fucking obvious what was starting to happen to him now.

It had been over thirty years now since he'd put out a hand and had it impatiently pushed away every time. He had very low tolerance for irrational behaviour and he considered it a complete waste of time to dwell on regrets. Which was exactly why he'd always despised the fact that the small creeping shadow of that early lesson had burrowed so deep. That he'd let people who'd long since lost his respect, let alone any chance at love, leave even the smallest scar. And that he couldn't deny it had chipped something away from even the most casual of his other relationships.

That voice when he was with her? Not gone. But so quiet right now as to be almost negligible.

When he actually had time to sit and breathe and let his mind and body properly settle, the significance of that was patiently waiting, ready to sink in hard.

He accepted the boxes of cheesecake that the staffer passed over the counter. "I'm not sure where you got the image of yourself as a timid rabbit who bolts from confrontation. Five minutes after we met, I copped a lecture on empathy and public relations before you wandered off humming 'Frosty the Snowman.'"

A fractional pause.

"That was different." A frown flickered between her brows. More quietly: "It's always been different with you."

It was a day for some ruthless home truths. "Likewise. Apparently to a far greater extent than I realized."

Their eyes met. Held.

Dominic's hand tightened around the cardboard boxes. "Sylvie—"

Behind her, the door to the kitchens opened and a young woman came out. Speaking of timid rabbits . . . The stranger's very large eyes widened, and he was surprised her nose and ears didn't twitch before she turned tail and shot back into the kitchen.

He frowned. "What was that about?"

"What?"

"A woman I've never seen before in my life, who just took one look at me and scarpered." He turned back to her thoughtfully. "Or one look at you."

"Probably a viewer," Sylvie said sweetly. "Your reputation precedes you."

"Well, well." The kitchen door had opened again, and a blond man walked out, green eyes and provocative grin fixed on Sylvie. He was probably midthirties. Muscular build. A uniquely punchable face. "The head of the coven herself. In my humble little establishment."

Not so long ago, Dominic would have said that Sylvie thoroughly disliked him. Clearly, that wasn't the emotion directed at him now. The exact degree to which her feelings had changed, he didn't know. But she'd never looked at him with the loathing she turned on this prick.

"'Humble' is not a word I've ever associated with you, Darren." Her gaze flicked dismissively around the gold-standard example of staggeringly bad taste. "Nor is it the first descriptor that comes to mind in this place."

"Always my biggest fan, Sylvie." Darren's smile didn't remotely touch his eyes.

"And apparently, you're still mine. Since half my menu seems to show up here. In a remarkably poor reflection."

"And yet you appear to be *buying* from my sad shade of a menu." Darren's mocking stare swung to rest on Dominic. "I *am* honored today. Dominic De Vere." He extended a hand. "Darren Clyde. Owner and proprietor. Your fellow judge and I have a history. Instant pals in class, weren't we, Sylvie?"

"Well, you did copy my answers on the very first quiz," Sylvie said. "Nobody can say you're not consistent."

For a person who kept insisting she lacked assertiveness, she was taking swipes with the same skill she applied to her sugar sculptures, verbally whittling Clyde down to reveal the little cockroach within. Dominic had developed an apparently endless supply of protective instincts where Sylvie was concerned, but absolutely none of them were currently required. It actually pissed him off that she would have had to curtsy at St. Giles, because this woman needed to bow to no one.

He didn't so much as glance at Darren's extended hand. After a moment, the plagiarizer's fingers curled and fell away.

"Funny." Darren divided a cool look between them. "I had the impression that you two weren't exactly fast friends. How deceptive TV can be."

Dominic scanned the other man from head to boots. "So this is the talentless twat who's been stealing your recipes."

Bristling, Darren stood taller, straightened wide shoulders.

"The one you offered to punch," Sylvie agreed chirpily, picking up the toss with effortless ease.

"He's a little bigger than I was expecting," he noted, and the rigidity of her body relaxed into a sudden bubbling of laughter in her eyes. "But I'll give it a go if you like."

The guy actually took a step back, to his own immediate, visible aggravation.

Sylvie tilted her head. After a considering moment, she said, "That's okay." She didn't look at Darren; only at Dominic. The dimple beside her lips peeped out. "I can handle myself."

His mouth lifted. "I never doubted."

The server came around the counter with two trays of drinks. "Here you go."

"Thank you so much." Sylvie took them. "I have two new sweets going into production next week. Clearly, your lonely brain cell is incapable of any original thought, Darren, so why don't I just type out the recipes and email them straight over. Save you the trip. Little early Christmas present."

Even the Duchess of Albany would fail to find fault with the way she exited the café.

Amusement becoming an outright grin, Dominic followed.

Outside in the bitter cold, he stood in a circle of warm light reflecting from the café windows and took one tray of drinks from her. "Such a spineless, retiring mouse."

Sylvie huffed a half laugh. "Even the confrontation-averse have their breaking point."

"Thanks for the drinks."

Her fingers folded tightly around her own tray. A thick strand of lavender hair fell across her eyes before she shook it back. "You're welcome."

A few snowflakes drifted down over his shoulders, falling to melt on the wet stones.

Sylvie's eyes searched his as their arms touched. When Dominic leaned in, her lips trembled under his as he kissed her. It was a lingering caress, light, gentle—until she pushed up on her tiptoes, pressing into him. They breathed each other in, the kiss deepening.

Her tongue had just stroked his, sending a pleasurable shock straight to his groin, when his phone rang.

He lifted his mouth with a muffled groan, and she dropped her head to rest briefly on his shoulder.

"I was expecting to come out of this experience sleep-deprived and hopefully many pennies wealthier," she said into his coat. "Not internally sobbing from sexual frustration."

Ruefully, she stepped back. "Answer it." She took back his tray of drinks to free up one of his hands.

Dominic straightened, breathed deep. Joking comments aside, he got the frustration. His body was taut with aborted sensation, his skin prickling as if it had stretched too tight across his bones. In just a few seconds, he was infinitely more aroused than he was comfortable with on a public street, relatively deserted or not.

With a jerk, he pulled his phone from his coat pocket, checked the screen. He swiped to answer. "Liam, I hope you're clocking out."

"Nobody is clocking out." Liam's voice shot down the line. "We've got a problem."

His movements stilled. "What's the matter?"

Sylvie had been kicking her feet along the ground, also keeping moving to stay warm. She looked up swiftly.

"Last month, when Aaron was still . . . preoccupied, he took an order from Grosvenor Park Hotel." Paper rustled. "Twelve dozen cupcakes, six hundred chocolates. Mostly Pointillist Caramels." Their most time-consuming sweet, which had to be produced and consumed fresh. "And a five-tier cake. He forgot to record it."

Foreboding was a hard pulse in Dominic's blood. "And when is the delivery date for this order that we haven't started yet?"

Sylvie came close, obviously concerned.

Liam dropped the expected hammer. "Nine o'clock tomorrow morning."

"Fuck," Dominic said emphatically.

What's wrong? she mouthed, and he grimaced.

"Who's still there and who's prepared to stay?" he asked Liam. "Triple pay."

"Everyone here is staying. Regardless of overtime pay," his friend said firmly. "You're a bit of a dick sometimes, mate, but we're all pretty loyal to our boss, you know. Go team."

His boots squeaked over the falling snow as he turned with a small sound of amusement, but the sincerity behind the words didn't pass unnoticed. Or unappreciated.

"But we're already short-staffed because of the flu bug. Pete left early for a dental appointment and his phone is off. Lizzie's on annual leave as of this afternoon and is probably at the airport by now. And we still have to finish the remainder of the Farquhar's order for tomorrow afternoon." Liam had earned his position at the salon through finely honed talent and years of hard work—and because he was routinely unflappable. Right now, he was flapping. "There's no way we're going to finish this on time. It's intricate work, and we don't have enough hands."

As Liam added each dire pronouncement to the situation, Sylvie had put down her armload of drinks and extracted Dominic's car keys from his pocket. Taking the slices of cheesecake from him, she beeped the lock on the car and put the boxes and trays on the back seat, coming back to touch his arm.

And in a moment of stress and bone-deep tiredness, on a freezing-cold street outside the tackiest establishment in London, he realized that for the first time, his instinct when things went wrong really *was* to reach out, metaphorically and physically. After years in sole charge of every aspect of his life, of feeling the honor and the weight of so many livelihoods standing on his shoulders, he put out his hand and Sylvie took it in hers without the slightest hesitation.

There was nothing wrong with a solitary life. In fact, even if you didn't intrinsically *want* a solitary life, there were still times when it was fucking bliss to spend long hours in your own company. Essential. Bonus points if the cat was upstairs in his own room. However, the feeling of absolute faith that when the cracks started to appear, someone else would be crouching at your side, helping to bail out the water, and that you could do the same for them—

Pretty indescribable.

He rubbed warmth back into her chilled fingers. "Start the mixing," he said crisply to Liam. "We'll be there in fifteen."

"'We'?"

The surprised query was cut short as Dominic swiped his thumb, ending the call. He looked down into her questioning face. "Sylvie," he said. "I need help."

She looked back silently.

And her fingers moved to interlock with his.

De Vere's
And, temporarily, quite a lot of Sugar Fair.

"Duck," Sylvie sang out, swinging a tray of chocolates out of the way as Dominic's sous-chef Liam slipped past her holding a huge bowl of Vienna buttercream.

"A word from you that sends shivers down my spine." Dominic was transferring the final cake layer onto the racks to cool. The moment it was secure, he turned back to the conveyor belt of chocolates, picking up a mold. As Sylvie took three seconds to roll out her shoulders and neck, she watched him hand-painting the multitude of tiny dots that would form the crisp surface of De Vere's Pointillist Caramels. Several of his team had already completed trays of these and done so adeptly, but as soon as the brush was in Dominic's hand, it was as if the universe had a hit a fast-forward button. He was working so quickly she couldn't even catch the individual techniques.

Now that the more irritating parts of his personality were dramatically losing the battle against his reluctant and increasingly overwhelming good side, she could appreciate his skill without prejudice.

However, they were on the clock here. This was not the time for musings as to whether her more sensitive patches of skin would tolerate chocolate paint.

"Last time, it preceded a fairly dramatic explosion," he murmured, setting his brushes in their stand and pouring molten chocolate into the mold. He tipped and rolled the mold, coating each casing in a thin layer of chocolate.

"Well, fortunately this is one of your cakes." Sylvie eased around another of his team with a polite "Excuse me" and set a large pot of sugar syrup on the stove. "And the only soulless robotics involved with a De Vere's commission"—she clicked on the gas and turned to smile blandly at him—"are the clientele."

At the cupcake station, a grinning Liam made a hissing sound between his teeth. "Bit unfair," he said over his shoulder.

"Farquhar's?"

"All right. Fair."

Dominic joined her at the stove with another pot. The moment they stepped foot in a kitchen, regardless of whose name was above the door, they were both in their professional zone, concentrating on the task at hand. But as he turned to meet the teasing glint in her eyes, out of the others' sight and for the merest flicker of a moment, he angled his head as if he were going to whisper in her ear—her ultimate weakness. His lips touched the hollow beneath her earlobe. The tiniest butterfly nuzzle. He was gone and back to work before the last shiver had skittered down her spine.

The man didn't make a practice of spontaneous physical affection. Clearly, he was one of those people who excelled at literally every bloody thing they tried. If she weren't thoroughly enjoying the near-constant sensual annihilation, it would actually be quite annoying.

With a mostly steady hand, she stirred the sugar solution and adjusted the temperature, then joined Liam and the rest of the staffers spinning out cupcakes. Most of the team were Dominic's, but a number were her own people. The rivalry between the two bakeries extended right down the staff line, but every member of her team who'd been about to pack up this evening had taken up the offer of overtime. They'd dashed across the street to help, with no more than lighthearted jabs.

She wasn't in the least surprised. She and Jay hired for skill— and they hired for integrity.

Even Mabel had agreed to lend a hand and was currently using a lethal-looking syringe to shoot filling into chocolates. Naturally, she'd made a beeline for the sharp and pointy.

And frankly, the whole night would be worthwhile just for the first meeting between Mabel and Dominic.

Her assistant had marched her diminutive self into the kitchen as if she owned it, cast a disparaging look around, criticized his choice of lamps, and skewered him with a comprehensive stare. "I'm Mabel," she'd said. "Those of my choosing call me Mabs." Another pointed sweep up and down his body before she reached her verdict. "You can call me Mabel."

Sylvie hadn't missed the immediate acquisitive gleam in Dominic's eyes. She saw it again now as Mabel finished a row of chocolates almost as quickly as Dominic himself.

When he walked past the cupcake station, she caught hold of his belt and leaned close. "If you try to headhunt my Mabel," she said, incredibly silkily, "the next balls floating in my cocktails? Will not be made of sugar."

He raised a brow. "I'll pay her more."

"She's very well paid and will shortly be getting a large Christmas bonus. You can try to coax her away." She smiled at him. "She'll never come. She loves me."

They both looked over Mabel, who was—with an air of *extreme* martyrdom—helping Dominic's apprentice Aaron to correct his technique. The poor guy still looked on the edge of tears over his error with the order.

"Or she doesn't trust me to run the business successfully without her supervision," Sylvie said. "Either way—the terrifying misanthrope is mine."

Liam edged past them with another rack of cupcakes. "Oh?" His face was alive with devilry, his dark skin creasing into lines of amusement around the light in his eyes. With a pointed chin jerk toward Dominic and very precise enunciation, he asked, "Which one?"

"The strawberries are infusing in cherry brandy." It was the return of Dominic's most hard-nosed judging voice. Liam's grin widened. "Pulse them with the icing. We don't want it completely smooth."

"That's fortunate." His sous-chef got out a last shot before Aaron tentatively called out to Dominic. "From all I've seen so far—it won't be."

Dominic's look was sharp with warning; when it briefly moved to Sylvie, it became a lot more complex.

She watched him walk over and bend to help Aaron. But not before he rested a light hand on his miserable employee's shoulder.

"He's a really good boss."

Sylvie turned. All vestiges of shit-stirring were gone from Liam's expression. Very seriously, he repeated, "He's a great boss."

"I can see that."

Dominic's staff viewed him with obvious awe, with a clear desire to meet his very high expectations—but with zero intimidation.

With the exception of one irreverent sous-chef, the atmosphere was more formal than Sugar Fair, but in its way, similarly supportive.

"He doesn't suffer fools," Liam said. "But when it comes to mistakes, it's nowhere near one-and-you're-done." A renewed spark of amusement. "Possible exception for incendiary unicorns." He jerked his head toward the busy stations. "There's not a person in this building who isn't exponentially better at their job now than before they stepped through that door."

There was nothing of the casual, throwaway comment about that information.

He looked at her squarely. "I'm not just his employee. I'm his friend. And it might seem like there's never been a man less in need of protection—but I'm a pretty protective sort of guy."

Sylvie didn't drop her gaze. She didn't even blink. "Noted."

A short silence. "You're pretty badass with a piping bag your-self."

"That is what they write on the bathroom walls," she agreed solemnly, and took the cupcake that he proffered with a great ceremony.

At one in the morning, while the rain hit against the roof in steady sheets, Sylvie piped another intricate line of curlicues around the bottom tier of the cake. She switched off the bag to Dominic, who completed a delicate ribbon of sugar lace while she used tweezers to set a cascading river of pearls in place.

"Even?" He made a minute adjustment to the lace.

She scanned the effect. "Slightly more on top."

They switched places, swapping tools again, and Sylvie stepped up on a low stool to reach the utmost tier. She started piping. "Tell me when."

"Yeah. That's good." Dominic's eyes narrowed as he scruti-nized the cake in all its crisp, white, beautiful dullness. Without looking away from the pearl drapery, he reached up a hand and balanced her as she hopped down. "Well?"

She took a few steps back, joining the few remaining mem-bers of their staff. Most had left with the completion of the cupcakes and chocolates, Mabel so quickly that Sylvie had literally blinked and she'd gone, winking out like *I Dream of Jeannie*.

"You know those DIY craft kits for kids, where they supply the blank ceramic base and it's just screaming out for the paint and glitter?" She relented when he cast his eyes ceiling-ward. "It's lovely. Elegant, chic, and perfect for the brief. And inspir-ingly executed. If I had my *Operation Cake* crown coin, I'd award you the thousand quid."

He addressed her with typically crisp brevity. "Your ingenuity was never in question. But your technical ability now—"

"Is neck and neck with yours." Sylvie lacked confidence in several areas of her life; this wasn't one of them.

When the moment between them drew out a little too long, Liam cleared his throat loudly. "And *now* I'm clocking out and toddling home to my lonely bed." He stuck out his hand to Sylvie; she took it. "Without the neighborly assistance, we'd still be racing against the clock at dawn—and I doubt we'd have made it."

"We wouldn't have." Dominic nodded at the assembled members of her team. "Thank you very much."

Sylvie saw several pleased flushes.

When the door closed behind them, she leaned back against a countertop, a flicker of restlessness igniting low in her belly.

Dominic was securing the order away. He picked up one of the cupcakes she'd decorated, holding it under the light and turning it to see a telltale iridescent shimmer. "Glitter is contraband in these premises."

"There's nothing wrong with a little sparkle."

That dark intent gaze switched to her face. "On a cake? Yes, there is. In other areas—maybe not." He set the cupcake in the box with the rest. "No sign of your business partner tonight."

"Jay had a family commitment. I texted and let him know I was offering some unscheduled overtime for the team. And where."

"And what did he say to that?"

She felt a bit uncomfortable, and she wasn't sure why. One of her shoulders lifted in a half shrug. "Not much. He thought there might have been an insurance issue. Having the staff working in someone else's business."

"Did he." She couldn't read Dominic's voice at all.

There were a few spare scraps of fondant on the countertop. Turning abruptly, she collected them, squeezing and rolling until the strange tension in her muscles eased. As her fingers moved quickly and she reached for a paintbrush, Dominic shut and locked the fridge.

She sensed his body heat before he said over her shoulder, "What are you doing?"

Keeping her wee project concealed in the palm of her hand, she flickered her brush. Changed to a different color.

"Sylvie—"

"Just a second." A third brush, the addition of a few spiky eyelashes, and she turned to extend her palm. Her fingers opened. "You're welcome," she said graciously.

Dominic looked down at the miniature fondant version of the possessed Betty Boop clown. He was totally expressionless.

With the end of the smallest paintbrush, Sylvie poked the side of the leering mouth, tugged it upward into an even more disturbing grin.

Dominic's lips pressed together.

She stroked little BB's head with her pinkie finger.

His chest started to shake.

Carefully setting the ridiculous fondant clown on the counter, Sylvie reached up, slipped her arms around his neck, and brought his smile down to hers.

There wasn't a scrap of hesitancy this time, no gentle exploration and circling each other. One moment of awkwardness when their noses bumped, before his hands came up to hold her head and they were kissing—long, deep, hungry kisses.

Her hand stroked his neck, sliding over his chest, and she murmured when he tore his lips from hers long enough to drag a jagged breath and kiss her cheekbone, her jaw, her Cupid's bow.

Her lashes fluttered as their mouths were drawn irresistibly back together.

His heart was thumping under her hand as they moved together. Sylvie traced a light pattern over his shirt with her fingertips. Breathing deeply, she whispered, "You don't taste the way you smell."

Dominic shifted, his own fingers trailing down her neck, skimming a tantalizing path over her breast that made her legs shake. "I'm not sure how to respond to that." His voice was deep. Husky.

"The sugar scents cling to your hair and the fibers of your clothes." She moved her head, gently nuzzling into the silvering hair at his temple. "I thought you might taste like cake twenty-four seven."

Less husky. "I do brush my teeth."

"I know. Minty fresh. Delicious," she assured him. "I'm just saying, I like cake. It would have been nice."

He shook his head.

She kissed the satiny skin under his ear, and with a sudden movement, he lifted her onto the edge of the counter, parting her legs with his knee. His big hand gripped her hip, pulling her into him. She kissed him, or he kissed her; it was urgent, heated, all shivery sensation, and she didn't realize she'd hit the point of literally ripping his clothes off until her fingertips were startled by sudden contact with an unfamiliar nipple.

She froze with her hand trapped under the remaining buttons of his shirt. The taut skin over his shoulder joint was hot and smooth; his chest was roughened with hair. It rose and fell quickly beneath her touch. His teeth lightly scraped her neck as his fingers went to her own buttons. "Wait."

Dominic's whole body stilled. When he lifted his head, his face was dark and taut with desire—but concern was edging in.

She wrapped her fingers around his forearms, holding him. "We can't."

His eyes closed for a second. He breathed in deeply. Twice. "Okay."

He was still touching her, but she could feel him retreating.

"I'm sorry, but . . ." She bit her lip, and his expression changed. One brow started to lift. Her sigh was an art form of resignation and regret. "No matter how stringent your cleaning regime, it would be *very* unhygienic."

She was up and off the counter in seconds, grabbing her purse and bolting for the back hallways. She made it to his office before he tackled her, catching her laughter in his mouth as they stumbled through the door.

With his hand tangled in her hair, he kissed her hard as he kicked it closed behind him.

"You're a bloody menace," he said against her lips.

"You can't say you weren't adequately warned."

He groaned suddenly. "I don't have any protection here."

She waved her purse before she threw it down to start unbuttoning her shirt. "I do."

She yanked open his belt, and they kept walking back until they collided with the couch.

Outside of vampire novels, Sylvie had never understood the inclination to involve too many teeth in lovemaking, but the curve above Dominic's collarbone was so inviting that she had the distinct urge to nibble.

Or just curl up and hang off him like a bat.

As he unclipped the front clasp of her bra and pressed a kiss to the damp skin between her breasts, she asked, "Are we going slightly down or all the way down?"

He stopped kissing. Raised his head. "The latter was the

plan," he said drily. "But I'm happy to take direction if you have preferences otherwise."

She was standing in Dominic De Vere's office with her boobs out, he had just expressed an intention to put his mouth between her legs, and she was fully going to laugh out loud. "I meant, couch or floor?"

His forehead dropped against her chest. "This is going well."

As she laid her hands on his silky hair, any inclination to giggle slipped away.

There was a lovely fluffy white rug on the floor in front of the couch. Slowly, Sylvie lowered to kneel on the ground, tugging on his hands to pull him down with her. Their fingers twisted together. "It is," she said softly. "Going well."

An emotion she couldn't quite read flashed through Dominic's eyes. And then they were kissing again, and he was pulling away her dangling shirt and bra, tossing them aside. They kicked away the rest of their clothes, and he stretched out at her side, looking at her. The dimly lit office was nicely warm, but Sylvie could feel goose bumps rising on her skin.

She both really wanted to do this and had never felt more self-conscious in her life.

When his fingertips brushed her temple, smoothing back a fallen strand of hair, her shiver was more violent than it should have been.

"Sylvie."

She finally raised her gaze higher than the scattering of hair and freckles on his bare chest—and saw, in that cool, experienced, always imperturbable face, a reflection of everything she was struggling with.

At sea with the intensity of feeling. The uncertainty of the new. The fear of not being enough.

Her eyes closed when their faces touched. For a moment, they just breathed, Dominic's fingertips tracing a small, soothing circle on Sylvie's upper arm.

When their lips met, it was so perfectly natural—and her heart started to beat harder. She stroked his chest and felt him shudder, made a small sound in her throat when he cupped her breast.

His mouth closed over her nipple, and she drew in a sharp breath, arching a little as her fingers wove through his thick hair.

His lips returned to hers, their breath mingling, tongues tangling as the intensity deepened. She was already wet by the time his hand slid up the sensitive skin of her inner thigh, stroked inside her.

His groan shuddered from deep in his chest as she closed her fingers around his erection, teasing the length, flirting with the head, before she increased the pressure, gave him the friction he needed.

For long minutes, his muscles were stretched taut, his fists closing, and his legs moving a little restlessly. Abruptly, he loosened her grip and kissed her fingers. It was her turn to tense up as his lips left a burning trail down her abdomen, nuzzling over the stretch marks on her hips, pausing to nip her belly button. His hair tickled her skin and Sylvie squirmed.

She felt a renewed spike of self-consciousness when he parted her legs, but it disappeared into incredibly intense pleasure when his tongue fluttered around her clit. Her breath coming so quickly she was starting to feel light-headed, Sylvie dug her fingers into the rug at her sides, clutching fistfuls of softness when he started to suck.

Two aspects of Dominic's personality had always been very clear: determination and completionism.

And holy shit, was she reaping the benefits.

She was snapping back, just about bowing in half as she came for the second time, when he at last sat up, breathing hard.

He crouched between her legs, the muscles bulging in his thighs, a thin film of sweat over his chest, as she stared, her arm draped bonelessly over her forehead.

"Okay." Her voice was a broken mess. "Just give me a second. The condoms are in the zipped pocket."

While he found one and suited up, she inhaled. Exhaled. Repeated, until her lungs no longer felt like collapsing bagpipes.

"Right." Swiftly, she sat up and went straight into his waiting arms, onto his lap. And onto his cock. She hadn't actually intended that movement to be quite so fluid.

They both grunted; there was no other word for it. Dominic swore under his breath, his hands tightening on her. Lengthwise, he was perfectly, beautifully average in size, but he was *thick*, hard and pulsing, and almost uncomfortably full inside her.

"That was . . . impressive." He sounded a little strangled.

"That was the single most athletic achievement of my life." Sylvie couldn't help wriggling. At the slightest movement, her nerve endings exploded happily, and Dominic groaned again. "Four years on the school netball team and I never shot a single goal."

She gripped his shoulders as his hands went to her hips, pulling her into him as his hips gave an involuntary first thrust. "Score," she murmured, shakily teasing against his lips, and his half laugh was cut off as the kiss immediately deepened.

If her life and business depended on it, she couldn't have said how much time passed as they moved together. His mouth was on her neck, his hands stroking up her waist, cupping her breasts as his thrusts grew harder, faster. She wrapped her arms around his head.

When they stared into each other's eyes, it was so intense, so intimate—too intimate. She had to look away, burying her head in his shoulder as he lifted her, lowering her to her back. His weight was heavy on her as he pulled one of her thighs around his hips, and she felt the beads of sweat rolling down the backs of her knees. She was caught between sensation and awareness and the sudden shockingness of clarity that this was *Dominic* moving inside her, bringing her more pleasure than she'd ever had—and that was a judgment formed with the authority of an entire catalogue of toys. It shook her enough that she tensed up at the end, and the building third orgasm slipped out of her grasp.

When he came, his face against her neck, she cupped his head and breathed in the scent of his skin. She couldn't stop shivering, and his arms tightened around her.

His hand slipped down her belly when he regained his brain cells and motor skills, but she caught his fingers, gave them a little squeeze as she shook her head. "Too sensitive. And too exhausted." She turned her head, smiling into his eyes. His irises were very, very dark. "And trust me, I did good."

His mouth tipped up. "I'll say."

They were stroking each other's skin, apparently mutually unable to stop. Dominic tugged her into his chest and they just lay there for some time, sprawled half-dead on the rug.

But a growing, nagging feeling was becoming impossible to ignore. At last, she had to say it. "Dominic."

A slight rustle as his head turned on the rug. His fingers played with hers. "Hmm?"

"I'm starving."

He pushed up on one elbow and looked down at her. That expression in his eyes was back, the one she couldn't quite get a read on. She was distracted from her speculation, however, when he opened his mouth and uttered the sexiest words a man had ever spouted in the history of orgasms. "We have cheese-cake in the fridge."

"I was already ranking you a solid nine and a half, De Vere, but that's straight up to ten."

"It *is* Midnight Elixir cheesecake."

"And we're back down to nine and a half."

Chapter Thirteen

The Flat of Humphrey the Cat
(Some big, grouchy dude also sleeps here. No idea who he is, but at least he knows how to work the can opener.)

They took the cheesecake back to Dominic's flat for what remained of the night. When he unlocked the door and held it open, Sylvie slipped past him with a small, very private smile. Her cheeks were flushed. He'd wondered if stiffness would creep back into his reactions, that instinctual need to withdraw and recalibrate.

Yet his body and his mind were at ease. Relaxed.

Cautiously, tentatively . . . happy.

Endorphins played havoc on the brain, but that wasn't why he was constantly drawn close, why he reached out and cupped her cheek, rubbing his thumb over the heated skin.

And he didn't think it was why her fingers closed over his wrist, holding him.

"We had sex," she said, that smile deepening in her eyes.

"Yes, we did."

"*We* had sex." Sylvie moved her head, the slight shake of a person adjusting to a game changer. "And it was really good."

His mouth curved. "Yes, it was."

She released his wrist to take a gentle hold of his shirt, pulling him toward her. When her soft lips brushed his, a renewed skittering of arousal clenched his abdomen.

Sylvie's hand brushed down his chest as she turned, looking around his lounge with avid interest. She had been making a quiet humming sound. It stopped. Her gaze moved over the exposed beams, the open fireplace, the built-in bookcases, the piano, brick walls and spiral staircase. Her fingers rose to cover her mouth. "Oh my God," she said behind her hand.

He put the boxes of cheesecake on the table and went to turn on the kettle. The kitchen was attached and open plan. The previous occupant of the flat had modernized it, but installed electrics that mimicked the appearance of antiques.

He'd put in an offer on this place within an hour of the first viewing.

"Weep." Sylvie dropped her handbag on the couch. "I was feeling all smug because my bakery is so much cooler than yours, and then you pull out my dream house. I currently live in a concrete box with an authoritarian rental agreement, and you have a living room straight out of the posh, antique-y villages in *Midsomer Murders*."

"Hopefully with a lower body count." Dominic heard a telltale thudding on the stairs. "Although at the first opportunity, Humphrey would like to begin that tally."

Sylvie swung around as the enormous cat thumped onto the last step. With an audible groan, Humphrey rolled sideways to the floor. As evidenced by the noise he made every time he went up and down the stairs, he had perfectly adequate paws, so why he couldn't just walk down the remaining step instead of collapsing like a Victorian heroine on her fainting couch remained a mystery.

"Oh." Sylvie started forward with totally misplaced concern. "Dom, I think your cat's sick."

That shortened version of his name slipped out again. Even as a kid, nobody had ever called him Dom. Evidently, his demeanor didn't encourage a friendly nickname. Like more and more things right now, it was unique to Sylvie.

He liked it.

He took down two mugs. "Just give him a minute."

As she ignored him and went to crouch by Humphrey's side, the tabby menace flipped over, with admittedly impressive agility for his age and stature, and stared beadily up at her.

Dominic could already see she was about to repeat Pet's error of judgment on meeting his cat. And as he hadn't managed to intercept his sister's urge to grab and cuddle, the scratch down her arm had been inflamed for a week.

Pet had since nicknamed his pet Humphrey "Boggart." In normal circumstances, he might protest at a member of his household being compared to a malevolent spirit. In this case, it was not only accurate but bordering on generous. Pet sarcastically inquired after Boggart's welfare on a semiregular basis. *Maimed anyone else lately?*

"Don't pat him," he warned sharply, moving quickly around the kitchen bench as Sylvie made an incomprehensible enamored sound and stretched out her hand. "He doesn't like people and he scratches—"

The moment Sylvie's fingers touched his cranky, diminutive head, Humphrey hunched his body, drew himself up—and collapsed into a boneless puddle. He expanded across the rug like dough spilling out of a bowl. A noise like a rusty hacksaw undulated through the room.

He was purring.

The little shit hadn't even purred for Sebastian.

"Oh, you're so sweet," Sylvie said, getting right down on the floor to scritch under Humphrey's chin. The cat batted against her hand. Affectionately. What—and Dominic could not overstate this—the fuck? She looked up. "*This* is your terrifying satanic cat?"

Humphrey peered up from beneath her rubs and strokes. And smirked.

"You are the feline Iago," Dominic said flatly.

"Don't listen to him." Sylvie pretended to cover the flicking ears. "You're so handsome."

Rolling his eyes, he returned to the kitchen to pour the tea. Sylvie still had her heart set on cheesecake, but he couldn't face anise-flavored cream cheese at two o'clock in the morning. Regardless of the time crunch to confirm the Midnight Elixir recipe, he stuck a piece of bread in the toaster.

When he took a slice of cheesecake and a fork into the living room, she was curled up on the couch with Humphrey draped over her chest, his purrs rattling louder with every stroke down his back. "Food." He passed her the plate and she took it with murmured thanks. "Feel free to have the cat, as well. Permanently."

"Dominic." Sylvie cupped her hand around Humphrey's neck. "Is that any way to talk about your son?"

He supposed he should be honored that when he returned with the tea and his toast, she nudged the annoyed cat onto a cushion so she could curl up against him instead. She did so with apparently instinctual ease, resting her head on his shoulder, and he breathed in deeply as he slowly lifted his hand to sift his fingers through her hair.

Her hairline was still a bit damp. He could smell the remnants of her perfume. Lightly, he ran his fingertips over her temple.

In his peripheral vision, Humphrey's paw stretched toward his plate. He wouldn't eat the toast—although he'd lick the butter just to be a dick—but it was one of his favorite pastimes, knocking other people's life sustenance to the floor.

"Don't even think about it." Dominic moved the plate out of reach.

The cat's response was to turn around and stick his backside out.

"With every passing day," he mused, "I become more of a dog person."

"You're too busy for a dog." Sylvie forked a bit of cheesecake into her mouth. "A temperamental, pessimistic cat is your ideal pet. Don't be so ungrateful. It sounds like your grandfather knew you to a tee."

With a faint huff of a laugh, he tilted his head tiredly back against the couch. Between an already long day, the unexpected order, and a fairly mind-shattering orgasm, he could easily drop off right here. "How's the cheesecake?"

"Gross." Sylvie was clearly not devastated on Darren Clyde's behalf. "There's a horrible aftertaste that's not present in the drink. But . . ." She put a bit more on the tip of her tongue, considering. She swallowed. Twisted in his arms to face him. "Pomegranate. The missing ingredient is pomegranate."

He tipped his head in acknowledgment, and she turned to burrow more comfortably, looking highly satisfied.

The rain was hitting the windows and increasing drowsiness crept over them.

"Raspberry syrup," Sylvie said softly, and he opened his eyes. "What?"

"A tablespoon of raspberry syrup for every cup of Sorceress emulsion."

The ingredient he'd missed.

He looked down at the top of her head, where strands of pink and purple caught the light overhead. "Thank you."

"Mmm." She finished the rest of her cheesecake and pushed the plate away. Humphrey crept forward and extended his tongue. And was so offended by what it encountered that he leapt off the couch and stalked back toward the stairs. Darren Clyde proved useful in at least one instance, then. "Dominic?"

"Mmm?"

"I'm worried this wedding isn't going to happen."

They were both currently investing hours of work every day into crafting cake proposals for this wedding. They were both exhausted. And both of their businesses could receive a huge financial boost from a successful contract.

But it wasn't even a question where Sylvie's main concern was directed. Not at a potential lost contract, but at the welfare of two people whom they both liked a great deal.

He stroked the side of his thumb over her cheekbone. "Is Rosie getting cold feet?"

There had been obvious underlying tension in the princess's body language today—or rather, yesterday; it seemed like eons ago now. Ditto Johnny, when it came to that. And Sylvie had been in private consultation with Rosie for a long time.

In the car, while Pet put on her headphones to continue the audiobook she'd *also* started debriefing for him, Sylvie had told him in a low voice what Rosie had said about Jessica Maple-Moore. Dominic had always thought Johnny was walking an unenviable path, purposefully eschewing all privacy and a great deal of autonomy, forever. Once the marriage license was signed, there was no exit clause. He'd always be connected to the royals, a public figure, fair game in the eyes of the tabloids. And even his reason for it all—their relationship—would never be entirely theirs alone. So Jessica's ultimate decision that she had to walk away was entirely understandable. In her shoes, he'd probably—

Sylvie's breath was lightly fanning the hollow of his neck. He looked down at where she lay with her cheek against his shoulder. Her long lashes were lowered as she watched her fingers playing with his shirt buttons. Her nails were painted midnight blue, and she'd painted a dozen tiny silver stars on her thumbnails; she'd told him that she'd have liked to stick on actual crystals, but even with glove use, she didn't want to risk them falling into a batter. She'd sweated off most of her makeup making love with him, during a night he hoped he'd still remember as a very old man, and the thin blue veins standing out on her temples had an appearance of vulnerability that made his arm tighten.

Would he? Would he walk away if he were in Jessica's position or Johnny's position? If, hypothetically, he'd held someone in his arms who could become the center of his life, if he suddenly had that knowledge deep inside, if he'd felt their heart beating close to his, and to be with them would involve that level of sacrifice—would it be too much?

"Not cold feet in the usual sense," Sylvie said. He'd pulled a blanket around her as the air turned chillier with the advancing night, and she was plaiting the fringe. That knee-jerk stress tic that he'd always found reluctantly endearing; even four years ago, he remembered he'd found it oddly relaxing to watch Sylvie at her station, nervously plaiting offcuts of dough as she waited for her turn in the judging. "She's . . . I don't think it's an exaggeration to say 'tormented' over what even this engagement is doing to Johnny's life. And clearly Patrick was such an influence over her own life that the precedent with Jessica is looming large. I feel like at this point it's fifty-fifty what happens next, whether she'll fight to have a life with Johnny. Or whether she'll act so he can have a life without everything that surrounds her."

Her arm suddenly slipped around his ribs, holding him tightly, and he ran his fingers down her forearm, again that instinct to comfort overriding all else.

He thought of Johnny standing stammering in the Captain's Suite at that first meeting, his obvious misery at dealing with his future mother-in-law, the bullying demeanor of Edward Lancier. In retrospect, he couldn't even use the Father Christmas epithet; there was something so genuinely unpleasant about the man, it was totally inapt.

And he thought of the expression in Johnny's eyes every time he looked at Rosie.

"He doesn't want a life without her," he said. "I don't have a fucking clue why he looked so shifty yesterday, but he's going into this with his eyes open. And beneath the bumbling puppy exterior, that man has a heart of gold and, I suspect, a core of iron. If Rosie won't fight for their relationship, I'd lay a bet he will, like hell."

Sylvie kept her head lowered for some time. And then she looked up at him, searching his eyes, and smiled faintly. "Four years ago, if someone had told me that one day I'd never find greater comfort than in the sound of your voice and the scratch of your stubble, I'd have questioned their sanity."

So lightly, so easily, she could say things that he'd never forget.

She had finished plaiting an entire section of blanket. He flipped the end around so she had more to do.

"Ultimately, we can't control what anyone does," he said at last. "All we can do is keep working on the proposals. Keep looking for a key to unlock the Patrick design. One thing at a time. One *day* at a time."

Her fingers had stilled when he moved the blanket for her. Usually, Sylvie's expression was very open. She seemed to live life in its entirety that way, appreciating and inviting in experiences. But occasionally, that enigmatic shadow slipped into her eyes. "Yes," she said. "One day at a time."

With her hands wrapped in the blanket, she reached up and kissed him.

"As much as I love your lounge and was hoping you might play the piano," she whispered when their lips parted, "I think I'm ready for bed."

The shadows had slipped into pure desire.

And his body was at least ten years too old to react this swiftly.

Pushing off the couch, he swept her up into his arms and carried her toward the door. She was still clutching the blanket. "Over three decades and it's finally happened," she said, sounding totally thrilled. "I'm going to be carried upstairs and ravished."

He walked past the spiral staircase.

"Why aren't we going upstairs?"

"Because my bedroom is this way." He nudged the door open and walked down the short hallway.

"Oh." She kicked her feet, making it difficult to keep a firm grip on her. "What's upstairs, then?"

"Humphrey's room." Balancing her weight, he managed to get his bedroom door open.

When he laid her on his bed and saw her face, her lips had tucked in between her teeth.

She cleared her throat. "The cat has a bedroom?" There was a quiver in her voice.

His brows drew together. "Yes."

She levered off one of her boots and toed the other free. Her head was ducked low while she gave the task more attention than it needed. Dominic watched narrowly as her breath caught in a suspicious hitch.

He opened the drawer in his bedside table, found the box of condoms, and tossed it onto the bed. At her continued silence, he found himself saying in his own humiliatingly heated defense, "It's a cramped, poky little box with a window better suited for a prison. It's too small for an office."

Sylvie had already stripped off to her underwear. She came up on her knees and started unbuttoning his shirt. "You gave your despised cat his own bedroom. Despite everything, this day is great."

She shoved his shirt the rest of the way off, took his face between her hands, and pulled him down on top of her.

They landed and rolled, Sylvie straddling his hips. The laughter in her face softened as she stroked patterns over his stomach, making him go rigid in reaction.

Everywhere.

"Dominic." She flattened her palms over his ribs, holding him. Bending, she touched her nose to his. "I'm starting to suspect you might be kind of okay."

Their lips touched.

"Deep, deep down," she murmured.

They were so mutually exhausted that he'd expected the sex

to be a slow, lazy build of pleasure, but the moment he held himself still for her and she slid down on him, her internal muscles a wet, hot fist around his erection, the intensity spiked.

She leaned forward to grip the headboard as she rode him, her eyes closed. He held her hips, rubbing her against his pelvic bone with every thrust. Through the prickling ecstasy in every nerve ending, he watched her lashes flutter, her chest flushing red as her breaths quickened.

Slipping his thumb between their bodies, he touched her lightly, gradually increasing the rolling pressure to follow the cues of her body and the sounds she made.

"*Dom.*"

Sylvie orgasming was, without question, the sexiest thing he'd ever seen. She shuddered, her thighs spasming to clasp him tightly, her hands scrabbling for his.

He linked their fingers as she rocked back and forth, unable to stop pushing against him.

When she had her breath back, she finished him in her mouth, her fist tight around his length as her tongue lapped and tickled under the head, drew him in, sucked hard, and brought him to such an intense release that his knee jerked up and his vision whited out.

It was after three by the time they pulled the covers up and she cuddled close under the curve of his arm. She lay with her lips against his skin, her fingers idly playing about his nipple, tickling down to his navel. He had now officially pushed his body beyond the ability to rouse sexually, but her touch still provoked a tingling, drowsy pleasure. She fell asleep almost immediately, her weight against him lax and warm and trusting, and—no.

If he were in Jessica's shoes, he would never have walked away.

An Unfortunately Short Time Later
Still in the flat of Humphrey the Cat.
More specifically, the en suite of Dominic the Human.
Who's really kind of okay.
Deep, deep down.
Many regrets about vomiting in his loo, though.

On balance, it was still a great day. She'd worked herself into exhaustion and she was deeply worried about the royal couple. She would also be disappointed if the cake contract became redundant; she was only human. On the flip side, she'd collaborated with Dominic professionally, which had turned out to be almost as enjoyable as competing against him, and she'd shagged him into exhaustion. Definitely more ticks on the plus side.

However, the current situation was admittedly a low point.

Taking deep, gulping breaths, Sylvie turned to sit against the vanity, resting her sweaty forehead against her knees. Nausea was hot, roiling distress in her stomach, rising up her throat. She swallowed repeatedly.

She'd had about ninety blissful minutes sleeping in Dominic's arms, clutching his pec like a teddy bear, before she'd become ill. From dreamless, comfy oblivion to throwing up in his en suite, all in the space of sixty horrifying seconds.

Her mortification was complete when a hand came to rest on her hair, stroking her gently, but even now, she was shocked by how much comfort his touch could give her.

Her eyes wet, she turned to press her face against his chest with a little sound of misery, and felt his palm tighten on her head.

"When did you start feeling rubbish?" His voice was low and soothing, and her eyes prickled.

Through clenched teeth, she managed, "I felt fine when I went to sleep and then . . ." No. Wasn't going to be able to finish that sentence.

Her stomach had clearly been biding its time since the assault of Byron's scone and was now exacting its revenge. As she put her hand over her mouth and surged upward again, Dominic tucked her unraveling plait out of the way and held her.

The next half hour was a blur. She was making the executive decision to strip all thirty minutes from her memory. They had never happened.

After the experience of which she had zero recollection and definitely wouldn't still be cringing over in her aged care home, her grand plans for the rest of the night involved curling in a ball and awaiting the arrival of the Reaper. When Dominic picked her up in his arms and carried her back to bed, it wasn't *quite* as sexy as the first time he'd swept her off to his room.

Yet, for every kiss earlier tonight, every thrust of his body, every time her neck had arched and her lips had parted, somehow as she crawled beneath the sheets and he lay beside her—*this* was the most intimate and significant moment she'd ever had in bed. As he tucked the blanket around her shoulders, touched his lips to her temple, and held her hand.

She couldn't think of a single man from her past that she would want anywhere near her when she was sick. And if she had the energy to move her limbs, she'd probably wind them around Dominic like an octopus.

For the remaining dark hours of the night, he didn't leave her side. He murmured comfort in her ear, he held her up through the utter bliss of a shower and found her one of his shirts to wear. Finally, when her continuing misery left him repeatedly pacing, he wrapped her in a quilt and took her out to the lounge. Settling her on the couch with the most infinite care, he sat down at the piano and he played her favorite Bach for her.

As a pianist, he wasn't quite at the level of Patrick. But it was very close.

And as Sylvie lay drifting with her cheek against a cushion, the music wrapping around her, and tears slowly sliding over the bridge of her nose, she felt the tether on her heart start to fray, that guarded thread that had kept it in her own possession, lonely but secure. Protected. At no risk of shattering into infinite pieces like the little glass deer.

By half past six, her stomach felt raw and battered, but finally like the calm after the storm. Back in bed, she lay like a rag doll, barely able to lift her hand and scratch the itch on her nose.

When she vocalized that thought, Dominic, stretched out on the bed beside her again and looking equally tired, rubbed the tip of her nose with exaggerated care.

The backs of his fingers touched her forehead. He frowned. "You're not hot, at least. Still no sore throat? Headache?"

She shook her head. "No. Just the nausea."

"Some of my staff are out with the bug that's going around, but it doesn't sound like . . ." He broke off. "Just a minute." He slipped off the bed. "I'll be right back. Rest."

He touched her curled hand as he strode out with enviable vigor.

While he was gone, the door creaked, and Sylvie heard the sashay of fur brushing past wood.

Seconds later, her second main man Humphrey came flying onto the bed in a blur of tabby bulk and immensely long whiskers. He marched triumphantly up and down her body a few times, kneading her through the covers.

"You look right at home for a cat I suspect is not allowed on this bed," she informed him, scratching his ears.

An assumption confirmed when Dominic came back in and exchanged looks of mutual loathing with his reluctant family member. The irascible furry son with the best feline real estate this side of Notting Hill.

"Since she's relaxed for the first time in hours," he said to Humphrey, "you can stay for exactly five minutes."

Humphrey flicked an insouciant tail.

Dominic held up the box in his hand. "The cheesecake with the 'horrible aftertaste.' Which also has a strange smell that doesn't belong to any of its myriad ingredients."

Sylvie put a protective hand over her poor stomach. "But we put it in the bakery fridge right away."

"I suspect it came complete with off taste and smell at point of purchase."

Unbelievable. "So he's given me food poisoning now."

"I wish I *had* punched the prick," Dominic said, coming to sit on the side of the bed again. Despite the cold dislike in his words, his hand was very gentle on her skin as he ran it down her upper arm.

Sylvie tucked her arm under her head. She was too exhausted to indulge her usual Darren wrath. Too exhausted even to argue when Dominic had told her he'd left a message with her staff that she wouldn't be in this morning. She closed her eyes. "He's bigger than you thought, remember."

Lips on her browbone.

"He could be the size of a fucking double-decker bus."

She drifted into her nap smiling.

It was her phone that woke her. Dominic must have set it to

silent, but the vibration disturbed Humphrey, who dug his claws into her arm. She opened her eyes with a jump, lifting her head. Her cheek felt hot and sticky, the room a bit too overheated. For a moment, she had no idea where she was.

Voices drifted through the open door. She recognized the cadence of Dominic speaking, and she was fairly sure the feminine response was Pet.

Her phone writhed more insistently, and she blinked away the remaining confusion, snatching it up. Jay's name was flashing.

"Jay?" She spoke huskily, crackling over the syllable, and coughed as she pushed up against the pillows.

"Syl? Are you okay?" His concern came through clearly. "Mabel took a message that you're out sick today, but she said you seemed fine last night when you had to pull De Vere's out of the shit. Very charitable of you, by the way," he added with a dry edge. "I believe her words were '*more* than fine.' Have you come down with something?"

"Just ate something that didn't agree with me." On a number of levels. "My body rejected it fairly gruesomely. I feel like a deflated balloon," she said frankly. "And as I'm supposed to shoot *Operation Cake* tonight and the producers would have my head on a platter if I have to pull out, I think I'd better take the rest of the day away from the bakery if you can cope."

Tonight was the always-feared night episode—also operating as the semifinal, thanks to Nadine's early departure and the rescheduling of the location shoot—in which the contestants had to prepare a five-course dessert banquet for a number of celebrity guests. Which this year included the footballer Chuck Finster. Name of a Rugrat, kick of a stallion, thighs of a god.

What a time to be alive and probably looking like something that had recently dragged its way out of a tomb.

And how fortunate that her mind and body appeared to have lost all interest in any other man. She was no longer dancing around it, as she sat here in his crumpled sheets, with her bed-hair sticking to her face and a vile taste in her mouth. She was absolutely mad about Dominic De Vere.

"Of course we can manage. You rest up. But are you sure you're up to working on the show tonight?"

She didn't even want to think about tasting baked goods right now. One bonus of the night episode, however—most of the eating was done by the guest panel. She could probably get away with a handful of minuscule bites for the camera.

The acid on her tongue was a sour burn.

"I signed a contract. I'll see it through."

"They're lucky to have you." The warmth of Jay's response made her smile faintly. "Okay. Go back to sleep. I'll talk to you later."

"Bye, Jay. Love you." She ended the call as Dominic came into the room, Pet following behind him with a bunch of gerbera daisies in her hands. The flowers were beautifully arranged and tied with a polka-dot ribbon.

When her eyes met Dominic's, the flip-flop in her stomach had nothing to do with dodgy cheesecake. She lowered her lashes for a second, feeling a rush of that ridiculous shyness that sometimes caught her off guard lately when he looked at her. When he'd been a total stranger, she'd gone toe-to-toe with him without a second thought. Now she knew him intimately—for God's sake, she'd sucked on the man's cock like a lollipop and was still blushing like a Regency deb.

"I heard your voice," he said, "so I thought it was safe to let your visitor in. Although foisting Pet *and* Humphrey on you—you've already got an upset stomach; you don't need a migraine."

"Oh, ha-ha," Pet said. She thrust the bunch of flowers at Sylvie. "I hope you're feeling better. You look awful," she added, with the blunt brutality of a soigné twentysomething.

"What an effusion of warmth and compassion. Florence Nightingale walks again." Dominic came over to the bed and, after the slightest pause, bent to kiss Sylvie's cheek. Very low, with just a tinge of roughness to cover his glaring discomfort, he murmured, "You always look beautiful."

Sylvie had to blink away yet another stupidly wet burn in her eyes.

Still with uncharacteristic awkwardness, he said something about tea and left her with Pet. The Road Runner had made slower exits from a room.

Self-consciously, she looked down at the flowers on her lap. She gently stroked a petal. "These are lovely. Thank you so much, Pet."

The side of the mattress compressed, and when she raised her head, Pet was smiling at her. It was a genuinely affectionate smile, but just slightly twisted.

"It's been pretty obvious since he kept that silhouette of you on his desk," Pet said. "Dorian Gray couldn't take better care of a portrait than Dominic. Someone tried to touch it with dirty hands last week and he reacted like a dragon guarding his hoard."

Sylvie couldn't help a small smile in return, but she said frankly, "It sounds like there's a looming 'but.' Is this the precursor to a warning from a protective sister?"

Pet snorted. "Please. Like Dominic needs me running interference for him." She played with the end of the bouquet ribbon. So inaudibly that Sylvie may not have been meant to hear, she muttered, "I still don't know that he needs me at all." She looked up. "It looks like he's taking good care of you. I know he cares a lot about his people in his own . . . brusque way, but to be honest, I didn't expect *him* to do such a good Nightingale impression. He almost *cuddled* you."

There was, again, an odd little edge to those words.

"Pet," Sylvie said, and hesitated. This felt beyond overstepping.

"You're partly responsible for scoring me an invite to a royal ball," Pet said. "Unless you leave my brother for a man who smiles more than once a month, we're buds for life, you and me. Go on."

"Dominic's told me just a little about when he was younger."

Pet's smile faded, and Sylvie selected her next words very carefully. "I know he finds it difficult sometimes to . . . to physically show he cares."

"And yet that doesn't seem to be an issue with you," Pet said, apparently before she could stop herself. She bit her lip.

Yeah—that was what Sylvie thought she'd seen in Pet's manner.

She grimaced, feeling as if she were walking on very fragile ice. She didn't want to break Dominic's confidence; nor did she want to put any pressure on Pet here, but—"Pet . . . If you went out there right now and gave him a hug, I honestly think it would make his whole fucking month."

Pet looked at her unblinkingly. And then she lifted one eyebrow, and again looked so like Dominic it was momentarily startling. "How to put this tactfully . . . You haven't been inhaling buckets of cold medicine or anything? He'd be legging it down the street before I'd finished raising my arms."

"No," Sylvie said. "He wouldn't."

Pet just shook her head.

Sylvie touched the slim, curled fingers. "He does need you in his life. Very badly, I think."

The other woman's face worked for a moment before she got herself under control, the frothy, flirty exterior slipping back into place.

They sat in silence.

And then Humphrey, who had been snoring against Sylvie's knee, bolted up and screamed.

Both she and Pet jumped violently.

The cat, totally unbothered at the close of his dramatic scene, plunked himself back down and went back to sleep.

Sylvie hadn't even known a cat could make that sound. Hyenas, maybe. The odd owl. Mabel, the time Jay had accidentally used her best brush to touch up a spot of paint in the staff bathroom.

"What the fuck was that?"

Pet had recovered from the fright and just looked annoyed. "She leaned on your tail for two seconds, Boggart," she said to Humphrey. "She didn't go after you with a chain saw. Jesus Christ."

Dominic came back into the room with a mug in each hand. "Who sat on Iago?"

"Me," Sylvie said, fighting a smile. She took the mug he offered. "And you're both awful."

"Slow sips," he warned. "Your stomach needs time to recover. And I don't think you should be going to the studio tonight."

"I'll be fine."

"Stubborn."

"Pot and kettle, De Vere."

Pet moved to sit cross-legged and pulled out her phone,

thumbing open an app. "I'm glad you're feeling a bit better, because I've got an email from Kathleen Maple-Moore, your Jessica's younger sister."

Sylvie paused with the tea mug halfway to her mouth, and Dominic turned his head sharply.

"Kathleen inherited Primrose Cottage after Jessica's death and must have changed its name," Pet went on, scrolling down her screen. "She runs amateur art classes from there now and hires out studio space." She lifted her head and smiled at them. "I've booked us in for a tour on Friday."

Humphrey's snores echoed through the room. It was like a cross between a wheezy donkey and a rusty seesaw. *Hee-haw. Hee-ho.*

It was Dominic who got over the blank surprise first. His eyes narrowed. "You had your headphones on in the car. You said you were listening to your book."

"I turned it off to eavesdrop," Pet said with absolutely no shame. "Everyone was being very furtive at that meeting. I was unacceptably confused."

Sylvie eyed the phone. Clearly, Dominic had told his sister nothing on this subject, and Pet hadn't seen the photographs Sylvie had taken at Abbey Hall—as far as she knew. Patent mistake to underestimate the sheer balls of Petunia De Vere. But she probably hadn't had access to the envelope with the Oxford address. "If the name of the property is different, how do you know it's Primrose Cottage?"

"And what do you mean, you booked 'us' in for a tour?" Dominic added pointedly.

"Maple-Moore is hardly a common name. And there are very few members of the family living in England. Most of them are still in Ireland, FYI. Jessica was born in County Clare. Once I found Kathleen's website, I ran the records of her property and found it was legally retitled twenty-six years ago. It took about ten minutes. I'm a very good PA," Pet said with a roll of her long-lashed eyes. "Incidentally, I'm currently *your* PA." A pointed aside to her brother. "And this concerns bakery business."

Complacently, she finished, "Also, Primrose Cottage is now Petunia Park. Which is even *more* twee, frankly, but I took it as cosmic confirmation that I ought to tag along."

Tucking his hands into his pockets, Dominic raised his eyes to the ceiling.

Sylvie couldn't help a giggle, which turned out to be a mistake. Her abused abdomen was not sufficiently recovered. She puffed out her cheeks at the twinge of residual nausea.

Pet studied her with alarm. And edged back a few inches. "Are you feeling poorly again? Did you say cheesecake was the culprit?" Yes, and she would thank everyone never to mention the word again. "Dominic said it came from the Starlight Circus. Whose owner, by the way, put up a trash post about De Vere's on Facebook this morning."

Sylvie stopped counting the rhythm of her deep breaths. She looked up. "He what?"

Pet was thumbing through her apps again. "Someone tagged me. Don't worry—he sounds like a moaning dickbag. Nobody will take it seriously. But you must have pissed him right off, big brother."

She turned the phone around and handed it to Sylvie.

Sylvie read the post with increasing fury. While skating around the edges of libel, Darren had insinuated a number of things about quality control at De Vere's—ragingly ironic from the man selling salmonella. He'd thrown around terms like "overrated" and "overpriced," and he'd called Dominic a "hulking thug who dominates the industry with all the integrity of a Corleone."

First of all—Dominic was not "hulking." He was broad-shouldered, huge-handed, and terribly elegant.

And secondly, *Oh, I think* not.

Ignoring the lingering weakness in her limbs, Sylvie calmly handed Pet back her phone and reached for her own. She started typing and soon found the number she was looking for.

Dominic had scanned the Facebook post with no interest at all. "Who are you calling?"

"The Food Standards Agency." She lifted the phone to her ear. "I think Darren is due a surprise inspection."

Chapter Fourteen

Hartwell Studios

The *Operation Cake* semifinal.

Will a single dish survive intact? Will any contestants make it to the final?

We're all undoubtedly on the edges of our seats.

Dominic knew Sylvie was still hoping for some epic romantic ending to the series, no doubt with Emma and Adam embracing beside their future wedding cake as the credits rolled. But unless the couple commenced a grand seduction scene in the next half hour, those hopes were sinking fast.

Emma's chance of making it to the final currently looked slim. She'd had a decent night initially, with relatively minor errors—a concave soufflé and a separated topping on her toasted marshmallow butterscotch pie. But her star dish, a gingerbread dollhouse, should have pushed her close to the top of the leaderboard tonight.

It currently lay scattered across the studio floor, shattered into at least fifty pieces.

"I'm *so* sorry," Libby apologized again, her hands to her mouth as the two women stood amidst the biscuit carnage.

"It was my fault." Emma was still clutching the empty platter on which the previously impressive structure had rested, her knuckles taut. She was clearly wresting back tears. "I tripped."

A piece of the dollhouse had rolled to rest against Dominic's shoe. He picked it up, laying it against his palm. It was a miniature Tiffany lamp, constructed entirely from molten sugar. The candy "glass" had cracked, but he could still see the structural lines. Slightly clumsy in places, but—

"Really quite beautiful," he said, turning it to watch the light shimmer and sparkle through translucent pink sugar that reminded him of Sylvie's hair. Crouching, he collected a few intact pieces from the wreckage—a gingerbread table, a beam covered in spun sugar cobwebs, a fondant teapot—and carefully set them on Emma's tray. She let out a long, shaky sigh. "Visually, it was a triumph, Emma." As he spoke, her wet eyes jerked to his face, widening. "One of the best bakes of the season. I'm truly sorry that we can't award you the points." It was engrained in the competition rule book—they could only score what was placed on the judging table, or in tonight's case, the banquet table. Emma had literally fallen short by about four feet. "Nevertheless, you should be very proud of yourself tonight."

She swallowed hard, but gave him a quavering smile. Sylvie and Adam had also bent to salvage what they could of the dollhouse; and Sylvie paused where she crouched, a piece of tiled roof in her hand. She looked worryingly ill still, her face sheet-pale, but she was looking thoughtfully at Dominic—and as Emma straightened her shoulders and touched a finger to the Tiffany lamp, Sylvie skewered him without warning. She had a variety of smiles, and he'd always been able to tell whether she liked the recipient by which she pulled from her repertoire. He'd been on the receiving end of Sylvie smiles from both ends of the scale over the years, but very few people were ever hit by her ultimate weapon, the one that seemed to start in her heart and encompass her entire being.

For a good five fucking seconds, he was almost prepared to believe in her spells and potions, because he literally couldn't move.

When Sylvie's gaze traveled to his left, that gorgeous smile immediately slipped into a small scowl. Despite being absolved of guilt, Libby was still fluttering and tossing out apologies, keeping herself in the camera frame.

In fairness, the collision had occurred so quickly that Emma *might* have tripped entirely by accident. Once again, there was no evidence to suggest otherwise, and even she seemed genuinely convinced of her own culpability.

However, throughout his career—both in the kitchen and here on set—Dominic had encountered his fair share of life's natural cheaters, the people whose sense of morality, if it existed at all, was easily overridden by ambition and greed. He recognized the behavorial patterns. He knew the verbal tells. And Libby wasn't even a particularly subtle instance; nobody was legitimately that artless. She was consistently overacting the part, and unfortunately it usually worked on television.

Aadhya called a break then, and Sylvie released a breath and reached for the nearest chair. When she almost stumbled because her legs were so weak, his patience snapped. He took a step forward, ready to carry her out of there and straight home to bed if necessary, but Chuck Finster had already broken away from the cluster of celebrity judges. The footballer leaned over her, his brow creased with obvious concern.

He'd done a surprisingly decent job tonight. As each contestant presented their work, Finster had engaged them all in conversation, offering thoughtful, legitimate feedback. He was built more like a basketball player, standing over two meters tall, and possessed very symmetrical features for a man who'd taken a ball full to the face during the World Cup. When off the field, he raised millions of pounds for children's charities and was reading history at Cambridge.

And could still spare the time to guest-judge *Operation Cake* and flirt with Sylvie all night.

"Are you growling?" Mariana asked mildly at Dominic's side. Her gaze followed his as Finster stroked Sylvie's shoulder with his thumb. Sylvie looked down at his hand. "Ah. Poor Chuckie. A veritable god amongst us mortals, yet he still hasn't noticed he's shooting his shot at a brick wall. When Sylvie's not tottering about half-dead, she's eye-fucking you." Across the room, Sylvie firmly removed and returned Finster's thumb. "No need for the jealous alpha wolf act."

Coolly, he said, "Jealousy is a destructive, pointless emotion and a complete waste of energy."

"Fairly annoying, then, that it's seeping from your pores right now?"

"Very." And apparently he could add pettiness to the score of new emotions Sylvie was foisting upon him, as she delivered a severe-looking comment and Finster's handsome face fell.

"Imagine thinking that woman is in any mood for seduction right now. She's so pale her makeup looks like someone smeared lipstick on a porcelain doll. Is it definitely food poisoning or have you two been guzzling absinthe again?"

He didn't immediately reply. Sylvie had taken out a water bottle and was sipping from it slowly. Whatever she'd said to Finster had sent the footballer packing. Her eyes met Dominic's over the bottle, and she lifted her free hand, touching it to her cheek in a quick gesture. More studio-speak. The sign for *keep going*. All good, carry on, continue filming, ignore the horny, overpaid athlete.

Subtext: *And drop the unexpected mother hen act; it's freaking me the fuck out.*

When he narrowed his eyes, so did she.

A little smile tugged at her mouth, and he couldn't help the twitch of his own.

When he turned back to Mariana, the amusement and teasing in her expression had faded. She looked at him silently for several moments before she said, "Do you know what's strange? I would rank you as one of the most inscrutable people I've ever met. For the entire first year on this set, I wondered if you were adopting a deliberate persona. The requisite Demon King in the pantomime."

"I have as many failings as the next person. Possibly more—"

"Since *I'm* the next person, definitely more," Mariana mused.

"But dishonesty isn't one of them."

However, even as he heard himself say the words, his eyes were inexorably drawn back to Sylvie. She was sitting in almost exactly the location of her onetime workstation, where he'd seen her for the first time four years ago. When his usual brief glance across the new contestants had paused for three thudding heartbeats.

Just that handful of seconds, and later that night, as the taste of her garish glitter-bomb cupcakes stuck to his taste buds like superglue, her face had been similarly fixed in his memory. He'd seen the freckles on her nose, the mole on her neck, even the way her Cupid's bow curved fractionally higher on the left side.

Maybe he'd always tried to be honest in his dealings with others.

But clearly not always with himself.

"Oh, I know you're honest," Mariana said with intense wryness. "Footnote: honesty is a more palatable virtue when paired with tact. But you give nothing away. By comparison, Sylvie is an open book."

Something in her tone made the muscles in his gut momentarily tighten.

"Your heart was in your eyes just then, *mi amigo*." He turned his head, and Mariana held his gaze with great frankness. "It was always at least fifty-fifty odds you two would eventually hit a mattress. For the most part, even when people dislike each other, they don't strike palpable sparks every time they meet. Chemistry—true, strong, wild chemistry—is the biggest rush in the world and rare as hell, as I'm sure we're all sadly aware. It would be a missed opportunity if you didn't burn up the sheets for a while." Her scrutiny was piercing. "But it's not just an affair, is it? On your end."

Those last three words were a mere echo of his own growing apprehension. He still felt them like an iron fist in his chest.

And yet another self-revelation: in a million years, he couldn't have imagined divulging any details of his private life to a colleague, but he found himself unable to deny Sylvie in any way. What happened between them was nobody else's business, yet he couldn't just dismiss her as if their changing relationship were something to be ashamed of and not the greatest blessing of his life right now.

Potentially ever.

"I've had many feelings where Sylvie is concerned." The note of irony slipped in, a well-worn protective shield. "None of them have ever been casual."

For all her digs about his own lack of tact, Mariana rarely

beat about the bush herself. "And Sylvie? Is it only an affair for Sylvie?"

His jaw clenched. Again, he looked across the room, where Sylvie was still sipping water. She wrinkled her nose at him with gentle playfulness, and he inhaled sharply.

He couldn't reply. For a number of reasons, not the least of which was that he didn't know the answer to that question. It wasn't that Sylvie was hiding her feelings. She obviously cared about him. From her expression last night, she cared quite deeply.

But as to the future—

One day at a time. Their mutual words last night applied in this and every situation.

Logical. Unsatisfying.

Perhaps reading the tension in his expression, Mariana diverted the subject. "Word in the greenroom is that you two are nose to nose on a very lucrative commission. Is it a bit strange to be . . . personally collaborating, shall we say, while you're competing professionally?"

It was so bloody bizarre that it *wasn't* strange. And not only were they "personally collaborating"—if that were the polite term for kissing her mouth, nuzzling in the scent of her skin, feeling her nipple bead against his thumb and her wet, silky muscles tighten around his erection, and a million tiny moments that were for the two of them alone—they were doing joint investigations for rival proposals. Somehow standard contract prep had turned into the adventures of Nancy Drew and Frank bloody Hardy.

And he couldn't remember the last time he'd enjoyed his work so much.

The camera crew had almost finished setting up for the final part of the shoot, and Aadhya called a five-minute warning before waving Mariana over.

Dominic crossed to Sylvie's side. Regardless of any watching eyes or cameras, he reached out and lightly stroked the top of her head with the side of his thumb. *One day at a time.* But whatever their future held, he'd never take that increasingly natural intimacy for granted.

She reached up and softly flicked his palm with her fingers. Her eyes searched his. "Are you okay? You look a bit odd."

"And you look like a wrung-out dishcloth." He touched the backs of his fingers to her forehead, checking her temperature.

"Wow." Reluctant humor sprang into Sylvie's tired eyes. "Less than twenty-four hours after the stupendous sex, and the romance is already dead."

"I think we can manage at least *one* more day. But I suspect you'd rather have a nap and slightly less of an audience."

"Mmm." So quickly even he barely had time to register the movement, she slipped her fingers under his tie, between the buttons of his shirt, and stroked a fiery line up the trail of hair between his abs. His muscles jerked, and she returned her hands primly to her lap and looked over at the contestants. Her mouth turned down. "Emma's out, right?"

At this age, it was good to know he wasn't entirely at the mercy of his hormones. Despite the reactive twitch behind his zipper, his brain shut down for two seconds at most. "Unless something goes even more catastrophically wrong with the last presentation."

"Why would it?" Sylvie muttered. "Libby's already secured her place in the final. Please God that Adam takes out the title. Or at least Terence." Her fervent prayers were interrupted by a large yawn, but as her hand went to her mouth, her eyes widened. "What's that?" she asked faintly.

Like everyone else in the studio, Dominic was already looking.

It was a little hard to miss the man wheeling a tabletop cannon into the room.

To what Dominic now suspected would be the detriment of them all, Terence, the middle-aged naval officer–turned–cupcake fanatic, had opted for a literary theme for his presentation. He'd declared it an homage to his favorite novel, *Treasure Island*, and apparently he'd taken the idea and run all the way into the realm of rudimentary ballistics.

"It looks like the baby version of those machines that fire tennis balls across a court," Sylvie said warily. "He also drew gingerbread from the flavor wheel, right? Please tell me he's not going to cannonball biscuits onto the celebs' plates."

"Little judgmental from the woman who built a sponge-cake siege engine."

Shooting small, hard objects at litigious celebrities. What could possibly go wrong?

On closer inspection, however, the cannon was constructed extremely well from fondant and blown sugar. Impressive. And upon being questioned, Terence responded with some annoyance, "I'm not going to shoot *anything* at people. What an excellent way to knock someone's eye out."

Incredible. Sanity finally prevailed on this set.

The celebrities, who had rapidly retreated behind their table at the sight of the cannon, all crept cautiously forward.

As filming recommenced, Terence produced his bake, a series of gingerbread cakes he'd designed as a map of Treasure Island, intricately decorated. Out of spun sugar, he'd woven the ghostly outline of a pirate ship, sailing elusively on a sea of twinkling crystals.

Sylvie was so enamored that some of the color came back into her cheeks.

Terence had clearly worked incredibly hard for hours. And if he hadn't set the studio on fire, he would have been a lock for the final.

The cannon itself merely spilled out a gust of rolling steam and crackling sparkles, but he simultaneously ignited the interior of the pirate ship. It was intended to melt, folding into itself, and sink defeated into the sugar "sea."

Instead, the entire front of the ship cracked in half moments after he lit the spark. Tiny flames licked along the sugar and reached the replica grog barrels on the adjacent dock. As it later transpired that Terence—experienced military sailor and apparently a bit of a fuckwit—had filled them with real brandy, the whole thing went up like kindling. Blue-tinged flames billowed outward in a *whoosh* of crackling heat, until the entire tablecloth was ablaze.

Dominic yanked Sylvie out of the way; she shoved *him* out of the way; and those respective immediate instincts almost canceled each other out as they lost their balance and collided.

Mariana's right hand grabbed the back of his collar, then she took hold of Sylvie with her left, and calmly pulled their entwined bodies clear of the flaming table.

"Time and place for canoodling, children," she said with mock severity.

"Thanks, Mamá," Sylvie said, grinning, and Mariana flicked her affectionately on the forehead.

As a crew member whipped out an extinguisher and blasted the desserts into soggy oblivion, the burnt and broken remains of the crow's nest drooped sideways, teetered and fell.

And it was Libby, Adam, and Emma for the final.

They had to follow protocol and evacuate, but nobody had their coat, and it was freezing in the outside courtyard. Ignoring the perpetually interested gazes of various colleagues, Sylvie huddled in Dominic's arms, shivering against his chest.

"Well," she said at last through chattering teeth, cuddling in closer, "that seems about par for the course."

"The studio's insurance premiums will be through the roof after this season." As Dominic's arm tightened around her, he added cynically, "If they forced you into a multiyear contract, expect further cost cutting disguised as efficiency."

"It's certainly had its moments." Sylvie made a humming noise under her breath. "Makes my tiny little miscalculation with the unicorn cake seem negligible, really, doesn't it?"

"Don't push it."

Chapter Fifteen

The road to ~~Primrose Cottage~~ the even more twee Petunia Park.

Shorter than the road to Calvary.

But with Pet along for the ride, it doesn't necessarily feel like it.

Sylvie was becoming increasingly fond of Pet. Dominic's sister was a sweetheart. A cheeky, cheerful soul with a razor-sharp brain. Despite the ten-year difference in their ages, she could foresee the development of a solid friendship.

However, she was also beginning to appreciate Dominic's point about the book recapping.

For all her many delightful qualities, Pet did not possess an appreciation for restful silence. Any pause in conversation seemed to rattle her completely. Sylvie suspected it was situation specific, Pet's transparent desperation to bond with Dominic emerging as relentless chatter. She was entirely sympathetic to both De Veres, and a psychologist would undoubtedly find the whole situation fascinating. However, she'd spent the past ten minutes mentally designing a pair of invisible noise-canceling headphones.

She'd been given to understand, through Dominic's absinthe-slurred whinge, that Pet was reading romance novels. Sylvie also enjoyed romance novels. Sylvie would fucking *love* to hear every last nuance of a romance novel right now. Unfortunately, the book club Pet had joined over the summer—and Sylvie could now recite the names, occupations, and personality quirks of all twelve members—had since moved on to a painstakingly graphic horror novel.

Although she'd mostly recovered from the food poisoning, Sylvie was now feeling slightly carsick. Her stomach was not ready for detailed descriptions of seeping wounds and wiggling maggots, especially recounted with a Pet level of enthusiasm. Despite numerous interruptions from Dominic's GPS app and the competition of the rain pounding the car windows, the gore from the back seat continued on and on. And if Sylvie was keeping track, they'd only reached chapter eight in the narrative.

A particularly twisty turn in the road coincided with an anecdote about severed heads, and she had to physically gulp. Dominic briefly took his gaze from the unfamiliar country lane and glanced at her.

"Pet, Sylvie's still not feeling a hundred percent," he said, taking one hand off the steering wheel to touch hers. She immediately twisted their fingers together. "Cool it with the blood and gore, all right?"

The rough pads of his fingers were gentle on her skin. Multiple times a day, she was still struck by the fact that she was holding hands with Dominic, kissing Dominic, having sex with *Dominic.*

With each passing second, every part of this had started to feel irrevocable.

And it no longer seemed so strange or unbelievable. Still surprising, definitely not the path she'd imagined her life would take, but a bit wonderful, really. Turning her head and looking at him now, the familiar stubble shadow on his jaw, the bump on the bridge of his nose, the thick, endearingly stubby eyelashes, she was overwhelmed by a sudden surge of feeling. Bubbling joy, possessiveness, protectiveness, lust, a thousand emotions all in a jumble.

Impulsively, she raised their joined hands to her lips and kissed his thumb. His grip tightened, and a strong flash of heat lit his mismatched dark eyes.

"Oh. Sorry." Pet's chastened tone brought her back to the reality of their surroundings, the stuffy interior of the car, the endless winding Oxfordshire lanes. The property formerly known as Primrose Cottage appeared to be located in a rural labyrinth.

"Petunia Park must be quite a drive for its aspiring artists," Pet commented after a twenty-second silence, shifting onto Sylvie's own train of thought. "Perfect love nest for a clandestine royal romance, though."

Dominic released her hand to make a sharp turn in the road, and Sylvie rubbed at the foggy side window with her sleeve. She couldn't see far beyond the glass, but the sporadic cottages and gardens they passed appeared to be thatched and pretty. It was a scene of quiet serenity and must be idyllic in the summer. Tapping her phone on her lap, she brought up the photograph of Patrick and Jessica, happy and in love on the stone steps, circled by primroses and sunshine.

Very lightly, she touched the relaxed lines of Patrick's face. A fleeting moment of perfect happiness, captured forever.

A short time later, Dominic turned the car through wrought-iron gates and drew to a stop. Jessica's onetime home was larger than it had appeared in the photo, sprawling backward in a charming hodgepodge of outbuildings. A sort of miniature barn had obviously been converted into studio space; Sylvie could see easels through the windows.

The rain had slowed to a gentle drizzle, so she left her coat hood down when she got out of the car. The cool air was refreshing after the drive. She stood looking at the front of the cottage, lifting her gaze from the photo to the stone stairs where the couple had sat all those years ago. The surrounding gardens were a tangled mass of bare branches, not a flower in sight, but otherwise—

She'd looked at that snapshot so many times over the past few days that the setting in person, so entirely familiar, gave her an eerie tingle. Even the crack in the stone by Jessica's foot was still there. She could see them in her mind, coming out of the house, laughing, kissing, setting the timer on the camera. For some reason, she was convinced they'd been alone in that moment.

Jessica holding the railing as she sat, Patrick turning his head to look at her, his eyes alight.

Pet looked over her shoulder at the phone screen and shivered a little. "It's a bit ghostly, isn't it?"

"Part of me expects that I'll look up from the photo and they'll be there," Sylvie murmured, and for once Dominic's practicality was a welcome shattering of the spell.

"You're both under the influence of severed heads and floating corpses. It's a house. Stones and thatch. Wherever Patrick and Jessica are now, they're not—"

"What did you say?" The startled voice came from behind them, and for one moment when Sylvie turned, it *was* as if Jessica had stepped out of time and back into the scene.

The woman who stood staring at them had short dark hair, threaded with silver. She was an age Jessica had never reached, her figure lush and curvy in a print dress and baggy cardigan. Her enviably muscular bare calves ended in muddy Wellington boots, a far cry from Jessica's flowing skirt and neatly laced shoes. Their faces were different shapes—Jessica's cheeks had been very round; this woman's face was long and narrow.

But their eyes were identical. Large and dark with tremendously long lashes, tilted at the outer corners like a cat.

Pet glanced at Sylvie and Dominic before she walked forward with a smile and extended her hand. "Are you Kathleen? I'm Pet De Vere."

Kathleen took her hand automatically, but her attention remained fixed on Dominic. "Did you say Patrick and Jessica?"

With a few beads of rain rolling down his temple, Dominic studied her for a moment before he spoke. "I'm Dominic De Vere, Pet's brother, and this is Sylvie Fairchild."

"I know," Kathleen said. "I've been watching you on TV." She continued to stare at him, recovering enough from her frozen shock that suspicion was creeping in. "I'm guessing you aren't really here for a studio tour."

"No. I'm afraid not." He glanced at Sylvie, and she stepped forward and held out her phone.

"If you don't mind," she said, "we'd like to ask you about Jessica and Prince Patrick."

Kathleen's frowning eyes were dragged down to the photograph on the screen. Her breath caught in a little hitch. Slowly, she reached out and took the phone from Sylvie, automatically scissoring her fingers to zoom in on the faces of the couple.

No sound other than the gentle padding of rain against stone.

Finally, she inhaled deeply and lifted her head. "Well. You'd better come in for a cup of tea."

The unraveling of a royal romance.

The front room of the cottage was delightful, cluttered and cozy, with paintings all over the walls and a fire crackling in the hearth. Sylvie sat on a well-stuffed couch next to Dominic and accepted the cup of tea Kathleen handed her, murmuring her thanks.

"She *was* the light," Kathleen said, sitting on an armchair opposite Pet's. Sylvie had just repeated the words Patrick had spoken to Rosie, Jessica's sister listening with tears in her eyes. "She was kind and beautiful, and everything he thought she was. And she loved him so much."

"Did you know him?" Sylvie asked quietly, and Kathleen shook her head.

"I never met him. None of her friends did. I believe I was the only one she told." She smiled a little. "I was eighteen, and it was the most romantic thing I'd ever heard. A secret romance with a real-life prince. Like something out of a book." Her smile quivered and faded. "It didn't end like the fairy tales."

She picked up the photo album she'd taken from a shelf and set it in front of Sylvie, who looked down at a large studio portrait of Jessica. Once again, a camera had managed to capture the lively spark in her eyes, suppressed laughter in every line of her face.

"She looks . . . joyful." It was the only word.

Kathleen nodded. "That's exactly what I associate with her memory. Joy. Pure joy in life, in people, in her hopes for the future. In her love." She shook her head. "She was a human being;

of course she had moods and moments. But if she lost her temper, it never lasted long and she'd apologize very solemnly, and hug you tight, and you'd be laughing again in minutes. I miss her," she said. "As much now as I did in the days after her death. Over a quarter of a century, and I never stop hoping she'll walk through the door. This is still her house, really. She always called it Petunia Park. In the summer, the field out the back is just a sea of petunias. She liked to curl up amongst them at night and look up at the stars. I can still feel her presence out there so strongly." Her voice turned thoughtful, abstracted. "I suppose that's why I moved here. Why I've stayed so long. I can't leave her."

She'll be alone. I don't want to leave her alone.

Blinking away a sudden burn at the back of her eyes, Sylvie cleared her throat. "According to Rosie, Jessica decided she couldn't live the life of a royal, that she wouldn't be able to bear it."

"She tormented herself over it." Kathleen was still clutching Sylvie's phone tightly. "She came to see me one night, in tears. I'd never seen her like that. I think she had to talk to someone, and there was nobody else she could trust. She'd seen how the press treated his previous girlfriends, you see. How the public tore their lives wide open. Eyes always on you. Scrutinizing every gesture, every outfit, every word. How many marriages in that family have survived with any love and happiness left intact? She'd walked away from him that day, and it was like part of her had died. The light in her eyes just . . . gone."

They were all very quiet. Instinctively, Sylvie slipped her hand sideways and back into Dominic's. She sensed him look at her, before his fingers tightened around hers.

"She didn't sleep a wink that night. She barely slept at all for four days," Kathleen went on. "Finally, five nights after she'd left him, I came here with her to Primrose Cottage, as it was then, and we lay out in the petunia field until dawn. I think she needed to be here, where she'd always found solace. And where she'd been happy with him." She exhaled shakily again, running her fingers over the image of her sister's face. "I remember dozing, waking on and off, and seeing her looking up at the sky. At some point, she stopped crying, and this look came over her face. I could hear her voice, just a breath in the breeze. *We can do it.* That was all she said."

She lifted her head and looked at them. "She would have been brilliant. Whatever situation life threw her into. And she adored him. I knew from the moment she turned up on the doorstep that she'd never be able to go through with it. She always would have chosen him, in the end."

It took a second for that to register, and Sylvie saw Dominic's own head lift.

Pet had been sitting quietly, one hand tucked against her cheek as she listened, but she pushed forward in her chair now. "You mean she changed her mind? She went back to him?"

"She was going back to him. That day." Kathleen's jaw worked. Her voice had the hoarseness of one who still, even after all this time, didn't quite believe the reality of loss. "Once she'd made the decision, it was like she'd . . . ignited. She was Jessie again, so excited and determined to see him right away. She packed a bag and left. I still remember her grabbing my face and kissing me, laughing." Her fingers flexed on the phone. "She was forty minutes outside of London when a truck slid out of control in an intersection. The cab smashed into the driver's-side door. She died before they could cut her from the wreckage."

There were tears on Pet's cheeks, and Sylvie felt the wetness under her own lashes. Dominic covered their linked fingers with his other hand.

"I tried to get in touch with Patrick, but I didn't have any direct way to contact him." Kathleen took a creased hankie from a voluminous pocket and scrubbed over her eyes. "If Jessie ever wrote down his number, I never found it, and obviously you can't just call the palace and ask to speak to the prince. We'd already had the funeral before I finally managed to speak to a royal aide, who—" Her voice cracked. "Who passed on the palace's deepest condolences and proceeded to politely fob me off. First, he wouldn't believe that Jessie had even known Patrick, and then when I wouldn't give up, he—he made it sound as if there were other women, that Patrick had any number of casual relationships on the go. I was only eighteen, and he was so . . . matter-of-fact about it."

Something in her expression became almost childlike, the confused, grieving teenage girl she'd once been.

"I believed him," Kathleen said. All that chilled nothingness fell away, leaving her voice raw with grief. "I thought Patrick had just been a typical playboy prince, leading Jessie on. Making her believe she'd found this great love, when really, he wouldn't even care that much that she'd—that she'd died. I was so angry for so long. I kept remembering her face that day when she was getting in the car. The weeks before then, when she was literally dancing as she walked. The months on end she spent making a sculpture for him, ignoring all her other work—she was the most incredible artist, did you know? Bronze, stone, glass, ceramic. She could draw the beauty out of anything."

She was speaking rapidly, changing course and continuing before anyone could reply. "She said he'd put it in his favorite part of the gardens at St. Giles Palace, the only place he could sit and think and *be*. It was his petunia field, she said. And after that conversation with the aide, I thought, *It's* all *a lie*. Jessie spent hours and hours making the mold for that bronze, and he probably just threw it in a cupboard. Just another dusty old relic in some dreary abandoned room."

The stream of words came to a halt. Kathleen's callused fingers were shaking as she stroked the sides of Sylvie's phone, staring down again at that photograph. At the transparent emotion on Patrick's face, the way his body naturally curved toward Jessica's.

"It wasn't true, was it?" The tears streamed down her face, and Pet got up and went to crouch at her side. She rested her hand on the older woman's wrist, rubbing gently in comfort. Kathleen lifted her eyes to meet Sylvie's. "He did love her."

"He loved her very much." Sylvie was squeezing Dominic's fingers tightly. "There was no one else. Only Jessie, for all of his life." She hesitated. "He never knew that she'd changed her mind, that she was coming back to him."

"Patrick notoriously hated the interference of senior advisors. If the aide you spoke to told him anything of that conversation, and that's not a given, he may have persuaded Patrick that Jessica's family wanted nothing to do with him. Perhaps that you blamed him for her state of mind that week," Dominic put in grimly. "Probably assuming the prince would move on faster if all lingering ties were cut. A clean break. From everything I've heard of Patrick, if he *was* informed of Jessica's death then, I can't understand why he wouldn't have come to see you, unless he believed he was respecting your own wishes."

Sylvie was mentally replaying her conversation with Rosie. The princess had spoken of her uncle mourning Jessie all his life. Mourning her loss, her absence in his life. Rosie had never specifically mentioned her death. Slowly, she said, "He may not have known anything about *any* of it. She'd told him she had to leave, and he'd done the last thing—the only thing—he could do for her. He let her cut contact between them completely, so she could go and live the life that he thought would make her happiest in the end. *A bird that was always meant to soar.*"

Kathleen made an audible gulping sound, the fingers of one hand curled against the brooch at her breast. It was a beautiful little bronze piece, two entwined hearts. A gift from a very talented, affectionate sister? "Oh God," she said, and her face crumpled. "That poor man." With another sudden sob, she clutched Pet's hand. "But I'm so . . . To know that she did find that sort of love, that she lived in perfect happiness even for a short time, and it was real and true . . ."

Her smile was shaky—but it, too, was almost identical to Jessica's.

"Thank you," she said, very simply.

Even Pet was very quiet on the trip back to London. When they were about twenty minutes from St. Giles Palace, Sylvie heard a muffled sniff from the back seat and stretched her arm back.

Pet's hand clasped hers. Her fingers were damp. "I wish I could go back in time and tell him," she said in a fierce, unsteady whisper. "It's so— It's *awful*. That he never knew she'd chosen him. That she was going to fight for them."

Sylvie looked at Dominic. His profile was grim and handsome and so very . . . dear. "Maybe he knows now," she said softly. "I hope he knows now."

He turned his head and their eyes met for a long moment.

It wasn't raining in the city, but the cold air was a sharp bite. Dominic found a parking space a couple of blocks from the palace, and Sylvie huddled inside her coat as they walked the distance to the west grounds. Although it was still a bit mad that she had the private cell number for a senior member of the royal family, she'd contacted Rosie before they'd left Oxfordshire. The princess was on her way to a royal engagement in the Cotswolds, but she'd granted them permission to enter the private part of the park.

Sounding preoccupied, a definitely tight note underlying her greeting, Rosie had given her concise directions to the location of Patrick's "thinking spot."

"I'll let security know you're coming. You might bump into Johnny," she'd said before hanging up. "He's needed quite a bit of breathing room in the garden this week."

That two-minute call had done nothing to alleviate Sylvie's growing concerns about this wedding.

A guard let them through a locked gate, and they followed a winding path through rain-soaked trees. It was lovely—she'd had no idea the gardens were so extensive; it was bizarre that a hop and a skip away were some of the busiest metropolitan roads in Britain. They crossed over a little bridge, Pet peering over the side at a large pond.

"No fish," she murmured with obvious disappointment.

Sylvie knew when they'd found the right place, even without consulting Rosie's instructions. Under the enveloping branches of an enormous mulberry tree was a small wooden bench, carved from a tree trunk, the legs a whimsical profusion of whittled leaves and flowers. On closer inspection, she saw a small carved mouse peeking around the left side. There were rosebushes everywhere, but arranged far more haphazardly than the precise landscaping elsewhere. In the warmer months, the ground would likely be a carpet of wildflowers.

There were artworks right throughout the grounds, but Sylvie found the sculpture in a small clearing beyond the tree.

Jessica's gift to Patrick was a cast bronze of two kneeling figures, a man and a woman. There were no facial features, merely smooth planes and deliberate mystery. They sat facing one another, knees and foreheads touching. Their hands were extended, the man's cupped beneath his lover's. On her upturned palms was an intricate trinity knot.

The edges of the knot were wrought from delicate ribbons of bronze, and Jessica had filled in the interior with stained glass. Even on an overcast day, when the sky was dull and heavy with rain clouds, the weak light sparkled in the glass, shimmering in a multitude of colors.

Dominic came to stand at her side, and for long minutes they remained there in silence. Pet had sat down on the bench at the mulberry tree, obviously giving them privacy.

At last, he said, "I can see why it gave him comfort to come here."

She pressed her cheek against his bicep, his wool coat scratchy against her skin.

He lowered his head to rest against hers.

They were leaving the peaceful copse with Pet, Sylvie flicking through the photos she'd taken of the sculpture, when she heard the low murmur of voices.

Frowning, she looked around, but saw no one. There were guards patrolling the park, but she hadn't seen them for some time.

"Who . . ." Pet began as they turned the corner, and then Sylvie saw them outside a small stone building.

Johnny stood in the doorway with a tall blonde woman. Spiral curls were poking out under her woolen hat, and her gloved hands waved for emphasis as she spoke. She was doing most of the talking, Johnny inserting a word here and there, shaking his head.

The body language on both sides was intense.

As the sky overhead gave an ominous rumble and the first raindrops began to fall again, the woman moved forward and suddenly they were clutching each other's arms.

Johnny fell back a few steps.

And as they disappeared back into the outbuilding, their mouths slammed together in a fierce kiss.

Chapter Sixteen

Sugar Fair

The bell gave a homey little tinkle as Dominic held open the door to Sugar Fair, and Sylvie slipped past him, looking grim. Pet—also in an unusually subdued incarnation—had headed straight across the street to De Vere's.

Inside, he absently noted the number of customers milling around and was satisfied for Sylvie's sake. Less thrilled about the people trying to take photos of them, and failing in any semblance of subtlety or manners.

He stared directly at a few of them. Cheeks immediately flushed, phones were flung into bags, and one person hid behind the sugar ice castle.

Sylvie's assistant—"You can call me Mabel"; subtext: *You total dickhead*—was sitting at her central table, humming classic rock against the background splash of the chocolate waterfall. The diamantés on her skull bracelet glittered under the overhead lights. She looked up briefly from the *amezaiku* flamingo she was painting a vivid fuchsia pink, surveyed Dominic with cold dislike from head to foot, and ignored them both.

If it wouldn't result in Sylvie castrating him with a pastry cutter, he'd offer Mabel a signing incentive to join his staff on the spot.

"I'll just be in the office for a while," Sylvie said, and Mabel grunted.

As she opened the bookcase of chocolate boxes, which he would vote as hands down the best part of her entire aesthetic here, the other woman spoke without looking away from her rapidly flickering brush. "Don't do it on the desk. The front left leg is wobbling again. Should the entire thing collapse, I *will* make sure your headstone says DEAD GIVING HEAD, SHOULD HAVE USED A BED."

Sylvie closed the door behind them with a *thud*. For the first time in hours, humor was a momentary flicker in her eyes. "If you still want her, I may be prepared to negotiate."

In the cramped office space, which was really too small for one desk, let alone two, she put her bag down. The room was overheated, and he shrugged off his coat, draping it over the back of a chair.

Sylvie was still holding her phone, on which were several photos of Johnny and his mystery companion, attached at the lips in every frame.

While they'd been standing there, Pet had whipped out her own phone and taken some rapid-fire shots. His baby sister would make a frighteningly efficient private investigator. And if he'd vocalized that opinion, she would already be heading out to the shops in search of a trilby and trench coat.

She'd AirDropped them to Sylvie, leaving it to them to decide what to do.

"The sculpture was beautiful." Sylvie's voice was very flat. Dominic could see exactly what Kathleen had meant about the light dimming in a very bright person, and the sight of her unhappiness was like steel wool on his nerve endings. "I can finish my cake proposal," she went on in those low tones. "I know the right design now." She looked at him. "You?"

"Yes. I've got mine, as well." Usually, he'd already be back in his office, getting it down on paper before his business meeting this evening, but he wasn't leaving her while she was blatantly upset. Leaning back against the wall, he tucked his hands into his trouser pockets. Exhaustion was creeping into his bones. He needed a decent night's sleep or four. "Sylvie—"

"Materially, socially, in almost every way, Rosie's an incredibly privileged person," she said suddenly, pushing up to sit on the edge of her desk as if she, too, felt drained. "She admits as much. But mentally, I think she has very little respite. Johnny isn't just her lover, her best friend—he's her sanctuary. She obviously feels completely and utterly safe with him."

"With good reason. He would literally take a bullet for her, and there's no way that was what it looked like. That man doesn't have an unfaithful bone in his body."

Sylvie looked down at a photo of the kiss; exhaling in a noisy gust, she brought the phone to her forehead, pressing the cool screen against her skin.

"Bone-deep, every instinct in me agrees with you," she said at last. "But there's *something* fucking dodgy going on. That was a private part of the palace, Rosie obviously has no idea he was meeting someone there, and you said it yourself at your flat—there was a shifty look in his eyes at that meeting. He's not a good actor." She lowered the phone to shoot it another narrowed look. "Am I right in thinking that woman—"

"Was last spotted having a massive tantrum outside the royals' private office?" There was a reciprocally grim note in his response then. He'd strip naked and cartwheel into the Thames if Johnny had willingly partaken of that vicious snog this afternoon, but—yeah. Admittedly, with no pun intended, things were not looking all that rosy for the royal engagement. "I can't be dead certain. Distance. Poor light." And increasingly fucked eyes from years of intricate detail work. He was heading for a pair of glasses the next time he saw an optician. He'd casually mentioned that to Sylvie last night, a passing comment that had somehow led to a blow job. Apparently, she was strongly in favor of the specs. So was he, now. "But I think so. Her height, her boots, the ringlets. All a match."

"You noticed her boots?" Sylvie was momentarily distracted. "Jesus. You and Pet should open a detective agency." In a moment of lightness, she fluttered her lashes at him, and welcome laughter crinkled his eyes. "I'll be the mysterious sexpot who seduces you on your desk."

He nodded at the desk beneath her. "Practice makes perfect. If you'd like to demonstrate on *your* desk—"

She touched the wooden surface. "This one is Jay's."

"Ah." Amidst the neatly arranged papers and pens was a framed photo of her and Fforde. It hadn't been taken in England; looked like the south of France. They were on the beach, Sylvie's arms wrapped around her knees as she beamed into the camera. Fforde sat at her side, turning to look at her, also smiling. Dominic rubbed his thumb over his jaw as he continued to study it, very thoughtfully, for an extended moment. "Maybe take a rain check until you're in my office, then."

Sighing, Sylvie dropped her phone on the desk and drummed her heels against the wood. "What do we do about it?" She in-

clined her head toward the screen. "We're about to submit proposals for their wedding cake. Rosie's already having doubts. I doubt
they'd be alleviated if I texted her a photo of her fiancé tumbling
around her massive garden with a temperamental blonde. This is
both none of our business and also *literally* our business. Businesses," she corrected belatedly, with a slight blink. She bit her
lip and her tone abruptly changed. "It's so bloody odd. I genuinely
keep forgetting that we're competing in this. I feel like I'm talking
to my partner."

In the beat of silence that followed, the air felt thick and
heavy with unspoken words, and a flush of the palest pink swept
through her cheeks.

He cleared his suddenly dry throat. "I know you care about
those two in a way that has nothing to do with this contract—"

"So do you," she murmured.

"Clearly, it's going to play on your own peace of mind if you
do nothing. The only thing I can suggest is that when we submit
the proposals before the ball, one or both of us speaks to Johnny
privately. Be honest about what we saw, and leave anything further to him."

After a moment, she nodded. Her eyes were searching his.
"Do you still have that business dinner tonight?"

He pushed his hand through his hair, cupping the back of his
neck. "Mm-hmm. And if I don't want to turn up looking as if
I've been dragged through a hedge, I need to get going." Drinks
and filet mignon with the CEO of Farquhar's, one of his biggest
clients. The networking would likely result in a high-five-figure
contract, and if he only had his own income to worry about, he'd
be very tempted to reschedule.

"Dom. When all the work is done," she said so softly, a whisper on a breath, "we need to talk." Her office window looked

onto a brick wall, but the definition of the moss-covered bricks was fading with the light, and her features were cast into increasing shadow. "About . . . about this." Her throat moved as she swallowed. "About us. I always like to know where I stand, and where I'm going. But especially when I'm in a place I've never been before."

From the moment their mouths had met in the Dark Forest, things had developed so insanely naturally between them, but the tension had wrapped around them now in ropes. Dominic vaguely heard a soft sound outside the closed door, but neither of them looked away.

In fiction, falling in love seemed to happen in soft focus, all cheerful montages of pop music and soulful glances. In reality, it was raw and confronting, powerful and passionate, shifting every goalpost.

The past few weeks had been so busy he'd barely had a moment of rest, and his head had been thrown into a total spiraling mindfuck where she was concerned. It was as if his usual, well-trodden path had begun to crumble beneath his feet, at first in pieces over a longer time than he'd ever admitted, and then he'd fallen so quickly he'd never had a chance to catch his breath. It was overwhelming, and it was disorientating.

And ultimately, he was thankful. He was incredibly grateful to know that he *could* feel like this about someone, and he was increasingly privileged that it was her.

But he also hadn't known how it would feel giving someone the power to cause him hurt.

How difficult it would be to take the last step, to let go of the need for control.

To take the biggest leap of faith there was.

He nodded, and her teeth sank deeper into her lip. With a

decisive movement, she pushed off the desk and came to stand before him. Without another word, she went up on her tiptoes, very lightly framed his jaw with her hands, and kissed him hard.

They continued to look into one another's eyes as the kiss deepened, then softened, feeling each other's mouths, darting the tips of tongues along the silky skin of inner lips, nipping and nuzzling. His hands were on the curves of her waist, feeling the warmth beneath her shirt, his thumbs gently stroking up and down.

When she breathed in deeply and carefully broke away, her cheeks were red, her pupils dilated, and his erection strained against his zipper.

He jumped when the old-fashioned clock on a shelf chimed, a small door opening in the dial and a cuckoo bird popping out once, twice, five times. Somebody—and he could guess who—had put a tiny pink baseball cap on its head. He couldn't help smiling.

"You have to go," she said quietly.

"I don't know when it'll wind up, and you need an early night, so—"

"I'll see you tomorrow at the shoot." Her fingers had drifted to his body again, plucking at his clothing, but she realized what she was doing and curled her hand into a fist.

He kissed her once more, very lightly, then went to the outside door in a swift movement, closing it quietly behind him as he stepped out into the rain.

God.

From pop songs to poems to personal experience, everyone knew how fun and dizzying and delightful it was to fall into infatuation.

Sylvie hadn't known how disorientating and terrifying it could be to fall in love.

When just out of reach, teasingly stretching out to touch her hands, tugging her forward, was the prospect of something so unbelievably wonderful.

She ran her hand over her eyes, walked to the internal door, and pulled it open.

And almost ran straight into Penny, who was standing in the hallway, so close they could have bumped noses.

Her intern's large eyes widened farther, but her usual vague smile made a rapid reappearance. She held up a stack of envelopes. "Mail. And just to let you know, I finished the bread rolls early and saw we were out of caramel truffles, so I made more."

Good grief. She'd done the task she'd been assigned *and* showed initiative.

Light was breaking through the clouds at last.

"I couldn't find the toffee crumbles, so I used the pretty crystals by the sink instead," Penny added, looking very pleased with her own ingenuity.

Sylvie paused. "The crystals in the jar?"

The younger woman nodded happily.

"Um. How many truffles did you make?"

Penny gave an excited little hop. "Five dozen."

Well, it could have been worse.

At least she'd only made sixty units of their exciting new variety of truffle.

Dark chocolate and crystallized oven cleaner.

Thank God Jay was out all day at meetings.

Before she could issue a tactful reminder that all edible ingredients *and* industrial cleaning products were meticulously labeled, Penny continued, "There's another reporter out front.

Asking the staff questions about the royal wedding cake. And Mabel's out on her break."

Joy upon joy.

"And your friend left his coat."

At Penny's blithe observation, Sylvie turned and saw Dominic's beautiful wool coat hung over her chair. Damn. It was already cold outside, and it would be freezing by the time he left the restaurant tonight.

"If you need to take it to him," Penny offered, "I'll get rid of the reporter."

"Oh, I don't think . . ." Before the polite refusal was out, Sylvie reconsidered. It was impossible to either fluster or coerce any information out of Penny. She didn't appear to retain any in the first place. Multiple people had just given up and noped out of a conversation with the intern, through the sheer frustration of talking to a wall of smiling indifference. "That would be great. Please do."

As Penny floated over to her desk to drop the stack of mail into appropriate sorting boxes, Sylvie hastily tapped her phone to vanish the photo of Johnny and Aggressive Blonde. She grabbed Dominic's coat and rushed out the side door into the alleyway.

He'd obviously hit rush-hour traffic, because he was only just heading into De Vere's when she emerged onto the street.

In a small break between cars, Sylvie dashed across the street, her boots sending puddles splashing up her legs.

"Dominic!"

He turned with a frown, the wind blowing his hair back from his face, but his expression cleared as he saw the coat in her hand. "Thank—"

Looking at the sharply hewn, arrogant features, she couldn't help herself. Her heart flooding with warmth, she flung her arms around his neck and kissed him again.

He stiffened for the most infinitesimal of moments—he obviously liked it when she kissed and cuddled him, but they were right outside their workplaces on a public street, and he was definitely never going to be a PDA sort of bloke to *this* extent—then his body relaxed. His mouth moved warmly over hers, his hand coming up to smooth her hair away from her cheek.

They drew back from each other. Rain was falling down his cheeks, over his shoulders. She was barely aware of the wetness of her own hair and clothing.

"Have a good dinner," she murmured, and was rewarded with a flash of that rare, genuine smile before he took his coat, brushed his lips between her brows, and went inside.

Sylvie touched her lips and bit down lightly on her thumb as she swung around, smiling, to cross back to her own territory.

The rain was starting to fall in sheets, sending mist and spray rising from the sodden pavement, throwing the entire scene into a soft, unfocused gray.

But there was nothing to impede her vision as she looked over the roof of a newly arrived taxi, into Jay's eyes as he stood, one hand tightly gripping the open door.

Clearly, he'd had an equally good view of her. And Dominic.

She wasn't moving. Couldn't move. She just stood there, getting more and more soaked, her chest rising more quickly with every breath.

His face.

Oh God, his face.

Suddenly, she knew exactly, finally, what Jay had wanted to talk to her about.

And that wobbling foundation stone in her life crumbled into dust.

Chapter Seventeen

They stood in their office, the desks between them. They were both holding on to the backs of their chairs, as if they didn't know what to do with their hands.

As if they needed the support.

The rain was hitting the windows hard, and the clock was ticking, and everything felt both unnaturally loud and painfully silent.

She couldn't look away from him.

He couldn't seem to bear to look at her.

When he spoke at last, it was with his head lowered, his hair falling forward. "You and De Vere." There was nothing in his tone. Literally nothing. Her stomach did a horrible, sickening little flip. "You're—with De Vere."

"Yes." Sylvie spoke very quietly, but with no hesitation. Even as she felt that every word would stab into Jay with a weapon she'd never imagined she possessed, she wouldn't deny Dominic. Couldn't. "I'm seeing Dominic."

Inadequate. Barely touching the surface. And already more than he wanted to hear.

"How long?" Jay asked, still expressionless. Under the stubble edging his sculpted jaw, a muscle jumped.

"Not long."

He finally looked up, and the moment she saw his eyes again, her heart hurt like hell. "I, um—I didn't realize. I wasn't expecting . . ." He took a visibly unsteady breath.

"Neither was I," she said softly. She had to cross her arms tightly to stop herself moving forward, reaching out for him.

She'd always held him when he was hurt.

And to do that, right now, would obviously gut him.

He seemed to be bracing himself. "Is it serious?" He forced those words out and raised a hand before she could answer. "Don't answer that." That frozen, hateful emptiness was leaving his voice. It cracked. Her eyes burnt. "I know you." His mouth twisted. "I know you."

Sylvie nodded once.

"The look on your face when you turned around. When you . . . left his arms." Jay pressed his lips together. "It's serious."

"Jay."

"I love you." He said it so simply, as he'd said it a hundred times before, all these years.

And for the first time in all these years, she heard him.

The first tears slipped past her lashes.

Her usual response, as deeply and truly as she meant it, would be another sharp knife.

"I didn't know." She managed to speak, but it was barely more than a whisper. They looked at each other. His face was white. Another tear fell down her cheek. "I'm so sorry. I didn't know."

He closed his eyes, tilted his head back. Exhaled.

"How . . ." She trailed off.

Slowly, he looked back down at her. He slipped his hands into his pockets, the fabric of his trousers pulling taut across his long legs. "How long?" He shook his head slightly. "I don't even know anymore. It crept up so gradually. For a while, I thought, *Nah, you love her so much that you're crossing wires that aren't there.* But no. And now I . . . I can't remember a time when it wasn't you." A single crack of horrible self-deprecating laughter. "And for some reason, I was convinced that we've been moving closer to a point where it would be *us*."

She didn't question how he felt. She never would. Jay knew himself; he knew his feelings. She had no right to invalidate that to try to make this situation easier for herself.

They'd flatted together for a few years after Mallory's death. Night after night, they'd curled up in the lounge, watching Mallory's favorite classic films, and talking for hours and hours.

There had never been a time when Sylvie couldn't talk to Jay, about anything.

She couldn't think of one word to say now.

Nothing that wouldn't make this even worse.

Even as she watched, his shoulders straightened, his face smoothing out, the professional suavity slipping over his features, the mask that had carried him through years of business negotiations.

He'd never used this version of himself with her.

It was as if he'd reached out and closed a physical door between them.

The pain was shocking.

"I have to leave now." His every syllable was measured and too calm, but as their gazes met again and held, the façade cracked. "And for everything that we are, all that's ever been between us that *wasn't* in my head . . ." A slight note of bitterness, swiftly quashed. "I need you to let me do that."

During that time back then, when Mallory had died, and her breath had been punched out of her chest and she'd felt she could never move again, she'd forced herself up and she'd thrown herself into work. Keeping her hands and mind busy until she was ready to face what had happened. Keeping herself intact until it was time to break.

She let him leave. Without a word. Her gaze averted. Her hands clenched into shaking fists.

When the door closed with finality behind him, the clock kept ticking in the silent room.

Chapter Eighteen

Saturday

Hartwell Studios
The *Operation Cake* final.
Life has a habit of throwing curveballs.
Sometimes things work out as expected and desired.
And sometimes they smack you in the face harder than a
sponge-cake unicorn hoof.

Something was wrong with Sylvie.

With six different cameras ready to catch the slightest change
in his expression and edit it into a fantasy narrative, Dominic
tried to give them as little as possible. He kept his face turned toward the contestants' stations, watching as the final three painstakingly decorated their final bakes of the competition.

Wedding cakes.

The universe loved a shot of irony.

No fear that Sylvie's favorite contestants would make a sneak
grab for the Albany contract. Adam had gone with a theme aimed
at love-struck bookworms, a stack of antique books with their
titles painted on the spines in gold curlicue. *Romeo and Juliet,*

Tristan and Iseult, and *Bride and Groom*, an insert-the-names-of-the-happy-couple-here proposition.

Nothing said "marital role models" and "everlasting happiness" like Shakespeare's melodramatic, hormone-driven teens and the doomed, bespelled adulterers of yore.

However, the choice of titles was less of an issue than the ill-placed dowels. The bottom two tiers had already collapsed into each other, the gold paint of the text blurring and running. As of two minutes ago, the spines now read *Juliet and Iseult* in just-legible writing.

Likely a more interesting story, but a disaster of a cake.

Emma had opted for a wishing well cake, with small biscuits crafted into realistic gold coins for the theoretical bride and groom to toss into the depths of the fondant stone structure, making a wish before they closed their hands around the nuptial knife.

And plunged it into their own chests to avoid having to put a crumb of that cake in their mouths.

Dominic had tasted a spare cutting during his contractual stalk around the studio. He did not fancy having to repeat that experience for the approaching judging.

Two major errors—and this time, neither of them could be blamed on Libby. The producers had set a ridiculously difficult time frame for the final round. If Libby *had* intended more mischief, she'd been far too busy at her own station to carry it out.

All three contestants had crumbled in their own ways under the intense pressure.

Sweating and racing against the clock, Libby had let the sweetness-and-light act slip several times. She'd snapped at crew members and dissolved into tears over a broken bottle of milk.

Unfortunately, unlike the other two, she hadn't let it affect her work—and when tested under fire, she managed to produce the best bake of the entire series.

She'd gone the classic route—four tiers, white icing, fondant flowers, sugar lace—which was risky. If a contestant chose to play it safe with the design and forfeit the ingenuity points, the stronger-weighted execution had to be flawless.

Visually, at least, this was.

It was also, he suspected, aimed at appealing directly to his own tastes.

He had absolutely zero respect or liking for Libby Hannigan, and if he weren't fully focused on the frozen misery of the woman at his side, he'd be extremely irritated that she'd succeeded in her ploy.

As Adam watched another piece of his cake break off and splatter to the countertop while he uttered a mild "Oh dear!" of consternation, Dominic couldn't keep his eyes from jerking back toward Sylvie.

She was staring fixedly at the unfolding action, but beneath the professional gloss of makeup, her face was set in harsh lines of tension. Her hands were continually curling into and out of fists at her sides.

He touched her restless fingers—and she jerked away from him. Her hand pulled away, lightning fast, and lifted to clutch at the fabric of her shirt, over her heart.

Obviously, even if a person *had* unexpectedly toppled head-first and deeply in love, they weren't going to be superglued to their partner. He designed cakes for besotted lovers on a regular basis, and they rarely sat through the meetings entwined like octopi. He was currently the happiest he'd ever been because of Sylvie, and he got a ridiculous amount of pleasure from even her most casual touches. But he still needed space, and so did she. Earlier in the week, she'd been tired, getting over the food poisoning, and when he'd reached for her on the couch, she'd mustered the energy to open one eye and nudge his hand away with her foot. He'd left her alone. End of story.

Although admittedly slightly galling when she'd subsequently smooched the cat.

This was different. The violent swiftness of that withdrawal twanged straight at the chord of his worst memories, the deep-buried hurt he'd always despised himself for retaining.

Reflexively, he took a step back.

The remaining color leached from Sylvie's cheeks. Her eyes were shadowed and deeply unhappy; briefly, she squeezed them shut as she released a shaky breath.

He could see the apology in their darkened depths when she looked at him again. She reached out and touched his arm, stroking the pad of her thumb over his wrist.

It was a featherlight touch, heedless of any watching eyes and cameras. Intimate.

And trepidation had a sudden creeping, cold grip on his gut.

Things continued to spiral downward during the final judging. Libby embedded one last tiny crystal on the top tier of her cake and set down her tweezers, while Adam and Emma stumbled over the finishing line in a *Monty Python*–level comedy of errors. If the production team managed to edit this footage to create any sense of uncertainty about the outcome, they ought to be in line for a BAFTA.

The series villain was going home with the prize money.

It was a teeth-gritting ending to a tumultuous series, and the most flagrant rewarding of self-serving behavior since the appointment of their current prime minister. But every episode was theoretically a blank slate, and they could only judge what was put on the table today. Libby's cake was infinitely superior to the others.

A shrewd-eyed Aadhya had Sylvie hold up her baton second, after Mariana had unenthusiastically cast her vote in Libby's direction, extracting any tiny thread of drama that they could.

Sylvie was a fundamentally good person with strong sense of ethics, who looked at the world and genuinely saw magic. She'd suffered deep losses in her life, but she still believed in happy endings. He didn't want Libby to win, either, but it would be even more intolerable to Sylvie that someone could cheat and still prevail.

However, Libby *had* prevailed today. The judging playbook was clear. So Dominic was genuinely surprised—and concerned—when Sylvie lifted her chin and voted for Emma.

Dominic was left to break the tie and award the title to Libby, who fucking *winked* at him as if there had never been the slightest doubt from day one.

If Adam hadn't tripped over his own bootlaces and knocked Libby headfirst into the sink, the entire experience would have been irredeemable.

They left the set in an atmosphere both tense and anticlimactic.

As Zack handed Dominic a wipe to remove the light coating of powder on his forehead and nose, the makeup artist grimaced. "Another series when the biggest bitch on set takes home the prize. Even more unsatisfactory than the second season, when that pompous prick of a banker won." He reached out and flicked an eyelash from Dominic's cheek. "Fortunately, he was swallowed by a hippo at the safari park in Derbyshire last year. The universe always rights a wrong."

Dominic's eyes were on Sylvie, who was listening silently to

Mariana's chatter, her body tauter than a quivering wire. At that casual revelation, however, he lowered the wipe. "He was swallowed by a hippo?"

"I mean, he didn't *die*," Zack said carelessly. "He only went in from the waist up, and it spat him out again. Probably tasted rotten. I saw him on the news covered in tusk punctures. I expect it's too much to hope that Libby wanders into a wildlife pen, but at least she's unlikely to score the big endorsement deals. I've been keeping an eye on social media since the show started streaming, and she's not popular with viewers. Everyone loves Emma and Adam. The shipping game is strong. Shame that didn't work out."

Sylvie had broken away from Mariana and was coming toward them, not quite meeting Dominic's gaze. She arrived in time to hear the conclusion of Zack's gossip.

"Did you notice them avoiding each other today? They hooked up the other night. And according to Suzie in catering—worst sex *ever.* Mutual agreement that the only pleasurable part was the postcoital shower. Apparently, the contestants' hotel has massage jets. Their scalps got a pounding. The mattress did not." He clicked his tongue against his teeth. "They were so cute together, too. Sometimes you don't know the chemistry's a fizz until you put it to the test."

Sylvie had been cheerfully invested in that budding love story for weeks. She frequently texted Pet with updates. And after all the hope and speculation and tongue-in-cheek bets with his sister, she heard out the demise of the great *Operation Cake* romance with not even a flicker of reaction.

She was completely silent as they walked down to their dressing rooms. By the time they reached the locked doors, he was so bloody worried about her that he resorted to the meaningless small talk that usually tested his patience.

"Not an ideal outcome for the series," he said, pulling out his key. "Every superhero narrative would lead you to believe that fortune eventually turns its back on evil. A theory supported by the time Humphrey climbed the curtain rail and it collapsed before he could execute a carefully planned decapitation. However, apparently there's an outside chance she'll be inhaled by a large semiaquatic mammal, so there's still hope."

Sylvie's head was down as she unlocked her own door. "I can't believe you voted for her." Her voice was low. "She didn't deserve to win."

He leaned his shoulder against his door and studied her profile. He said nothing for a moment. "Morally, no. She deserved to be catapulted headfirst into a sink full of red food coloring, and I'm not sure that was an entirely accidental stumble from our mild-mannered professor. She's an insincere opportunist and probably a cheat, but there was never solid proof, and we had to judge what was on the table today. Her work was far and away the best. You know that. Did Aadhya tell you to vote for Emma?"

There wasn't a trace of judgment in his tone, but Sylvie's jaw tightened. She was worrying at the doorknob with her thumb. "No. Her wishing well was an ingenious idea. Right up my street. Just like Libby's design was tailor-made to appeal to you. And you danced to her tune just as she intended."

That last accusation twisted in midair even as the words left her mouth, starting off knife-sharp and layered with acres of something that had nothing to do with Libby and Emma and this never-ending headache of a show. Ending in a hitch of breath.

Everything about this was so unlike her. He was completely bewildered, and when he was unsure of himself, sparks of temper tended to stir. He had to bite back a taut response, but that defensive reflex vanished when her hands came up to cover her face.

"Oh God." She was trembling now. "I'm sorry."

He couldn't take it anymore. Opening her door, he nudged them both inside, closed it behind them.

With his hands over hers, cupping her face, he pressed his lips to her forehead. They stood there like that, completely still, until those gut-wrenching catches in her breathing stopped.

"For the record," he said then, with a lightness he didn't remotely feel, "I don't dance to anyone's tune. I can do a lot of things with my hands. I make no similar claim about my feet."

Sylvie's hands slipped down to his waist. Under any other circumstances, she'd have jumped to the obvious double entendre, but any teasing in her eyes was merely a sad flicker.

"Sylvie." Yesterday, she'd clutched his face on a busy street, in front of God knew how many watching eyes, and kissed him as if he were the only person on the planet. And today she'd walked in here as if she'd disappeared into a world of her own, and wherever she was right now, it was dark and lonely. Something in her eyes was deeply, bitterly alone, and a fist closed around his heart in a tight grip. "Sweetheart, what's happened?"

The first time he'd ever used that endearment in his life, but he barely noticed. Her fingers tightened, her eyes darkening with tumultuous emotion.

"I . . ." Her face crumpled again, and he stroked his hands down her shoulders, back up to her cheeks.

He'd been told repeatedly throughout his life that he was a difficult person to read, that he was unapproachable, intimidating, closed off. He could see why his reserve sometimes frustrated the people who cared about him—because the woman he fucking adored was drowning right in front of him, and even as she stood in his arms, she was pulling away.

"I can't—" Sylvie's voice cracked. She was starting to shake again, and he made a rough sound in his throat. "I don't—"

Very slowly, she put her palms against his chest and turned her head to touch her cheek to his heart. It was a butterfly-soft movement; he could barely feel her weight against him.

Foreboding was a cold trickle through his veins. His heartbeat was a fast, painful thud.

When he lifted his hand to stroke her hair, he realized his own fingers weren't entirely steady.

Sylvie's hand closed into a fist in his shirt, then, holding the fabric so tightly that her knuckles blanched.

Somebody knocked on the door and it opened before either of them could react. Mariana stuck her head in, biting her lip. "Sorry to interrupt," she murmured, her eyes softening on Sylvie's averted face. "I did try next door first."

She'd also noticed Sylvie's preoccupation during the shoot. She was far more accomplished at offering comfort than he was, but Sylvie had withdrawn from all friendly overtures.

Mariana held up his phone. "You left this in the greenroom and it's been going off repeatedly. I wasn't intentionally nosy for once, but you've got a cluster of messages on the screen about an urgent situation at the bakery."

Without letting go of Sylvie, he reached out a hand and Mariana gave him the phone. "Thank you," he said, and she nodded.

With another glance at Sylvie and a brief pat on her back, she left them. Dominic grimaced. Five messages from Liam; the team was fulfilling a major order today and the primary oven had broken down. It had happened once before, an annoying quirk in the wiring that he'd managed to repair last time.

Sylvie reached up and tipped the screen to see, then pushed

away from him. Reflexively, he reached for her again, and she shook her head. Strands of brown, lavender, and pink hair had come loose from her plait. She shoved them behind her ear. Her body was still racked with quiet shivering.

"Your staff need you," she said in a low voice.

"You need me." The response emerged strongly, from the very heart of him. Her eyes jumped back to his. There was a sudden hard knot in his throat. "And I need you."

Her lips parted. Drawing in another long, quivering breath, she reached up and touched her palm to his cheek, gently cradling his face. She ran her thumb along his bottom lip, tugging it slightly before her hand fell away.

"How can I feel this much so fast?" she whispered. "I can't even remember looking at you and *not* feeling like this. And when I try to imagine my life without you now—"

Her hands fisted again.

That almost anguished whisper had hit him directly in the gut. And the heart.

It had also ended on a fairly alarming note.

"Sylvie—"

"You have to go," she said, backing away. Looking around with something suddenly close to panic, she grabbed her bag and coat.

He caught her hand, and she turned and looked at him.

He recognized what was in her eyes, then, and his grip tightened.

"Please." Sylvie looked down at his fingers and brought his hand to her mouth. As she had once before, she kissed his thumb, and his jaw flexed. "I just—I need to think."

He let her go. A year ago, while drinking at a bar with Liam after his sous-chef's latest breakup, he'd drunkenly referred to Sylvie as a fairy, to his friend's endless delight and recurrent teasing. She slipped lightly away now, in that moment somehow as ephemeral as the magical lore she loved.

With her hazel eyes deep and dark with fear.

Sugar Fair
Where the Dark Forest welcomes all those in need.
Most likely, you already know, deep down, what you want.
What you need. And what's right.
Beneath these branches, may it always become clear in the dark
of night.

And may Jay retire his poetry pen as soon as possible.

Sylvie had once looked at Dominic and seen a man without feeling. Cold, hard, impenetrable.

That felt like a different life. When she looked at him now—when she woke in the night and lay next to the warmth of his skin, tracing the lines of his face and body with eyes and lips and fingertips—she felt so much that it overwhelmed her.

It terrified her.

The moment the door had closed behind Jay yesterday . . . She'd forgotten how it really felt when the ground suddenly dropped out beneath her and she was left reeling in the cold and dark, alone.

How badly it hurt sometimes to love so fiercely—and to have it torn away.

And she'd walked into the studio this morning and seen

Dominic. Dominic, who was rapidly becoming the center point of her life. Dominic, whom she was giving—unexpectedly, without plan or any prescience at all—the power to rip the remains of her heart to shreds.

She'd been scared to her bones, in that moment, how much he could hurt her as well.

Instead, she'd hurt him.

Notting Hill was busy and congested as usual, and the studio car had dropped her a block from the bakery. She'd walked blindly up the street toward Sugar Fair, and now just stood outside.

Her haven, her safe place, today seemed woefully inadequate; she wanted strong arms and that deep, cynical voice saying things that filled her heart and made her cry. The arms she'd pushed away. The voice that had cracked, because she'd made *him* afraid, too.

Her eyes stung.

Before she went inside, she braced herself and checked her phone. No new messages. She hadn't really expected Jay to return her texts, but the blank screen was another cold ache. Everything between them, years of friendship and loyalty and love, altered completely—irrevocably?—in a matter of seconds.

So fucking quickly, life could take away everything that mattered.

He was meant to be working on-site today while she was at the final. Whether he had done so remained to be seen.

She pushed open the door, letting the warmth and sugary scents wash over her. Mabel was at her table, shaping a series of little candy people. She had full autonomy to go wherever her creative mind took her with the sugar craft and had randomly embarked on a Shakespeare kick. So far, she'd made the complete casts of *Othello* and *Hamlet*. Sylvie could see a small cauldron with two witches crouched beside it and a third taking shape in Mabel's fingers. She was working her way through the tragedies.

Which immediately sent Sylvie's mind shooting straight back to Adam's poor, sad *Juliet and Iseult* fiasco—and her own behavior in voting for Emma. Whose cake *had* been ingenious. *Had* been right up her street. And had been nowhere near the caliber of Libby's.

She had never let her personal feelings affect her professional behavior before. Dominic was right. She believed to her core that Libby was a cheat, and although she wasn't quite nasty enough to hope the young woman was chomped by a hippopotamus, fingers crossed for a quick backhand from a baboon.

But she'd undermined her *own* ethics today in voting as she had.

She'd undermined a lot of things today that she held incredibly dear.

Mabel had looked up without interest, but for once had not immediately returned her attention to her work. She was staring steadily at Sylvie as her busy fingers continued pulling and shaping, drawing out a hooked nose, a clawed hand.

"Is Jay here?" Sylvie was relieved that her voice sounded relatively normal.

Or maybe not.

Mabel's eyes narrowed.

All she said, however, was "He's in the office."

No sarcastic rejoinder. No referring to Jay by any of her many and varied pejoratives.

"Thanks." Steeling herself once more, Sylvie slipped through the bookcase and walked quickly down the hallway. She could hear Jay's voice before she reached the office, and when she let herself in, he was on the phone.

He was standing at the window, looking out at their inspiring view of the moldy brick wall opposite, and didn't turn around. But beneath his crisp suit, his broad shoulders stiffened.

Sylvie stood for long enough that self-consciousness didn't so much creep in as throw open the door, sashay across the room, and make itself at home on the couch.

Quietly, she went to her desk and set down her bags. She unzipped her work tote and removed a folder, opening it to look down at the sketches she'd made last night, throwing everything she had into the distraction of Rosie and Johnny's cake.

For the wedding that might or might not still go ahead. With relationships crashing and burning all over the place right now.

Forty-eight hours ago, she'd been making gorgeous love with Dominic on his kitchen table. On the premise that it was a home environment, so not infringing any health and safety regulations. She'd opened her eyes to admire his face as he came, and had instead looked over his shoulder and seen Humphrey on the kitchen counter, viciously shredding teabags into Dom's lovingly tended sourdough starter. New discovery: when she started giggling on the veriest cusp of an orgasm, it did something fantastic to her pelvic muscles.

She'd suddenly realized then how truly happy she actually was. Happier than she'd been in years. Perhaps ever.

Jay was schmoozing one of their overseas suppliers. He sounded completely normal, joking, laughing, but he still hadn't turned his head.

She ran her fingers over the sketch, remembering a gut-punchingly beautiful bronze statue in a frosty garden. Wrought by the hands of another woman who'd been desperately in love. Desperately happy.

Blithely unaware of how soon she would lose it all.

As she closed the folder, Jay ended his call and appeared to brace himself.

He turned. Placed the phone carefully on his desk. Finally looked at her. "How was the final?"

So even, so hatefully polite.

"Bit of a disaster, really. Jay—"

"I've been looking at the rosters. One of our groups for the Dark Forest tonight canceled; I've rescheduled the other. And I'm going to be taking some leave for a few days."

Her mouth felt dry. "We're submitting the Albany proposal tomorrow. And then it's the ball."

"I'm not going to the ball." Something flickered in his eyes. "And this proposal has turned into more your thing than mine. Yours and his, ironically, despite the fact he's meant to be our competition in this situation, not your collaborator."

At the coldness in his voice, Sylvie internally flinched. She couldn't refute the accusation. "This proposal is for a contract that will significantly benefit the business. *Our* business. You have as much investment as I do in this panning out."

He was playing restlessly with a ballpoint pen on his desk. It slipped out of his fingers, skittering across the wood in a sound that obviously irritated both their exposed nerves. He turned away sharply. "As to that . . ." His jaw worked. "I may need to . . . reassess my position in the business going forward."

She was honestly incapable of speech for a moment. His eyes dragged to hers.

"What does that mean?" she said at last, tight with disbelief. "You're pulling out of Sugar Fair?"

One of his shoulders moved in the barest glimmer of a shrug.

It was enough to provoke an unexpected echo of emotion within her. Through her sadness and horror and fear, a small bubble of anger rose.

"This wasn't just our dream, Jay. This is our livelihood, and the livelihood of every member of our staff. You can't just throw all that in the bin because . . ." She cut herself off.

"Because I'm in love with you, and you're infatuated with the emotionless bastard across the street?" Reciprocal temper was threaded through every biting word.

"He's not emotionless," she couldn't help saying very quietly.

And she'd never been infatuated with Dominic. She'd detested him. She loved him. Fleeting infatuations were a silly, fun phase of her life that had now passed. There was nothing transient about her feelings.

Which was exactly why she was so scared.

None of which she said aloud. She was upset, stressed, and honestly, starting to feel a little betrayed in return, but she hoped she wasn't cruel.

"Jay." She met his shuttered gaze. "I didn't mean to undermine the way you're feeling right now. I would never intentionally do that. But—you're my best friend." She saw the look that crossed his face. "Maybe that sounds inadequate to you right now. Maybe to you, that's nothing." She swallowed painfully. "It's not nothing to me. You're one of the most important people in my life, and you have been for over thirty years. You're my family. I'll always love you. I'll always be here for you. My—" Her voice broke, and she had to pause to steady her breathing and herself. He was watching her intently, the beginnings of a faint sheen in his eyes. "My love isn't romantic, but it's deep and true. It's valid and it's yours forever, and I can't let you devalue *that*, either."

She gripped the edge of the desk. "I don't know what to do here. I don't know what to say."

Jay looked down. He closed his eyes. "I just— I need some time."

A repetition of what he'd said before—but the change of tone made them very different words. That visceral sharpness was gone. What was left was torn and almost gentle, and it made her eyes prickle.

That core of ice in her chest started to crack.

Her response was soft and raw. "Okay."

The door clicked quietly shut behind him.

And she breathed in, and out, and went to where she'd always sought solace these past three years.

Her own field of petunias.

Under the branches of her favorite tree in the Dark Forest, she sat and watched the light play through the leaves and over the stone walls.

Her head was tilted back and her eyes were closed when Mabel came quietly down the stairs and stood looking at her thoughtfully.

Moments later, the front door jangled as her assistant left the building.

Chapter Nineteen

De Vere's

The Midnight Elixir cake on the bench was an appetizing color—difficult to achieve with this blend of ingredients—and had a perfect crumb texture. It was also delicious.

Dominic stood with his hands propped against the counter, his mind tightly directed on the task at hand. He'd managed to fix the oven in record time, and Liam was escorting the finished cakes to their banquet destination. He'd considered taking them himself, but he hadn't wanted to leave Magnolia Lane because Sylvie was across the street and she was hurting.

She also wanted to be alone, and he was respecting her wishes, so the reasoning was illogical.

Regardless. His jaw set firmly, he pulled out a fresh bowl and started making another batch of the batter, slightly adjusting the ingredients.

Pet spoke from the kitchen door. "What's wrong with that one?"

"Too much pomegranate."

Her high heels tapped as she walked to the bench, picked up the knife there, and cut herself a small sliver of cake. She took a bite, chewing slowly. "Dominic," she said after she'd swallowed. "Even for you, this is a ridiculous level of perfectionism. This cake is superlatively good. Why are you wasting more time and ingredients?"

He measured out the spices without a reply.

She sighed. "Oh, hell. What's gone wrong with Sylvie?"

A bolt of emotion made it through. Frustration borne of uncertainty and helplessness, which resulted in a very cool "I don't have a fucking clue."

Pet leaned against the wall. "Did you have a fight?"

He glanced up at her. She was biting her upper lip.

"Pet, I don't mean to be rude—"

"No, I'm sure you don't usually *mean* to be rude," she obviously couldn't help inserting.

"—but I don't want to talk about this."

She looked at him very directly then. "Yeah. There's always been a habit, in this family, of not talking about a lot of things. And maybe we should."

He set down the egg in his hand and straightened, but before he could reply, his phone rang. The name on the screen wasn't the one he was hoping for, and certainly not the one he was expecting.

Marigold. The code name Sylvie had entered into both of their phones.

He swiped to accept the call. "Dominic De Vere."

As on a previous occasion, he'd expected to be dealing with the snotty condescension of Edward Lancier and instead got the woman herself.

"Mr. De Vere—" Rosie began.

"Dominic," he said with just a hint of dryness. They'd worn this routine to death.

"Dominic," Rosie amended after the briefest of pauses. There was an extremely odd note in her voice. "I apologize for the interruption while you're no doubt working. But I've been unable to make contact with Sylvie. Her phone appears to be off."

Yes. He'd discovered that piece of intel himself.

"May I ask," Rosie went on, and the chill in the words made Lancier seem a comparative teddy bear, "if you've looked at a news site in the past hour?"

Again, not what he'd expected. He met Pet's inquiring glance and nodded at the iPad on the bench. "News," he said under his breath, and she immediately grabbed the tablet and started tapping.

Seconds later, he saw her shape the word *Fuck*.

She turned it around to show him the screen. Under a screaming bold headline—*Who's Been a Naughty Boy, Then?*—was the photograph of Johnny and his curly blonde assailant, last seen on Sylvie's phone. And on Pet's phone.

It looked even more incriminating in close-up, splashed all over the worst of the tabloids.

He echoed Pet's brevity. "Christ."

"I assume you're currently looking at a photo of Johnny having some 'alone time' in the garden." Despite the sarcastic words, Rosie's tone was very level. "We were tipped off this morning that the story was going live today but were unable to halt it in time. My team have been investigating the source of the photograph—and at the moment, I'm told all roads are leading back to Sugar Fair." For the first time, her incredible control wobbled. The princess cleared her throat. "I don't believe Sylvie would go to the tabloids about us."

"She wouldn't." Dominic's eyes lifted from the photo on the screen to Pet's worried face. "But we do have the original of that photograph."

There was a brief, taut silence at the other end of the line. "I see," Rosie said, and then: "I can't talk about this now."

Tightly, matter-of-factly, she proposed a private meeting the following evening at St. Giles, after they'd delivered their final cake proposals, before the ball.

That she was going ahead with the ball at all, with speculation likely exploding all over the country . . .

In a way, it was a pity Rosie wasn't higher in the line of succession, because he suspected she'd make one hell of a queen.

He ended the call, still looking at Pet.

"Oh, gosh," she said, digging her teeth into her lip again as she read through the accompanying article. "Poor Rosie. Poor *Johnny*. The stuff they've written is vile. It'll be everywhere by now. How the hell did they get the photo?"

She looked up—and stilled.

Pet was a source of perpetual motion and energy, the extent to which was only recognizable when she went absolutely motionless and quiet.

"God." In its sudden absence of all expression, her voice was impersonal. Almost unrecognizable. "You think it was me."

"Not deliberately. Certainly not maliciously. But did you show someone, or leave your phone somewhere where a friend might have seen it, a boyfriend . . ." He cut himself off at the look that came into her eyes.

"Yeah," she said slowly. "Silly, flighty, careless Pet, right? The queen of bad decisions. It's not like I've consistently proven my discretion and loyalty for weeks on end now." Pet folded her arms, almost hunching into herself. "You really don't know me

at all, do you?" The words were very quiet, and all the more powerful and damning for it. "Did you ever really want to? That time
you tried to see me when I was younger, was it just a guilt reflex?
Because you left without a second thought?"

Pet's eyes went to the small mural on the opposite wall. The
London skyline, out of step with the rest of the décor, painted
on a whim by Sebastian during a surge of excitement over a
big new contract. "I felt awful for *years*, for turning you away
that day, when . . ." A wobble, rapidly steadied. "When I so
desperately wanted to go with you, even then. It had been a
slow transition with Gerald. He was so affable and affectionate
in public. Behind closed doors, he criticized everything I did.
It was never enough." She blinked hard. "Whatever I did, I was
never enough."

Dominic could hear the rhythm of their breathing in the quiet
kitchen, in sync, equally light and ragged.

She looked at him. "He used to say you'd turned your back on
us. On me. That if you ever reached out, it would just be under
obligation from Sebastian."

"That wasn't true," he said roughly. "It was never true."

Pet's mouth tucked in at the side, a desperate attempt not to
cry in front of him that made his chest hurt. "Mum used to keep
a photo of you, did you know that? In her drawer."

His jaw clenched.

"When I was little, I would go and look at it." Pet pressed her
thumb under her eye. "I'd tell you things."

There was a lump in his throat, as well.

"Gerald found the photo and really kicked off right before my
eighteenth birthday, right before you asked me to meet with you.
Mum closed down. The whole thing was just . . . too much. So

I told you I didn't want to see you again, and I regretted it from that day forward." She shook her head, and her eyes when she looked at him again were dark pools. "The thought of you, and Sebastian, and this bakery, was like a dream for me. This magical safe haven somewhere. A place that would be there, if I ever needed it."

The sound she made wasn't quite a laugh, and had nothing to do with amusement. "This thing with Patrick and Jessica—of course I wanted to know more about them, it's romantic and tragic and beautiful, but all I really wanted was to spend time with you. To get to know you better, when it's been so hard to do that. And to get to know Sylvie, because it was obvious that she's going to be a big part of your future." Pet forced the words out and they hit like spears. "I would never, *ever* run around spilling out information that's going to hurt you or anyone else. I would never be careless with something like that. Honestly, I'm gutted you would ever think I would."

He stepped forward instinctively, but she stepped back and lifted her hand. "No. Not now."

When Aaron pushed open the kitchen door, looking harassed, she took the opportunity to escape. Making it two for two on completely alienating the most important women in his life.

He was going after her despite that cool warding-off when Aaron caught at his arm. "Sorry, Dominic," he said, with a darting glance behind him. "I've said you're busy, but she's—"

The diminutive figure of Sylvie's assistant Mabel steamrollered past his hapless apprentice, waving him out of her way with an attitude that strongly reminded Dominic of his cat.

She noticeably looked him up and down, and audibly sighed. Her tone was, as usual, all sweetness and light. "Look, motherfucker. You gave her space when she asked for it. Clap, clap, well done, surprisingly sensitive. But she's had time to be and to think." She jerked her thumb over her shoulder. "She's in the Dark Forest. Move it. Your woman needs a fucking hug."

The Dark Forest
Where two people both need a fucking hug.

Sylvie was on her feet, on her way to find him, when she heard the footsteps on the stairs.

She didn't even question it was him.

Her Dominic Bat-Signal kicking in.

She was almost running when he strode through the door, and she flung herself at his chest. He caught her, pulling her in tightly, and she wrapped her arms around his neck.

"God. Dom. I'm sorry." She buried her face in his throat, closing her eyes and breathing in the comforting scent of his cologne. His jaw was prickly against her temple, but the skin under her lips was so silky. He felt hard, and warm, and sexy. He felt like home. "I'm so sorry."

He shook his head against her, his hand coming up to grip her head. "Don't" was all he said.

She could feel the damp warmth of her own breath against his neck. "It just—all hit me at once. I was totally overwhelmed." She reached up and touched the sharp line of his cheekbone. "I hadn't realized how much I've been keeping my life locked down. Safe. And suddenly, everything's flipped upside down. Nothing's what I thought it was, or what I expected to happen."

He pushed back her hair from her forehead and her hand drew down his body to press against his heart. There was something hard under the fabric of his jacket, a bump in the inner pocket. Momentarily distracted, she frowned.

He realized what she was poking at, and her brows pinched closer at the change in his expression. Concern lined his face; it was joined now by caution. He hesitated, then he released her to reach inside his jacket.

Without a word, he took out a small, well-wrapped bundle and handed it to her.

With another quick glance upward, she took it and unfolded the layers of protective silk.

And for a moment, she stopped breathing.

Nestled on the cloth was a small glass deer. The Arielle Aubert sculpture from Middlethorpe Grange.

"How did you—?" The words rasped from her parched throat. She touched the deer's head, cupped trembling fingers protectively over its fragile body.

Dominic was still very tense. He was watching her with that shrewd closeness, obviously unsure of the wisdom of this gesture. "Lady Middlethorpe is a far nicer human being than her husband. When I rang and explained that the little glass deer in her gallery would mean a great deal to someone, she was happy to sell it to me. She brought it to the bakery herself."

He moved one shoulder in a quick jerk. "You said the deer brought back more good memories than pain, but if it's going to make things worse, I'll return it to her."

Sylvie stood frozen.

Then, lifting the deer to her cheek, she lowered her head and went down to the floor. On her knees, hunching over. And she cried. Not light, polite tears. The sort of heavy, deep sobs that hadn't wracked her body for over a decade.

Dominic was also rendered momentarily motionless. She

heard him swear viciously, before he was down on his knees beside her.

"God," he said. "My darling."

He wrapped his arm around her head, tucked his head back against her, and they crouched there together. The lights in the trees danced around them, eerie shadows flickering around the walls.

It was a short, violent release. As the sobs dwindled to the occasional hiccup, Sylvie's nose was running and the beginnings of a headache pressed between her brows. With her head on his shoulder, she said croakily, "I always thought you were the rigid one. Like I was this soul of spontaneity. When, really, I've played it so safe since Mallory died."

"You put all your finances into a food business in London," Dominic murmured. "That's hardly playing it safe."

"I don't mean work." She scrubbed her wrist under her eyes. "When Sugar Fair struggles, obviously the stress is huge, and it would gut me if I lost it. But it can't . . . shatter me."

Holding the deer close, she watched the ghostly shapes moving amidst the leaves.

"That night in the hospital, when Mallory was gone, I felt as if I'd been cut adrift. I've never felt out of control like that. My biggest safety net was gone." A sharp pain in her chest. "But I had Jay. I had my friends. And I . . . kept going. I rebuilt a life. One day at a time." She exhaled. "But I've realized now how much I've protected myself because I didn't think my heart could survive another loss like that. And when Jay . . ."

She stopped, and felt Dominic stiffen.

He said nothing, however, and she went on haltingly, "Suddenly, I might be losing Jay, and I've been completely knocked off my feet by what's happening between you and me, and it hit home how—"

"How badly you could be hurt again."

"It was . . . horrific, the first time." She picked her way very carefully now. Neither of them had ventured into direct "L-word" territory yet, and she'd just wept all over him. She needed to be honest, but self-consciousness was prickling. "I suspect it would be even worse now."

His arm tightened reflexively.

"Thank you for the deer," she said. "It's one of the nicest things anyone's ever done for me."

"If it's going to make you sad—"

"No." She looked into the little carved eyes. It had a more piquant expression than Mallory's, a glint of mischief that made her smile. "No."

The lighting scheme in the Dark Forest was changing, softening to a warm glow, the spooky effects fading into flitting fireflies and the gentlest rustling whisper of the trees.

Evidently, Mabel was making a few adjustments upstairs.

Over the rustling, Sylvie heard the *snick* of the automated door lock clicking into place—keeping out any further visitors.

Mabel had definitely earned that Christmas bonus this year.

With his hand tucked up under her messy hair, his palm warm against her neck, Dominic kissed her cheek and the corner of her mouth. Sylvie turned her head obligingly, and their mouths met.

Unlike the usual flare of passion, desire was a slow burn, flickering under a surge of comfort and growing intimacy.

She carefully set the deer aside and Dominic took her all the way down to the floor, the kiss starting to deepen as the hardness of his body lowered onto hers, his hands slipping up under her top as he pressed closer.

They slid away layers of clothing, undoing buckles, lifting and arching. Their skin was a bare, shivery glide against each other when he belatedly hesitated, removing his lips from her throat.

"What's wrong?" she asked huskily, her hips moving just a little restlessly against his shirt, spread on the ground beneath them as an impromptu, inadequate blanket.

"You're still upset." A bit of sex growl nonetheless roughened his voice. "It's in your eyes, and I can feel it in your body. I don't want to take advantage if you—"

"I want you." It came out as more of a significant, final statement than she'd intended. But she meant it, in every respect. More quietly, holding his gaze, she murmured, "I want *you*."

As they continued to look into each other's eyes, seeking something and mutually finding it, Sylvie took his hand and brought it to her mouth. His breath coming faster, he slipped his first two fingers between her lips and she wet them, a sensual tug, before she slid his hand down her body.

In the dim, dancing light, under the trees, he stroked her as they lay side by side, heads turned to watch the tiniest changes in each other's expressions. The hitches in breathing, the deepening flush in their cheeks and chests. Sylvie arched her head back with a small sound when he carefully slipped a finger inside her. Blindly, she reached for him, ran her own hand down his slightly damp abdomen.

"Can I—"

"You can touch me wherever you want." A rasp. "Whenever you want."

Words that she might have taken lightly from another man. That meant a very great deal from him.

His head jerked to the side as she teasingly ran her fingers down his erection, cupped him, curved her thumb and forefinger as far as she could around his length.

Neither of them had a condom or any real desire for penetration. They lay for a long time just touching each other, looking at each other, existing in a bubble of slow, lazy, helpless pleasure and unbelievable closeness.

Their lips were just touching when she cried out, and he went rigid against her when she got her breath back and slid down to take him in her mouth.

She had no idea how long it was later when they sat together under her favorite tree, Sylvie tucked between Dominic's legs as he rested back against the trunk, her cheek nestled on his chest.

"I need to finish my proposal," she murmured, her whole body feeling deliciously limp and lethargic.

His muscles, however, tensed. He stretched out an arm toward the crumpled pile of clothing and extracted his phone. "About that."

She sat up, curling her legs to the side, and stared in horror at the news headline on the screen as he recounted the call from Rosie. But when he got to the part about Pet, she reached up and curled her arms back around his neck, a tight hug of comfort.

"She wouldn't do that," she said quietly, kissing his throat.

"I knew that the moment I said it, but the damage is done." The words were bleak and grim. "To a far greater extent than I realized." He ran his fingers through his hair. "She left the bakery before I did. I don't know if she's coming back."

She puffed out a breath. What a total sodding disaster all round. "She'll come back," she said with certainty. "She loves you."

He jerked his head to the side, not quite a shake, but a negation, nonetheless. She held his veiled gaze. "She loves you," she
repeated, and after a moment he touched her cheek.

And very unsubtly changed the subject. "Sylvie." The serious-
ness in his tone and renewed tautness in his body warned her.
"What did you mean about losing Jay?"

She couldn't respond immediately. With the way she felt
about Dominic, it was—and should be—completely natural to
talk to him about something that was eating away at her like a
corrosive burn.

It also felt like the most colossal betrayal of Jay's feelings.

No matter how dismayed she was by his threat to leave the
business, she cared, very much, about that.

And bluntly, she still found it totally surreal, such a shift in
viewpoint, to realize he was even looking at her like that. Vo-
calizing the surreal—it suddenly solidified into reality before a
person was necessarily ready to cope.

She continued to hesitate; and in the end, as he'd done so
many times lately, he made it easy for her.

Dominic pulled away far enough that she could see his face
and he hers. His expression was nothing like what she'd expected.

Gentleness. Sympathy. The sudden burning of tears caught
her by surprise.

He bent and touched his mouth to hers. "He's in love with
you."

It wasn't a question.

Her fingers curled into the scattering of hair on his bare chest.
"He says he is." She shook her head slightly. "He's family to me. I
thought I knew him to his core. I thought I knew *us*. How could
I not even *notice*?"

"Because he's family to you," he reiterated simply, his thumb moving in a featherlight stroke.

"In the true meaning of the word, to me, which has nothing to do with biology. And which is unconditional. Forever." She searched his eyes. "Did you know?"

"I wondered. The way he looked at you."

One tear slid free. "Dom, he's already slipping away."

He caught the tear with his lips. His forearm flexed, warm and strong, when she wrapped her fingers around his wrist.

"Sylvie." He spoke very low, their browbones touching. "I don't know what to say. It's less surprising to me than it is to you." When she lifted her gaze, he smiled faintly. "Nobody understands better where he's coming from than me."

She'd experienced multiple emotions after Jay's confession, none of them positive. When Dominic spoke, however— butterflies.

Or perhaps, like the pinpoint lights flitting around the walls, "fireflies" were a better description. Bright little sparks of joy, lighting up the darkness.

She'd fallen so much in love with him that it hurt.

"Where is he now?" Dominic asked, his voice going husky in response to whatever he saw flashing in her eyes then.

"I don't know. He asked for some space. Time off."

In an absent reaction to the *caw* of the raven clock on the wall, they had both stirred to get up. The raven popped out to announce the fifty-minute mark in each hour and no other time. The utter randomness had appealed to her for this room. That particular *caw* meant that the last of the staff should be signing out upstairs, and she needed to make sure her Midnight Elixir cake sample was secure for tomorrow before she locked up.

At this point, who bloody knew what was going to happen

with the royal wedding, but—she had to have faith in Rosie and Johnny. And right now, all she could do was fulfill her part of the commitment.

She had a responsibility to the people upstairs to see this through.

She had a responsibility to *herself* to bloody rock this.

They had almost finished dressing when she voiced the last painful revelation about Jay. "He talked of pulling out of Sugar Fair."

This time, Dominic went completely rigid. Not in the good way that usually culminated in mutually shaking thighs.

"He what?" His voice was sharp. He was *not* impressed, and was still informing her of that fact, as if she hadn't already said three times she agreed it wasn't acceptable to throw that at her and at the business, and that it bordered on emotional blackmail, when they entered the kitchen—and almost walked straight into a wrathful dandelion.

A patronizing description of a human being, nevertheless accurate as Penny faced them with streaks of red in her cheeks. She was so cross that her hair seemed to be quivering, yet even in her towering rage she maintained that vague vibe, as if one strong puff of breath would send her thoughts scattering every which way.

"How *dare* you have the Starlight Circus shut down," she snapped, her hair wiggling more vigorously as a punctuation mark.

It was such a bizarre moment that it took a second to absorb the words.

"They shut it down?" Sylvie had vindictively hoped Darren would cop a whopping fine for his shoddy hygiene practices; she hadn't dared to hope they'd actually hazard-tape the door.

Having consumed multiple foodstuffs from his bacteria den, she didn't want to think too hard about how bad the kitchens must have been.

Otherwise—what a delightful twist in an otherwise shit of a day.

Between that and the orgasm, and the confirmation that she was utterly, bone-deep, soul-hard in love with the man beside her, it was definitely ending on an upward curve.

"Thanks to you."

"Thanks to the hygiene failures and probably dangerous cost-cutting of your . . . boyfriend?" Dominic was using the face and voice most calculated to send *Operation Cake* contestants scurrying around corners. Sylvie could have told him not to bother—all variation in tone bounced off Penny like an impenetrable shield in a video game.

She also didn't mention that the space between the concentric circles of Stern Dominic and Sexy Dominic was rapidly narrowing, lest he become perversely affable in response.

She looked sharply from his very icy face to Penny's. "Boyfriend?"

"She was coming out of Darren Clyde's kitchens the other night," he said, without looking away from the other woman. "And made a very fast retreat when she saw you."

"You're connected with Darren?" Sylvie was trying to fit those pieces together in her mind. Failing miserably. "A *relationship* with Darren?"

What in the actual fuck was going on at the moment?

At this point, if Pet suddenly popped out from a corner and revealed herself a secret agent for MI5, she wouldn't even blink.

"Why did you say it like that?" Penny asked defensively. "Why *wouldn't* we be a couple?"

Sylvie just looked at her, totally wordless, before she turned to Dominic. "I don't want to be alarmist, but I believed I've single-handedly cracked the space-time continuum. This is a parallel universe after all. And it's very odd."

"Penny Pops." Dominic had decided to add verisimilitude to her theory by making nonsensical statements.

"I'm sorry? Pops what? Pops who?"

"On Clyde's god-awful menu. There was an item called a Penny Pop. I assumed it was a nod to old-fashioned penny sweets."

Penny had the almighty nerve to clasp her hands over her navel and sway in love-struck gratification. "No, it was a nod to *me*. In recognition of all my help with the development of the menu."

Her intern might be falling out of her rage and back into walking dreamworld, but Sylvie was taking a swift turn down the path of being seriously pissed off.

"Did you take this job just to pass information along to Darren?"

Penny blinked at her. "Of course. But I did appreciate all that advice you gave me. I don't really remember much of it, but . . ."

A shrug.

Sylvie lifted her hand to her temple. *For Christ's sake*, said she in her head and Dominic aloud.

"It was Darren's idea that I apply." Penny looked suddenly proud. "But I'm the one who realized in the interview that if I said I had no family, either, you'd probably feel sorry for me. And you did." She was patently delighted by her own manipulation.

Sylvie immediately slipped her hand sideways and pressed her palm against Dominic's ribs as he took an instinctive step forward.

As tempting as it was to cheer him on, he really couldn't chuck her staff members out the window.

With a slightly aggrieved note, as if Darren had been claiming all the credit for their misdeeds, Penny added, "And it was *my* idea to get the photo off your phone and give it to that reporter."

Sylvie's breath caught, and Dominic went very still.

Behind Penny, the door to the shop floor had opened silently. Mabel stood there with a lollipop in her hand, also listening.

"It did get rid of her," the intern pointed out, as if Sylvie ought to be grateful. Her smile widened. "She wasn't interested in the *cake* at all after that. If you're going to have such private discussions in your office, you really should have spent less on tacky kitsch and more on soundproofing."

"You took the photo off my phone? You *broke* into my phone?" Sylvie's voice lifted in pitch, and Penny lifted her nose.

"You left it on your desk, unlocked. Again, poor security, boss."

At which point, she fucking *tutted.*

Sylvie breathed in deeply.

Rosie and Johnny's relationship was being ripped to shreds, with the press and public pawing over the pieces like wild dogs.

The emotional chasm between Dominic and Pet had been torn even wider.

Apparently, Sylvie had been wasting time, money, and ingredients for months, constantly defending this woman to Jay.

And someone intimately connected to the Starlight Circus had just called *her* décor "kitsch."

"Penny," she said very calmly, with a smile just as vague, just as airy, and just as malicious, "get the fuck out of my home."

Penny tossed her head—and froze as Mabel walked toward her, hips swinging, also smiling.

That smile had more eerie impact than every lighting effect in the Dark Forest combined.

The intern took a step back, but halted in momentary confusion when Mabel offered her the lollipop.

She took the candy skull automatically, and then shrieked as Mabel—tiny, deceptively delicate Mabel—made a blur of a movement with her foot and Penny tumbled across her shoulders.

Whistling, Mabel walked toward the back door and out into the alley, wearing Penny around her neck like a scarf. Through the window, Sylvie watched as her assistant calmly threw the intern into the dumpster.

As a stream of profanity drifted from the piles of rubbish—most of which, incidentally, was all the ingredients Penny had purposely wasted—Mabel returned to the kitchen.

"I'll be off, then," she said, collecting her bag and coat from their hook.

"Have a good night," Sylvie returned serenely.

As Mabel passed her, without turning her head or altering her expression, their hands fleetingly clasped.

The door swung closed, leaving Sylvie alone with Dominic in a lovely, clean kitchen, while her former intern made a third cross attempt to clamber from the trash.

Locking the back door, Sylvie transferred the bland smile to him.

His dark gaze shifted from the window to her face, his handsome features expressionless. "I'm equal parts terrified and aroused."

"What an excellent relationship motto for us. I think I'll embroider it on a cushion."

The death blow to his composure.

He had to hold on to the countertop, he was laughing so hard, and despite the chaos surrounding them at every turn, Sylvie grinned.

Chapter Twenty

"Though she be but little, she is fierce."
—William Shakespeare

St. Giles Palace

Sylvie had never found it so difficult to draw a line and consider a design done.

She had tweaked her work over and over again since last night, would likely still have been fiddling with it down to the wire if she hadn't needed to stop and dress for the ball.

But it was done. She and Dominic had both delivered their final tenders ten minutes ago, casting shrewd looks at each other's folders and the accompanying cake boxes of samples.

Whatever decision the royal couple made, she was happy with her proposal. The whole thing was tinged with shadows over Jay, who was still screening her calls, but she was proud of herself and her team. It was a cake that could well and truly hold its place in the historical records.

And regardless of who got this contract, this experience had changed her entire life. Dominic stood at her side and their fingertips brushed.

Unfortunately, it was looking increasingly doubtful whether there would be a wedding to *require* a cake.

Once before, she'd sat in this palace, watching as Rosie and Johnny continually reached out to each other with hands and eyes. She'd rarely seen a couple with such a tangible connection. Such obvious affection.

They stood now on opposite sides of a small meeting room. In the fraught minutes since an odiously pleased Edward Lancier had ushered Sylvie and Dominic inside, Rosie hadn't looked at Johnny once.

He, on the other hand, couldn't take his eyes from her face. His desperation was visceral.

Much like last time, the Duchess of Albany was doing most of the talking. She looked more like a majestic iceberg than ever. "After the *extremely unfortunate* photograph that emerged yesterday, there will naturally be questions and comments this evening. You will ignore the atrocious manners of others and make no response. Any decisions and public statements will come at the appropriate time, through the appropriate channels. Do I make myself clear?"

"That's right," Edward decided to pipe in. "With the personages present this evening, this is hardly the occasion to publicly sever this engagement."

Rosie jerked visibly, but she was already following her mother's directive. She made no response, even to her family.

"We're not s-severing anything," Johnny burst out. He moved then, lunging forward to grab Rosie's hand. She didn't pull away, but her fingers were limp in his. *"Rosie."*

The princess's navy eyes had been frighteningly blank and flat, but as they lifted to meet the urgency in Johnny's, a spark of pure anguish flared and extinguished.

"I'll thank you to not raise your voice in this room, please, John," the duchess said frostily. "Most of this situation has been entirely your own doing. Although there has clearly been an unacceptable breach of privacy."

The chilling pale stare speared Sylvie. The moment the door had closed behind them, she had explained—quietly and succinctly, and to Rosie and Johnny, not the watching sharks—the circumstances that had led to the publication of their private pain. As Rosie knew, they had been in the grounds near Johnny. The photograph had been taken; Sylvie had left Pet's name out of it. And a member of her staff had leaked it to the press. That person's employment was now terminated, and she could only sincerely apologize.

Johnny had merely shaken his head, his face white.

Rosie had briefly looked at Sylvie, and said in an unnaturally calm voice, "I know you didn't intend for it get out."

Her mother was less forgiving, but as the aristocratic lip curled, Dominic shifted. Angling his body so that he was partly shielding Sylvie, he looked at the duchess—who actually flushed.

Even royalty couldn't withstand the De Vere Glare.

The older woman drew herself up and redirected her fury, but for once Johnny didn't quail under her disapprobation. He was otherwise occupied, obviously geared up for the fight of his life.

The fight *for* his life.

"Fidelity may not be a highly prized virtue in this family," opined the duchess, who was strongly rumored to have at least four lovers herself, "but you are expected to act with a *minimum* of discretion. Cavorting in the palace gardens, for goodness' sake."

"I wasn't *c-cavorting* anywhere," Johnny snapped. He was still holding Rosie's hand tightly, and he shook it gently as he spoke, urging her. "I would never be unfaithful. *Never*. It makes me feel sick even thinking about it."

Even Edward Lancier, who clearly despised Johnny, must have heard the ring of truth.

Rosie drew in a shaky breath.

Johnny jerked a glance at Sylvie and Dominic, but although he spoke to them, he looked at Rosie. The princess's head was down. "Her name is Helena. The woman you saw on Friday and making a scene outside our offices." He was speaking with uncharacteristic matter-of-factness now, so focused on his fiancée that the connection between them might be a visible cable, zipping with electricity. "I've known her all my life. She lives in the village adjacent to my parents' estate. There's never been anything romantic between us, but she's told members of the press otherwise. She's built up a fantasy narrative in her head, and she's been s-systematically harassing me for months, from the moment my relationship with Rosie first hit the papers. She's not well, and I'm trying to see that she gets the help she needs."

"Load of nonsense," Lancier sneered, and Rosie turned on him in a sudden burst of anger.

"Oh, shut up, Edward." Red flags appeared in her cheeks. She lifted her chin, as regal as her mother when she wanted to be. "Of course Johnny isn't having an affair. He's got more integrity than most of this family combined." She looked at Johnny then. "But I still can't believe you told me nothing about any of this before yesterday. This woman has been sending you, what, twenty messages a day sometimes? Thirty? She's got hold of your schedule and is ambushing you outside our home. Getting past security. Physically throwing herself at you."

"You already had Lancier and the rest of your family dripping constant poison in your ear about how temperamentally unsuited I am to this life." Johnny shot the seething Lancier a forgivably nasty look. His eyes were burning with emotion. "I didn't want to lay what seemed at first a ridiculous, petty s-situation in your lap." His expression hardened. "And when it became progressively more serious and . . . concerning, I didn't want to potentially expose you to any danger."

"You truly think this woman is dangerous?" Rosie looked torn between anger and concern, equally understandable.

"Even a few weeks ago, I wouldn't have said so," Johnny said. His fingers curled tighter about hers. "I felt sorry for her. Frankly, I *still* feel s-sorry for her. She was always a bit of an odd bird out in her family, like I am in mine. But she seems to have spiraled since we announced our engagement. She honestly believes we have this long-standing passionate history and I've betrayed her." His mouth twisted. "Before she kissed me on Friday, the only time I remember ph-physically touching her was ten years ago, when I helped her into a carriage during the village heritage festival."

"She didn't *kiss* you. She assaulted you. *Johnny.*" Rosie turned in a sudden surge of frustration. "We're engaged. We love each other. You need to be able to tell me anything. Lean on me for *anything.*" She threw up one hand in a gesture almost of despair. "God."

Lancier made a final, ill-advised attempt. "He's clearly *not* suited to the public rigors of this role. Encouraging the delusions of a mentally ill—"

Johnny had finally reached his limit.

"That's it." Releasing Rosie, he walked to the door and pulled it open. "Your Highness. Lancier. Get out."

Sylvie couldn't repress an instinctive snort at the look on the duchess's face.

Every affronted, outraged GIF in history had just come to life in this room.

If the Prince of Wales never had a child, it was possible that the Duchess of Albany could one day become Queen Consort.

At the very least, she would hopefully much sooner become Johnny's mother-in-law.

He did not give one single shit.

"*Out*," he said again, his entire demeanor brooking no opposition.

The duchess was the most stereotypical type of bully. When faced with a dose of her own medicine, she retreated.

With a malevolent glare at the offspring who'd foisted this man on her.

Sylvie strongly suspected that if Edward Lancier hadn't followed suit, Johnny would have happily given him a helping hand, via a fist in his collar. Lancier might be a snobbish, interfering dickhead, but he wasn't completely without a sense of self-preservation. He scuttled out like a bristling squirrel.

Johnny shut the door firmly. He immediately turned back to Rosie. "You're deliberately picking a fight," he said with that unaccustomed coolness, and her lips thinned.

"We'll give you some space, as well," Dominic began, belatedly startling Sylvie into realizing that she shouldn't just stand here gawping at them and openly eavesdropping.

Alas.

"We all have to get out there." Rosie's hand fisted in the skirts of her spectacular black gown. Sylvie was in sparkling pink, and the combined effect was a little more Elphaba and Glinda than she'd intended. "We're going to be late. And there's nothing I enjoy more than waltzing with a room full of people who'll be thrilled my fiancé is cheating on me. It enlivens the supper."

Sylvie winced, but the cold sarcasm made no impact on Johnny. He shook his head. "You don't give a shit about any of them. All your Christmases came at once when that story broke yesterday."

A flash went through Rosie's defiant eyes.

That shot had hit home.

"The perfect reason to end things," Johnny went on. His hands were shaking, and he stuffed them in the pockets of his crisp tuxedo trousers, but his voice was rock-steady. And all of a sudden, it gentled. His next words were so soft he might have been humming a lullaby. "So determined to save me from myself."

Rosie blinked hard. There was a wet glitter behind the thickly mascaraed lashes.

"Decent play, my love," Johnny went on in that low murmur. "But I'm afraid it's game over. I'm not going anywhere."

Her breath was expelled in a long sob, and the genuine torment in that sound made Sylvie flinch. She imagined it had ripped the guts out of Johnny.

"I'm not going to ruin your life." The words wrenched from Rosie. "I can't. I *can't*."

"I love you," he said simply. "I don't care about the opinions of strangers. I don't give a shit what people like Lancier think. My loyalty is to you. Our duties will be plenty, but my highest priority is to keep both of our hearts safe. I'm walking into this freely, of my own volition, with my head held high and my hand in yours."

"That's probably what Jessica thought with Patrick at first, and—"

A sudden surge of exasperation tore from him. "Stop comparing us to your uncle and his girlfriend. We're *not them*. I don't care if she didn't choose him. I fucking choose *you*—"

Sylvie cleared her throat. "She did choose him."

She could now appreciate Dominic's attempt at a discreet exit. She'd intended to tell Rosie the truth about Jessica at a more appropriate time, and it was very awkward interrupting a declaration of undying love.

Johnny's mouth snapped shut. Silence followed, so for a moment they all had nothing to do but really *feel* the anticlimax.

"What?" Rosie was understandably thrown by the abrupt change in atmosphere. She'd been about to be thoroughly snogged. Johnny's hands were still on her face. He didn't seem to know what to do with them now.

Dominic came to the rescue with a matter-of-fact explanation. "Sylvie was going to speak to you later. We went to Jessica's former home and spoke to her sister, Kathleen. Jessica changed her mind. She didn't even make it through a week without him. She was killed in a car accident on her way back to London. Back to Patrick."

Johnny's hands slowly fell away from Rosie's cheeks.

The princess's face was very pale as she looked at Sylvie. "Is that—is that true?"

Sylvie nodded. "She loved him, Rosie. According to Kathleen, she'd never been so happy."

Beyond the door, she could hear the distant murmur of voices and music. It felt as if they were in a bubble, a snow globe, temporarily hovering away from the rest of the world.

The words came from the very heart of her and she looked up at Dominic as she spoke. "She knew it was worth fighting for. That they would have been stronger than everything that tried to break them." Her fingers twisted into his when he silently took her hand. "That sometimes you have to overcome your fears and reach out for what you really want. Because no matter what happens in the end, you'll never regret a single moment. It's *always* worth it. It's the only thing that matters, really."

Rosie made another soft sound.

Someone knocked on the door, just once, very politely.

Nobody moved; then, finally, Johnny bent to straighten Rosie's skirts for her. "Duty calls," he said quietly.

Unlike Pet, Dominic considered this ball a final hurdle in the competition, not a reward for said work. He would admit, however, that the premier ballroom in St. Giles Palace was a stunning example of Georgian architecture, he appreciated excellent food that he didn't have to prepare himself—and he had the most beautiful woman in the room in his arms.

He looked down into Sylvie's eyes as they moved to the music of the band. In the dim, romantic lighting, her irises looked dark. Given all the circumstances, this felt a little like dancing while the ship burnt around them, but he wanted the comfort of her body and touch.

God, they'd come a long way.

The woman who had driven him absolutely batshit four years ago, who had opened a rival business in direct view of his own, who was solely responsible for over a million people watching a YouTube clip of him being unicorned in the face, was the love of his life.

Still totally surreal.

The band switched to a more up-tempo song, and he startled a peal of laughter from Sylvie when he suddenly twirled her.

"I should have known you were full of shit when you claimed

to be a poor dancer," she said when he brought her back in against his chest. "With the possible exception of people-ing, you're good at everything. It's very irritating."

But "people-ing" was a pretty significant thing to fuck up, when it resulted in the sort of hurt he'd seen in Pet's face yesterday.

He was determined to be a good partner, but he continued to prove an absolute bloody failure of a brother.

The drummer launched into a solo, and Dominic glanced over at the mocked-up stage.

In the unlikely event that Pet showed up tonight, she'd be thrilled. The average person streamed their favorite music for their birthday. Princesses scored the Grammy winners live and in person, and this particular group had been playing on Pet's phone on repeat for weeks.

Sylvie's fingers touched the back of his neck above his shirt collar, and that shiver wound down his spine. Increasingly familiar, yet never failing to startle in its intensity.

"She'll come," she said softly.

He pulled her closer. Spoke into her hair. "I hope so."

Over her head, through the crowds, he saw a familiar figure come through the main doorway and look around with an air of intense anxiety.

Sylvie shifted to look up at him. "You okay?"

He turned them so she could see where he was looking.

She saw Jay at the same time her best friend spotted them. She took a quick breath as her mouth quivered.

Apparently unconsciously, her hand slid across his shoulder to hold on to his bow tie.

Jay also seemed to take a steadying breath before he moved toward them. He edged through the well-dressed crowds, wrinkling his nose when he passed the woman who must have bathed in her perfume.

The closer he came, the more Sylvie tensed.

"It's okay," Dominic said. "It'll be all right. All of it."

Her eyes moved to his. "Promise?"

The question was forcibly light, half ironic.

He didn't look away from her. "Yes. I promise."

Her fingers tightened on him.

A few feet away, Jay cleared his throat. "May I cut in?"

Sylvie squeezed Dominic's arm before she nodded.

Jay looked at Dominic. His expression was completely unreadable, but it was clear that Dominic wasn't high on his list of favorite people. The feeling was mutual.

And for the sake of the woman standing between them, it was something they'd both have to get the fuck over.

"I assume you're not looking at me for permission," he said coolly. "Because she doesn't need me to give it, and I'd probably get another cake to the face if I tried. But of course she wants to dance with you. You're a vital part of her life and always will be."

Jay blinked.

As Dominic stroked his fingers calmly, gently, down Sylvie's back and moved away, he said in a low voice, "As much as you hate my guts, we both have a vested interest in Sylvie's happiness. She's so worried about you that she's physically shaking. If you hurt her—*then* you and I have a serious problem."

He left it, and them, at that.

Sylvie hesitantly took Jay's hand, resting her other arm lightly on his shoulder as they moved into the dance.

He looked typically tall and handsome in his tux, the lights playing over his hair and cheeks.

Their eyes met—and she could have cried in the middle of the dance floor.

Because the man looking back at her wasn't a cold, distant stranger. He was Jay.

"'If Sugar Fair ever closes,'" he quoted her huskily, from what now seemed a million years ago, "'it'll be at our instigation.'" His hand tightened on her waist. "But it won't ever be at my instigation. I'm sorry I even went there, Syl. And after all the shit I've given you about keeping emotions out of business. I promise you right now—I will give one hundred percent to our company, now and always. We will share those decisions, and successes, and all the bloody stress that comes with it."

Her eyes briefly fluttered closed. "I'm so glad to hear you say that. Because it wouldn't be Sugar Fair without you. This is *our* journey, to take together." She hesitated, tried to relax her fingers against his shoulder. "But—"

Jay broke in before she could put the rest of her fears into words. "I—" He cleared his throat. "I couldn't sleep last night because I felt so shit about everything that happened. And the . . . the barrier that suddenly sprang up between us, it just felt—"

"Wrong."

"So wrong." His lips pulled into a grimace. "Sylvie, I love you."

She didn't flinch, didn't look away from him.

"And there's one aspect of that love that is not what you need, and is not going to be good for me, either. It's something I'll be talking about with a family member I trust and with my therapist as I move forward and I hope past it, but this is the last time I'm ever going to talk about it with you." A muscle in his cheek leapt, but his voice was now very firm. "I can't pretend that in the short term I'm going to find this easy, especially when . . ." He jerked his head very slightly toward the bar, where Dominic was now talking, extremely unenthusiastically, to the Chancellor of the Exchequer. "But above all else, I'm your best friend. And the rest of my love? It's unconditional, it's everlasting, and I fucking want you to be happy."

A tear slipped down her nose and she impatiently brushed it away. She'd shed enough tears. "I want you to be happy, too. So much."

Jay nodded, just once. "I will be. You've found your path, and I'm—I've taken the first step toward finding mine."

He gave her hand a little shake. "But De Vere is already drilling a hole through me with his eyes. If you keep sobbing with sympathy over all those blind dates I'm going to have to sit through before I either meet the person of my dreams or decide I'd rather be a single cat dad, I don't fancy my chances of leaving this ballroom intact."

Their smiles were shaky but genuine.

"Come on," he said, gently steering her off the dance floor. "You can introduce me to the birthday girl. It would be nice to meet her in person before she provides us with the contract of the decade."

Rosie and Johnny had been making their social circles of the room with very complicated body language, but they'd now reached Dominic at the bar, and had both noticeably relaxed in the company of someone who was on their side.

They all looked up as Sylvie and Jay joined them, Dominic's eyes immediately searching Sylvie's.

Whatever he saw there made something ease just fractionally in his expression.

As Johnny shook hands with Jay, Sylvie saw his personal

protection officer come to stand a few feet away. The security appeared to be extremely heavy at this party, and she wondered if it was solely down to Johnny's unwelcome admirer or if the royals were alert to other specific threats.

Not for the first time, she was *so* grateful that her own stint in the public eye was minuscule by comparison. The fact that Johnny was willing to step into all of this by choice spoke volumes about the reality and strength of his commitment to Rosie.

His PPO was eyeing Jay with sharp suspicion. Obviously, he was meant to be a visible deterrent, not a covert one, because he wasn't exactly blending into the crowd. The guy was a walking tank, with hands the size of plates and a stare that could laser through titanium. His bone structure was brutally sharp, his features quite uneven, and she'd heard a snotty-looking woman with a probably real fur cape giggle under her breath about "the ugly brute at the bar."

So many people right now who should be stepping on Lego every day of their lives.

Rosie had regained the composed face of a well-trained person under a lot of stress. She was probably dying to retreat to her private apartments, kick off her shoes, and curl up with a very large cup of coffee. And—Sylvie was crossing all fingers and toes—knock down that visible wall still between her and Johnny.

The princess looked past Dominic. "I'm glad to see your sister made it."

Dominic immediately turned, and Sylvie released an audible sigh of relief when she saw Pet walking toward them. *Oh, thank God.*

Pet was wearing a long flapper-style dress with strings of beads that bounced with the hesitant *tip-tap* of her stiletto heels. Her hair was in its usual sleek bob, her red lipstick perfect as always, but as she came closer, Sylvie didn't think she'd taken the care with her makeup that she would expect of Pet. The younger woman had been so excited about this ball, but she looked as if she'd just thrown on the nearest dress in her wardrobe and grabbed a taxi. Clearly, this had been a last-minute decision.

She still looked hopelessly pretty—and Sylvie wasn't the only one who thought so.

Her eyes happened to be passing over the inscrutable, suspicious face of Johnny's PPO, and she saw that laser gaze fasten on Pet. Naturally. Anyone barreling toward his charge was a potential threat, even pint-sized twenty-first-century flappers.

But when he saw her, he inhaled—and he didn't immediately exhale.

And he blinked, three times in a row, very quickly.

Hmm . . .

Sylvie was dragged out of intrigued speculation as Pet reached them. She sent a fast, faltering smile at Sylvie and bobbed an awkward curtsy at Rosie and Johnny, but her eyes were fixed on Dominic. She ran her tongue over her carmine lips and spoke in a wobble. "I—"

Dominic immediately stepped toward her. "Pet—"

The royal couple were watching the scene with interest, probably relieved to focus on someone else's tense situation for two seconds.

And in that moment of abstraction came the attack.

It happened so fast that Sylvie still found it hard to piece together all the fragments of memory later. The fire alarm went off first, a sudden piercing sound that first froze and then scattered the crowd.

It distracted the security team for mere seconds. That was long enough.

Sylvie saw, vaguely, the curly blonde hair in the moving crowd right next to them before the woman rushed at them.

But she didn't see the knife in her hand.

Rosie and Johnny's PPOs were just a beat too slow in intercepting Helena before she silently, expressionlessly, slashed at Johnny with the long, slender blade.

Instead, it was Pet who pushed Johnny out of the way, shoving him into Rosie's arms.

And as the blade sliced into bare, vulnerable skin, Sylvie would never forget the sight of blood splattered across antique satin and beads.

Chapter Twenty-One

St. Agnes Accident & Emergency
Around Ten O'Clock
Seconds, minutes, and hours tend to blur together within
these walls.

Sylvie carefully carried the cup of steaming hot tea back from
the small kitchenette. She sat down next to Dominic, on chairs
that made the backbreakers at Hartwell Studios seem like plush
recliners, and put the cup into his hand before he could refuse
it. "Just a little bit. Please."

Dominic's lips turned up very slightly, but it wasn't a smile.
"Good old England. When in doubt, when in crisis, when
awake—a cup of tea."

"Look, it's a thing for a reason." She leaned in to touch her lips
to his cheek. Against his skin, she whispered, "She's going to be
fine. The paramedic said it was mostly her arm. The cut over her
ribs wasn't deep."

He flinched slightly, his hand tightening around the cup and
threatening to squeeze boiling-hot water over his hand. She put
her fingers over his, stroking him.

"She'll be okay. I promise you, she'll be fine. I don't think they come much stronger than your little sister."

The silver in his hair and beard, the fine lines around his eyes, all seemed more pronounced under the harsh hospital lights. Her heart aching, all she could do was hold on to him.

"She's been through a lot," he said harshly. "More than I realized. Gerald spoiled Lorraine, treated her like a fucking princess. I thought he'd do the same for Pet. I let myself believe she would be okay there. I failed her."

"You were a *kid*." She took the tea and set it on the floor before it spilled. "Dom, you were just a kid. You couldn't have done anything more. She's okay."

"She's hurt. And I think I've been the last straw."

"No, you're going to be a part of the wonderful life she has coming for her now." Sylvie held his darkened gaze squarely. "We all walked very different paths that have converged together in this hospital tonight, and we'll all be there for one another going forward."

She could just imagine what cynical rejoinder that statement might have prompted from him in the past. Now, he looked at her for a moment, before he reached out and cupped her head, pulling her forward to kiss her mouth.

"I love you." Stated so simply, as a straight fact, without emphasis or frills. So perfectly Dominic, and so unexpected just then that she could hardly breathe, let alone speak.

Her hand was resting on his thigh. Her fingers tightened, hard, on the muscle flexing beneath her palm.

"Mr. De Vere?" A nurse with a calm face and compassionate eyes came to join them, and Dominic took Sylvie's hand as they both stood at once. "We've moved your sister to a private room, as requested, and you may see her now."

"Is she all right?" he asked, his fingers tight around Sylvie's, and the nurse—Dahlia, according to her badge—nodded.

"The cuts to her arm were deep and required stitches, and it's possible she'll have some residual tendon damage that may require physical therapy. But the wounds to her side were superficial. We're giving her a course of strong antibiotics to ward off any possible infection from the blade, so she'll be in for a night or two, but she'll be just fine."

Dominic exhaled, but the tension remained in his body, and Sylvie didn't think it would begin to drain away until he'd seen Pet for himself. His mind was at least able to focus enough that, as they followed Dahlia to Pet's room, he asked with a small frown, "You said Pet has a private room as requested? I didn't—"

"No." Dahlia looked back at them with a raised eyebrow. "I believe that request has come, shall we say, from quite high up the chain? We've also been warned of an increased security detail tonight. Your sister has one or two VIP visitors requesting entry."

Rosie and Johnny.

The royal couple had been whisked away with the rest of their relatives in the pandemonium that followed the evacuation and Helena's arrest, but Rosie had already rung Sylvie's phone twice to ask for an update on Pet.

Dahlia brought them to the small room with Pet's name beside the door, and stepped back to let them past.

Sylvie also tried to hang back and let Dominic have some privacy with his sister, but he still had her hand in his and he didn't let go.

They walked in together and found Pet propped up against the raised head of the narrow bed. Her right arm was heavily bandaged, resting against a pillow, and a few smaller plasters were visible under the neckline of her hospital gown. Without her red lipstick, she looked very young and very pale, but she smiled when she saw them.

With her left hand, she was spooning brown goo into her mouth that Sylvie hoped was chocolate. She spoke around the plastic spoon. "Please tell me nobody cut my dress off. It's genuine twenties vintage and it cost a fucking arm and leg. I can get blood out, but if someone shredded my baby, I'm *livid*."

Dominic shook his head. Both in answer to her question and in admonishment. "An arm full of stitches and that's your first question."

Pet shrugged her left shoulder. "Hey, I have morphine and chocolate pudding. I'm good." The lightness left her face as she looked into his eyes. "Really. I'm okay."

The clock on the wall *tick-tick-tick*ed in the silence.

Then Dominic walked forward swiftly, bent over the bed, and put his arms around his sister. He was very careful not to bump even the tiniest of her cuts, but his hold was nevertheless firm and encompassing.

Over his shoulder, Sylvie saw the tears rush into Pet's eyes. Very carefully, she put down her spoon and reached up to put her arm around her brother's neck.

Their first hug in twenty-five years lasted for a long time.

Sylvie started to back out of the room, keeping her steps light, and both De Veres spoke without looking up. "Don't even think about it."

Rolling her eyes, she went and sat in a chair on the other side of Pet's bed. At least the chairs in here had cushions. Useful to have royals pulling strings.

As Dominic straightened, Pet bit her lip. "Dominic." Her voice sounded strange. "Lorraine rang me this afternoon."

He hooked the other chair with his boot and pulled it closer, wincing as the legs made a terrible screech against the linoleum.

"Funny, that's the noise my soul makes when I see her number in my call log," Pet cracked.

He couldn't help a small grin, but he looked at her expectantly, with a certain grimness. "What did she want?"

"To complain about her life, mostly. Sounds like everyone else she knows is wisely avoiding her, including her husband. She also tried to talk me into investing the money you gave me from Mum's estate into a start-up. I think she's having an affair with some tech bro who's conned her out of her share."

Dominic absorbed that for a microsecond. "You're too smart to even hear out the pitch."

"Correct. I have other plans for that money, anyway. But she also talked about you. Bad-mouthing you as usual. Ungrateful cow. She . . . wasn't happy to hear that we're back in touch." Pet hesitated. Then, as she touched the skin above her bandages, lightly rubbing, the words fell out in a rush. "Is it true that when you left home and came here to London, you took me, too? That Gerald tried to have you charged with abduction, when you were just a little kid?"

Even when Dominic's face revealed nothing at all, Sylvie thought she had some grasp on what was going on behind that studied blankness now.

He was rapidly considering if telling the truth here would further damage Pet's idea of her family.

There had been too much deception lately.

As she watched, he came to the same decision.

"Yes. It is true." His words were taut. "I can't begin to tell you what a fucking *light* you were to me in that house. This funny, clumsy, loving baby. When I couldn't take any more, when I *had* to leave, I took you with me. I brought us both to Sebastian, and with thirteen-year-old logic, I thought he could keep us both. It didn't work out that way. And when Sebastian took you back there, and came home with the certainty that you would be happy with Lana and Gerald in a way I hadn't been—that was the only way I could reconcile that outcome."

Pet was crying silently.

Dominic reached out and took her left hand, squeezing her fingers.

"I'm sorry," he said, very evenly, "that didn't turn out to be the case. More sorry than I can ever say. But I will say it again: it was *never* true that I turned my back on you without a second thought. It was never true that I didn't care about you. I loved you. I still love you."

Pet took a shuddering breath and took the tissue that Sylvie held out to her.

"And I love you." Her smile wobbled to life, casting beautiful lights into her wet brown eyes. "Big brother. Which is why I'm asking you one last time if you'll accept the money Lana left."

She correctly interpreted Dominic's expression. A short-sighted person standing five kilometers away without their glasses could have correctly interpreted Dominic's expression.

"Not as *your* money," she added. "As mine. I'd like you to take it and give me shares in De Vere's in return. It's always been a family business, and I'd like to be a small part of that."

"You *are* part of that, without needing to put money in," Dominic said, but he was studying her now with both the big brother and the businessman faces. "You're serious."

"Yes, I am," she said, very firmly. "I'll pay market value on the shares. You'll let me come up with some social media campaigns and general promo ideas to help De Vere's continue on a strong trajectory. You'll invite me around for a family dinner every fourth Sunday. And I will keep at least a couch length from your demon cat at all times."

A bubble of welcome laughter was rising in Sylvie's chest, and something in her own body relaxed as she saw the amusement slipping into Dominic's eyes.

"Is that the full list of demands?" he asked mildly.

Pet tilted her head, considering. "Don't check the small print, because there may be something about a lifetime supply of chocolate in there, but basically—yes."

"Then—yes."

She had been fiddling with the top of her bandage, but her head lifted. "Really?"

"Really." He smiled faintly. "Does this mean you want to work in the bakery full-time, too?"

"Oh God, no." Her return smile was rueful. "As fond as I am of you, bro, I don't want you as a boss. And as I've said, approximately six hundred times, I like being a PA, and there's no full-time vacancy in your joint."

"That's fortunate," a new voice said from the door, and they all turned as Rosie and Johnny knocked belatedly on the frame and came quietly in.

They were flanked by Johnny's huge, muscular, silent PPO, who stopped at the door. He was as towering and menacing as ever—and he was holding, in one massive hand, a tiny teddy bear.

Sylvie tore her gaze from the incongruous sight as Rosie went on, "Johnny is in need of a new PA. A full-time, permanent position with excellent renumeration and travel opportunities, that we'd like to offer to you."

Pet had gone understandably flustered, having the royals arrive at her sickbed. At that, her mouth literally dropped open.

"We already checked you out and you have fantastic credentials. You also have a lovely personality, we both feel comfortable with you, and I suspect you'd not only be very good at this job but enjoy it very much." Rosie's hand went out and linked securely with her fiancé's. "And you might have saved the life of the man I love tonight."

When they looked at each other, their faces said everything.

Rosie finally recollected they weren't alone in the room and dragged her eyes back. "Tonight put a lot of things in perspective. It was a pretty strong reminder of what's truly important. What I was lucky enough to find and will never throw away. And I can never thank you enough."

Pet shook her head. "You don't have to thank me. But what's going to happen to Helena?"

The security team had taken Helena out of the room before the police were called, but they hadn't needed to restrain her. After she'd cut Pet, she'd gone completely limp, her face frighteningly empty.

Even in the horror of it all, Sylvie had felt intensely sorry for her, and a similar concern was evident in Pet's voice.

It was Johnny who answered. "She *will* get the help she needs."

Looking at him now, standing tall and exuding both protectiveness and compassion, Sylvie thought there was every chance he would defy expectations and become an indispensable asset to the royal family.

There was no doubt at all he would be a loving and supportive husband to the woman beside him.

"And I told the fucking leech press trying to take photos of Helena and Pet exactly what I thought of them," Johnny added.

Rosie winced slightly.

Of course, there was an equal chance that Pet would have her hands full working for Johnny, if she took this job. By the look on her face, that contract was going to be signed.

Behind the royal couple, in the shadow of the door, Johnny's PPO took a step forward, and Rosie turned with a start.

"Oh my goodness, I'm sorry. This is Matthias Vaughn, the head of Johnny's protection team. He's off shift now, but he wanted to speak to Pet."

Pet's eyes widened as Matthias came farther into the room, within sight of the bed.

The bodyguard stood looking at her, his wide chest rising and falling a little too quickly, the only sign of disturbed emotion in his body.

"If I'd been doing my job correctly, you wouldn't be here now." He had one of the deepest voices Sylvie had ever heard. His words were clipped, not wasting a syllable. "I apologize."

"It was a split-second distraction, an unavoidable human re-action to the fire alarm," Rosie began, and Matthias shook his head in an abrupt motion.

"That 'split-second distraction' can be—and tonight almost was—the difference between life and death. I made an error. It won't happen again." He looked back at Pet as he repeated, his voice defying the laws of physics and anatomy to become even deeper, "It's my fault you were hurt."

He paused—and then he thrust his hand out.

The room had gone very quiet.

Pet's eyes traveled from his face to the little teddy bear on his palm. It was wearing a waistcoat with a teeny-weeny pocket square.

At Sylvie's side, Dominic's eyebrow had lifted. She watched with total fascination as the very tips of Matthias's ears turned red.

"I . . ." It was not impossible this was the first time the man had ever been remotely flustered. "The gift shop was closed. They didn't have much at the corner shop—"

His fingers closing around the bear, his hand started to fall away.

Pet shot forward, sticking her own hand out and almost dislodging the drip in her arm.

After another hesitation, Matthias stepped forward to give her the bear, and she lay back against the bed, holding the toy tightly against her chest.

"Thank you." Her smile was sudden and blinding, and the bodyguard moved one shoulder in a rough, apparently uncontrollable jerk.

With a stiff nod, he bowed to Rosie and retreated very quickly from the room.

Pet had been determined to find a new path. Wherever her life went after today, it was shaping up to be interesting.

Rosie smoothed out her smile before she addressed Sylvie and Dominic, slipping back into her professional princess gloss. "We've made a decision about the cake."

Sylvie drew in her breath. She hadn't expected that, not tonight. Her eyes went immediately to Dominic, and they exchanged a long look.

Whatever happens, it changes nothing between us.

They didn't even need to say the words aloud.

"I know it's late and it's been a sh-shit of a night," Johnny said, "but we wondered if you'd like to accompany us back to St. Giles. We won't take up much of your time."

"We're happy to schedule a meeting for tomorrow." Rosie spoke emphatically on that point. "But a lot of things seem to have come to a pass tonight. Lines have been drawn. It seems fitting that this part of the journey also now comes to a close."

She looked at the three of them. At Johnny.

"And I hope," she said, "that the best parts of our respective stories begin from here."

Chapter Twenty-Two

The Primrose Room, St. Giles Palace
The end of one journey.
And the beginning of all the rest.

"Thank you for coming here so late," Rosie said in the quiet, almost shocking serenity of a comfortable sitting room in a rear wing of the palace. She'd walked straight past the businesslike efficiency of the Captain's Suite and brought them to this little haven of warm light and surrounding bookcases. Much of the floor space was taken up by a grand piano, there were framed music awards on the walls, and she hadn't needed to tell them that the room had once belonged to Patrick. She settled herself more comfortably in her chair, spreading her papers and tablets out on the table between them. "We looked at both of your proposals and tasted your samples of the Midnight Elixir cake."

"For 'tasted,'" Johnny put in, "read: 'ate every crumb.' We loved them both. It was hard to choose between them."

Rosie picked up an iPad. "Impossible to choose between them in the case of the utmost-tier flavor. We don't have the developed dessert palates that the two of you do, but quite frankly, your Midnight Elixir cakes tasted identical to me."

She tapped the tablet screen, bringing up two images, positioning them side by side. "And your designs . . ."

Sylvie leaned in, her attention immediately going to the unfamiliar sketch, the De Vere panel. At her side, Dominic was intently studying her own submission.

"It's evident which drawing came from which mind," Johnny said with a small grin, and certainly, the sparkling *pâte de verre* flowers and spiraling tiers of Sylvie's cake said "Sugar Fair" as distinctly as the clean lines and elegant piping pointed to De Vere's. "But . . ."

But at the essential level, the cakes were remarkably similar. They had both chosen a stained-glass effect, constructed entirely from blown sugar, each tier designed to catch the light and cast a shimmering cascade of color. Peony poppies, primroses, and petunias glittered within the sugar glass.

And on the highest tier, the Midnight Elixir cake, they had both incorporated a trinity knot.

Rosie had a photo of Jessica's sculpture on the table. She rested her fingers on the stained-glass knot, where it was kept safe, held forever in the joined bronze hands.

"I always loved this sculpture," she said softly. "But I never knew the identity of the artist. Patrick was forever in that part of the grounds, but I didn't ever want to disturb his privacy while he was there." Very lightly, she stroked the photograph, where the foreheads of the bronze figures touched, and echoed Dominic's own sentiment about the work. "I can see why it gave him comfort. I just wish . . ."

She didn't finish the sentence. She didn't need to.

Sylvie also looked down at those cupped metal hands and silently made her own last wish for the man and woman sitting together on the steps of Primrose Cottage, with love and laughter and life shining from their eyes. Two entwined souls, forever.

Rosie coughed to clear the crackle in her throat. "Obviously, there are quite a few similarities between the cakes—surprisingly many." She shot Dominic a quick smile. "I know this isn't your own taste at all, and I really appreciate how much you set aside your own preferences for this design."

Dominic was not appreciative of being singled out there. "It's a commissioned work, not my own birthday cake. Of course I design to suit the client." High-level irritation.

Rosie bit back a widening grin as she returned to her tablet. "We like elements of both cakes." Whatever app she had scanned their designs into, she now started fiddling. In a center, separate panel, she pulled Sylvie's lower tier. Dominic's middle tiers. Sylvie's top tier. She kept moving and shifting elements from each drawing.

A little like being at school, watching a teacher attack a personal-best essay with a red pen.

Finally, with a significant look, she put one finger on Sylvie's trinity knot and another finger on Dominic's trinity knot. She drew them into the central panel.

The knots touched and locked together.

And became a Serch Bythol.

The symbol for everlasting love.

"We'd like you to combine these designs," Rosie said simply. "And we're offering you a joint contract."

Neither of them said anything for a moment. Sylvie strongly suspected they were having the exact same silent reaction—mostly a sense of *Yes, this is right, the perfect way to close one door and open another, with a single, meaningful collaboration.*

And a little bit of mutually competitive anticlimax.

She was opening her mouth to agree, nevertheless, when Dominic took the tablet into his hand, looking closely at the drawing.

"No," he said.

The eyebrows of both Rosie and Johnny shot up in unison.

Sylvie watched him calmly. She had no idea what was coming next, and not the slightest qualm.

"Over seventy percent of the details you've highlighted are Sylvie's." Dominic turned the screen back to face the couple. "The Midnight Elixir cake itself is based on a flavoring emulsion from Sugar Fair. And any remaining feature from the De Vere's proposal that needs to be included, Sugar Fair is equally capable of executing. By merit, this is not our contract."

It possibly wasn't royal protocol to stand up first, but it was getting on for midnight, after an incredibly tumultuous forty-eight hours that had culminated in the violent assault of someone she was coming to care about very much. Sylvie wanted nothing more than to go home and curl up in bed with Dominic.

And tomorrow, together, they would start finalizing the details for this cake of all cakes.

She got up from the table. "I'm sorry to cut this short, but I'm about to fall asleep where I sit. We'll be available to discuss next steps at your earliest convenience. Or just to join in on a gaming tournament if asked. And we happily accept the offer of a joint contract."

Dominic had his freezing look on. He was clearly unaware that all it did was heighten her urgency to get to bed.

She continued breezily. "Enjoy the experience, De Vere. After this collab, the moment we step foot on Magnolia Lane every day, the battle of the bakers continues."

Rosie was suppressing laughter, but she put out her hand. "Before you go . . ." Her smile fading, she chewed on her lower lip as she opened a folder on the table and very carefully removed a thin sheaf of papers. With a quick glance at Johnny, who put his hand on her back, she turned to Dominic. "Patrick wrote this a short time before he died. I've never shown it to anyone. And I've never heard it played. It was so personal to Patrick, I was the only one who'd know what it truly meant—and I think I was afraid," she murmured. "I'd already seen his sadness over Jessica, and his music was always so— transportive. I was grieving and I couldn't bear to be immersed in the depths of his pain."

At the top of the musical score, in Patrick's distinctive handwriting, was the one swirling word. *Jessie.*

"I know you're a talented pianist. It was in your background check." Rosie's hesitation lasted only a moment. She squared her shoulders and inclined her head toward the piano. "Would you please play this for me?" Again, she looked at Johnny. "For us."

Dominic still looked slightly tense and irritated, and was clearly more interested in continuing their argument—which he obviously thought he'd win.

So cute.

He took the score from Rosie with the greatest of care, however, and looked down at it. As his eyes skimmed across the page, reading the notes, following the tempo, a faint frown tugged at his brows. He turned the page, his eyes lifting briefly back to the tense woman before him. "Yes. If you want me to, I'd be honored. But I'm not sure it's what you're expecting."

He crossed to the piano and sat down, placing the papers on the music stand before he pushed up the sleeves of his jumper. Sylvie just had time for a spike of lust—honestly, all Dominic had to do in the future was bring out his forearms and plop down at his piano, and half the work was done for him where foreplay was concerned.

But as he set his long fingers to the keys and began to play, any light amusement faded. Patrick's composition, the music that had poured from him in his dying days, the story of his life and his love, wasn't the wrenching sadness Rosie had feared. It was deep and rich, first fast and lilting in tempo, then slow and passionate—a man falling in love, finding himself, seeing the world differently. Somehow, as Sylvie stood listening, the music twirling around her, she heard nothing but gratitude. The sheer thankfulness of having known her, of having been *them*. It didn't matter for how long.

It was happiness.

It was joy.

By the time the last note drifted away, as if a final bittersweet ghost had slipped out through the window and into the stars beyond, Rosie was in Johnny's arms, her arms wrapped around his neck, her head buried against his shoulder.

And her body free of every last scrap of tension.

Dominic rose from the piano, looking at Sylvie. Silently, they left the other couple in their own world, following a security guard back through the halls of the eerily quiet palace.

In the deserted courtyard outside, in the shadow of Abbey Hall, they stood on stone steps and looked at each other in the light of the streetlamps.

The rain had stopped today after what seemed like weeks,

the ground hardening with a thin layer of ice, and a hint of the moon shone through the dark clouds above.

Dominic finally spoke. "Competitors at work. And outside of Magnolia Lane?"

His face was difficult to read in the weak light and shadows, but his hands took hers, his grip tightening immeasurably as she spoke.

Simple words for something so wondrously immense. "On and away from Magnolia Lane, you're my business rival. My friend." Their fingers linked. "The man I've fallen in love with so hard that sometimes I look at you and I can't breathe."

The look in his eyes was one she'd never forget. And there was a lump in her throat as he spoke.

"You walked into my life, tipped it upside down, and when it finally righted—you were right there in the center. In a very short space of time, you've changed everything." He lowered his head. Against her mouth, he said, with a lightness he obviously didn't feel, "Bane of my existence four years ago. The best part of it now."

Her breath shuddered inward. "This really is . . . it. The real thing."

His hands came up to cup her cheeks and he kissed her again.

She was kissing him back, but tears were a thick burn in her chest, and she had to break off to press her closed eyes against his neck. "Still a little scary."

His arms locking at the base of her spine, he rested his cheek on her head. "Still fucking terrifying."

"I'm so glad I saw your forbidding scowl on TV and decided to apply for *Operation Cake* anyway."

"Clearly, so am I, but don't expect a follow-up that I'm grateful your version of Cupid's arrow was a unicorn catapult."

Her laughter was echoed in his eyes as they stood entwined under the night sky, the ice glittering on the ground beneath their feet, the growing moonbeams slipping through the faint mist.

Despite everything, as the Sugar Fair motto said, *Vita est plena magices.*

Life is full of magic.

Epilogue

The cake stood towering and majestic on the gold state table. Six feet tall, it had come in at eight tiers, arranged to wind upward like the circular staircase that Rosie adored in St. Giles Palace. A photograph in the records at Abbey Hall had shown Rosie and Patrick sitting together on the landing, hand in hand, feet crossed. During her childhood, Patrick had apparently propped his great-niece on that banister and slid her down as they laughed and laughed, her mother and their advisors looking on in frozen disapproval. The cake stand had been designed to reflect the same Georgian carvings etched into that stairwell.

Both the top tier—Rosie and Johnny's portion, to be preserved for their first wedding anniversary—and the largest bottom tier were flavored with Midnight Elixir; the remaining cakes alternated dark and white chocolate, with one obligatory fruitcake to appease the traditionalists.

The overhead lights hit the Serch Bythol sculpture on the utmost tier, the sugar crystals shimmering and dancing like a cascade of diamonds. The planes of the cake beneath were clean and crisp, and the sugar stained-glass panels caught every light on the ceiling, throwing back shimmering rainbow rays. Sylvie was most proud of the silhouette that circled the middle stained-glass tiers—the skylines of London and Johnny's family estate in Lancashire. Only when viewed at close range did a second, hidden skyline emerge from within the reflective depths—the fantasy lands of *I, Slayer*, complete with a tiny flying dragon. It was a work of art—and even now, she was taken aback by the level of harmony they had achieved, twining together two very different styles.

In honor of the union of two very different people, whose lives would hopefully interlock just as successfully.

She stood at the edge of the crowd, watching Rosie and Johnny doing a very decent Charleston in the center of a ballroom that had probably seen far more scandal over the centuries than the starchy décor would suggest. Dominic's warmth pressed behind her before his hands came to rest on her ribs.

His fingers moved as if he was enjoying the sensual glide of her silk dress—or just the feel of her body, which he traced with lips and hands almost every night and treated with more reverence than the most beautiful and valuable of masterpieces.

His mouth touched her neck, making her shiver as he said into her ear, "Quite a contrast to the public part of the proceedings."

Eye-openingly so. She put her hands over his, unconsciously stroking his knuckles. On the dance floor, the band switched to classic rock and Johnny started undulating his hips. The intention was presumably Elvis; the execution was more like an emu that had just been stung by a bee. He was doing extraordinary things with his neck. As a mating dance in the wild, it would have netted him eternal bachelorhood, but his new wife seemed genuinely impressed. Definitely true love.

After the pomp and solemnity of the day, the ceremony at St. Paul's Cathedral beamed out to millions across the globe and the carriage procession that had packed the streets of London, she wasn't sure what she'd been expecting for the private reception—high tea and a cotillion, probably. However, the moment the gates of St. Giles Palace had closed and Rosie and Johnny had completed the obligatory balcony snog for the screaming crowds—Rosie passing off the moment smoothly when Johnny came in too quickly in his nervous state and very obviously bit her lip—the vibe had jumped straight to the level of Ibiza nightclub.

To the dour disapproval of the bride's grandfather, the Prince of Wales had kicked off the proceedings with a risqué toast, and they'd now reached the portion of the evening when the Duke of Albany was attempting to jive with his daughter.

Even the duchess cracked a brief smile when her husband and daughter collapsed into each other, giggling helplessly.

A lot of champagne had been consumed this evening.

"I think they've enjoyed their day," Sylvie said, folding her arms over Dominic's.

"Good. They deserve it after the tabloid pile-on. I expected it to be ugly, but . . ." He grimaced, and she nodded.

The infamous kiss photograph would be dragged into every remotely relevant article for years, and the tabloids had been having a field day for months. Sylvie felt awful for all three of them, Rosie, Johnny, *and* Helena, who was receiving intensive treatment. She knew Pet still felt guilty for snapping it in the first place.

"Apparently, Johnny's planning to focus on the arts as his first major patronage. I hope the public gives him a proper chance," she murmured. Helena's family had released a statement and public apology, but Johnny had still lost a lot of public sympathy. "I think Pet's in for an interesting ride this year with Team Marchmont."

"She can handle it." Dominic spoke with cool certainty. His lips brushed her earlobe again. It was a massive honor to have been invited into the inner sanctum tonight—and frankly, she was ready to leave now and go home to celebrate their own milestone.

Six months to the day since they'd taken each other by surprise with that kiss in the Dark Forest. Thousands of kisses since, and it still felt like the first time, every time.

With his body hard against her, his arms warm around her, she wanted to turn and kiss him now, but a light peck usually ended up with her legs around his waist and her back against the wall.

Sighing, she leaned back, feeling the fatigue slipping through her bones as she admired their joint achievement again. Months of planning had gone into that cake, weeks of practical work as they began the sculptural components, culminating in a near all-nighter in the palace kitchens to complete the finishing touches to their mutual satisfaction.

Even transferring it safely to the ballroom today had been an eyebrow-whitening experience. But the task was done, with barely a smudge of icing to fix when it was finally in place.

And their checks had already cleared.

Dominic swept a professional eye up the cake. They weren't usually guests at the weddings they catered, and it was difficult to stop checking for problems. "We came through the collaboration with staff, kitchens, and relationship intact."

"Touch and go there for a while." She could feel rather than hear his quiet laughter. "It's probably a good thing we're not joining forces professionally on a permanent basis—"

"And personally?" His voice was a little gruff as he spoke into her hair, gently nuzzling her.

Softly, she said, "The *important* partnership? Unbreakable contract."

His arm tightened around her.

They were silent for a while, just enjoying the music and the happiness in the air, watching the lights twinkle up and down the cake display as the room darkened with the night.

On the floor, through the crowds, she saw Jay dancing with Emma Abara. The pattern designer was doing a spot of contractual work at Sugar Fair. Despite the disastrous outcome of the *Operation Cake* final, her knack for design and unfailing patience had unexpectedly made her an unbeatable team with Mabel. The two of them were already coming up with ambitious and bizarre ideas for new sugar craft—all of which looked insane on paper and had so far been wildly successful when they came to fruition.

She and Jay had hit it off right away. They'd discovered a mutual desire to learn to play Dungeons & Dragons and had just joined a local team. So far, it was a solid friendship forming, but Sylvie was cautiously optimistic. There were definite sparks of attraction there, and his only hesitation about inviting her as his date tonight had been her employment status with them. That was temporary, however, and Emma was—fantastically for her and unfortunately for them—shortly starting a new apprenticeship elsewhere.

Dominic was rubbing his cheek against her head when his body stiffened. "What is that?"

"What?" She was trying to wiggle her fingers in between his shirt buttons without anyone else seeing. She liked the feel of his chest hair beneath her skin.

Although her onetime comment comparing it to petting Humphrey was a mistake she wouldn't repeat.

"In the sugar bubble on the second tier." Dominic was dropping into his *Operation Cake* tone, which only made her want to open *all* the buttons. "What is *that*?"

"Probably another dragon," she said airily, rubbing him and making a shiver run through his big body. "We agreed on including Caractacus."

"Yes. We agreed on the dragon. We did not agree on other crea . . ." He couldn't seem to help running his fingers down her spine, but she felt the moment he realized what he was looking at. His words became dangerously even. "It has a horn."

"You're seeing things." A soothing pat on his pec.

"It has *hooves*." Unmistakeable outrage.

"I have no idea what you're talking about."

In public, he was still usually a little more reserved, but he swung her around now, properly into his arms. His brows had lifted pointedly, but he was unable to fully repress that laugh she loved so much. His forehead came down to rest on hers. "God, you're lucky I adore you."

Sylvie was smiling as she slipped her arms around his shoulders. "And despite your hopeless lack of imagination and tragic inclination toward minimalism, I love you madly." The amusement in her tone faded, and his eyes darkened as they always did when she said those words. It never failed to bring a lump to her throat, that she somehow had the power to give another person that much pleasure. That much quiet, wondering happiness. "Endlessly."

His hands came up to cup her head with that same gentle reverence, and their lips brushed. Once. Twice. Teasing. Lingering.

Perfect.

As the kiss deepened, someone cleared their throat pointedly.

Reluctantly, Sylvie broke away and turned her head, her arms still circling his neck.

Pet stood a few feet away in another of her gorgeous flapper-inspired dresses, holding her phone. She was shaking her head in heavy disapproval, but her eyes were sparkling.

"Pardon me and the rest of the room for interrupting yet again," she said smoothly, "but I was just having a word with my new boss. He put his neck out with that interesting dance maneuver and is now drinking alarming quantities of highly boozed punch. And clearly discretion is not going to be the name of the game moving forward, because he not only spilled the beans on yet another royal headline breaking tomorrow, he even AirDropped me the announcement before it goes to press. I've given Rosie a nudge to make sure it goes no further than us, but I think you'll find it of interest."

She held out the phone, and Sylvie let go of Dominic with one hand to take it.

With their heads still close, they both read the drafted press release.

His Majesty King James III is delighted to announce the engagement of His Royal Highness Prince Alexander, the Prince of Wales, to—

"The bachelor prince—soon to be a bachelor no more. Rosie and Johnny's wedding was a big deal. But the heir to the British throne?" The glint in Pet's expression intensified as she tilted her head meaningfully. "Hell of a cake contract, folks."

Sylvie's gaze rose to meet Dominic's.

The drumbeat of the band was quickening in pitch.

He lifted a brow.

And the curve of her mouth deepened.

Let the battle (re)commence . . .

Acknowledgments

Writing is often a solitary process—unless you have a new puppy walking over the keyboard every five seconds, as I've recently discovered—but the support and hard work of so many people go into bringing a story to life on the page.

Firstly, I'm incredibly grateful to my amazing editor, Elle Keck, and the entire team at Avon. You made me feel so welcome from day one, and have all been supportive beyond measure throughout the whole process. While dealing with the extreme difficulties of a global pandemic, you worked so hard, always offering valuable insight, helping me to take these characters and make them who they needed to be.

Thank you, as always, to my agent, Elaine Spencer. You're at my side on every step of this journey, an expert voice when I need one but also a constant cheerleader. You believe in me even when I don't.

I'm so thrilled to have Liza Rusalskaya illustrating the cover, bringing a whole new, gorgeous, colorful dimension to Sylvie and Dominic, and their respective bakeries.

The friends I've met in the book community have been one of the greatest blessings since the beginning. It's a privilege to know all of you, I'm so lucky to have you in my life, and I think about that every day. You're the kindest, most talented people, and the very definition of friendship.

To the book bloggers, YouTubers, and Instagrammers who work tirelessly and often don't receive the thanks and respect they deserve: I cannot thank you enough. I'm forever grateful for everything you do.

This is a book about family, biological and found, and I couldn't do anything without mine. You've taught me the meaning of unconditional love, you're my whole world—and you've had to put up with me brandishing pieces of paper and plot points scrawled on whiteboards for a second opinion, keeping frequently unsociable hours, and worrying over details large and small. I love you very much.

Teddy, my newest and furriest family member: you may have introduced me to Extreme Editing, in which all of my worldly possessions were destroyed around me while I revised, but you're an adorable (and very mischievous) light in my life.

And to every person who reads my books, thank you so much. I appreciate you all.

And don't miss Lucy Parker's next
delightful romantic comedy

Starring Pet De Vere and Matthias Vaughn

Coming Summer 2022